OVERLORD

Volume 13: The Paladin of the Sacred Kingdom Part II

Kugane Maruyama | Illustration by so-bin

YEN ON

NEW YORK

OVERLORD

VOLUME 13

KUGANE MARUYAMA

Translation by Emily Balistrieri
Cover art by so-bin

This book is a work of fiction. Names, characters, places, and incidents are
the product of the author's imagination or are used fictitiously. Any resemblance
to actual events, locales, or persons, living or dead, is coincidental.

OVERLORD Vol.13 SEIOKOKU NO SEIKISHI GE
©Kugane Maruyama 2018
First published in Japan in 2018 by KADOKAWA CORPORATION, Tokyo.
English translation rights arranged with KADOKAWA CORPORATION, Tokyo,
through Tuttle-Mori Agency, Inc., Tokyo.

Yen On
150 West 30th Street, 19th Floor
New York, NY 10001

Visit us at yenpress.com
facebook.com/yenpress
twitter.com/yenpress
yenpress.tumblr.com
instagram.com/yenpress

First Yen On Edition: April 2021

Yen On is an imprint of Yen Press, LLC.
The Yen On name and logo are trademarks of Yen Press, LLC.

The publisher is not responsible for websites (or their content)
that are not owned by the publisher.

Library of Congress Cataloging-in-Publication Data
Names: Maruyama, Kugane, author. | So-bin, illustrator. | Balistrieri, Emily, translator.
Title: Overlord / Kugane Maruyama ; illustration by So-bin ; translation by Emily Balistrieri.
Other titles: Ōbārōdo. English
Description: First Yen On edition. | New York, NY : Yen On, 2016–
Identifiers: LCCN 2016000142 | ISBN 9780316272247 (v. 1 : hardback) |
ISBN 9780316363914 (v. 2 : hardback) | ISBN 9780316363938 (v. 3 : hardback) |
ISBN 9780316397599 (v. 4 : hardback) | ISBN 9780316397612 (v. 5 : hardback) |
ISBN 9780316398794 (v. 6 : hardback) | ISBN 9780316398817 (v. 7 : hardback) |
ISBN 9780316398848 (v. 8 : hardback) | ISBN 9780316398862 (v. 9 : hardback) |
ISBN 9780316444989 (v. 10 : hardback) | ISBN 9780316445016 (v. 11 : hardback) |
ISBN 9780316445016 (v. 12 : hardback) | ISBN 9781975311537 (v. 13 : hardback)
Subjects: LCSH: Alternate reality games—Fiction. | Internet games—Fiction. | Science fiction. |
BISAC: FICTION / Science Fiction / Adventure.
Classification: LCC PL873.A37 O2313 2016 | DDC 895.63/6—dc23
LC record available at http://lccn.loc.gov/2016000142

ISBNs: 978-1-9753-1153-7 (hardcover)
978-1-9753-1154-4 (ebook)

1 3 5 7 9 10 8 6 4 2

LSC-C

Printed in the United States of America

Contents

OVERLORD

Chapter 4   **Siege**

Chapter 4 | Siege

1

The end of winter was still far off, and the air was cold. But thanks to copious amounts of body hair, a certain creature felt none of the chill. His shiny black fur and the clothes he wore provided more than adequate protection from the elements. Even if he donned metal armor, the cold wouldn't seep through.

His body trembled for a different reason.

Anger.

Even the word *rage* would not do it justice.

He let out the instinctive growl of a carnivore before catching himself and clicking his tongue in shame.

For a member of the zooostia race, growling was a sign that he wasn't in control of his emotions. Rather improper conduct for an adult.

But that was only when among those of his own race.

If one of his peers had heard him, the low rumble that came from between his sharp, closed teeth might have made their blood run cold and paralyzed them with fear.

In any case, he turned away from the human city wall he had been staring at and returned to his camp.

An overwhelmingly powerful demon called Jaldabaoth held sway over the many different races that had gathered here, but his control did not stem the arguments that were constantly breaking out.

The allied subhumans numbered over a hundred thousand strong and had been roughly split into three groups.

Forty thousand were arrayed against the Sacred Kingdom's southern army.

Fifty thousand were defending and managing the prison camps in the seized territory of the Sacred Kingdom.

The last ten thousand were performing odd jobs such as scouting the northern lands in search of supplies.

The zooostias were currently in a detachment of forty thousand that had been drawn from the prison camp group.

With that many thrown together, trouble was only natural. This time, though, there was no one blocking his path. Nothing would stop or slow him down.

Who would voluntarily stand in front of a rolling boulder?

No one here had the mental fortitude to disturb him when he was this determined.

Advancing as if strolling across an empty meadow, he soon spotted a tent up ahead that was grander than all the rest.

There were subhuman soldiers at the entrance, but they weren't for guard duty. They were simply standing by in case the one inside needed errands run—in other words, they were gofers.

The soldiers gave way, shuddering in fear. As he passed between them and brushed aside the fabric overhanging the entrance, the five inside turned sharp gazes on him.

He had just drawn the attention of some of the most powerful members of the entire subhuman army, not counting the demons. All their glares were so intense that the pressure was almost palpable, but the zooostia retained his composure, unfazed.

In fact, he also stood among the top ten strongest, making him one of their peers. He sniffed derisively at their glares and dropped into an open seat. He didn't have the lower body of a humanoid, so technically he lay down.

Though he noticed one of the five bob his head at him, he ignored the greeting and instead opted to scowl openly at the most powerful subhuman in the room.

The target of his ire was a serpentlike creature with arms.

Appropriate to his nickname Rainbow Scales, his scales shone in all the colors of the rainbow, glittering curiously, almost as if they were wet. This flashy exterior wasn't only visually striking—as rumor had it, those scales were as hard as a dragon's. What's more, they were resistant to magic as well. On top of that, Rainbow Scales wore enchanted armor, wielded a large shield, and was a capable warrior. Little wonder he was regarded as the most formidable inhabitant of the Abellion Hills.

He was a nagaraja named Rokesh, the one chosen by the demonic emperor as commander in chief of this army.

Lying next to him was the famous weapon he wielded, known for its terrifying special ability, a Trident of Dehydration.

"—Why aren't we attacking?" the zooostia asked Rokesh in a low, restrained tone.

It had been three days since they had reached the city held by the pitiful human resistance, yet there hadn't been a single clash.

"…I realize their walls block our way, but with our numbers, breaking through should be no problem."

There were plenty in the subhuman alliance who would not be hindered at all by these simple fortifications. If they pressed that advantage, there didn't seem to be much issue.

"You're not losing your nerve on us, are you?"

"Sir Vicious Claw."

At the sound of his name, Vijar Rajandala frowned as he glanced at his fellow zooostia before turning back to the nagaraja.

The name Vicious Claw was known throughout the hills. It had been for nearly two hundred years—not because zooostias lived a long time but because there was a clan that passed it down.

Having only just inherited the title from his father, Vijar was fully aware that he wasn't worthy of it yet. Hence his eagerness to do battle and gain some renown. But so far, there had been few opportunities to show off his power as the newest successor to the name Vicious Claw.

Most of the opponents he had fought were weak. None of them could withstand even two blows from his enchanted battle-ax, Edge Wing.

That wasn't good enough.

He couldn't let this war end as just another mere underling of the peerless demon known as Jaldabaoth. He needed a chance to distinguish himself. And that chance had finally arrived.

Yet, Rokesh refused to attack. Vijar's discontent was plain to see.

"I heard the Mighty King was the one who guarded that city. Are you scared that our opponent was able to defeat him?"

The Mighty King—the leader of the bufolk.

He had been another one of the most powerful ten subhumans.

Vijar knew the Mighty King had been known for using a vexing weapon-breaking ability, but even so, he was confident the two of them were equal in power. If this new challenger had defeated the Mighty King, perhaps he had finally found a worthy opponent.

"I'll take care of the upstart, so let's attack already."

He suspected he already knew the identity of the one who had slain the Mighty King.

It must be that human paladin. If the rumors I've heard are true, she could have pulled it off.

He pictured a holy knight with a sword of light.

"Sir Vijar, you arrive late without so much as an apology and then go so far as to make demands? As commander, I'd like to give you a piece of my mind…but for now, I simply ask that you contain yourself. Rest assured, I understand your intent." Rokesh denied his request quite generously, although it was still firm.

"What a joke. Listen to this clueless nestling twitter on."

The one snickering at Vijar was the queen of the four-armed magiroses, Nasrenée Berto Cule—sometimes better known by her title Elemental Storm.

Vijar frowned.

He had no intention of losing in hand-to-hand combat, but Nasrenée was adept at magic; the idea that the battle could be decided in a way he couldn't even imagine made him nervous. But he would be too ashamed to face his ancestors as inheritor of the name Vicious Claw if he simply stood by while someone openly mocked him.

"Maybe I wouldn't need to if you would get off your ass, you old crone."

Magiroses had relatively long life spans, but considering she had already made a name for herself in the hills when he was still a child, he figured she must be middle-aged at least. It was impossible to tell her age by her complexion, since she applied makeup to her face. But perhaps it was also a sign that she was concerned about how the passage of time had affected her looks. And maybe the perfume she wore was more to mask the natural musk of an aging body than for its flowery scent.

"Oh-ho."

As Nasrenée narrowed her eyes, the temperature in the tent seemed to suddenly drop. This was no trick of the mind.

"I'm just stating the facts," Vijar replied as he sat up slightly straighter.

This subtle but clearly aggressive gesture was no empty threat. His quadruped lower half could muster prodigious amounts of instantaneous muscular power and agility. In combat, he used this to his advantage, often lunging forward from a deep, low posture. It was notable that he didn't drop into that stance. Between the two of them, he held the higher status, so he wanted it to be clear he was letting her make the first move.

"True or not, there are certain things that you simply shouldn't say. I think you need a lesson in how to properly treat a lady, nestling—and that's a job for someone older and wiser."

Rokesh headed off the volatile situation.

"Would you two cut it out? If a fight breaks out at the war council meeting, I'll have to report it to Emperor Jaldabaoth."

After he invoked the name of absolute power, the pair decided against it, though they didn't neglect to send parting shots with their eyes, signaling, *It's not as if I've forgiven you* and *I'll fight you anytime!*

"*Sigh...* I realize the strong have a compulsion to prove yourselves, but I'd like you to appreciate the meaning of the word *cooperation*."

"Hee-hee-hee. Not like you can talk." An apelike creature with long white hair laughed as he ribbed Rokesh.

"Fair enough. In any case, Sir Vicious Claw, regarding your previous question, no, it's not that I've lost my nerve. Certainly, the Mighty King was a fierce warrior. But each of us here is a match for him, are we not?"

Rokesh looked pointedly at Vicious Claw and Elemental Storm before turning to the other three as well.

The primate with the long, snow-white hair wearing a plethora of enchanted gold accessories was king of the stone eaters, Harisha Ankarra.

The elites of his race could discretely obtain special abilities depending on what gems were included in their diet. For example, by eating diamonds, they could gain temporary resistance to all physical attacks except sheer blunt force. Normally, it was possible to hold only three of these attributes at once, but Harisha could possess many more. For that reason, he was considered a different variety of stone eater.

Then there was the orthrous general who had greeted Vijar when he joined the meeting. The one clad in armor covered in ornate carvings and bearing his equally splendid helmet and lance lying next to him was Hectowyzeth a Lagara.

The acknowledgment he offered earlier was due to the orthrous race's alliance with the zooostias, not recognition of Vijar's personal strength. That was why it had bothered him.

Still, that was no excuse to come to blows with Hectowyzeth. Certainly, Vijar would win if they got into it, but Hectowyzeth was known for more than his own strength; he was a famous general who had been victorious despite being outnumbered ten to one. It was clear who held the advantage in any fight that involved leading troops. Any boasts Vijar could make about his individual martial prowess would just seem pathetic, knowing that. He was often at a loss about how he should interact with this orthrous.

Finally, there was another zooostia, who had stayed quiet—Muar Praksha.

Known by the epithet Black Iron, he was an accomplished ranger often likened to a shadow slipping through the darkness.

Though rangers were rare among the physically blessed zooostias who usually relied on brute force in battle, Muar used his terrifying skills as an assassin to approach stealthily, launch a surprise attack, and quietly finish off his enemies before they had a chance to respond. Once he targeted someone, his iron will never faltering, he would end them without fail, hence the nickname.

Vijar didn't think he would lose, but a fight against any one of them would be no easy win.

"And as for the reason we're not attacking, it's because of the order I received from Emperor Jaldabaoth at Limun."

"What? Really?"

The reason Vijar asked was because out of the forty thousand who had been gathered to form this assault force, only Rokesh had spoken to Jaldabaoth directly. Once the others had been called to the city of Karinsha, preparations were made, and all that remained was waiting to move out.

Jaldabaoth kept teleporting between multiple cities, so there hadn't been any further contact from him.

"Emperor Jaldabaoth said to give the humans occupying the city a few days."

"Why should we do that?" asked Vijar.

"To make them afraid. There aren't even ten thousand of them. If we only count the few who can fight, then the number goes down further. Meanwhile, all of us are battle hardened... I can only imagine how terrified they must be."

"I see... Our emperor is truly terrifying."

"Hee-hee-hee. Yes, exactly. But I do understand how you feel, Sir Vijar. How much longer until their time runs out?"

"Well, he left the number of days up to us. That said, though we have two months of food, we shouldn't give them too much time."

"And the prisoners have to be managed, too."

The huge number of prisoners was currently being supervised by a mere ten thousand subhumans. Though they were stronger than humans individually, numbers had a strength all their own. If any kind of mass disturbance occurred, they most likely wouldn't be able to contain it.

"That's right. Which is why I've gathered us here—to make the final decision. I propose we attack in two days and finish this once and for all. Any objections?"

No one objected.

"Good. Then we'll attack after two more days. Continue observing until then."

It seemed extremely unlikely, but there was a nonzero chance that the enemy moved first.

"Should we finish off the humans we brought with us?"

Some subhumans ate humans. And those races liked their food fresh. Zooostias weren't particularly fond of human meat; they preferred beef. But if it was a choice between beef jerky and fresh human meat, most would choose the latter.

Meanwhile, Elemental Storm made a sour face. Magiroses didn't eat humans, probably because their appearances were relatively similar.

"Hee-hee-hee. So how about we eat them alive right in front of the city tomorrow? That'll scare the ones inside."

"Good idea. And if we announce our attack tomorrow…"

"Don't make them despair too much. What'll we do if they surrender? It's when they cling to hope and struggle that makes the fight any fun. There's no bigger bore than killing people who have already resigned themselves to die."

Vijar wanted to fight strong opponents. There was no sport in combat with the weak.

"Oh. There's one more thing—an order from Emperor Jaldabaoth. He doesn't want us to kill everyone; we should let some survivors escape. It doesn't have to be a lot. My plan is to kill everyone on this side guarding the west gate and then chase off the ones by the east gate."

"Meaning the one leading the offensive on the east gate needs to be someone who can control their troops. Otherwise, they'll just massacre everyone."

When Nasrenée said that, everyone's eyes gathered on one individual.

"I see… Then is it all right if I take all my fellow orthrouses?"

"I'd like to use some as messengers, so could you spare a few?"

"Understood, Sir Rokesh. Then I, Hectowyzeth a Lagara, shall handle the east gate."

"I'd also like to have smaller detachments positioned at the north and south walls for added pressure. There's no need to mount serious attacks, but I do want them to do some damage. I'd like someone who's used to fighting at range to handle it…"

There were three present who could be relied on in long-distance fights. The one Rokesh chose was the taciturn zooostia.

"Sir Muar Praksha."

"Understood," he replied sulkily.

"The rest of you will focus on the west gate. I doubt there will be much for you to do, but if someone strong shows up, I'm counting on you all; I'll be overseeing the operation, so I won't be on the front lines."

Vijar and the others nodded.

"Then we're in agreement. We seize this city in two days. Take it easy and conserve your energy until the moment we make those foolish humans scream."

2

As she headed for the King of Darkness's room, Neia swallowed the sickening taste that rose from the pit of her stomach. An inescapable sourness spread throughout her mouth.

She took the leather pouch on her hip and drank some of the water inside.

The contents had acquired the distinct flavor of the leather, so the water wasn't very enjoyable, but it soothed the irritation in her throat and washed away the foul aftertaste that had lingered. Her nausea remained, however, and the water couldn't bring the color back to her pale face.

Neia recalled what she desperately wanted to forget—a scene that made her sick to her stomach.

Three days had passed since the city came under siege by a giant subhuman army.

There hadn't been any attacks or negotiations since it started, but on this day, the subhumans had brought out some Sacred Kingdom prisoners to a spot just beyond the walls of Roytz, the small city they were currently in. The invaders had been close enough that someone well trained could have attacked them with a bow or sling, but unfortunately the humans didn't have anyone like that inside the walls.

Neia was sure that she could hit them with the bow the King of Darkness had lent her. Sadly, an overt attack like that could have sparked a battle, beginning a fight of ten thousand against forty thousand. And they would have to open the gate to rescue the prisoners.

That simply wasn't an option, since the subhumans would flood in the moment they tried, so all they could do was watch.

There were a little fewer than twenty prisoners made up of a variety of men, women, and children. No elderly, however. They were all naked and worse for wear.

The Sacred Kingdom citizens who had gathered to see what was going on assumed they would be used as some kind of bargaining chips. Then the bloodshed began.

The subhumans casually killed them all.

Ripping their throats out, subhumans nearly ten feet tall held the bodies upside down. Neia could see clearly as a huge amount of bright-red blood suffused the soil.

Then the dismembering began.

Neia had seen her father butcher animals a few times. But it looked completely different when it was being done to humans, and the sight shocked her deeply.

After that, what remained of the prisoners was devoured while they were still fresh.

The worst part was that some of the victims were still alive when the eating began.

Neia could still hear the shrieks of the infant whose stomach was torn apart by ravenous mouths and the wails of those having their innards yanked out.

It was thanks to Gustav's smart thinking that they had left Remedios behind under the pretext of having her guard Master Caspond. If she had been there, she would have started the battle for sure.

"*Sigh.*" Neia took another sip of water and forced it down.

Some say it's better to just throw up if the urge comes, but she figured it would be rude to visit the King of Darkness's chamber smelling like vomit.

After exhaling and checking her breath a couple of times, she stood before his door.

There was no one standing on either side of it.

It meant that under siege by the subhumans as they were, there weren't enough personnel to assign the king proper guards.

Neia knocked and called out. "Your Majesty, it's Squire Neia Baraja. May I come in?"

"Yes, come in."

Having received permission, Neia quietly entered the room.

Most of the furniture had been ruined by the subhumans, so his quarters were simply appointed. That said, the room was still better furnished than probably any other in the city.

The King of Darkness was standing with his back to Neia, looking out the window.

"It's quite hectic out there. So many people running below my window. It's the fourth day since we've been surrounded, but I don't think there has been this big of a commotion since the first. Has there been some sign they'll attack soon?"

The king had been spending his time quietly in this room as if to emphasize that he didn't wish to participate in the fight. He didn't attend the war council meeting they held when the subhumans first moved into position outside the town, either.

The leadership of the liberation army weren't too thrilled about that, but when he pointed out that in the long run, it wouldn't really do them any favors to have another country's king butting in, no one was in any position to make demands.

Instead, Neia was dispatched to various meetings. She knew the army leaders were trying to share information with the king through her, and she could see why they were doing it. But that was also how she ended up witnessing the massacre.

"...No, there hasn't been any major enemy movement. But they did carry out what I suppose you could call...a demonstration. I think there's been a change of the guard and so on."

"I see. I take it the showdown is imminent? The subhumans must have wanted to hurt your people's morale... By the way, do you think you can win?"

No. She could reply immediately; the answer was so obvious.

First, they were far too outnumbered.

Ten thousand humans against forty thousand subhumans.

And that was only if they included children and elderly. Plus, it wasn't as if everyone was well rested and had a chance to properly recover from the wounds—both physical and mental—they had suffered in the prison camps.

Common wisdom said that the defenders held the advantage in a siege, but that didn't apply when both sides were never evenly matched to begin with.

It was practically pointless to compare subhumans to ordinary, run-of-the-mill humans, considering how fragile they were.

The only ones who could put up a decent fight against subhumans were paladins, priests, and the career soldiers known as servicemen, but naturally they didn't have many of those. Against a subhuman army of forty thousand, their pitiful numbers would be as powerless as splashing water at a fire dragon's breath.

But was it actually impossible for them to win? Not necessarily.

Even without the trump card of the King of Darkness, it was possible for one person to repel the enemy.

If there weren't any extraordinary subhumans in their ranks, then the Sacred Kingdom's most powerful paladin, Remedios Custodio, could probably sweep away forty thousand of them. At least if fatigue and sustaining critical hits weren't taken into account.

But there was no guarantee that there wasn't a warrior as powerful as Remedios in the attacking army. If anything, it was more likely for there to be one present.

Neia remembered Mighty King Buser, who had ruled this town previously. He had fallen like a sack of trash before the King of Darkness, but that was because the king was simply that much more powerful. Overwhelmingly so. No matter how Neia tried, she would never manage to win against someone like that.

There could easily be another subhuman lord just as strong as the Sacred Kingdom's strongest paladin—and maybe even stronger. To Neia, that much power couldn't even be measured accurately.

And in reality, fatigue couldn't be left out of the equation, either. Not even the strongest warrior was immune to fatigue. It was possible to recover temporarily with magic, but the problem wouldn't go away indefinitely.

If the enemy attacked Remedios while she was still exhausted after slaughtering an army of ten thousand, it would only take an average-strength subhuman to defeat her. Numbers were truly powerful.

But if there was a way to negate that... Neia's gaze moved to the great king whose back was still turned to her.

An absolute power.

An overlord, a being who transcended this world.

The King of Darkness, Ainz Ooal Gown. He was their only hope.

Captivated by the sight of his regal back, Neia realized she hadn't answered his question and blurted out a response. "I-I'm not sure!" Her voice came out a bit louder than intended because she was flustered. Blushing, she reverted to her regular volume. "All we can do is give it our best shot."

The king seemed not to notice her distress and followed up with another question. "I see. And is there any new information about the enemy? Or if Jaldabaoth is present?"

"Nothing has changed from the other day. We haven't spotted him among their ranks."

"Hmm, then sorry, but it would be difficult for me to aid in the defense. We'll be in trouble if I don't recover the mana I've used. We need to consider the fact that he may be aiming to strike when I'm low."

"Of course. Everyone understands your position on this matter, Your Majesty."

Once someone reported they had spotted a demon that seemed like Jaldabaoth, but when Neia said she would confirm, she was suddenly told that it was probably a mistake. Judging by the mood during that meeting, it was clear the members of the war council had conspired while Neia wasn't present to attempt a ruse by feeding the king false information.

These guys who would lie to another country's king just because they detest undead are completely devoid of good faith… Even trapped like this, shouldn't we conduct ourselves with pride when we engage with someone deserving of respect?

"How do you think the subhumans are likely to move?"

"Well, up until today, they were only at the west gate, but they've split their forces and maneuvered a smaller group to the east gate. It might be in preparation for the coming battle."

"So they've had enough time to build a siege weapon? Well, I suppose we can say that's a good thing. Mostly because they didn't try to starve you."

Neia wasn't sure if the current situation was good or not, but it was true they had no recourse if the enemy chose to let them wither on the vine.

The surrounding area consisted mostly of featureless, flat land. Sallying out would just end with an instant, crushing defeat. Holding the city wall against an assault, considering the number disparity, would still only make it a little more of a fight. Of course, that was simply a change from over-whelmingly bad odds to fairly bad odds.

"It might be because they have no way of knowing how much food we have, but more than that, they probably don't think this minor city will be very hard to take."

"They did overcome that wall we saw when we entered the Sacred Kingdom, so it makes sense that these fortifications seem like nothing to them... If you put up a good enough defense to the point where the sub-humans feel like they're losing the advantage, they'll switch to starvation tactics. Then things will get really tough."

It was like he was saying that what lay beyond this unwinnable battle was the *true* battle.

"Your Majesty, what do you think will happen next?"

"How will things develop from here? I don't know any better than you. Frankly, being besieged like this may very well be checkmate. You should only hole up if you know you have reinforcements coming. Or if your opponents have a time limit for some reason. But we're solidly in enemy territory. Merely holding the city doesn't help your chances very much."

"We did send the nobles who were imprisoned here to the south, so the chance of reinforcements isn't exactly zero."

That's what she said, but she knew they couldn't count on getting any substantial aid.

In order for forces from the south to reach them, they would have to break through the subhumans on the southern front. And even if reinforce-ments somehow arrived, they'd have forty thousand subhumans to fight the moment they got here.

"Well, that would be nice."

He didn't seem to believe her one bit.

Well, why would he? The only way to get through this without a single casualty would be—

Neia dismissed the idea that came to mind unbidden.

The King of Darkness came to this land to fight Jaldabaoth. Making him use up his mana and lower his chances of victory would be unforgivable.

"…It'll take a while before I can use the teleportation I used on the orcs, but the one I was using to return to the Nation of Darkness occasionally is still available. I could probably move a few dozen people, but you probably can't choose. You probably don't want to."

"I'm glad you understand my feelings, Your Majesty."

She thought maybe she should have him take Caspond away somewhere, at least. But at the same time, she wondered if that would really be a good idea.

The king of another country was braving the battlefield to confront a horrifying demon. Meanwhile, here were the leaders of her country, asking him to help a man of royal blood escape. She could hardly imagine anything more shameful.

As Neia was preoccupied with these musings, the king turned around for the first time since she had entered the room.

The red flames in his vacant orbits were facing her directly. At first, those eyes had scared her, but now that the initial shock had gone away, she actually found them rather striking.

"This is what I think, Miss Baraja. You clashing with the enemy here is a result of the foolishness your higher-ups invited. A single squire can't overcome that. Have you considered pursuing your own interests? …If you like, my nation would accept you. Training to be a paladin, you could make use of your skills there, too, I'm sure."

Neia hesitated, unsure how to respond.

Though she was incredibly moved by his worry for her, the thought of what she would lose if she accepted his offer made her tremble with fear.

The sacrifices her parents must have made for the sake of the kingdom.

Her love for her hometown.

A future where she would never be able to return to the country of her ancestors.

Memories of her few friends.

A whirl of thoughts bubbled up and then faded. But one remained, and it was the most important thing of all.

I'm a member of the Paladin Order.

She wasn't sure what justice was yet, but there was one thing she could say with her head held high.

"Even so, as a subject of this kingdom, I need to save as many people as I can. It's only natural to rescue the weak—to help those who are struggling."

The King of Darkness stopped moving. It was so abrupt, it was as if he had been frozen.

"…Mm."

With that murmur, he put a hand to his chin.

Apparently, what Neia said had affected him. He was watching her very closely.

But it was a totally normal thing to say… She felt a bit awkward.

"You're stationed on the west gate wall when the subhumans attack, right? The left side of town from here? That's a dangerous position. You're making a big mistake if you think I'm going to save you."

"I'm aware of that."

Due to her archery skills, Neia would be fighting on the front line. It was practically a given that she would die. This was war, and she had steeled her resolve.

Pursing her lips, she looked straight at him.

"Ah, those are his eyes. I like those eyes."

He seemed to be talking to himself, but Neia blushed in spite of herself. She was sure he didn't mean anything by it, but hearing the word *like* directed at her from someone she respected so highly did quite a number on her.

"Well…I suppose I'll lend you some items, Miss Baraja. Use them well."

He drew a surprisingly large object out of thin air. It had occurred to her before when he first shocked her by producing the bow in the carriage, but Neia was realizing once again the wonders of magic never ceased.

The magic item that appeared was one Neia had seen before. The green enchanted armor with the turtle-shell-esque pattern had been worn by Mighty King Buser.

"I-it's...!"

"I'm sure this will come in handy. For your protection, I mean."

It was too large for Neia to wear. In fact, it wasn't human-size at all. But from what she knew about magic armor, she figured it would work out.

Refitting normal armor would require smithing. And there was a limit to how much modification could be done; frankly, resizing something this drastically would normally be impossible.

But magic armor was different. If no special conditions were needed to equip it, just about anyone could wear it. There wouldn't be any major changes in its functionality, but it would conform to fit the user.

Theoretically, it was perfectly feasible to create a thumb-size suit of armor and later equip a giant with it. That said, the durability of the armor still depended on the amount and quality of materials used. If the armor was originally the size of a ring, its enchantment would not be even half as effective, making it weak against magic or corrosive attacks, and it would succumb easily to gear-breaking abilities.

The world simply wasn't that convenient and lacked such obvious loopholes. If nothing else, she was sure that Buser's armor was very durable after seeing how large it was despite no one wearing it.

"I have three other things for you." The King of Darkness handed them over. "This crown, these gauntlets, and this necklace. They don't overlap with anything you have, do they?"

"N-no. I didn't have any enchanted items to begin with."

"Excellent. Then I'll briefly explain what they do."

The Crown of Psychic Defense was fairly self-explanatory. It protected the user's mind from attacks with attributes such as charm or fear. The only catch was that while it completely nullified incoming magic, it did nothing against special abilities. It was also important to note that it prevented positive effects as well.

The gauntlets were Archer's Gauntlets. Apparently, there were some spells that required shooting skills, and that's why the King of Darkness originally had them made, but he later stopped using that type of magic, so all that equipment had just been languishing in storage.

And the necklace was an item that consumed mana in exchange for casting the tier-three faith magic healing spell Heavy Recovery. As long as the wearer had mana to spare, the spell could be cast any number of times, but apparently it required far more mana than the spell usually cost, so with Neia's meager store, she figured she could reliably use it only once. She would have to be judicious with the timing. This item was not one that the king and his people made but apparently something he had bought because he found its appearance attractive.

She could see a lot of care had gone into crafting the necklace; it looked like a goddess holding a green gem. No wonder the king had found it aesthetically pleasing.

Presented with such a stunning set of items, Neia shook her head.

"M-my apologies, Your Majesty. I can't borrow these items."

Each of the things he was offering had to be extremely valuable. If she died in battle with them equipped, they would undoubtedly fall into the hands of the subhumans and only make the enemy stronger. Or her body could simply be lost in the tumult of war, and all the precious items would go with her. Plus, she was already borrowing the bow. Was it acceptable to take further advantage of his kindness?

If anything, she should have returned the bow before going into battle.

"Why not? They'll be useful to you in the coming battle, you know. Well, as a warrior, you may not have enough mana to use the necklace, but it's worth a shot."

In response to the king's question, Neia expressed her anxieties honestly. He answered with a chuckle.

"Then let's do this. Go out there with the firm intention of returning them to me."

Of course, that was her intention, but she didn't think mindset alone would be enough to overcome the dire situation. But when she told him that, he waved her off.

"It's fine; just take them. I have a spell that can locate my magic items. I'll remember that you have them, and if you lose them, I'll just cast the spell to find them."

"Are you sure, Your Majesty?"

"I am. Now…no need to be shy. Take them."

If he had expressions, she was sure this one would be a smile—that was how gently he spoke to her.

It would be rude to refuse such benevolence. After thinking about taking advantage and how to apologize if she lost them…

"Well? Aren't you going to promise that you'll return them to me?"

"!"

Come back alive. The significance his words held made her tear up. There hadn't been many people in Neia's life besides her parents who had been this kind to her.

The Nation of Darkness is fortunate to be ruled by such a kind king, she thought as she bit her lip and bowed her head.

"Thank you! I'll be sure to return them!"

"…………Good."

When she raised her head, she wiped the tears out of the corners of her eyes.

She couldn't immediately put on the armor, but the necklace, gauntlets, and crown she could equip right away. First, she donned the necklace.

The moment she draped it around her neck, she could sense the knowledge of how to use it flow into her as she gained the item's ability. It felt like an extension of her own body, and just as she wasn't frightened of her arms and legs, the sensation seemed utterly natural.

Next was the crown. There wasn't any particularly special feeling when she put it on. But given the explanation she had heard, she figured it would be clear when something triggered it.

Finally, the gauntlets.

These, on the contrary, made for quite a vivid change.

Power welled up from inside her.

She had been on the receiving end of strength-boosting spells before, and this felt identical to that. Her movements grew faster and sharper, as if the amount of muscle in her body had suddenly increased. Not only that but she could make out smaller details, and it seemed like her heart and lung function had noticeably improved, giving her better stamina.

It was almost as if her body had suddenly gotten much stronger.

"Wow…"

She hardly noticed changes that resulted from training, since those increases were incremental. But this was such a dramatic improvement in ability that it was impossible to ignore.

The other surprising thing was that she didn't feel any incongruity between herself of a moment ago and now; it had been a seamless transition.

"Magic is amazing…"

Hearing her murmur, the King of Darkness shrugged. "It sure is. Magic for daily life is what surprised me."

"It did?"

"Because you can make stuff like sugar and pepper. It's possible to produce ice, and you can even create ores, though it's supposedly not worth the mana. Magic items can provide daily essentials and even fulfill an entire city's water needs… It seems like those sorts of objects play a big role in the development of this world's culture."

"Oh…do you think so?"

She didn't understand why a caster as great as the King of Darkness would be surprised by something so ordinary. But if he believed it, she had no reason to doubt it was the truth. And she readily acknowledged that everyday magic really did come in handy in all sorts of ways. Without it, quite a lot of regular activities would become rather arduous.

"The sewers that make use of slimes—or rather, the way they coexist within… Ah, I've started rambling. You've probably got better things to do, Miss Baraja. Don't worry—I won't keep you from your work."

Frankly, it wasn't unreasonable to say that she considered nothing more important than being his aide, but given that the defenders needed all the help they could get, there actually was quite a lot for Neia to do. Keeping watch was her main task—something anyone could do, but nonetheless critical.

"Thank you, Your Majesty. I'll make sure to come back alive."

"Right. If you get in trouble, run for the east gate. I imagine that's the only place you'll manage to survive."

With Buser's armor in hand, Neia bowed and left the king's room.

•

In the war room, Remedios Custodio was meeting with three other paladins to consider how to best allocate their troops.

Contrary to how Remedios tended to bungle almost everything else, she had a keen edge when it came to battle. Her little sister would say, *There's nothing wrong with your brain; you just need to study*, but if she had listened to that advice, she probably never would've excelled to this degree in all things related to combat.

She was different from her sister, who was endowed with intelligence, aptitude, and beauty.

We have ten thousand. Estimates put our opponents at forty thousand. Victory conditions are either holding out until reinforcements arrive from the south or forcing the enemy army to retreat... Maybe if there were ten of me, we would have a chance...

If the members of the Nine Colors, chosen for their strength, had been present, the defenders might have been able to put up a decent fight, but the reality was harsh.

For any chance of buying time, we need to counter the enemy's first attack in a way that will deal major damage. That should put them on guard and give us a little breathing room. The enemy shouldn't have any way of knowing the true size of our force.

There was also serious consideration given to the idea of launching a preemptive strike.

That would involve concentrating their troops at the east gate and sallying out to annihilate the enemy forces there in one fell swoop. After that, they could shift to the west gate.

But the outcome of any attack was clear. Such a plan would no doubt end in failure. They wouldn't be able to defeat the small detachment of enemies in the east before the enemies' main force breached the west gate, which would mean the fall of the city.

The disparity in numbers was a real problem. In order to win, they had to find a way to close that gap.

But there's no chance of that happening.

Remedios frowned and moved the pawns on the map arbitrarily.

She was hoping for a flash of inspiration. But no path to salvation revealed itself.

"Any good ideas, guys?"

"Well, I…"

After listening to the other paladins' proposals, rejecting them, asking for more, and repeating that cycle, everyone had run out of ideas. A heavy silence had descended on the room when there came a knock at the door.

To Remedios, it felt like being saved by the bell.

"So this is where you were, Commander."

The one who had entered was her deputy Gustav Montagnés. His timing couldn't have been better. Everyone else in the room seemed to feel the same way, given how their gloomy expressions brightened slightly with hope.

"Yes, and you've come at a perfect moment. I want you to give me your thoughts on the situation."

She jerked her chin toward the map of the city spread out on the table. He glanced in that direction briefly and seemed to quickly grasp what she was getting at after a moment.

"If I have any, I'm more than happy to offer them all. But before that, I have a few things to get your thoughts on, if you don't mind."

"Hmm? Why would I mind? Go ahead."

"Very well…" Gustav lowered his voice slightly. "To be frank, there's been an inconvenient development; some of the citizens are requesting that the King of Darkness participate in the battle."

The King of Darkness was not planning to fight this time. He needed to recover the mana he had expended, and they were still on guard against the possibility that Jaldabaoth was scheming to force him into using more here.

Her sister, Kelart, recovered mana in a day, so the former reason didn't sit right with Remedios. But when the king said it was problematic to compare the amount of mana he had used retaking the city with the same amount a human had, everyone else accepted the explanation, so she didn't bring it up again; as there had been priests present, she had no reason to think otherwise if everyone else found it reasonable.

The latter reason, meanwhile, was one Remedios could heartily agree with.

Who could say whether Jaldabaoth was hiding within the subhuman army?

They had brought the king here to fight Jaldabaoth. Remedios would be happy if they took each other out, but it wasn't as if she wanted the king to lose. It made sense for her, even though she absolutely hated the undead, to make sure he could fight at full power. The few nobles in the city offered to pay what they could—a sum that made even Remedios's eyes bulge—if the king would participate in the battle despite his protests, but he still refused.

"Well, what's the problem? We already know that he won't be fighting. Just be up-front with the people."

"Commander, I can't tell them that. If we're unlucky—or not even—there's a chance that this will set off something much worse."

"Why?"

She couldn't understand. What was the problem with him not participating?

Gustav frowned in reply to her innocent question.

"The people who witnessed us retake the city saw that what's impossible for the paladins on their own is easily within the realm of possibility if the king is helping."

She really didn't see what he was getting at.

"It's not a pleasant thing to admit, but it's true, right? What's the problem?"

"The key point is they trust the King of Darkness more than they trust us. If they find out the person they believe to be the strongest one present isn't participating in the defense of the city, morale will drop like a rock."

"Trust him…? He's an undead!"

"True, but he's also the one who liberated the city and rescued the prisoners. To them, the King of Darkness is a hero."

"A hero?" she shot back while blinking furiously. "They think *he's* a hero? An undead, hater of life, lover of death? He abandoned hostages—no, it's fair to say he outright killed them!"

"Even so. At least they still only consider him a hero. At the rate we're going, it might not be long before the people will begin to see him as their savior. Or even the holy king's—"

"—The Holy Lady's." Remedios grimaced. "I've said this countless times, but Holy Lady Calca is being held prisoner somewhere. I'm sure of it. After the battle with Jaldabaoth, there were paladins and priests strewn all over, but Kelart and the Holy Lady were nowhere to be found. If they really were dead, there would have been no reason to take the corpses. He must be planning to use them as hostages."

"I beg your pardon, Commander, but we're at the point that the Holy Lady may have trouble governing."

"What do you mean?"

"…We allowed the wall to be breached and were on watch when the subhumans poured over our borders. There will be those who wish to serve an absolute ruler who can guarantee them protection."

"But he's… He's an undead!"

"I'm repeating myself, but that doesn't matter. He is the one who rescued them from their suffering!"

Remedios could not accept this point.

"He wasn't the only one fighting! We were there under the Holy Lady's banner, weren't we?"

"Yes, we were. We and the citizens all fought. But even taking that into account, if the king achieves further successes, he will only rise in popularity, and I fear many will welcome him as their new ruler."

"What?!" Remedios shouted. "Why would that happen?! Who would consider him not just a hero but superior to the Holy Lady?! What are you even saying, man?!"

"But from the people's point of view—"

"How could anyone in their right mind think that about an undead?! Do they know how hard the Holy Lady has worked, the sacrifices she's made to make them happy? The people—"

"Please, Commander!"

"How can I stay silent?! Tell me how, Gustav! Are you being serious right now?!"

Swept up in a torrent of violent emotion, Remedios pounded her fists on the table.

A living legend herself, she struck with prodigious force. Her blow was so powerful that it tore clean through the table, sending only what she touched flying to the ground. The strange deformation, looking like a giant had pinched the edge of the table and pulled, spoke volumes to her fury.

"Commander, please calm down! We know how great and compassionate the Holy Lady is. There's no way an undead could compare! But we know that because we were close to her!"

"Are you a buffoon?! Just because they never had an audience with her doesn't mean people would respect an undead from another nation more than the leader of their own country. You're jumping to conclusions!"

"Commander!" he practically shrieked. "The King of Darkness is the monarch of another nation and an undead, but he freed them from their pain! That was something that we—that the Holy Lady—couldn't do for them!"

After Gustav shouted all that in a rush, the only sound that filled the room was his panting.

"...What do you guys think?"

When Remedios quietly addressed the other paladins in the room, they exchanged glances. Then one of them answered after summoning up the courage to speak.

"We certainly don't think of the King of Darkness as a hero. But we were aware that there are some commoners who feel that way."

Then another spoke.

"Many people know he took the city with the help of only one other—on his own, really. And as word of mouth spreads the story to people who didn't witness the fight, he's only becoming more lionized."

And another.

"It's true that the King of Darkness came on his own to the aid of a country in crisis that isn't even an ally or friend. If you ignore the fact that he's an undead…it's quite a heroic thing to do."

It seemed Remedios was the only one who couldn't accept the truth. Knowing that, what was the right way to answer Gustav's question?

Certainly, if a hero refused to participate in battle, morale among the defenders would drop, and it could lead to a serious issue developing if the people were left to wonder why. The enemy outnumbered them four to one. Considering the mental stress of standing against that army with those odds, perhaps getting upset was only natural.

"…Then if the king becomes a villain, we'll have killed two birds with one stone. What if we told the people he had no intention of helping us anymore?"

"Such a lie would be quite damaging," said Gustav. "The mental state of the people is like a dam ready to burst. If they learned the truth at some point and realized we had deceived them, there would be no coming back."

"But we could tell them in a way that it wouldn't be a lie."

"If the people consider it a lie, that's what it'll be, no?"

"Then we just have to prevent the king from ever meeting them."

"…If a riot broke out and someone asked explicitly to meet him, would you kill them?"

"…I don't want to do that."

Gustav heaved a sigh. "We're out of moves. The King of Darkness has already done too much. It wouldn't have come to this if we had been able to take back the city on our own… In the worst case, the country might actually split. If the King of Darkness was to declare this land to be an enclave of his nation, who would be able to stop him?"

"This country belongs to the Holy Lady and the people who live here, not to some undead! Do you think the neighboring countries would even accept that in the first place?" She slammed her fists against the table again.

Gustav replied calmly but firmly. "Yes, I think they would. You saw them, too…the monsters in that city. No state would want to have a nation with such terrifying military power as an enemy. To them, it would be smarter to turn their backs on us as we slip from power… And if he claimed an enclave in our lands, that would mean the Nation of Darkness would have to split its forces to defend its new holdings, which many of the surrounding countries would see as advantageous. And if the locals wish for it, the king would have the perfect justification to follow through."

"…You mean they'd rather be part of an undead country than one that can't protect its people, sir?"

Gustav nodded and answered the paladin's question. "That's exactly what I'm saying."

"Tell me, Gustav, was it a mistake for me to bring him here?"

"No, Commander. At the time, it was the best choice. But it's true that we've relied on his power too much. Like I said before, if we had managed to liberate those two prison camps on our own, things wouldn't have turned out like this. The masses might have still been frightened of the King of Darkness and harbored hostility toward him."

"…What should we do?"

"We'll think of something to tell the people, buy some time, and then repel that huge army without the king's help. If we can't manage that…the fighting might continue even if Jaldabaoth is defeated in the future."

Remedios stared up at the ceiling.

"…Then I guess that's what we have to do. That King of Darkness… I wonder if he had this in mind all along."

"I don't know… I honestly don't. But he may have calculated that much out."

"So he might have ambitions to expand his holdings? The Nation of Darkness is pretty small, right?"

"I don't think it's quite that small, but it's just one city and its surroundings, plus lowlands where the undead are said to spawn in large numbers."

It was easy to conclude that was the main motivation.

"That awful undead! We should have just gotten Momon's help."

"The same thing might have happened with Momon. But he probably wouldn't have had the impact the King of Darkness has. Seeing a king come alone leaves a deep impression. Plus the fact that he's an undead, someone who should be our country's natural enemy."

So if it's a bad guy who does something good, he looks extra good?

"…Shit."

When she realized, in the silent room, that Gustav was asking her opinion, she gave him instructions.

"Let's consult Master Caspond. If—yes, *if* because I doubt it's true, but *if* the Holy Lady has perished, then he would be next in line, right?"

"None of the other royals have been found, so yes. Let's do that."

Leaving the other paladins, Remedios took Gustav and went to Caspond's chamber.

The conclusion they reached was to do as Gustav had proposed: delay their response to the people, and when the enemy attacked them in the meantime, they would defeat the besieging army without relying on the King of Darkness's power and demonstrate that the Sacred Kingdom could still be counted on.

3

Major movement has been detected in the subhuman camp—the report told Neia that the time had finally come.

This was, without a doubt, a sign of an impending attack.

Clad in the items she'd borrowed from the King of Darkness, she raced through the city.

She knew the people she passed were staring at her with wide eyes.

They were captivated by the splendid bow and shocked to see her wearing armor that had belonged to the previous ruler of the city, Mighty King Buser. With her sharp ears, Neia could hear people murmuring, "Who's that warrior?" She also heard their responses: "The King of Darkness's attendant" or "A lady from the Nation of Darkness."

I'm not from the Nation of Darkness, though…

Whenever she heard mistaken information like this, she both wanted and didn't want to know what kind of rumors were going around. If there was one that would cause trouble for the king, she would have to make a clear denial.

But "the King of Darkness's attendant," huh…?

The thought made her sort of happy, and she found herself laughing under her breath—which made the people she was passing by scream.

I realize I look like my dad, but come on…

With those things on her mind, Neia was racing for her position on the wall by the west gate, which was also where most of the subhuman troops were massing.

Eighty percent of the paladins, priests, servicemen, and able-bodied males were stationed at the west gate and adjacent wall. The other 20 percent were at the east gate, while the women, children, elderly, and other noncombatants were assigned to keep watch on the northern and southern stretches of the city walls.

Remedios Custodio was in command at the west gate and Gustav Montagnés at the east gate, while the commander in chief was Caspond Bessarez. Of course, the commander in chief was stationed at the commanders' lodge in the city and didn't venture outside.

It wasn't long before Neia could see the west gate come into view.

The portcullis the King of Darkness had blown to pieces was a part of the east gate, so the west gate was intact. Still, subhuman strength easily surpassed that of most humans. If they rammed the gate with a huge tree, it wouldn't be hard for them to break it down.

Neia clenched her fists to stop her hands from shaking.

If this position was breached and the enemy flowed in through the opening, it would quickly become impossible to contain the attackers, and the city would fall in short order.

If that happened, Neia would have no way to flee and would probably end up dying in battle against countless subhumans.

She brought a shaking hand to her mouth and bit it.

Calm down! Otherwise, you won't even be able to make the easy shots!

The magic item the King of Darkness had lent her would guard against magic attacks that targeted her mind, but it couldn't help her with the fear that came from within. Still, if she wasn't wearing it, she probably would've been even more terrified.

Feeling the throbbing in her bitten finger, she entered the tower that was on the left when looking out from the city and bounded up the stairs leading to the top of the wall two at a time.

Coming from her meeting with the King of Darkness, Neia was the last to arrive, it seemed (with permission from her superiors, of course, so no one would complain). The many citizens who had been gathered to defend this location were already there.

As she was about to hurry to her designated position, the paladin in charge of the west gate's left flank stood in her way.

"The King of Darkness doesn't seem to be here..."

For a moment, Neia looked at the holy knight's face in confusion. She had told her superiors he wouldn't be participating in this battle. For the paladin to bring this up now...did that mean he hadn't heard?

But Neia realized right away that wasn't the case. He must have harbored a shred of hope the king would change his mind at the last minute and come.

Neia studied the army of subhumans arrayed outside the city. There were over thirty thousand of them, but their overwhelming presence made it seem like there were more.

Up against an army like that, she could understand the temptation of hoping the peerless King of Darkness would show up. Honestly, she felt the same, but…

"His Majesty isn't coming. This is our, the Sacred Kingdom's, fight."

The paladin hesitated for a moment.

Neia slipped past him to run to her position when—

"Wait, Squire Neia Baraja!"

"Sir!" She halted and straightened up.

"I want you to stand by here for now."

"What?!"

She glanced around. This was near where the tower opened up onto the wall. There was an awful lot of people coming and going. Wouldn't she simply be in the way? And it was quite far from her appointed position near the center.

"M-may I ask why? Is there something you need me to do?"

"N-no, it's not that, just… There's a bit of an issue… Squire Baraja, you're to stand by. Got it?"

"Uh, okay…"

She didn't understand, but he must have had a reason. Otherwise, he wouldn't put a soldier with proper training in a place like this when the battle could start anytime.

Was my assignment changed? Like they want me to snipe the enemy commander or something? It's easy to tell at a glance that the bow the King of Darkness lent me is high-quality equipment, so maybe they want to keep me in reserve as a sort of trump card?

"Understood. How long shall I wait? And where should I stand by?"

"Uh, hmm. Until the enemy attack begins, I guess. And for the position…"

"Huh? You want me to cut it that close?"

Yeah, this is weird, Neia was thinking, perplexed, when several militiamen came up the stairs carrying a huge pot. It was probably food for those already standing by on the wall. She could tell from how much they were sweating despite the cold that they had already made several trips—a matter of course when there were hundreds of mouths to feed.

When she moved against the wall to make way for them, they bustled past in front of her. But one of them glanced up and saw her face.

He looked surprised.

She thought it might have been because she resembled her father, but that wasn't it.

"Huh? You're the one always hanging around the King of Darkness, aren't you? I mean, you're his attendant, right?"

"Oh, that's why... Er, I beg your pardon. Yes, I'm His Majesty's aide."

Perhaps the other men carrying the pot overheard their conversation because they stopped to stare at her in surprise as well. Probably for the same reason as the one talking to her.

The thought that everyone knew her as the king's attendant was embarrassing, but she also felt proud.

Having no idea what sorts of emotions he had invoked, the militiaman asked somewhat hesitantly, "Actually, there's something I'd like to know about him—"

"—Wait! Er, I mean, hang on a second. She's busy. Please continue with what you were doing." The paladin abruptly jumped between her and the men.

That was a bizarre reaction. No matter how she looked at it, she could tell he obviously didn't want her talking to the troops, but...

Does this have something to do with his earlier order? He doesn't want to let me talk to them... But why? Because they were asking about the King of Darkness?

She didn't know the reason, but it would be easy to reach the answer.

"I'm fine. What can I help you with?"

If the paladin didn't want them to talk to her, then she just had to talk to them.

"Squire Baraja!"

"Are you interrupting a question about the King of Darkness?!" she shot back at the same volume he had been shouting at.

Frankly, it was shameful to keep leaning on the king's reputation, but she figured she should confirm that the Sacred Kingdom wasn't trying to undermine him. She didn't want them to behave so ungratefully.

Neia spoke kindly to the militiaman—though she knew that even if she treated him kindly, he would still be frightened of her.

"If it's about the great King of Darkness, I'll answer with whatever I know. That said, I'm not from the Nation of Darkness, so there are a lot of things I don't understand in detail."

"Huh?! But I thought you—er, m'lady—came from the Nation of Darkness!"

"Huh?! N-no, I'm a squire of the Sacred Kingdom's paladins."

"What? Really?"

"Yes! And I'm not a 'lady' or anything…"

A storm of chatter ensued. Looking around, she saw that everyone stationed on the wall had turned to watch them, perhaps drawn by her shouting match with the paladin.

It was a rather awkward situation, but since the King of Darkness had come up, she couldn't let it end embarrassingly. She puffed out her chest, thinking she might as well let all the soldiers hear. The paladin, for his part, seemed to have realized he couldn't suppress the dialogue anymore and simply glared at her in irritation.

"Huh, then first of all…I think that armor is the same armor the boss of the goat monsters was wearing. Did you defeat him?"

"No. The King of Darkness slayed Mighty King Buser with a single magic spell."

"*Ooh,*" the crowd marveled.

Mixed in were comments like, "That monster?!" "With one spell? Nah…," "He really took the city on his own…from all those subhumans…," "Whoa… I might be in love…," and "He's not like the undead I know…"

Maybe they were whispering to one another or murmuring under their breath, but with Neia's sharp ears, she could hear them.

It really felt good to have other people respect him as much as she did. It made her especially happy that they shared her feelings despite knowing he was an undead.

His Majesty's actions do mean something. There are people out there who understand.

"S-so is His Majesty going to save us again?"

In a complete reversal, the buzzing gallery fell silent. That reaction told Neia instantly that this question was the heart of the matter.

"…His Majesty the King of Darkness won't be participating in this battle. This is a fight the people of the Sacred Kingdom must take up to save our own country, not something that should be left to another country's king. And he needs to conserve mana for his eventual duel with Jaldabaoth."

The faces of the men listening to her fell. Neia braced for angry shouts to fly, but—

"That makes sense… Normally, a king wouldn't go to another country on his own. If we can't be thankful for what he's already done for us, what would that make us?"

"Yeah. And if it's because he needs to conserve his energy to fight Jaldabaoth, well…"

"…That king has a heart of stone, but he's also a man—er, undead—who chose the path that saved the most people… So if he's not fighting now, it must be for the same reason. I saw what he did that time, you know."

"Yeah, I did, too. And we're the ones who value this country the most. I'll be the one to protect my wife!"

"What are you talking about?"

"We got saved before this city was liberated, and…"

Neia could hear approving comments springing up.

Some were surely upset that the king wouldn't save them. But the fact that there were more who accepted his line of thinking warmed Neia's heart.

"May I take up my post now?" she asked the paladin. She understood perfectly well why he hadn't wanted her to before. That shouldn't have been an issue any longer.

Without even attempting to hide his sour expression, he curtly told her to go.

Passing by the soldiers murmuring about the King of Darkness, she reached her post and gazed out at the enemy camp.

Before her was a massive army, a force that seemed capable of swallowing them up whole. And it was about to attack them.

Her stomach felt like it was about to turn upside down.

Had her father felt this way any number of times when he stood on the fortress line at the border?

Neia peered up, musing that the cloudy sky seemed to mirror how she felt.

•

It was afternoon when the subhuman army began to move in earnest.

Neia gulped down her porridge.

Due to the winter conditions outdoors, the barley warmed in hot milk had already gone cold by the time the bowl it was in made it to Neia's hands, and to be frank, it tasted pretty awful. But if she didn't eat, she wouldn't last long in this crucial battle. Besides, it wasn't as if there were any other food options. Additionally, though there were reserves, she didn't think relief would be coming anytime soon, so she figured it would be quite a while before she would have an opportunity to eat again. That was also why the lunch portions were so large.

Using a crude wooden spoon, she shoveled the white mush of the milky barley porridge into her mouth and forced it all down.

Though it was plenty enough to fill her stomach, the thought that this gross meal might be her last was depressing.

Neia took the cloth from around her shoulders, balled it up, and put it on the parapet facing the subhumans. Then she protected herself from the cold with a gray coat. Though the militiamen had started eating at the same time she had, they were still slurping their porridge.

Everyone had downcast faces. There couldn't be anyone who found that flavor particularly pleasant. But there was nothing to be done about it.

And the porridge probably wasn't the only reason they looked so gloomy. Their mood wasn't being dragged down by their food but the subhumans who were beginning to stir.

Faced with the violence of overwhelming numbers, it was impossible to feel anything approaching hope.

And the former prisoners who had already endured so much suffering at the hands of the subhuman conquerors were branded with a distinct fear. It was not surprising that the stress made many of them lose their appetite.

What would His Majesty the King of Darkness do in this situation?

Would he have given a rousing speech to boost morale? Or laughed it off?

Neia couldn't imagine what sort of heroic action he would take. But even if she could have, she wouldn't have been able to replicate it. She was neither a hero nor a king.

And these guys probably wouldn't want to be subjected to Neia's attempts to lift the mood. Besides, a certain amount of tension could work in their favor.

The most important thing was that despite their dark expressions, they didn't appear to have given in to despair or seem like they were ready to break and flee. They had whatever it was that made a person a determined soldier.

The reason for that was a story that some people, who seemed to be liberated prisoners, had spread about the King of Darkness. Word had traveled like the wind through the militia stationed on the wall.

A story about the difference in the value of lives.

The people who learned secondhand that the king had killed hostages along with their captors wore a uniform look of disgust. *A heartless thing to do, typical of an undead*, many thought. But the people who had been there argued they were wrong. Even the great, matchless King of Darkness said he would end up losing everything, too, if he encountered someone with more power than him.

Neia remembered it. He had seemed terribly human with his determined resolve that even carried a hint of tragedy. It was indescribably persuasive, backed by an intense drive to protect what was important to him.

And it made everyone remember what would happen to the people important to them if this battle was to end in defeat.

Their will to fight was strengthened by the powerful resolve to never again let their loved ones suffer so hellishly.

Could His Majesty have known back then that this was how things would turn out…?

Without those words to steel the people's resolve, the army might have given up before the battle even began and collapsed.

Neia had only seen the Holy Lady once. She knew hardly anything about her personality or abilities. But she could already declare that the King of Darkness was superior. No, perhaps of all those known as kings, the King of Darkness was supreme.

"In the Nation of Darkness…the people are ruled by an undead, and I felt sorry for them, but…" *They might be happy…* Unable to say the words aloud, Neia rolled them around on her tongue. It wasn't something she could let anyone hear her say. Just then…

"Enemy advancing! All those assigned to defend this location, prepare for battle!" a voice in the distance shouted.

Everyone inhaled the rest of their porridge and took up their positions.

When the army of more than ten thousand moved all at once, the air itself shook, and it almost seemed to make the wall sway. Neia felt as though the pressure of their advance alone threatened to crush her.

And amid the clamor of the earthshaking march, Neia could pick up the hoarse shrieks of militiamen with her sharp ears.

Their morale was flagging.

But there wasn't anything Neia could do about that, and she wasn't high-ranking enough to try even if she did have an idea. Neia's sole role was to barrage the enemy with arrows as soon as they were in range.

Since the city's liberation, any moment she wasn't occupied attending the king she spent on training with her bow. Thanks to her efforts, she had grasped the quirks of Ultimate Shooting Star: Super and had grown fairly confident of her accuracy.

But why are the subhumans making their move in the middle of the day? They would have had the advantage if they attacked at night… Do they have a specific goal in mind? …If His Majesty was here, I would be able to ask what he thought…

Without the caster who had walked in front as if to guide her or stayed near as if he didn't want her to be alone, Neia felt sad, as though she was missing something essential.

No. I can't rely on him too much. I need to stand on my own two feet... Anyhow, I may not know what it is, but the subhumans must have some reason for attacking during daylight. I can't let my guard down.

Frowning at the enemy army from her perch on the parapet, Neia felt her eyes drawn to the subhumans leading the advance.

"...Huh? Those are..."

At the head of the enemy forces were ogres nearly ten feet tall. They were equipped with massive weapons.

They were ballistae with what seemed like wooden shields fixed to the front. The size was appropriate considering how massive the ogres were, but they were probably large enough to make them useful as siege weapons. Normally they would be set up and fired from a stationary position, but these ogres were carrying them in their hands. There was a whole row of them.

Had they plundered some city and modified them so they could be fired from a standing position?

At the sound of a giant drum, the ogres readied their ballistae.

Then—

—the wall shook with undeniable force. In some places, the parapet even crumbled a bit. Luckily, it didn't seem like anyone had been killed, but that was the only silver lining.

The huge bolts that had struck the parapet would probably more accurately be described as lances. Thick missiles that seemed longer than Neia was tall had been launched at high speed at the city wall, driving deep into the stone. At this point, they could be considered only siege weapons. There was a mere handful of humans in the whole world who could take a hit from one of those and still live.

She saw the ogres readying their second volley.

"Crap!" Neia scowled.

The ogres were too far away.

Given the poundage of her bow, her arrows would probably make it.

Unfortunately, the energy of her shots would have greatly decreased by the time they reached their targets. What's more, she hadn't been able to practice hitting targets at such a range while cooped up inside the city. Since it was an unfamiliar distance, she wasn't confident she could reliably land a killing shot between the wooden shields of the ogres.

It wouldn't have been strange for a city of this size to have its own ballistae, but the bufolk who had been in charge until the other day had destroyed them all, and there was no timeline for their repair.

At this rate, the only way they could crush the ballista unit would be to open the gates and engage in a field battle, but that would be the height of folly.

That meant they had no choice but to stay on the receiving end of these uncontested attacks.

All we can do is take shelter…but then we won't be able to stop the assault. What kind of strategy will our superiors come up with?

For the moment, all the subhumans were doing was shooting, but if the soldiers fell back from the wall, the subhumans would surely advance and occupy it. Once the enemy took control of the wall, the fall of the city wouldn't be far off.

By that point, the attackers would only need to hold the stairs leading to the wall and push their way through the remaining soldiers to open the gate, welcoming the main force into the city. All they had to do was muscle through each step in order. There was no way for the humans to stop them. It would be chaos within moments, and even Remedios wouldn't be able to last once she was surrounded on all sides.

At that point, the people's only choice would be to abandon the city and flee south, with Neia and the other survivors serving as a rear guard; however, as they had concluded in the strategy meeting, that course of action would simply lead to the enemy catching up with them on the plain partway to safety or end with the attackers joining up with their allies currently facing off against the southern army to deliver an even more devastating strategic blow.

What will the paladin commanding at the west gate choose?

Retreat? Or a battle of attrition where we fight to the bitter end?

As those thoughts occupied Neia's mind, the enemies loosed their second volley.

The lancelike bolts slammed into the wall, causing another large jolt. It surely wasn't her imagination that this felt more severe than the first impact. At the same time, she heard an indecipherable cry.

"Ogoboahhhh!"

When she turned toward the source, a horrific scene filled her eyes.

One of the bolts had pierced the parapet and skewered the soldier taking cover behind it. Bloody froth poured from his mouth. After twitching for a few moments, he crumpled like a rag doll. Actually, he couldn't crumple because he was pinned by the thick bolt like an insect specimen, so his limbs just went slack.

What a horrible way to die. Several people screamed.

Neia squeezed the necklace the King of Darkness had lent her and bit her lip.

That was a fatal wound. There was no saving him, even with healing magic.

One militiaman could die without compromising the integrity of their formation. But the death sent out ripples of intense fear. The reality that *I could be next*—that this wasn't merely someone else's problem—triggered survival instincts all along the line. Many were trembling.

"Under Divine Flag!"

It was a spell.

With that, the militiamen's nerves instantly settled. The magic had boosted their resistance to fear. The faith magic spell Lion's Heart would give full protection, but it could be cast only on an individual. Under Divine Flag worked on everyone within a certain radius centered on the caster.

That was why there were paladins among the common rank and file.

"Don't be afraid!" cried the one who had cast the spell. "Take up your arms to rescue the suffering!"

If it had been fear forced on them by a spell or skill, they might have been lost to it, but the fear assailing them simply came from within. With their terror suppressed by the spell, their eyes blazed with determination once more.

But that was only a distraction. They still had to figure out how to prevent untold thousands of subhumans from overwhelming them. If they didn't do something soon, they were nothing more than casualties waiting to happen. Sadly, Neia didn't have any bright ideas.

"Take cover! Ammunition runs out! They can't have brought that many!"

Ah, thought Neia. Most of the supplies the enemy had seized must have been taken south for the fight against the large southern army. There was a good chance the forces surrounding them weren't left much. While the ballistae themselves were out of the question, someone with the right skills could supply them with quite a lot of ammunition, so that assumption was a bit of a gamble.

The third volley came.

The ogres weren't used to shooting bolts, and many of them missed. Even so, the latest attack had damaged much of the parapet, and several more militiamen died.

The giant lancelike bolts had no trouble going through their initial victims and impaling those unlucky enough to be behind them as well.

Under Divine Flag was an area-of-effect spell. That meant the soldiers had to gather around the paladin in order to gain its protection. That wasn't going very well for them.

Before the enemy could launch a fourth volley, angels swooped overhead.

They were the lowest tier of angel, but they went straight for the subhuman ranks. In their right hands were lit torches, and in their left hands, urns with a piece of fabric hanging over the lip of each one. Without a doubt, the urns contained either oil or strong alcohol.

In other words, they were equipped with firebombs that would explode on impact.

Of course, these bombs wouldn't so much as singe an enemy with resistance to fire, and it was unclear if they would have much effect against subhumans with large bodies and thick skins or those who had honed their skills and abilities.

But on the other hand, some beings were vulnerable to fire, and if the ballistae were damaged, the barrage would cease.

The angels positioned themselves over the ogres carrying ballistae and lit their urns. But predictably, they weren't given the time to drop them.

Several subhumans spread their wings and rose into the air. It was a contingent of pteroposes. Their arms had webbing that formed wings of skin. The way they soared upward without flapping must have been the work of some magical power.

At the same time, something like a white net flew toward the angels and quickly tangled around them. It must have been created with a spidan special ability.

Like butterflies trapped in a spider's web, the angels were incapacitated and plummeted to the earth, where they were immediately surrounded. It went without saying what happened to them.

But the angels didn't go down without a fight.

Some of the urns hit the ground, scattering flames.

Up to this point, the shields attached to the ballistae prevented Neia from getting a good shot at the ogres. It would have been hard to deal a killing blow if she took aim at an unprotected area, like their feet.

Her father could have probably threaded an arrow through the tiniest crack and still hit an ogre right in the eyes, but Neia didn't have that kind of ability. That being said, either because they hated the firebombs or were afraid their weapons would burn, the ogres had lifted the ballistae up, which left the shields facing the sky. On top of that, they were distracted by the flames, not paying Neia even the slightest bit of attention.

This was as good a chance as she would ever get.

Neia drew her bowstring as far back as it would go and loosed an arrow.

The enchanted items she had borrowed from the King of Darkness boosted her skills to the point that they started to approach her father's.

The arrow crossed a surprising distance, and her aim was true, striking an ogre in the head.

She had wanted to avoid the hard cranium and pierce the soft eyeball instead. She knew some monsters had films that protected their eyes, but she figured the shot still had a higher chance of being fatal than a blow to the skull.

But it didn't go quite as she had hoped.

Her arrow was sticking out of the ogre's jaw.

She saw it roar and shake in pain.

The ogre dropped its ballista and held a hand to its face near where it had been hit. Then it began to stagger away, its back to Neia. She hadn't delivered a fatal blow, but she had chipped away at its will to fight.

If the subhumans had someone who could heal, the ogre would be back on the battlefield in no time.

"Tch!"

Even with the splendid magic items she had borrowed from the King of Darkness, this was all Neia was capable of.

With a click of her tongue, she ducked behind the parapet. Hugging the wall, she began to change locations. When she noticed the militiamen were surprised to see someone leaving their post, she addressed them in a firm tone. "Run! There's going to be a counterattack!"

It wasn't as if the subhumans had heard Neia's shout, but retaliatory ballista shots followed soon after. Sure enough, many of them flew way off mark, but a handful hit the wall and cracked the parapet where she had been standing.

If her luck had been any worse, she might have been impaled right then and there.

When she peeked out from behind new cover, she confirmed that the confusion from the angels' fire attack was dying down and the ogres were aiming their ballistae once again.

Word had probably spread that someone with a crossbow had shot at them, so they wouldn't make the same mistake of raising their shields again. Should she expose herself for a follow-up attack and hope that she would conveniently develop skills comparable to her father's? Or should she be like a turtle and bide her time until another chance came along?

As she hesitated on what to do next, the bow from the King of Darkness caught the sunlight and glimmered majestically.

You don't get points for being reckless.

Right. She was borrowing a valuable weapon. She had to do everything in her power to return it. This wasn't the time to be taking dangerous gambles.

They can't have that many of those special bolts!

The subhumans were apparently trying to destroy the parapet and were launching a continuous stream of the oversize bolts. But their aim was all over the place, meaning their shots often landed in random places off target, and some even disappeared into the city without hitting any part of the wall.

She would keep a low profile and wait for the enemy attack to end.

As she lay low, broken bits of wall occasionally rained down on her. Every now and then, an unfortunate militia member was struck by a bolt and died instantly. All she could do was silently pray for the attack to end.

Eventually the *boom* of the drum sounded once. Then it rang out four more times in succession. In the distance, probably somewhere along the enemy's left wing, she heard the same pattern.

…The number of drumbeats signals what plan they're executing. It's how the left and right wings stay in communication. If I could infiltrate the enemy lines, steal a drum, and beat it randomly, I could disrupt the— No, that would be impossible…

The subhumans had to be aware of the drums' importance. They would inevitably be heavily guarded. Who would be able to set foot anywhere near them?

If an adventurer was here, maybe they could use Invisibility and Silence to wreak some havoc.

Not that there's any point in wishing for what we don't have…

At any rate, it was clear that the enemy was up to something new. Neia—and most of the militia for that matter—cautiously peeked through gaps in the battered parapet.

A stifled commotion broke out.

Astonishment, terror, and seething anger.

The massive army that had been standing by on the other side of the wall had begun to advance. The right and left wings of the subhumans maintained their ranks and simply marched forward. Their center advanced in wedge formation, ready to smash through the gate.

Eager to kill all the defenders, the subhumans charged, their footfalls practically shaking the earth itself.

Another group—a smaller one—was circling around to the side. Were they planning on climbing over the wall at a different location? Or was it a feint?

In any case, the enemy's attack had entered phase two. What came next wouldn't be one side simply taking potshots at the other. A battle where blood would flow on both sides was about to begin.

But that wasn't the problem. The humans weren't happy at all even though this was the development they had been waiting for. What enraged the militia along the walls was seeing the mixed units at the front of each wing made up of all different races. The units lacked discipline, but they had two things in common.

One was that they carried ladders for rushing the wall.

These were scaling parties, the enemies Neia and the others would be fighting in moments.

And the other was that they had human children strapped to their bodies.

Some of the children cried and wailed; others were limp and exhausted. All were naked, and all were alive.

Neia pursed her lips tightly.

Surprisingly, she was utterly calm.

Keeping an eye on the encroaching wave of subhumans, she slipped an arrow out of her quiver and nocked it.

Even when the front of the formation came into range, she waited.

It was still too soon.

After a few deep breaths, she inhaled and held it, then drew her bowstring back with a quick twist of her body.

She took aim for a brief moment. Her target was a single point.

—*There!*

She loosed a shot.

The arrow flew true, piercing a child's chest and driving into the subhuman behind.

If she had shot an ogre or another race with similar toughness, one arrow might not have brought it down, but the subhuman she hit didn't seem to have been endowed with such vitality.

Paying no attention to the crumpled subhuman, Neia drew her next arrow.

She had killed a human—an innocent child hostage.

Her hands shook. Her field of vision darkened at the edges, and her mind was roiling.

Though she had prepared herself for this moment, she couldn't stay calm.

Without thinking, she reached for the hilt of her sword out of habit, but her fingers caught on her bowstring.

It was as if the bow were telling her this wasn't the time.

A moment later, something flickered in Neia's nearly frozen heart before spreading like wildfire, eradicating all traces of the howling wind that had been clouding her mind.

Her shaking ceased, and her field of vision returned to normal. All that was left were the words of the one who embodied unwavering justice.

Wow, it really works.

Neia reconfirmed that the King of Darkness had been speaking the truth.

The attackers who were around her first kill had noticeably slowed their advance; they were shaken to find their human shields not working as planned.

Then she yelled—at the militiamen gaping wide-eyed at her.

"What are you doing?! Throw your rocks! We can't save the hostages!"

It was true. There was no way for them to save the hostages. And it was clear what the subhumans would do to the now unnecessary humans. What choice did the defenders have?

Only to visit another arrow upon their enemies.

With her keen eyes, she saw as her next shot went straight through a young boy's forehead. Whether because the subhuman was an armat or because the hostage's skull had slowed her arrow, one shot wasn't enough to bring her target down. But it did disrupt the formation. Of course it did. Human or subhuman, when something doesn't go according to plan, it's enough to sow confusion and chaos.

But the enemy ranks stretched from one corner of her vision to the other.

The area she had shot into slowed, but the rest of the enemies continued marching, unaware that anything had happened. She had made only one tiny dent in the long, straight line.

"Throw your rocks already!" she shouted again.

If the soldiers continued to hesitate, Neia's actions would be meaningless. As she had already taken human lives—robbing children of their futures—that was unacceptable.

The left, right, and center were all attacking at once. If the humans simply clashed head-on with this army more than double their size, the numerical disparity alone assured their defeat. But if they could slow down the assault, that would take off some of the pressure.

If the subhumans reached the wall, they would undoubtedly climb up with their human shields still held in front of them. And once they were over the top, it would be impossible for the militia to resist them. It was a question of how many they could thin out before the enemy reached them on the wall.

It'll be hard to convince them to kill children, no matter how much I scream at them! That's why we need someone to take the initiative and dirty their hands as an example!

Neia glared at the paladin in the distance.

You understood when we took the camp and this city! The King of Darkness did the right thing! And you know there was no other way! Instead of clinging to the lives you can't save, you have to do everything possible to save the ones you can!

She loosed another arrow.

This time, she succeeded in killing the subhuman as well as the little girl in front.

"Hurry u—!"

"Rrragh!"

A battle cry drowned out Neia's shout as a sling sent a rock flying.

The rock hit a confused subhuman. It was far from a fatal injury, but it did seem to deal at least a little damage.

"You guys! It's fine—just attack them! You have to give up on the hostages!"

Neia recognized the militiaman giving directions.

It was the father of the boy who had been killed by the King of Darkness at the first camp.

You're out here, too? she wondered in surprise.

"If the enemy gets past us, the women and children inside will meet a horrible fate before we can save them! If you care about your kids, attack!"

The voice dispelled everyone's shock, and a few rocks flew. The arcs they traveled made her wonder what they were aiming for, but they did fly.

By the time Neia was aiming her next shot, everyone was hurling rocks at the subhumans. A few of the subhumans with human shields at the front were hit, though it would've been more accurate to say the children were hit, not the subhumans.

The children were crying. They wailed inconsolably. And then another volley of missiles flew at them. These children, brutalized by both armies, were the most tragic victims.

Neia prioritized shooting them.

They were forsaking the few to save the many—the dearest sacrifices of all.

As she was about to lean out and scan for her next target, she noticed the sound of something slicing through the air, coming toward her right, as a curtain of light fell around her.

An enemy magic attack?!

For a moment, she froze. But at that same moment, she felt the slight shock of a tap against her abdomen. Like she'd been poked lightly.

When she took a step back, surprised, she heard a loud clang at her feet. She peered down only to find what looked like a huge lance—one of the ballista bolts. The head of the bolt was flattened, as if it had been pummeled with a hammer.

In a panic, she ducked behind the parapet. That was when she heard the *ka-thonk, ka-thonk* of something huge thudding into the wall.

A sheen of sweat coated her back.

She found herself fingering the point of impact.

And she remembered the curtain of light that had defended Buser when the King of Darkness had thrown his sword at him. That must have been it. The armor she received from the King of Darkness had protected her. She had just narrowly avoided death.

So it defends against projectiles?! My chest, shoulders, and abdomen are covered by the armor, but what about the rest of me? Does the power extend beyond the armor? No, more importantly, how many more times can I use it? Could it have been just this once?

Without the armor from the King of Darkness, Neia had no doubt she would've been skewered.

That realization made her whole body tremble.

"*Phew*, breathe, *haaaah…* Hang in there. You're fine!"

Neia wasn't within range of Under Divine Flag. She figured the crown she was borrowing would be enough. But as a result, it was hard to ignore the fear of death that sprang up within her. Though tears had formed in the corners of her eyes, she still gripped her bow and raised herself up again.

She had decided she would continue fighting even if she had to rob children of their lives. There was no way she could let a single attack scare her into submission.

The children may have been beyond rescue, but she refused to let them suffer. And she would deliver deaths to the monsters who had resorted to such despicable tactics. That was all that filled her mind as she loosed arrow after arrow.

The determination to fight even if the hostages died in the process, which had taken hold on only a single area of the wall at first, had spread to all the units. Every defender was attacking the advancing subhumans with slings. It seemed like even the paladins were throwing rocks.

"Dammit! Dammit!"

"Ah, fuck. You monsters…!"

"I'm sorry! I'm so sorry!"

"There's no choice… Please forgive me…"

Some begged the children for forgiveness, but the rocks kept flying.

It was the attack of people who had agreed that in order to save the most lives possible, a certain amount of blood had to be spilled.

But there were so many enemies. By the time they had taken out the vanguard using the children as human shields, the rest of the encroaching army had nearly reached the wall and were already in the business of setting up ladder after ladder.

Without much technology to rely on, the best siege weapons the subhumans could muster were battering rams and ladders, but there wasn't a perfect way to neutralize them, either. A few men with poles shoved some ladders back, and several angels destroyed what they could, but there were simply too many.

"What happened to the firebombs we kept in reserve? Tell the priests to support us with magic!"

"Crap! There's a ladder over there! I'll get it, so keep an eye on this spot!"

"Drop stones on them!"

The top of the wall was a hive of activity. Wherever a ladder went up, the defenders started throwing rocks and jabbing with spears to knock off anyone who climbed up, but soon it was impossible to fend off all of them.

Some of the subhumans were able to nimbly dodge the thrusting spears or even grab them and pull defenders off the wall. Others, like armats and bladers, who made use of their natural resilience that was comparable to plate armor, ignored the jabs outright and continued to climb.

The paladins, who had been trained in close-quarters combat, focused on fighting the subhumans with high defense, but the number of enemies who had reached the top of the wall grew steadily. If there was a breach in any one location, the outcome was all but decided.

Steeling her nerves, Neia leaned about half her body out from the parapet and shot into the flanks of the climbing subhumans.

It was due less to her ability and more thanks to the power of the weapon, but many of the subhumans she hit went down in one shot. Ultimate Shooting Star: Super let her slay even the tough armats and bladers. Eventually, stone eaters started spitting rocks, and since Neia was half out in the open, she sustained a hit. It was thanks to Buser's armor that she survived the hail of missiles. Even so, she was sure to have bruises and maybe even some fractures.

Despite the cold sweat that broke out, she didn't pause her attacks for so much as a second.

I'm still okay… With my mana, I can only use the healing necklace His Majesty gave me one time. I have to save it for later!

As she landed shot after precise shot, part of her was trying to figure out how much longer she could hold out. Her healing spell was the ace up her sleeve, so she couldn't waste it.

Drawing an arrow from the quiver, nocking it, aiming for a target's head or heart, and then letting it fly. How many times had she repeated those motions?

Bang! Suddenly, the impact of a rock hitting her forced the arrow she was holding from her hand.

The reason she dropped it was that her entire body was screaming after enduring a stone eater attack, but that wasn't all.

A paladin's main weapon was the sword. As a squire, she was drilled in swordsmanship. Even though she had some familiarity with archery, she hadn't been training with the bow for long. That lack of practice was clear from the spasms of her arms and the pain in her fingers.

If she couldn't use her bow and arrow anymore, she would only get in the way. She had the feeling it was too early to use her last resort, but there was no other way to recover her combat ability.

She wavered only briefly.

"Activate Heavy Recovery."

Neia's mana was consumed so abruptly, she felt slightly dizzy. She knew she wouldn't be able to use the necklace again. But at the same time, all the soreness in her body disappeared. The spasms stopped, and the pain went away as well.

"Yes!"

She leaned out again and loosed another arrow.

Jaldabaoth's army seemed to be rather well disciplined. Neia was sure that if it weren't, one of the ballista-wielding ogres would have shot her. Fortunately for her, they were concerned about hurting their allies on the wall, and none of them attacked.

Neia was completely focused on loosing arrow after arrow until eventually her hand grabbed nothing but air.

Looking in a panic, she realized her quiver was empty.

And at the same time, she could hear the screams of the nearby militiamen.

On the ladder was a powerful-looking subhuman. Neia knew it had to be one of the stone eaters who had been spitting at her, but this one was heavily built. Maybe not as strong as Buser but still formidable.

In his right hand, he held a giant, crude sword like a thick meat cleaver. In his other hand was a helmet with something inside—the head of the commanding paladin.

"I, Jajan of the Ragon clan, have taken this commander's head! Now, kill them, you louts! Kill the humans!"

•

The situation took a sharp turn for the worse.

There weren't very many paladins. For one of them to be killed meant that the strength of the defenders in this area had just plummeted—and this was a clear sign of something else.

There is a definite gap in ability between paladins and militia, even without comparing one to the most highly skilled knight. The levies didn't have a chance against a subhuman who had slain a paladin.

While the militiamen were frozen in fear, more subhumans climbed up the ladder behind the stone eater Jajan. The flood of bodies made it seem like a dam had broken. One became two, two became four—the growth was exponential.

As the number of subhumans on the wall increased, the presence of the militia rapidly diminished.

The power disparity between the subhumans and citizen soldiers was clear.

Alarmed, Neia surveyed the area.

Arrows. Without arrows, she couldn't do anything.

Scanning with bloodshot eyes, like a wanderer in the desert searching for water, she finally found a quiver with some arrows in it next to a soldier who was slumped against the parapet.

There! I'll take his arrows and have him fall back!

But when she ran over to him, she gasped. The man who appeared to be an archer had lost half his face and was unmistakably dead.

One of the stone eater's rocks must have struck him in the head. With his brains seeping out and his remaining glassy eye staring into space, Neia knew that if things had turned out slightly differently, she would've ended up just like him.

She realized there were similar corpses scattered all around her. Her normally keen sense of smell finally picked up the thick stench of blood. No, her nose had been working fine. Her brain had simply refused to register it.

It took all Neia's might to keep her porridge down. She wasn't sure if it was luck or if she had built up some strange resistance after seeing people get eaten alive.

Gritting her teeth, she transferred the arrows from the dead man's quiver to her own. As her quiver filled up, she could feel her will to fight recover, too.

I can keep going. There are still ways for me to fight…!

Having finished the task at hand, she crossed the dead archer's arms and closed his eye. She knew there was no time to waste, but she insisted on doing this much.

"I'll fight enough for the both of us. Till the very end…"

By the time Neia had turned around and gotten to her feet, there were no longer any extraneous thoughts in her mind.

She was more alert than ever before, and her senses had never been sharper. She felt as if the bow in her hand had become a part of her.

The fight on the wall had turned into a brawl. Between Neia and Jajan, who was still holding the paladin's head aloft, there were several other enemies, so it was basically impossible at her skill level to get a shot in. But...

I have these gauntlets! And I have Ultimate Shooting Star: Super from His Majesty! I can do this!

She loosed an arrow with absolute conviction.

By the time Jajan heard the sound of the missile slicing through the air, it was too late.

Neia's shot punched right into his head, and he collapsed just like that.

"I, Neia Baraja, have killed Jajan of the Ragon clan!" she shouted, but no one cheered. Of course they didn't. Everyone was busy fighting—they didn't have time for a leisurely round of applause. When Neia realized that, she felt a little embarrassed, but she had still managed to rattle the subhumans. The aggressiveness of their attack had noticeably lessened.

Her announcement didn't appear to have been totally ineffective.

Neia nocked another arrow and let it fly at the next subhuman she saw. Taking a direct hit to the head like so many others, her victim tumbled off the wall and fell.

She grabbed another arrow from her quiver. There was nothing special about it, but the motion was smooth and efficient. *Right now, am I getting close to the mastery of archery my father had?*

Neia felt like her skill with a bow had increased dramatically during this fight. That was why she was able to kill Jajan, though admittedly he had also been injured in his fight with the paladin.

She hunted for more prey she could target in this melee.

I'm an archer. Why aren't they trying to eliminate me first?

She got her answer the next time an arrow went through a subhuman's head.

"Don't accidentally get close to that human! It's wearing the Mighty King's armor!"

"The Mighty King's?!"

"Mighty King Buser? His armor?!"

She heard with her sharp ears the murmur spreading among the subhumans.

"No doubt about it! That's Buser's armor!"

"No way. So the Mighty King was…? And by that human…?"

Oh! So that's why! The King of Darkness wasn't thinking about the magic protection against projectiles; he figured the reputation of having defeated Buser would protect me!

Apparently, Mighty King Buser was well-known among the subhuman forces. The subhumans who had arrived atop the wall must have thought, albeit mistakenly, that they had come face-to-face with the warrior who had beaten Buser. It couldn't have hurt that she had just taken out that higher-ranking stone eater in one shot.

Though they realized she was an archer, they were on guard and couldn't charge her.

The King of Darkness is always so brilliant. How impressive that he thought all that out…

Even if she turned tail and ran, only a few of the subhumans would follow. It was surely higher priority to secure the area than to chase someone they assumed was a powerful enemy. Neia was probably fairly safe. For a moment, the King of Darkness's words, *Run for the east gate*, crossed her mind, but she didn't feel like she could do that.

A person who would do that wouldn't have gotten this far.

Neia drew an arrow and killed another subhuman.

"Wah! There it goes…with those piercing eyes again…!"

Piercing…? I mean, I am glaring at them, but…

"Those eyes thirst for slaughter! That…female, I think, is a real threat!"

What was…with that pause…?

"Look at that bow! It's a terrific bow! It's not all her!"

Neh-heh!

"The Wild-Eyed Shooter!"

………*Huh?*

"What's with the name? You know her?"

………*Hold up!*

"That female human has a nickname?"

………*Wait a—!*

"I always heard there was an amazing archer with the face of a demon… Is that the one?"

No, that's my dad!

"The Wild-Eyed Shooter! The archer who killed Buser!"

For some reason, the words *Wild-Eyed Shooter* rippled through the subhuman ranks. *It's sticking!* she thought, but she didn't have the wherewithal to deny or amend it.

As she loosed another arrow, the militia began to move.

"Everyone—defend! That's the one! Don't let the subhumans get anywhere near her!"

"Right! Form up! Remember your training!"

"I'll take the front row!"

About twenty citizen soldiers came over to shield Neia.

"Shoot them down! We'll protect you!"

"Understoo—"

Then the sound of flapping wings came from the enemy side.

Neia twisted her body instantly to aim the nocked arrow at the source of it.

She spotted pteroposes taking flight. A whole flock of them.

Their main objective seemed to be to fly over the wall, but a few of them dove for Neia.

The thoughts of which to aim for had already fallen away. In a blank, soundless world in which she could see only the enemies, her sole action, having gone past coolheaded to cold, was to send arrows toward them one after the other. Her shooting wasn't human—the precision was machinelike.

The pteroposes who had been flying at Neia fell, and she relaxed slightly. Her sense of sound returned as the moment of hyper focus faded.

Right next to you—

She tried to dodge, but a sharp pain ran through her left arm.

An armat that had come right up close had slashed it open with its claws.

"Gaaagh!"

Even as she screamed, she went to reach for an arrow, but she worried whether her left arm would be able to keep the bow steady or not. *Then wouldn't it be better to draw my sword?*

Taking Neia's hesitation as a huge opening, the armat with the hideous face, still in front of her, raised a hand to aim a follow-up slash at her.

Neia tried to back up to avoid it, but her opponent's ability as a warrior was superior to her own, and the creature nimbly closed the distance so she couldn't completely evade.

A searing pain coursed through her face. Luckily, she managed to turn her head and save her eyes, but a gaping wound was ripped open, gouging through the meat of her left cheek into her oral cavity.

A massive amount of blood gushed into her mouth, the taste of it coating her entire tongue. And it wasn't only that. She could feel the hot liquid running down her neck and chest.

With no time to draw her sword, she whacked the armat in the face with Ultimate Shooting Star: Super.

The subhuman probably hadn't expected her to do such a thing with her bow. The armat leaped back out of range.

With her bow still occupying her partially immobile left arm, Neia used her right hand to draw her sword.

Resolved to die an honorable death, she unleashed what was basically a body check. The armat swiftly countered, but thanks to a militiaman cutting into its leg from the side, it missed. In exchange for getting part of her ear sliced off, Neia thrust her sword through the armat's throat.

Watching the armat fall out of the corner of her eye, she surveyed the situation.

While she had been focused on loosing arrows, most of the citizen soldiers shielding her had been killed, and the subhumans had reached her.

There were only five militiamen left, stubbornly holding out on the part of the wall that faced the city.

The nearest reinforcements were fighting some distance away, separated from their position by more subhumans who had climbed the ladders, so it didn't seem like they would be able to assist. With enemies behind Neia's group as well, there was no easy way for them to maneuver.

There were over thirty-four subhumans at Neia's position. Versus six humans.

When she shot her piercing gaze at them, the pressure eased off, and they backed away slightly.

"'Scuse us, ma'am!"

The few militiamen got into a defensive formation in front of her.

"They'll only get past here by walking over our dead bodies!"

The one who made that declaration was a weak-looking man in his forties with a potbelly. That said, his face, flustered from the rush of combat, was spattered with blood; whether it was his own or someone else's was unclear, as he was covered in so many wounds. Despite all that, he stood in front of her, determined not to sink to his knees.

He was the very picture of a dependable warrior.

"Thank you!" Neia said as she spat out the blood in her mouth. "I appreciate it!"

It wasn't just him. The bodies of citizen soldiers scattered around told her that they had all held their ground and died protecting her. Besides conveying her trust in them, what more could she say?

The man's gaze shifted to Neia's shoulder, and he winced. "You can see the bone."

"Please don't tell me stuff like that. Now it hurts an awful lot."

"Oh, ahhh, sorry."

A paladin with a bit of skill could have used a low-tier healing spell, but for Neia, a squire, that was an impossible feat. There were also no paladins or priests nearby. She hadn't recovered enough mana to use her magic healing item again, either. It was probably best to give up on using her left hand for the rest of the battle.

Neia scowled at the subhumans. Even just moving her eyes made her face throb.

The pain made her gaze even more severe, and the subhumans braced themselves.

"Thanks to the way you took so many out with your bow, that one before is the only one who has rushed us. It's thanks to you that we're still alive."

If the subhumans before her had all charged at once, the militiamen defending her would have been scattered. But since they were wary of Neia and her bow, they hadn't been able to move freely. And when she listened to what they were saying to one another, she understood why.

"The Wild-Eyed Shooter...isn't so great with a sword?"

"Don't let your guard down. She's probably trying to make us let our guard down."

"Could we call the snakemen and have them kill her at a distance with their spears?"

Neia laughed in her head. They seemed to overestimate her quite a bit thanks to her borrowed bow.

"...Can you take them?"

Neia smiled in response to the question asked in a voice low enough that the subhumans couldn't hear.

"...With this bow...if I could shoot them with Ultimate Shooting Star: Super, which the King of Darkness lent me, maybe, but..."

The man rolled the words *Ultimate Shooting Star: Super* around in his mouth and smiled sadly. "I see...so we're in trouble. Miss Baraja...you should jump down and run. We need you to survive."

Neia looked at the man.

"Eeegh! S-sorry. Of course you'd be mad I said something so presumptuous. I—I don't know what kind of hell you've gone through to survive, but it's just... You're about the same age as my daughter, and I just can't bear to see someone so young die..."

I'm not mad; I just looked at you normally, Neia thought, but she had gotten used to the reaction and didn't let it bother her.

What the man said was probably true. Rather than swing her sword impotently, it would be smarter to fall back, rest up, and return ready to shoot her bow.

But what will happen to them if I do that? I already know. But even if I fight here, I can't save them. They would only die in vain. Still…

Neia glanced at the bow in her left hand.

I have to return this weapon. There are tons of reasons I should make a run for it. But if I fled carrying the bow His Majesty the King of Darkness lent me, what would his detractors say? In that case…

"Who would run?" she bellowed. "You think I'd run after borrowing this weapon from His Majesty?!"

She tightened her grip on the sword in her right hand.

Kindness is meant to be repaid in kindness. That's only natural for a human being.

She would be hard-pressed to say that this country—especially the leadership of the Paladin Order—had repaid the kindness they'd received. But Neia wanted to show the King of Darkness that not everyone here was like them.

"Uraaaaaagh!"

With a cry like a wail, Neia made a decisive charge. If the militiamen defended her even though she couldn't use her bow, they would die for no reason. So now, while the subhumans were mistaking her as some immensely powerful opponent, she had a chance to prevent the enemy from fighting at full strength.

And they didn't seem to have expected that she would rush such a large group. They weren't ready. Even Neia, who wasn't so great with a sword, could hit a target this slow to react.

An instant after Neia, the militiamen followed her.

She swung her sword.

It was parried, and her weak stance invited the subhumans to shower her with attacks. Buser's armor took the brunt of the hits.

Neia lunged with her sword.

It plunged into a subhuman body. As she drew it out, innards spilled forth. Before her victim had even hit the ground, another slashed at her face with their claws. Now she had a gash on her right cheek as well as her left. Blood streamed into her eyes.

There was a horrible throbbing in her foot.

A subhuman dagger stabbed deep into her.

One militiaman fell.

She whirled her sword around.

Another subhuman went down.

The militiamen were wiped out.

Whether in front or on her flank, she could see nothing but enemies.

Her breath grew ragged, and her heart pounded.

Her ripped-up body grew warm, and her every movement tormented her with throbbing pain.

I'm scared.

Neia was afraid.

I'm going to die. The thought was unbearably terrifying.

Certainly, she had prepared herself. She knew she would die here.

The enemy army was multiple times the size of theirs. And the enemy was also superior in individual combat ability.

It was impossible to count all the disadvantages they faced; their only advantage was that they were the defending side.

It would be stranger to expect to live under such circumstances.

But even with that resolve, once death was right in front of her, it terrified Neia to her core.

Then she remembered what the person she respected most had said about the east gate. Even with her resolve.

As a child, Neia had wondered what became of people after death.

The holy book said that after souls returned to the great current, the gods would judge them, and those who had performed good deeds would be sent to the land of repose, while those who performed evil deeds would be sent to the land of suffering.

But even if she had accumulated enough good deeds to go to the land of repose, the end of her life was still frightening.

She swung her sword.

With her strength flagging, it was now impossible for her to kill an opponent with a single blow.

Even when she tried to follow through on her attacks, in her current situation, the counterattacks bit back far harder.

A dagger stabbed into her armor, gouging her.

It was thanks to the armor the King of Darkness had given her that she was still alive at all. Without it, she would have died long ago. Yes. Just like the civilian soldiers who were strewn around the wall, whose bodies had also been thrown into the city because they were in the way.

I must look awful…

She laughed—that she was able to think something so out of place as the next world was coming into view.

When she swung her sword, her foot slipped. Her left thigh cramped, and her right thigh was injured, so when she tried to plant her foot, it didn't work.

Losing her balance, she nearly fell. Leaning back on the parapet and staying on her feet was the most she could manage.

The world turned a foggy white, and she heard a distant wheezing.

Be quiet, she thought, wondering who was breathing so hard, but she realized it was her.

This was it.

Neia was going to die.

"The Wild-Eyed Shooter is on death's doorstep!"

"Yeah! Let's gang up on her!"

The subhuman voices sounded far away.

Shut…up…

She couldn't hear what they were saying anymore. But with the scattering fragments of her mind, she thought, *It can't be anything that would benefit me anyhow.*

Her sword remained in her hand, and she waved it around.

Don't come near me.

All it did was keep the surrounding enemies back, or perhaps it did even less than that.

I-I'm so scared... But you're all...waiting for me...right?

In this hazy, milky world, she saw her parents smiling. And her friends from home.

Who is that? Oh, it's Bou and Mo. And Dan—she was like a big sister to me. I'm...scared. Your Majesty...

Her lungs, heart, arms, legs, and brain wanted to rest.

Neia could no longer resist that temptation. So then why didn't she fall?

There was the fear of death. There was the belief that she had to fight till the very end as a squire.

But more than that, she wanted to be worthy of the gear she had been lent.

When all the weapons were thrust toward her at once, her body gave way.

And that's how Neia Baraja died.

4

The air of a battlefield is unique. All manner of things mix together to create a frankly sickening smell. But she was used to it.

Behind the lowered portcullis, Remedios breathed deeply, inhaling the air tainted with that stench.

As she watched, an army of well over ten thousand had begun to move.

At the head of the charging forces were ogres and some equine subhumans. Remedios tightened her grip on her Holy Sword.

Doing battle with a blade was very easy to understand, so she liked it. She loved it. The winner and loser were always clear, and if the loser was killed, there would be no more trouble. If only everything was that simple, life would be so much easier. Her little sister and her master would never have to worry.

"Sigh…"

Then she thought about what to do.

Gustav had made it sound complicated, but to summarize, they would be fine as long as they didn't let any subhumans past the gate.

There were thousands upon thousands of subhumans. The ones attacking this gate probably numbered around ten thousand.

On an open plain, it would be impossible not to let any slip through. But in a tight space like a gate, the number of enemies that can attack me at once is limited, too. So if I do my thing, I can keep them from getting past us, no problem! All I have to do is drink potions to cure my fatigue and kill ten thousand opponents in a row!

Gustav's face would have asked, *Are you serious?* if he had heard what she was thinking, but she smiled. Of course, Gustav stressed precisely because her ideas weren't entirely absurd, but…

My plan is perfect! For Master Caspond to transfer command to me—Lady Calca said it, too, but what a guy.

Yes. Remedios nodded.

And then she considered the one issue with her perfect plan of killing ten thousand solo opponents in a row: the existence of Jaldabaoth.

The plan fell apart if an enemy stronger than her appeared.

Remedios wasn't so great at using her head, but it worked well for her in combat.

Which is why she understood that it would be difficult for her to prevail against Jaldabaoth. Of course, she couldn't admit that in front of her subordinates. She was the strongest warrior in the Sacred Kingdom. If she admitted he could defeat her, everyone's will to fight would plummet.

That's why they had brought the King of Darkness with them.

The King of Darkness…

The idea of entrusting her country to an undead was so offensive, it made her want to vomit, but there was no other choice.

Tch. He could help out from the shadows and use that goat or sheep or whatever spell that killed all those Re-Estize soldiers. Then no innocent people would have to die. Do undead not grasp the logic that the strong should protect the weak? Is he really even that strong?

She applauded his single-handed capture of the city. And it was great that he had defeated Buser—whom Gustav had told her was a well-known subhuman warrior. But Jaldabaoth stood on a different level. Remedios wasn't even sure if a caster capable of capturing a city on his own was powerful enough to defeat the demon or not.

If she had sparred with him, she might have had a better idea of where he stood, but Gustav had been desperate to prevent her from doing that. As a result, she had no way to measure the King of Darkness's true strength.

Remedios doubted him.

When Jaldabaoth had shown his true form, she had felt his overwhelming power firsthand, but she never got so much as an inkling of that from the King of Darkness. If it was true that he annihilated the Re-Estize army, he should have had an aura of power that was impossible to hide even if he wanted to.

Maybe it had something to do with him being a caster. But if he was comparable with Jaldabaoth, she expected to sense something—anything.

I mean, I sure hope he's as strong as he says. Well, it's not as if we lose much if he dies. As an undead, he's sure to be a hindrance for the Sacred Kingdom in the future. The best would be if he and Jaldabaoth destroyed each other.

No matter how her subordinates tried to change her mind, Remedios remained firm on that. If anything, she had doubled down on her convictions when the king had killed the hostage boy. As a paladin, she could not approve of anyone able to casually do something so inhumane.

Couldn't it be that the people of his nation are actually ruled by fear?

When she thought about it, there were a lot of things that made it seem like that might be the case. Then maybe for those people, too, it would be better to have him die in the fight with Jaldabaoth.

The main issue is the people of our country. If what Gustav said is true, this is our chance. We have to prove the strength of the Paladin Order and get them to abandon their stupid ideas about the King of Darkness. But if Jaldabaoth shows up, we'll have no choice but to rely on him…

Remedios wanted to yank off her helmet and scratch her head in frustration.

She couldn't believe that the people of a kingdom governed by someone as wonderful as Calca would willingly choose an undead instead. The very idea of it made her sick.

And Squire Baraja—hmm? Could she be under some sort of spell, like Charm? Oh! Maybe he's using some kind of magic that forces people over a wide area to think favorably of him!

Dang, thought Remedios. *I hadn't considered that possibility.*

I should probably tell Gustav about this. Well, after I win this fight.

Remedios stared behind her.

Citizens had formed up with spears and shields.

"Brave subjects of Roebel! Sadly, our country is being overrun with subhumans—let's acknowledge that. But today we're going to drive them off and save our innocent friends who are suffering! This is the first step. Let's repel them here and take back the Sacred Kingdom!" In response to Remedios's rousing shout, the people looked nervous. "The grubby subhumans are attacking. You will block with your shields and thrust with your spears like a wall that won't let the enemy take a single step forward! There's nothing to be afraid of! After the first attack, your only job is to handle the subhumans that run from me! If you can slow them down for a little while, I and our elite paladins will defeat them!"

The tension lessened slightly. Becoming too relaxed was bad in battle, but being too tense was worse. As far as Remedios could tell, the militia was now in the perfect mindset for battle.

"You honed your skills all day yesterday! All we ask now is that you make full use of your training! No need to be nervous!" Remedios paused for a moment and then raised her voice even further. "First rank! Raise your shields!"

The front row of the militiamen surrounding the gate obeyed.

The shields were large enough to hide almost their entire bodies. The bottoms had finger-length spikes jutting out.

"Shields down!"

The people holding their shields up slammed the spike edge into the ground with all their might. Thus, an instant metal wall was built.

The Paladin of the Sacred Kingdom Part II

The previous day, this shield unit had been drilled in just three commands. One was to use all their strength to raise the shields up and slam the spikes down in a deep stabbing motion. The second was to never give ground no matter how strongly the enemy pushed them.

"Second row! Shields up!"

These shields were the same as those equipping the first row, except they didn't have any spikes. These were raised overhead to cover both the first and second rows, just like a lid. So even if attacks cleared the first row of shields, they would be protected.

Paladins stationed at fixed intervals in the second row cast Under Divine Flag. That way if the enemy put the pressure on, the troops would be protected from fear.

"Third-row pikes, advance! Next, fourth-row pikes, advance!"

The third and fourth rows were equipped with long polearms.

They stuck their pikes out between gaps in the shield unit members. They steadied the unsharpened ends against the ground in order to prevent the enemy from forcing their way through. The fourth row's pikes were slightly longer than the third row's. Normally, there would be more rows to make a dense thicket of pikes, but they didn't have enough people, so instead they overlapped the kill zones to make it harder to break through.

It was a perfect formation.

But it had one weakness.

This formation was effective against warriors, but it was weaker against opponents with special abilities such as certain subhumans or casters.

It was true that spells such as Fireball could be blocked by the shields, substantially reducing the damage they caused. But the attack spell Lightning would pierce in a straight line all the way to the back of their formation. There was no guarantee that the subhumans didn't have abilities like that.

The reason the paladins trained the people this way, despite those weaknesses, was that there was no formation more effective.

"Good! Now let's do this! Raise the gate!"

With Remedios's shout, the portcullis was raised. The attacking subhumans moved slowly, out of surprise. *The humans opened the gate themselves?* To an optimist, it meant surrender, while to a realist, it probably looked like a trap.

Remedios grinned.

"All right, you grimy monsters! How about I peel your skin off and use it to wipe my ass?!"

Getting cajoled by a squishy human provoked the subhumans, and they sped up their charge.

Remedios turned her back to the enemy and set off running. Placing a hand on one of the massive shields, she vaulted over the human lines.

The subhumans dashed forward, and several went sprawling over the ground after squeezing under the gate.

There was a ton of oil spread at the entrance. Tripping while charging could go one of two ways: Either the troops to the rear tripped, too, or they trampled the ones in front who had fallen.

Regrettably, the larger subhumans, such as ogres, invaded the city without tripping. The horselike ones seemed to be either falling or slowing down.

The charge of a larger subhuman would probably be on par with the attack of a warhorse. But if the humans couldn't hold here, their plan would go to pieces.

Though their gaits were out of step, the ogres continued their charge, waving their giant mauls. The pikes were longer, however, and some of the ogres failed to properly judge the distance and ran straight into them. But they weren't so weak that that would kill them.

"Now! Throw them!"

At Remedios's command, firebombs sailed over the humans' heads. They landed in the vicinity of the gate with a crash of breaking bottles and a burst of flames. The enemies that had gotten bunched up as they entered the gate were enveloped in an inferno.

The subhumans might have anticipated this attack, but Remedios was sure that the fire was more powerful than they had imagined—due to all the oil coating the ground and clinging to their bodies.

The ogres facing off against the shield wall were alarmed.

With a huge fire blazing up behind them, that was only natural.

They may have had thicker skin than humans, but that didn't mean they couldn't get burned.

Shouts and shrieks echoed around the gate. But as might be expected from subhumans with their exceptional resilience, being wrapped in flames wasn't enough to prevent most of them from continuing to fight.

The subhumans had two choices: advance or retreat.

The black smoke obscuring their view robbed them of any other choices. Many subhumans could see in the dark, but that didn't mean they could see through smoke.

Being seared in the fire while hardly able to see, struggling while blinded by the smoke, not very many of them could act with a clear head.

It was difficult to retreat in this situation; other troops had arrived behind them, thinking to invade the city via this gate. Actually, the ones outside the gate were hesitating due to the intensity of the fire, but since they were enveloped in smoke, it was impossible to tell.

For that reason, the subhumans chose to advance.

It was just as Remedios expected.

Relying on the natural toughness of their bodies, the subhumans undertook an impossible attack. But—

The third thing the shield unit had been taught to do was maintain the wall even in billowing black smoke.

"Pike unit, pull!"

The pikes were all pulled back.

"Pike unit, thrust!"

Everyone pushed their pikes forward at once.

The subhumans who had just leaped out of the smoke with ferocious growls, having difficulty defending or evading, were greeted by a thicket of pikes. But even so, it was difficult for someone with the strength of an ordinary human to pierce the body of a subhuman—especially when the attacking party was undoubtedly chosen for their toughness to break through a gate.

But that didn't matter.

Remedios never expected these people to kill their opponents in a single attack.

They could attack repeatedly for as long as the shield unit could hold.

"Pull! Thrust!"

As she repeated those commands, Remedios vaulted back over the shield unit and sliced into the subhumans who were out of range of the pikes.

The dark smoke stung her eyes and throat. But she wasn't at leisure to worry about that. There weren't many enemies who had gotten through the portcullis and past the oil—only about fifty.

First, she would slaughter all of them and chip away at the enemy's will to fight. This was the vanguard, so they had to be strong soldiers with high morale. Mowing them down would have a greater effect than killing regular members of the rank and file.

Without missing a beat, Remedios cut down one enemy after another.

Large subhumans like ogres weren't able to make full use of their abilities in the crowded melee.

The Holy Sword danced.

Eventually, through tears, Remedios could see that the subhumans had disappeared from the area. But she could hear the racket all the rest were making on the other side of the smoke. They may have been reorganizing their ranks.

As she was slowly retreating, she spotted a few enemies beyond the black smoke.

"Commander! Come back this way!"

A subordinate paladin who was using Under Divine Flag called out to her.

But Remedios felt instinctively that she shouldn't fall back.

In the gradually dissipating smoke, she saw that three subhumans were slowly walking toward her, which confirmed her hunch.

One was a warrior with the upper body of some animal and the honed lower body of a carnivore.

One looked like a woman with four arms.

And the other was a primate subhuman with long snow-white hair wearing a plethora of gold accessories.

Remedios's original plan was to clash with ten thousand subhumans, and she had a decent chance at winning. But the idea of facing these three at once seemed extremely dangerous, even to her.

Only three of them. She couldn't see them very well through the smoke, but their leisurely pace indicated an abundance of confidence. Even the mob of subhumans that should have been their allies left everything to those three and didn't take so much as a step toward Remedios.

…They're strong. I'm not even sure…if I could beat them one-on-one. There's no way I could win against all three.

Her gut told her that it would be better to run than take on the trio. But she had no idea what she should do after running. Conversely, if these three could be defeated, it seemed likely to mean that this part of the fight, at least, would be a complete victory.

She gripped her Holy Sword tightly and said, without turning around, "Sabicas, Esteban."

The two acknowledged with a "Ma'am!" and she knew from the sounds that they were making their way through the group of citizen soldiers to come forward.

"Can you keep two of those busy until I kill the other one?"

The two of them shouted, "Leave it to us!" but Remedios's intuition whispered that it was impossible. Buying her a few minutes would be a job well done. But what would happen if she brought out more paladins?

No. She shook her head.

Their opponents were the type to show up on the front line alone. They were most definitely the confident sort who wanted to stand out, and those guys tended to seek out one-on-one fights. It was the streak of pride the strong possess.

And the arrogant ones were apt to torment the weak. Even if they could end the fight within seconds, they would try to prolong it.

Entrusting her faint hope to this plan, she figured arranging three duels was the way to go.

"Paladins, if either one of them falls, take up their place in single combat. One at a time. After Sabicas and Esteban, the order is Franco, then Galván."

Not attacking in numbers could mean they were buying time, but it could also be interpreted as an order to sacrifice themselves. Knowing that, the holy knights accepted the plan with no hesitation.

This was what it meant to be a paladin.

These were true embodiments of justice.

It means sacrificing yourself for others.

This was quite possibly the last time Remedios could ever see them alive and well. Yet, she never took her gaze off the three subhumans. She didn't want to miss a chance to glean any information about them.

I can't see them clearly, but those two have the strength of warriors. The ape one might be a monk. The four-armed one is a caster, I suppose? Or something else maybe?

Subhumans who brute forced their way through battles didn't frighten her. The frightening ones were those who had honed various skills. Because if a subhuman was trained as a warrior, even if they didn't work at it for very long, they had improved the body they were born with, which meant they could grow to surpass the Sacred Kingdom's experienced warriors. In fact, the worst wound Remedios had ever gotten, aside from her fight with Jaldabaoth, had been against an opponent like that.

She could remember being impaled through the abdomen even now. That was why she was wary when fighting subhumans and relied heavily on her instinct.

Subhumans who can use magic are the worst. If she can fly, we're screwed.

If Remedios activated her armor's power, she was actually capable of flight for a limited time. But it didn't give her complete freedom; taking off, landing, and turning took time and effort, so she couldn't fight in her usual style. An opponent who could use Fly or a similar ability might be able to maintain a position out of her attack range. She had an art that would allow her to launch a ranged blade attack, but considering the decreased impact of the blow, it would be difficult to win quickly that way.

The three subhumans paused upon entering the gate.

"I can't believe we have to cooperate against a mere human."

Though Remedios still couldn't see them completely, a relaxed voice reached her from beyond the smoke.

The hand around her Holy Sword grew clammy. The bitter taste specific to approaching danger spread across her tongue.

Now that they were closer, she was certain.

The beast and ape were strong even among the strong. The four-armed one she was less sure about, but if she was standing alongside these two, it made sense to assume she was of a similar caliber—all three were as powerful as Remedios.

"Honestly! This smoke is just in the way. A real pain in the ass."

Wind roared past, blowing the rest of the smoke away.

Now the subhumans were fully visible. The one in front was holding a massive battle-ax.

"Zooostia as I thought!" shouted Esteban.

Zooostia? So this subhuman is named Zooostia? thought Remedios.

"Ohhh…? Well, it's no shock that you'd know." A beastly grin appeared on his face. "But all right, considering how knowledgeable you are, I'll let you go—in order to have you tell everyone how powerful I am."

"Hee-hee-hee. Sir Vijar, Emperor Jaldabaoth will scold you if you do as you please like that. Let's trash his weapon and take him prisoner—you've got to do at least that much."

It was the ape one who replied to the zooostia.

Remedios was completely confused. There was practically a question mark over her head as she asked no one in particular, "Zooostia? Vijar? Zooostia Vijar? Vijar Zooostia?"

She was asking what his name was, but the zooostia himself didn't seem to take it as such. He let out a comfortable laugh.

"Kha-ha-ha-ha-ha! Are you calling me that because you've acknowledged me as a representative of my race? I guess you humans have good eyes!"

"Surely it's flattery, Sir Vijar," the four-armed subhuman a step back to his left said with a sneer.

"Th-that's right. I only meant it as flattery, Vijar." Once the word *race* came up, even Remedios realized she had made a basic error.

Vijar's face warped in offense. "Hmph. I would have asked for your measly life to be spared if you were able to entertain me. I don't care if you regret it now!"

"Who would regret it? I'm sure you'll reflect on it once you're in the next world."

"Hee-hee-hee. This young lady's got some spunk. Is 'young lady' correct, age-wise? It's hard to judge with other races…"

"You're probably right, but I don't care."

The subhumans were being serious. Without knowledge or experience, it was impossible to tell with other races.

"Very well, young human lady. Shall I make the introductions? My name is Harisha Ankarra. And he may require no introduction, but this is Vijar Rajandala. And finally, this is Nasrenée Berto Cule."

"Those names! White Elder and Elemental Storm!" the paladin Sabicas yelped in surprise.

"Keh-heh-heh-heh-heh. Seems even the humans have heard of me. Meanwhile, the nestling—"

"Human. Haven't you heard of me?"

"I haven't heard of Vijar Rajandala. But there's a famous zooostia with a similar battle-ax. Vicious Claw. 'Vicious Claw' Vaju Sandiknala."

"That's my father." Vijar sniffed condescendingly. "I'm the inheritor of the name, Vijar Rajandala. I'll have to make sure that when you think of Vicious Claw, you think of me."

"Hee-hee-hee. Then shall we leave the human leader up to you, Sir Vijar?"

"Yeah. You made us come out here rather than use magic from a distance, so you can do that much. Frankly, I'd like you to take them all on."

"Hee-hee-hee. But we were ordered to work together, weren't we?"

"But it must be tough for you in your old age! I don't mind!"

"Tch!" Nasrenée clicked her tongue and glowered at Vijar.

Frankly, the hostility was so intense that Remedios wondered if they would start killing one another if she just left them alone.

"Now then, I really wouldn't mind fighting alone, but…" Vijar glared at Remedios. "But first I'd like to know your name. I don't need to know the name of every bit of rabble, but that's quite a sword you have."

"Remedios Custodio."

Vijar's and Harisha's faces twisted up—for different reasons.

Vijar was smiling, thirsty for the blood of a strong enemy, while Harisha was surprised.

Nasrenée's expression didn't change.

"You, huh? You're Remedios Custodio? The strongest paladin in this kingdom. Ha-ha! Great. If I kill you, word of my skill will spread all over. The zooostia who defeated Roebel's strongest paladin. And as the one who inherited the name Vicious Claw."

"Hmm. So that's a Holy Sword, then? Hmm. Hey, Sir Vijar. Any interest in trading opponents? If we swap, I'll have my tribe spread word of your achievements far and wide."

The other two subhumans reacted immediately.

"Hee-hee-hee. Is your plan to give that to Emperor Jaldabaoth and then pester him for a child?"

"Hmph. It's already decided that I'm fighting the leader. There's nothing for you to do."

"—You'd beg a demon for his seed? I feel sick." Unable to simply let that remark pass, Remedios cut into the conversation, only for Nasrenée to shoot her a look of disappointment.

"You can't even grasp the value of bearing the child of an absolute ruler? Humans really are stupid creatures."

"I'm sure even that great being…would favor the race of the one who bore his child. In that sense, women have a certain advantage."

"Hmph. And with such a distinguished father, I'm sure a fairly amazing child will be—" Vijar puffed out his chest. "No, an even greater child will be born! Hmm? Well, I might be an outlier."

Despite standing on a battlefield, these three subhumans seemed to have no sense of danger. Their casual chatting started to piss Remedios off.

"I'm amazed at the nonsense you're all spouting. What's the use in thinking of the future? Your ridiculous dreams end here. No, not just yours. All three of you are going down!"

"Hee-hee-hee. Oooh, I'm so scared." Harisha flailed his arms and legs, but he didn't look frightened at all—because he was confident he could win against Remedios. And knowing that offended Remedios even more.

Remedios ordered the paladins loudly enough that the subhumans could hear. "You guys, one-on-one battles. I'm taking Vijar. You—"

"Then for me…" Sabicas turned to Harisha.

"In that case…" Esteban stood before Nasrenée.

"…Oh? …I'm not a warrior, so I'm not sure I understand, but I get the feeling we're being underestimated."

"Hee-hee-hee… But is it the truth or a ruse? Better to stay on your toes, Lady Nasrenée."

Sensing Vijar laughing through his nose, Remedios shouted, "Let's go!" It was clear they had noticed that the other two paladins were weaker than her, but no good would come of letting them chat about it.

The initial attack would be critical. In order to assuage the fear of the militia watching from behind them with bated breath, as well as impress on their opponents how strong she was, Remedios needed to hit him as hard as she could without considering the pace of the fight at all.

With her Holy Sword in one hand, she rushed toward Vijar, swinging.

Vijar intercepted with his huge battle-ax.

When the two clashed, the air itself seemed to tremble.

There was a commotion among the people in the rear.

Remedios didn't have time to leisurely analyze whether it was admiration or fear—because the sword she'd put all her strength into had been repelled by a blow just as mighty.

Having unleashed attacks of even strength, neither weapon was dinged.

It was such a clash that a normal weapon would have bent or chipped slightly. In other words, Vijar's weapon was enchanted, too.

"Kgh!"

"Nrrrgh!"

Remedios's next swing delivered a shallow cut to Vijar's upper body, drawing a spray of blood. But at the same time, his battle-ax crashed into her chest.

Her magic armor protected her from the blade, but the impact knocked the breath out of her.

Remedios was thrown back by the blow, and Vijar rushed at her and swung his battle-ax to chop her down the middle.

Without the oxygen to counter, Remedios held up her sword to limberly parry. The ax gave her goose bumps as it came down a mere hair-breadth away before thumping into the earth. The ground jolted so hard, she momentarily felt like she had been thrown.

With his ax in the dirt, Vijar was defenseless, and Remedios jammed her sword into his face.

"Strong Blow!"

"Fortress!"

Realizing he had no time to raise his heavy battle-ax, Vijar let go of the handle and shielded himself with his arm.

Bright-red blood gushed from his right forearm.

But the blade of the Holy Sword didn't reach his face. There were two reasons for that.

One was that he had used a defensive martial art. The other was that Remedios's arm was numb, so she couldn't thrust at full power.

Well, then—, thought Remedios, but when she moved to shove the sword deeper, a flash of pain in her foot stopped her.

Vijar had used one of the forepaws of his lower animal body to swipe at her legs. His claws were mostly repelled by her greaves, but one of them managed to tear into her foot.

By that time, he had already raised his ax.

To prevent him from swinging, Remedios closed in a step. Her foot ached with every move.

"Strong Blow!"

"Strong Claw!"

With a dexterous motion of his ax, Vijar blocked Remedios's lunge.

And Remedios moved smoothly from glancing off Vijar's ax to swiping at his reinforced forelegs.

When Vijar fell back, Remedios rushed forward to close the gap.

Several exchanges of attack and defense ensued.

Both of them escaped fatal wounds, but with each blow, more blood flowed.

Remedios was convinced she was ahead.

If things keep going like this, I can win!

Joy welled up inside her.

If she could take out these three subhumans, it would mean she had protected all the people here. That would restore their faith in the Sacred Kingdom.

Then they won't have any use for that undead!

Roughly speaking, the difference between a regular warrior and a paladin is that warriors are the offensive vanguard and paladins are the defensive vanguard. It's extremely difficult to quantify the difference, but if a warrior's attack can be considered an 11 and their defense is a 9, then a paladin's attack would be 8 and their defense 11. Of course, paladins are able to use magic, but warriors acquire all sorts of martial arts, so it's ultimately not a simple comparison. Still, to explain it to someone who knows nothing about them, that sums it up.

As for which is stronger in a fight against a caster, that would be paladins. With their divine protection, they have higher resistance against magic than warriors. For that reason, if Nasrenée was a caster on the same level as Remedios, she didn't pose too much of a threat.

Then there was Harisha, who seemed in all likelihood to be a monk, judging by his gear and movements. They often had the upper hand against casters and thieves, but against a paladin, the paladin would come out on top. So the primate didn't worry Remedios much, either.

Which was why…

If I can defeat Vijar, there's a very good chance I can slay all three.

Given the choice between fighting Vijar after wearing herself out on the other two matches or fighting him unharmed, the latter gave her a better chance of winning, hence her decision to challenge him first. There was no problem there. Her calculation error—

"Oh dear, you're already dead?"

"Hee-hee-hee. This one, too."

—was not realizing how poorly her subordinates would fare against the other two.

"What?!"

Had she overestimated the other paladins or underestimated the sub-humans? Or was it both?

"Getting distracted during a battle with me is an insult!"

A furious blow struck Remedios.

"Guh!"

She just barely managed to block it, but the desperate defense had shifted the advantage from her to Vijar.

"It was Remedios, right? Standing before you is the powerful Vijar, whose name will soon echo across the land! If you don't run away as fast as you can, your life will end in mere moments."

As Remedios bit her lip, the sounds of the other fights reached her ears.

"Hee-hee-hee. This one's stronger."

"…Eh, he's no different than the last, is he? I'm not a warrior, so I'm not sure, but…"

"I'm Franco, a paladin."

"And I'm another paladin, Galván. You'll be fighting me now!"

Only a few seconds after she heard their voices, the clattering thud of a body in metal armor hitting the ground sounded twice.

Franco had been a good man. Though he still had a ways to go as a paladin, he valued harmony and was loved by most. He had been stationed here because Gustav trusted him, and since Remedios was familiar with his personality, she had entrusted him with the job of leading the people in this area.

Galván had just been married. But he didn't know where his wife was being held. He had suppressed his urge to go search for her in order to help the masses instead.

It was far too soon for either of them to die.

"You're distracted again!"

An even more vicious attack than before accompanied Vijar's bark. Remedios leaped toward him, accepting the blow, as she swung her sword in one smooth motion—at which point, Vijar deftly evaded it.

"Hmph. What's that? A bluff? Or have you trained your body over time to move that way?" Vijar growled ferociously—not out of wariness but out of glee.

"Nestling, we're done over here, but you seem to have your work cut out for you. How about it? Care for a hand?"

"Don't be ridiculous. If I accept help from you to kill her, it'll tarnish my legacy. The whole point is to win in single combat so word spreads far and wide."

"Yes, good point, Sir Vijar. Well, what'll we do, then, Lady Nasrenée? Perhaps rip through that shield wall and proceed—"

"You think I'd allow that?!"

Remedios ignored her opponent Vijar and raced toward the two unguarded subhumans. But...

"You insolent shrew! I told you, I'm your opponent!"

Vijar wasn't about to allow this to happen. Though Remedios had shown all her weak points, he didn't chop her with his battle-ax but sent her flying with a kick. Taking the full brunt of the attack, she slammed into the shields behind her.

For a moment, she lost her breath in the impact.

"Eeegh!" The people shrieked in terror.

"Don't get distracted, human! Fight me like you mean it!"

She heard his footsteps as he shouted and approached. If he swung that huge battle-ax, the people holding the shields would be thrown, and a giant hole, impossible to stitch back together, would rip open in the formation.

Nearly losing her balance, Remedios stepped firmly and charged back to meet Vijar, who had already drawn close.

If possible, she wanted to finish him off using only her own power. She decided to use the energy she had been saving for the other two.

This was the power of Holy Sword Safarlissia that could be used only one time per day.

It would unleash a boosted Holy Attack.

It was an incredibly powerful attack that only a paladin wielding this sword could perform.

Her gut said not to do it. But if she didn't kill Vijar this instant, many innocent people would fall victim to the other two subhumans.

This…is for Lady Calca!

"—!"

With a wordless battle cry, Remedios shook off her instincts crying out in alarm and mentally gave the command to her weapon. At the same time, she prepared the Holy Attack.

Sacred light suffused the sword, and its blade shone twice as bright.

Supposedly, the more evil one was, the more dazzling the light appeared when looking at the sword, and attacks in this state were difficult to evade or block. "Supposedly" because the glow Remedios saw wasn't very impressive.

She swung the Holy Sword from overhead with all her might.

With her balance off, it must have been easy to anticipate the arc of her blade, and Vijar had no trouble blocking it with his battle-ax, but—

"—!"

With another wordless cry, Remedios continued bringing her sword down against the ax.

She wasn't trying to land a hit by winning a contest of strength.

The light of her attack traveled along the arc, past the ax's blade, and into Vijar's body.

This was Holy Sword Safarlissia's greatest move.

A divine attack that disregarded all defense and protection.

The toughness of the armor, scales, or outer skin made no difference. It could even penetrate enchantments on equipment, so this was an unstoppable attack that could not be blocked with a weapon or shield.

Dodging instead of blocking would spare the target from a direct hit, but after being blinded by the dazzling blade, how could anyone reliably evade Remedios's attack?

As the blinding wave dissipated, the holy light in the blade went out.

But then Remedios's eyes widened.

Despite the direct hit, Vijar didn't seem hurt at all.

"…Huh? That was an awfully flashy move, but it hardly hurt at all. Is it all just for show? I mean, that caught me by surprise, but…"

Remedios was astounded.

He's not evil!

This attack was effective in proportion to the opponent's wickedness. Conversely, if they weren't very evil at all, it dealt very little damage. To someone who possessed a good nature, it would do virtually nothing. In other words, Vijar, who hadn't been hurt, was not a paragon of virtue, but neither was he evil.

But he's causing so much suffering! He's invading our country, yet he's not considered evil?!

"Hee-hee-hee. That was a tremendous light, Sir Vijar. Are you sure you're not hurt?" asked Harisha, bleary-eyed.

"That was so bright… The light is still burned into my eyes," Nasrenée grumbled.

That was a mistake. Her gut had been right; she shouldn't have used this attack on Vijar.

After moving his arms and legs to confirm nothing was wrong with his body, Vijar shrugged. He appeared unguarded, but there were no openings Remedios could spot.

"…Tremendous light? I dunno. Didn't seem like much to me."

"…Vijar, I'm surprised. If you could take that attack and be fine…I may have misjudged you."

"Hoh-hoh! So you finally get it? Ha-ha-ha. Now then, human. You've been an excellent foil for me. If you surrender now, I'll grant you a death free of suffering."

"Cut it out—that's not even funny! This match hasn't been decided yet!" Remedios raised her sword and shouted at the three subhumans.

And it was true. Remedios still had plenty of fight in her. Raising her injured hand, she cast a healing spell. A delicate warmth took her pain away.

If he's not evil, then I can't use most of my paladin skills against him…but the other two said the light was bright, so I can just save the skills for them.

She would simply have to face Vijar as a plain warrior.

"Hee-hee-hee. Then we'll leave it to you, Sir Vijar. I suppose we'll mop up the humans over there."

"What?! You dirty—!" All the paladins she had called to fight were dead. There was no way the levies could handle those two. "I won't let you!"

Remedios moved back to a position from which she could confront all three of the subhumans.

"You seem to want to fight all of us, but we told Vijar we'd let him handle it."

"Hee-hee-hee. Our objective is to exterminate the humans in this city. We can't just concentrate on you. Lady Nasrenée, what if you made all those humans behind her vanish with your power?"

"Yes, hmm…"

Nasrenée manifested magical energy in three of her four hands. One was chill, one was fire, and one was lightning.

"Shit!"

Remedios sprinted toward the female subhuman—

"I've been telling you over and over! Why do you refuse to listen? *I'm* your opponent!"

Vijar's roar was accompanied by a sweeping battle-ax swing that sent Remedios flying when she blocked it with her sword.

At this point, she knew it was impossible to deal with Nasrenée while facing Vijar. She could leap at Nasrenée, but in exchange for blocking one of her attacks, she would open herself up to Vijar.

Impossible…? I can't accept that! Saying I can't is just an excuse!

The groans of the people stirred her heart.

Remedios didn't want to embarrass herself in front of these ordinary citizens, who were standing their ground despite their terror because they believed in her.

She would never—she was the only one who would never give up on Calca's ideal: *a country where no one cries.*

"Militia! Full retreat!"

As she gave the order, she steeled her resolve.

One hit won't kill me. I'll use Fortress and rush that female!

Perhaps misunderstanding something, Vijar chuckled as Remedios set off running.

"Oh-ho? You seem so determined. That's it! Fight with all you've got! Make it a battle that will go down as legend! Duel Declaration!"

"Huh?"

"Gwaaaaaargh!" Vijar roared with a special power. Remedios had been changing course for Nasrenée, but now her feet carried her toward Vijar as if they'd gone haywire. And it wasn't only her feet. Her blade, her attention, and her gaze were all focused on Vijar, and she couldn't turn away.

"Fireball!"

A tier-three area-of-effect attack spell whizzed past her into the militia formation. Remedios may have been able to withstand such magic, but for the civilians, it would be fatal—

"Wall of Skeleton!"

A grotesque wall of skeletons appeared before the militia, and the Fireball spell splashed off it.

Someone yelped in surprise.

First, because the situation was incomprehensible. But the surprise gradually transformed—because they spotted a figure floating down to the top of the horrifying bone wall as if gravity didn't apply to it.

And its voice spoke with no bitterness and so much kindness, it felt out of place on the battlefield.

"I realize this could be a valuable lesson about war, but I can't watch a three-on-one fight. You don't mind if I join, do you?"

The owner of the voice was an undead.

There wasn't a single person in the city who didn't know who he was.

It was none other than the same person who had refused to fight on this battlefield because he needed to recover his mana.

It was the King of Darkness, Ainz Ooal Gown.

Whooooooo! An earthshaking cheer went up from behind the wall.

Remedios clenched her hand around her sword.

"Wh-who's this?"

"…Looks to be an elder lich. Apparently, some varieties don't have any skin. But…an elder lich that can block my magic? Plus, that magnificent robe… Could it be…? Or does he have an immensely powerful master controlling him from somewhere else?"

The voices of the subhumans didn't reach Remedios. The sounds entered her ears, but she didn't understand them. That was how hard she was trying to suppress her intense hatred. She didn't even notice that Vijar had let his guard down.

—Ahhhhhhhhhhhhhhhhhhhhh! Why is he here?! Why are they bathing him in applause?! Why?! Why?! This nasty undead!

On some level, the calmer part of Remedios knew it was a natural reaction, since he had saved them from certain doom. But the part of her that could never forgive them for cheering for an undead was far stronger. Before her lay the dead paladins, who had died for them.

You would cheer for the guy who showed up late, but not for those who fought to protect you?!

It made her want to rip her helmet off, hurl it to the ground, and roll around tearing her hair out.

Desperately suppressing her rage, she asked the undead perched on the bone wall, "Why are you here?"

The King of Darkness froze. Then the crimson flames burning in his vacant orbits turned from the subhumans to Remedios.

"…Why…am I here…? My intention was to help, but…?"

"…I see."

Why didn't you come sooner? You were waiting for the paladins to die, weren't you? Because you wanted to look cool in front of the people!

She wanted to spit those thoughts at him. But—

"Then I'll leave it to you." She couldn't say she was counting on him. She didn't want to. "Please remove the wall."

"Hrm?"

"I'll leave it to you!" she shouted before managing to control herself. "Please remove the wall. Can't you do that?"

"...Sure I can."

The wall beneath the king's feet disappeared. The reason he didn't fall must have been because he was using Fly or something.

Remedios opened her back up to Vijar completely. She didn't care if he cut her down from behind. She would be able to laugh at the King of Darkness for his failure to protect her.

But—perhaps unfortunately for Remedios, ruled as she was by this self-destructive despair—she made it back to the militia lines without being attacked by the subhumans.

The levies looked somewhat frightened. Was her face that upsetting?

"The King of Darkness can take care of this position! We'll go reinforce a location where the situation is more precarious!"

When she gave the order, the atmosphere was one of confusion, and the troops exchanged glances.

"Why are you hesitating?!"

When Remedios glared at them, one stepped forward and mumbled, "Ah, n-no. It's just...you're leaving His Majesty the King of Darkness...on his own...?"

"The King of Darkness is strong! Right? This'll be no problem for him. Let's go!"

•

Remedios set off with the militia who couldn't help but keep looking back numerous times. They headed for another battlefield.

Staring at the empty space where they had been, Ainz mumbled, "Huh…? That jerk, she actually saddled me with the whole fight."

The situation was so ludicrous, he let his true feelings show in spite of himself.

Wouldn't that normally be a "let's team up" sort of scene? How can you just shove everything off on the one who came to rescue you? You'd think she'd at least hesitate and ask if it was all right first… She didn't even thank me for saving her! What's up with that?

He felt the irritation in him rising. But he wasn't furious, so the emotion wasn't automatically suppressed. A smoldering anger remained, however.

It felt like he had to work overtime to cover for someone else's screwup, but then the person responsible left first, saying they had an errand to run. No…

I was more angry then. I mean, I had Yggdrasil to get home to… The guild had plans, so me being late caused trouble for everybody! Although everyone laughed and forgave me when I told them what had happened…

With fuel added to his smoldering anger, it grew into a blaze. And was forcibly extinguished.

"Hmm… My anger was checked just now, but I'm actually still upset. I don't think I've ever been treated so disrespectfully," Ainz mumbled to himself.

People had shouted at him to shut up before, but that was a completely different situation. For starters, he had raced to the rescue despite their understanding that he would not participate in this battle. Anyone with some common sense would have treated him a bit differently.

Everyone Ainz had met so far had an understanding of basic courtesy.

Maybe that was the reason for his surprisingly intense displeasure?

When he dug further back in his memories as Satoru Suzuki, he seemed to remember meeting a few people like Remedios. Not that that was any consolation.

Ainz glared at the three subhumans as if this was all their fault.

He knew he was just taking his frustrations out on them.

After being saved from such a dangerous situation, Remedios's opinion of Ainz *should* have improved a zillion percent; she should have apologized profusely for her past rudeness and set about working hard on all sorts of things for him. That was why he had waited up in the sky, using Perfect Unknowable, until she was in a tight spot and then swooped in to save her at the most opportune moment.

But this was the treatment he got instead.

Of all the results he could have gotten, this was the most incomprehensible.

If he hadn't met his quota as the end of the month drew near and a coworker came to save him, he would have been bursting with gratitude. Of course, his savior would have already finished their own work, so they would be going out of their way to help on their own time.

Watching the battle with a bird's-eye view, Ainz had grasped the whole situation. There were several areas more precarious than this one. He even knew the little girl who was always scowling at him was in danger.

Still, he had come here because he figured that if he was going to make someone indebted to him, it was better to hook the bigger fish—the commander of Sacred Kingdom Roebel's Paladin Order.

But...

"I really am a bit offended," he murmured in spite of himself. Just then, he heard a grating laugh.

"Hee-hee-hee. Seems like you've been left high and dry. Hee-hee-hee. How sad, how sad."

"An elder lich. And one with exceptional power as a caster. We need to be careful. I don't know that spell he created the wall with, but it must be fairly high tier."

"Hmph. So he's a caster? That doesn't make me very eager to fight. I can't get my praises sung in legends unless I defeat a warrior."

The three subhumans chatted away, seeming to have regained their composure. Ainz turned to the primate one who had laughed.

"That's no problem. We'll kill him and then—"

"Shut up," Ainz interrupted and silently cast the tier-eight spell Death.

The subhuman crumpled slowly to the ground with a twitching smile still on his face.

"…Huh? What did he—?"

"I said shut up." Ainz silently cast Death again.

The four-legged subhuman collapsed in the same way.

The lone survivor didn't seem to understand what was happening, but she knew who had caused it to happen.

"Y-you did this? Both of them…in an instant…?"

Her face was branded with fear, and her whole body was trembling.

"Yeah, uh-huh." He flicked a silent Death spell at her. "Hrm?"

She wasn't dead. Ainz's spell had been ineffective.

The moment he realized that, he immediately switched gears and entered the mental state that could be called combat mode.

Was it a racial trait that had blocked it? Or a magic spell? Did she just have resistance? Or did an enchanted item defend her? Could it have been something else?

A one in ten thousand fluke was not completely out of the question, but Ainz found it hard to believe she could have resisted the attack with her own power. He had been observing the three subhumans as they fought. Even if he hadn't seen them at full strength yet, he certainly didn't get the impression that she could weather the raw output of his magic.

When he wondered, *Now what?* he figured he should be cautious and give the enemy a turn.

And besides, it was possible this was a chance to acquire intel he couldn't get anywhere else. If this was an opportunity to see the cards of an opponent who could block his spells, he definitely wanted to take a peek at their hand.

"Hrm… It doesn't matter what she did. What a waste of time. If I had known this was going to happen, I would have forsaken that woman and gone to assist elsewhere. If I was going to fight alongside that one, then I should have taken some extra time to make it seem like I won after a rough battle…"

Before her stood a rambling undead.

What's with this guy…? There's no way an undead would naturally ally with humans. He must be controlled by a necromancer. But he's so powerful…

She had no idea what he had done, but the fact was, he had killed two warriors as strong as her in an instant. Who could control such a powerful undead?

If his fingers pointed her way, would death rain down on her, too?

Aside from Evil Emperor Jaldabaoth, the only ones she knew who could do something like that were maybe his great demon aides.

There's no way! Only a god could control an undead who compares to those mighty demons! There can't be a necromancer that powerful!

If the human world had a necromancer that strong, the subhuman alliance wouldn't have been able to invade like this.

Should I run? Should I run while I have the chance? Is it impossible?

She didn't have any spells that were handy for fleeing. She had never been in such a tight spot before, so she had never felt the need to acquire one.

Then…the only way to live is to press forward!

"Ahhhhhhhh!" With a battle cry to rouse her spirit, she cast a spell with trembling lips.

There was a tier-four arcane spell called Silver Lance. Though it did physical damage, it also had effects of the silver attribute and brought incredibly destructive power to bear on enemies vulnerable to silver. Not only that, it had the special piercing attribute and could do more damage to an enemy not wearing armor. The downside, then, was that armor could greatly reduce its potency.

Nasrenée's ace move was her own variation on that powerful spell.

Burning Lance, which dealt fire damage.

Freezing Lance, which dealt ice damage.

Shocking Lance, which dealt lightning damage.

All three dealt purely elemental damage that couldn't be reduced with armor, and they boasted the same piercing capability as Silver Lance, making them all brutal spells.

Naturally, such baleful magic came at a price, and they cost far more mana than a comparable tier-four spell.

She cast three of the strongest spells at her disposal all at the same time.

One would already drain quite a lot of mana, but she invoked three simultaneously. Combined with the fact that simultaneous casting itself consumed additional mana, using that much energy at once made her feel floaty, like her consciousness was fading, if only for a brief moment.

"Periiiiiish!"

The three lances flew toward the undead—and disappeared.

"Huh?!"

She couldn't understand what had just happened before her eyes. If he had taken the hit but endured it, that would have made sense. But the lances had vanished without a trace.

"Uh? Um? Wh-what?!"

"…I gave you time, and this was all you could come up with? I assume that was supposed to be your ace move? Hmph. I guess I didn't need to be cautious and give you a chance after all. I've spent enough time on this. Just die already. Maximize Magic: Reality Slash."

There's a raven-black world
    I don't know what I am
    My eyes seem open, but I don't know what eyes are
    I don't know the meaning of *raven-black* or *world*, either
    So I don't know why those things come up
    I don't know anything
    I'm disappearing
    I don't know what it means to disappear

But I'm disappearing

Suddenly, though, I feel something pulling me

Up, down, right, left, toward the middle, to somewhere…

The completed world draws me in

A poor soul who was made whole by friends' creations

A closed-minded soul who thought there was no greater treasure

And then…the world is awash in a bright-white light

A great sense of loss…

A break from solitude…

Neia Baraja blinked repeatedly, trying to bring her blurry vision into focus.

She felt like something had happened, but she couldn't remember anything. Just that she had been fighting with the subhumans. *What happened?*

"…That was a close one," said a quiet voice, and Neia turned her unusually piercing, half-open eyes toward the sound.

It looked like darkness.

Not the type of darkness that frightened children. The kind of darkness an exhausted person took comfort in.

It was the King of Darkness, Ainz Ooal Gown.

"Your…Maj…esty…"

Neia reached out without thinking, like an anxious child reaching for her father…

"Neia Baraja. Don't try to move too much. Leave this to me and rest."

Behind him, Neia could see subhumans frantically trying to attack him. They stabbed, slashed, and punched.

But the King of Darkness paid them no mind. He spoke kindly to Neia as if nothing were happening at all.

Neia recalled what had happened when he fought Buser.

Meanwhile, the king reached into his robe, and after seeming to hesitate for a moment, he pulled out a poisonous-looking purple potion. Potions were usually blue.

Even when he sprinkled the poisonous-looking potion over her, Neia didn't worry. Whatever His Majesty did had to be the right course of action.

Her prediction was right, of course. The purple liquid healed her wounds instantaneously. It seemed even the Nation of Darkness's potion colors were different.

"You seem pretty far from a full recovery, but first let's get rid of your fatigue… This is annoying, tch. It seems the militia has been wiped out… Ah, but it looks like there are some over there. In that case…"

The king turned to face the subhumans attacking behind him.

Combat was still raging in various locations throughout the city, and people were dying with each passing second. But for that moment, Neia forgot all about it. She was captivated by how heroic the King of Darkness looked as he stood up to protect her.

She no longer felt any worry or anxiety about the huge subhuman army.

This was the one she had hoped for.

So he was here. I see…

Neia felt certain that she had received a perfect answer to the question that had been on her mind.

The King of Darkness casually shot off a spell.

Dazzling lightning crackled in the sky over the wall. It was apparently a spell called Chain Dragon Lightning.

The subhumans on the wall were completely wiped out. It was over so quickly, it was hard to believe a desperate battle had been unfolding only moments ago.

"D…id…you…get them…all?"

"No, there is fighting still going on some distance from here, so I didn't catch them all. It wasn't— Napalm. Okay…now that's all of them. I guess I have to finish off the next fools who climb up, too. Widen Magic: Wall of Skeleton."

Outside, where the subhuman army was, a massive brace of skeletons towered as if they were reinforcements come to hold up the city wall. Her view was blocked, so she couldn't see, but she could hear the screams of the subhumans that had been coming up the ladders. And the sounds of them falling and hitting the ground.

"And then all that's left are the ones out there in formation… But I sent some undead out before coming here. They'll finish them off sooner or later."

As he said that, he took out another potion. This one was completely different from the last, in a stunningly beautiful, delicate bottle. She didn't know what the potion's effect would be, but she could tell by looking that it was valuable.

"I…I'm all right…Your Majesty…"

"…Don't hold back. I'm sorry I was late saving you."

Shielding the upper half of his face with his hand as if it was bright out, the King of Darkness sprinkled the potion on her. The weakness in her body melted away. But she still felt lethargic. It was as if something inside her had been whittled down. But in the same measure—no, to an even greater extent—she felt a warmth gathering at her core.

Like this, she could get up. She still hurt here and there so much it brought tears to her eyes, but she couldn't bear to remain in this impolite posture before the one who had saved her.

"Don't, Miss Baraja. There's no need to get up."

When she tried to move, a hand pressed her shoulder back down till she was lying flat again.

"We can have them carry you…as you are. Hey, over here!"

He must have been waving to militiamen.

Then Neia realized with a start—that she had been so moved, she had neglected to ask the question she absolutely had to ask.

"Your Majesty, will everything be all right? With you coming to save us. You used up the mana you were saving for the fight with Jaldabaoth."

"It'll be fine. I couldn't just stand by and do nothing."

"Your Majesty…" Something clicked inside her. "I understand."

"Hmm? You understand what?"

The King of Darkness waited for Neia to continue.

"I understand what justice is now."

"Oh, you found your sense of justice? Good for you... Is it about protecting the weak or something?"

His voice was kind, so she answered with confidence.

"It's you, Your Majesty. You are justice."

The King of Darkness froze for just a moment.

".........Hmm?"

"I understand now! You are justice, Your Majesty!"

"...............Oh, I see. You're tired. You should take a good rest. When you're tired, all sorts of crazy ideas pop into your head. You don't want to flail around in embarrassment after the fact, right?"

"I am tired, but more than that, I feel so much better knowing that I wasn't wrong, that you really are justice!"

"N-no, like I said before, I'm not justice. Look, justice is the way of thinking where protecting the weak is a matter of course—stuff like that. It's, uh, usually considered an...abstract concept?"

"No. Justice without strength is meaningless. And power alone, like Jaldabaoth has, isn't justice, either. So having power and using it for the right purpose, like saving others—that's true justice. And that means that you, Your Majesty, are justice!" Neia said, wide-eyed. The King of Darkness suddenly held a hand over her eyes as if he was putting an infant to bed. The cool touch of his hand's bones made Neia's cheeks relax into a smile.

".........Okay. If you talk too loud, you can feel it in your wounds, can't you? Let's put a pin in that and discuss it later."

"Yes, Your Majesty!"

Hearing multiple sets of footsteps, she shifted her gaze to see paladins and members of the militia jogging over.

"Your Majesty, thank you for coming to save us."

"Don't mention it." The King of Darkness slowly got to his feet as he replied.

Feeling lonely as he was about to go, Neia nearly reached out for his robe, but she realized what an embarrassing thing that would be to do and managed to hold back.

"Actually, do mention it. And then return the favor. I'd like you to take

Miss Neia Baraja somewhere safe. You can't see them from here, but the undead I created are out at the subhuman camp. I think it'll be fine to keep minimal personnel here for a while."

"Your Majesty—"

"Neia Baraja. And subjects of Roebel. Leave the rest of this to me. I promise I will save as many of this city's people as possible." He floated into the air. "Also, sorry—but could you transport those three subhuman corpses for me? They were powerful, so I'd like to examine them thoroughly."

He pointed at the three bodies. They seemed quite impressive.

"Collect them, gear and all. You can be rough with the bodies, but take care not to break their items. Thanks!"

After watching the king fly away, a paladin turned to Neia. "Squire Neia Baraja, we'd like to transport you as you are, but…we don't have anything to use as a stretcher. Are you able to stand?"

"Yes, I'll manage."

She slowly got to her feet. Her legs trembled, and when she put her weight on them, they hurt. One of the militiamen lent her a shoulder to hold.

When she peered over the side of the wall, the unit that had been guarding the west gate was gone, and there wasn't a single corpse, either. The clanging of swords she heard on the wind was fairly distant. It seemed like descending via the tower and taking the shortest route possible would be fine.

Scanning the sky for the king, who had flown off, and feeling disappointed to not find so much as an outline or blip, Neia entered the tower.

•

As Ainz visited attack magic down on the subhumans who had invaded the city, he thought over the events that had just occurred and frowned.

What a huge loss. I really went in the wrong order. I should have prioritized Neia Baraja over that horrible woman.

By choosing to rescue Remedios Custodio first, he had been late getting to Neia. And as a result, Neia had died. Which meant Ainz had to use a high-tier wand to resurrect her—because he didn't want her to turn to ashes like some lizardmen did in his previous revival attempts, and he didn't know what level she was.

To be frank, it wasn't clear if the cost of resurrecting Neia was proportionate to the benefits Ainz and Nazarick would receive. That said, having completely failed to put Remedios in his debt, he decided to resurrect Neia to at least have someone who owed him.

…Would a tier-seven Resurrection Wand have done it? Maybe I went overboard. It'll take another hour for the ring to free up…

Of his eight rings, Ainz was looking at the one on his right thumb.

A Ring of Mastery: Wand.

It was an ultrarare, boss-dropped artifact.

As a rule, wands containing spells could be used only by casters who had acquired magic of the same type. For example, a wand loaded with the tier-one faith magic spell Light Healing could be used only by a faith caster. Using a spell from a different type of magic required a staff, which was more expensive.

A patch later gave all players access to some wands, but a tier-nine True Resurrection Wand wasn't one Ainz could normally use.

Yet, his ring made it possible.

The only thing was he could use only one type of wand at a time. After that, there was an hour-long cooldown before he could switch. Using the ring consumed mana, too, so it was a costly item overall.

Since it was so rare, there weren't many Ainz Ooal Gown members who had one; the only reason Ainz did was because Amanomahitotsu gave it to him when he quit.

Well, I doubt I'll need to use that wand right away, so I guess I don't need to worry. Huh, but I just noticed if you cover her eyes, she actually seems to respect me. Her every word just… Does this mean she trusts me now? Hmm. I wonder.

Ainz recalled her reaction.

I feel like she was truly grateful…but also like she was glaring at me. Her face is so chilling. Maybe I should recommend she wear sunglasses.

But he figured he would never be able to say such a thing. He knew from their time in the carriage together that she was self-conscious about her eyes.

If he told a woman in the office who had BO, *You stink*, to her face and handed her a bottle of perfume, how would she react?

I get the feeling the respect I've cultivated would vanish, and all that would be left is hostility...

And Ainz—Satoru Suzuki—didn't have the stones to say such a thing.

At that point, he spotted some subhumans below and fired an area-of-effect spell to wipe them out. In response, the militiamen, who had been fighting them, waved their arms up at him in such huge arcs that a whooshing sound effect would have seemed natural. Ainz raised a hand—he would have moved it only slightly, but since he was so far away, he raised it higher—to reply.

That's right. I'm the friendly King of Darkness. Be grateful, everyone... But seriously, does resurrection magic drive people insane or make them act weird? If she was just excited, that's fine, but...

He was thinking of Neia.

No matter how he looked at it, that had been a strange interaction. When they parted before the battle, she had been normal, but once he revived her, she started acting like that.

Is she deranged? Can magic cure it? If it's an effect of resurrection, that's a bit scary. It would suck if her humanity warped over time or something.

Her murderous eyes had been abnormally rapt and seemed to shine with a disturbing inner light.

I mean, she was mistaking me for justice. Will she recover after resting...? Oh, almost forgot.

Ainz turned his gaze toward the enemy camp.

It was partially destroyed, and soul eaters raced through the mess of fleeing subhumans. That was all it took for their instadeath aura to wipe them out. And after devouring so much, the soul eaters grew even more powerful.

When soul eaters appeared in *Yggdrasil*, players generally encountered them at a reasonable level, so they only dealt instant death once every few hundred times. Which is why they were never able to eat any souls.

But this time was different. Their chance to really flex their ability had arrived.

"Souls… Dang, I should have done an experiment."

Ainz quickly descended to the ground. Then he used Create Middle-Tier Undead to create a soul eater.

Go.

When he gave the mental command, the soul eater set off running. At the same time, he gave an order to the soul eaters already trampling subhumans to their hearts' content outside—to leave enough prey for the new one to eat its fill.

Undead made from corpses didn't disappear after a set time. But why was that?

If it's the soul that's the medium, not the flesh, then it's possible that soul eaters, having eaten souls, won't disappear. Not that I have a particular use for the answer either way. But it's better to know than not.

He flew into the air again to confirm the safety of the city. He had mopped up the vast majority of the subhumans, but it was best to take every precaution.

Urk, that aggravating woman is down there. I'll just ignore her.

Shifting his attention away from Remedios, Ainz flew around.

Wherever he went, he heard cheers. Waving back at the people as he confirmed there were no subhumans—that the combat had been brought to an end—he headed for the war room. He would return to Nazarick if he had time after getting through all the annoying discussions he had to have.

"This had better all go well…"

An overpowering anxiety welled up within him until it was automatically suppressed. But the feeling like a gradual seeping of icy water remained.

I need to Message Demiurge and tell him I'll see him in Nazarick.

•

Once Ainz had made his move, victory was all but assured. After wiping out the subhumans in the city and tending to two other matters, Ainz returned to his room.

His first errand had been to pop into Caspond's quarters and ask him to take care of the little odds and ends that were left. Mainly, he told him they could have all the food and other items—besides anything enchanted—that were left at the subhuman camp after it had been overrun.

Common sense would dictate that whatever the subhumans had possessed would belong to Ainz now, since he had single-handedly annihilated their camp. Throwing everything into the exchange box would probably yield some decent income, but keeping it all for himself could make the people feel less indebted to him after he had worked so hard to set up this situation. So he decided to take a strategic loss and yield most of the loot to the Sacred Kingdom. Of course, there might have been valuable magic items in the mix, and he had no intention of giving those up.

Really, Ainz should have gone to the camp on his own to scope things out using Magical Vision Boost or See Through Mana along with other investigation spells, but he didn't feel it was necessary. Demiurge was already aware of what magic items the subhumans possessed. Even if he had missed one, it wouldn't be something that could pose a threat to Ainz. If there had been something dangerous, it would have stood out.

His other errand had been to pick up the items the three stronger subhumans had been carrying. As expected, no one had swiped anything, and he was able to acquire their enchanted gear without a hitch. Of course, he had an idea how valuable the items were from the amount of mana they contained, but he still wondered if there might not be something that made them unique.

Dropping the items in a heap on his bed, his plan was to appraise each one using magic, but he had something he needed to do first.

"It's time!" he said out loud.

Partly it was to psych himself up, but that wasn't the only reason.

It was a necessary step before contacting Demiurge with Message.

When Ainz pulled out a scroll—Demiurge brand, naturally—and activated it, rabbit ears sprouted from his skull.

He used them to listen in on his surroundings, but there didn't seem to be anyone snooping. But that wasn't enough to give him peace of mind. Given the existence of magic that erased sounds, such as the tier-two spell Silence, and similar thief abilities, the lack of noise alone wasn't enough to declare the coast clear.

It's all thanks to Demiurge and the ranch he runs that I can use so many scrolls. And the money for creating the scrolls can be acquired by just tossing a bunch of produce into the exchange box. I've felt this way for a while, but Nazarick is starting to become pretty efficient...

For tier-one spells like Rabbit Ears, he had been able to make do with regular parchment that could be found in this world, but for anything much higher, it had been necessary to use materials left over from the *Yggdrasil* era. Now their production covered some of that resource consumption.

Yes, they could swap out materials for only up through tier-three spells, but Demiurge's work was still a huge contribution. He was, without a doubt, the one who had accomplished the most. In second place was the one who perfectly managed Nazarick's day-to-day, Albedo.

Continuing with his preparations, Ainz used Create Lower-Tier Undead to create a wraith.

Take a look around and see if there is anyone watching me.

Following his orders, the wraith exited the room without opening the door. Since wraiths had astral forms, they were able to pass through walls. There were limits when it came to thick or dense obstacles, so they didn't work in every situation, but the walls of this building posed no challenge.

Ainz focused his attention to his magic ears.

Could any thief, even one extremely good at hiding, stay completely still without moving so much as a muscle in the presence of an undead who had appeared all of a sudden scattering an aura of Fear? They would need enough concealment skills to evade the wraith as well. Of course, it wasn't hard to trick a lower-tier wraith, but doing it all at once would be quite a feat.

In the first case, Ainz didn't believe anyone was that capable. If someone like that existed in this country, they would have been sent to fight in the two most recent battles.

Still, I can't rule out the possibility that the people of this country are still on guard against me and are hiding their hero. But given that woman's personality, I highly doubt it. If there was someone like that around, I assume Demiurge would've told me about them by now.

But as soon as he finished the thought, he wondered if that was really true.

Was it possible Demiurge thought Ainz would know even if he didn't inform him?

…Agh, the more I think about this, the more my stomach hurts.

If there was an oversight that big, he would have to brace himself and call Demiurge and Albedo together for a talk.

Soon the undead returned.

"Spot anyone?"

The undead replied, "Negative." And Ainz didn't hear anything strange, either.

"Got it. Then hide in the wall and patrol the area."

Watching the undead enter the wall, Ainz made up his mind.

Okay, now I have to Message Demiurge.

It was a simple matter, but he was having trouble getting himself to do it.

He felt just like an employee on business who knew he would get chewed out by his boss when he got back to the office.

But he couldn't put it off forever, and Demiurge contacting him first wouldn't be any more pleasant.

"C'mon, me, let's do this!"

With that small cheer for himself, he sent Demiurge a Message. He had simulated the conversation plenty of times in his head. All he had to do now was actually say the words.

But before he had a chance to go through the motions of taking some deep breaths to relax—and only mere moments after he triggered the spell—Demiurge connected. The response time was insanely quick.

"Demiurge?"

"This is he, Lord Ainz."

"Mm." He had rehearsed this over and over. Essentially, all he had to do now was recite his prepared lines. "I figured you might be wondering about the disparity between the reports and my actions. I know what you want to say, but if I'm going to explain all the details, I think Albedo should be present as well. Go back to the Great Tomb of Nazarick at once. I will also return immediately. Let's meet at the log cabin on the surface."

"Understood. I will go ahead and contact Albedo."

"Okay, thanks."

Ainz cut off the Message without further ado. Then he emitted a long, heavy sigh.

Ahhh, phew. He didn't seem angry. Ack, that was terrifying.

Ainz had been fairly afraid that he would anger his outstanding subordinate, so his body practically crumpled with relief before he tensed up and stared at the wall.

The wraith's work was done. Since friendly fire was possible, he could destroy his undead like Shalltear did, but there was no need to waste the energy; it was simple to return them to where they came from. Incidentally, he didn't even have to voice the command; just thinking it was plenty. That was enough to know which tenuous connection to break.

That said, he had countless connections stretching out in the direction of E-Rantel. For those, he wasn't as confident that he could do what he wanted if he didn't give orders vocally, but in the immediate area, he had created only a few undead, so he could tell them apart with no trouble.

Be gone. Now then, back to Nazarick for a day…

Now Ainz had an extremely unpleasant job to do, which could be filed under fabricating excuses or cajoling. If he could have delegated it, he would have, but that wasn't possible. Who would even do it?

Running his hands over the items on the table that had belonged to that trio of subhumans, he tried to forget about his anxieties.

Hrm. They're weak and not worth much, but I'm still happy to have acquired some enchanted items from this world... While I'm not as bad as Pandora's Actor, I admit I might have a bit of a thing for collecting them...

First, he appraised the items that had belonged to the four-armed subhuman. He discovered how she had blocked his instadeath attack—an Armband of Death Guard. It offered perfect resistance against an instadeath spell once a day.

Holding it up, he turned it around in his hands a few times before placing it back on the table.

Boring. I wish they had better stuff... Anyhow.

Just as he was about to leave, there came a knock at the door and a voice: "Your Majesty King of Darkness, it's Neia Baraja."

Ainz did a quick appearance check. Then he glanced around the room to make sure everything was fit for an absolute ruler. After that, he slowly sat down and assumed posture number twenty-four.

"Enter." He said it in as dignified a voice as possible. That voice, too, was the fruit of rehearsal after rehearsal.

The door opened, and Neia, fully healed, entered. Then she bowed.

"Thank you very much for allowing me in, Your Majesty. I'm here to perform my role as your attendant."

"Hmm, good of you to come, Miss Baraja. But there's no reason for you to bend over backward to attend me today. It seems like your wounds have been healed, but you must be tired from the battle..."

Oh, wait, I'm stupid..., thought Ainz. The potion he had used on her would have removed all her fatigue. It was the one Nfirea, with his dry, flaky skin, had raved about.

"No, thanks to Your Majesty, I'll have no problems performing my attendant duties. And besides that, it makes me very happy to be near you."

Neia grinned, or was it more of a smirk? It was hard to not detect some hostility or malice in her hair-raising smile. Ainz nearly braced himself, but he managed to rein it in and avoid disrupting his kingly bearing.

"...I see. But today I need to return to the Nation of Darkness and get some work done. I feel bad that you came over here for nothing, but..."

"Oh…"

She moped, but there wasn't a single thing cute about it. He simply felt like she was glaring at him. Ainz decided to employ a countermeasure.

He closed his eyes. That way he didn't have to look at hers.

"At any rate, I'm glad you're safe—or rather, that you were able to make it back alive, Miss Baraja."

"Thank you, Your Majesty! That's also thanks to you. Without this armor, I don't think I would have lasted until you arrived."

You didn't last… You were definitely dead… Well, all's well that ends well. But it appears I was right about lending her armor that protected her against projectiles for a fight on a wall!

"Ho-ho. Good. How did the bow work for you? Were you able to impress a lot of people?"

"Yes… Many people saw the awesome power of this bow…but then they all died."

"What?! …Ah, I see. So that's what happened. A sad state of affairs."

Another failure. Ainz was disappointed in himself. Everyone who had seen the weapon in action was dead, so it was the same as if no one had seen it. *Maybe I should just give up on trying to promote rune weapons.* But then after a moment, he thought *No, there's still a chance.* More importantly, he wouldn't lose anything even if the plan failed, and he stood to gain a lot if it succeeded.

"Without the gear Your Majesty was kind enough to lend me, I would have been invited to heaven with the others… I'm truly grateful, Your Majesty."

Yes! thought Ainz; her thank-you seemed to have come from the bottom of her heart. Of course, he couldn't openly celebrate. It was important to show her only an attitude befitting a king.

"Don't concern yourself. You should know that it's a master's duty to protect his followers."

Ainz opened his eyes for a peek and saw Neia's face warp a bit at the word *follower.* She didn't look angry, but on the other hand, she did seem offended. All he could do was trust that wasn't how she felt, based on the context of their conversation and past interactions.

In any case, he felt that opening his eyes had been a mistake, so he closed them again.

"Thank you, Your Majesty. Also, the people you saved all feel the same way. They wanted me to tell you how grateful they are."

"Ohhh?" He had to suppress the desire to shout, *Sweet!* "I didn't do anything so special. I was simply at the right place at the right time to aid them. I don't want them to assume that luck will hold. I used a tremendous amount of mana in that fight. Next time, I really won't be able to save them."

"Understood. I'll let everyone know."

"Very good. But, hmm…yes. Do tell them that if I meet them, I would be happy to hear their thanks in person… Anyhow, sorry, Neia, but I need to get going. I'll see you later, uh… Could you come again in about four hours?"

"Yes! I will be waiting! Then if you'll excuse me, Your Majesty."

Neia left the room, and Ainz opened his eyes.

Yes, she definitely seems to be immensely thankful. With this, I finally have one person. But every long journey starts with a single step. Should I give her some healing potions free of charge as a sort of promo campaign? That would make her even more grateful… The rune weapon didn't do much, but what if I gave her this…?

Ainz took out a purple potion.

It was one of the ones Nfirea had made. His potions were still under development and paled ever so slightly in comparison to those made in *Yggdrasil*. Still, maybe they would be just as effective soon; it might not be long before he could even make the red ones from the game.

I didn't use any Yggdrasil stock because I felt like revealing the existence of red potions here would be a waste, but…I'm still a bit unsure that people used to blue potions will accept purple ones. It wasn't a bad idea to use one here and establish a track record.

The potions Ainz was having Nfirea and his grandmother make were hidden away in Nazarick, and he had no intention of letting the technology get out. But it was possible the time to start selling them would eventually come. He figured a little setting up in advance couldn't hurt.

I'm not too sure what's the best move. Either way has its pros and cons. And Nfirea...

Frankly, getting asked advice on the things married people do at night was bothering him. Not that he got all the lurid details, but Ainz thought it might be awkward if it came out that Nfirea was discussing those sorts of things about his wife with him.

And besides, how had Nfirea come up with the idea to ask him in the first place? Ainz could only assume it was due to the fact that the young man had no father figure and had left behind the town he was from; he simply had no one else to turn to. Maybe he thought Ainz had that sort of relationship with Narberal.

Even though he knows I'm a skeleton...

Ainz eventually got so curious, he considered spying on them one night, but he had the feeling he wouldn't be able to treat them the same way afterward, so he refrained. Still, every time Nfirea inquired about something, he had to shrug off the renewed interest that flitted across the back of his mind.

When she realized it felt good, she wanted to do it more and more, or whatever, so... I can't believe he asked me for that kind of potion... What would you even call it? A performance recovery potion? Anyhow, I have a ton, so I could give him some, but, like...

Ainz decided for the time being he would give them to the lizardmen and have them do their best to produce more rare children.

What is it people say? Tech is first applied in the military, then to sex, and then the medical field? Is that true? ...Anyhow, I guess I should head back.

Chapter 5　Ainz Dies

Chapter 5 | Ainz Dies

1

There were four people in the room.

Two had come straight from the fighting and were still wearing blood-spattered armor—the paladins Remedios Custodio and Gustav Montagnés; one was the leader of the surviving priests, the cleric Ciriaco Naranho; and the last was the brother of the Holy Lady, Caspond Bessarez.

Two who had been on the battlefield, one who had tirelessly healed the wounded... Thanks to them, the royal master's quarters reeked of blood.

Remedios hadn't even taken her helmet off. That was no way to enter royal quarters—it could even be considered insolent—but Caspond seemed unperturbed.

Even so, the atmosphere in the room was awful. The smell hanging in the air was bad enough, but the mood felt so heavy that even the sunlight streaming in through the window seemed somehow overcast.

This was far from what most would expect from people who had just avoided what should have been certain defeat.

The first one to break the oppressive silence was Caspond. That was only natural. Who else would?

"Why don't you start by telling me our losses?"

"Yes, sir. About two thousand four hundred of the six thousand militiamen on the battlefield died of their wounds."

"...Adding to my second-in-command's report, about a thousand are injured. We're having the priests heal them, but if they don't provide treatment in time, around half could die."

"...And we lost about half of the remaining paladins as well as eight priests."

Caspond shut his eyes and shook his head.

"I'm not saying I'm glad we only lost that many, given what we were up against, but maybe we should be thankful that was all. Or should we be sa—"

"The latter," interrupted Remedios. "It has to be the latter."

"...Lady Custodio is right. We should grieve our losses."

At Caspond's comment, Gustav and Ciriaco lowered their gazes.

It was unquestionably a miracle—albeit man-made—to have so many members of the Sacred Kingdom Liberation Army forces return alive despite how outnumbered they were. But it was painfully obvious that saying so in this situation would only cause friction.

"The King of Darkness also took out the forces staging at the enemy camp as well, right?"

"Yes. Since it happened during the chaos of defending the wall, there aren't many witnesses. We don't have the details, but what we've heard is that some undead wiped them out."

"I see. That aligns with what I heard from the King of Darkness. He said he created some undead creatures and ordered them to take out the enemy... To think that he really eliminated such a massive army... It's probably safe to assume that the King of Darkness can win against Jaldabaoth, eh?"

Caspond glanced at Remedios, but she remained surly and silent. The strongest paladin in the kingdom was so intimidating at the moment that anyone but the strong would have been afraid of staying near her. When Caspond turned from her to her second-in-command, Gustav could only lower his gaze again apologetically.

"*Hahhh*... Then should we simply bet everything—every last pebble of our country—on him? Or should we have a plan for the scenario where he loses? Does anyone have an idea for that case?"

Silence was their answer. But then Remedios spoke.

"What if we tried to convince Sir Momon to come?"

The other three looked at one another with expressions that said her proposal was tricky at best.

Remedios thought it was a great idea, so she frowned. "What? Do you have any other ideas? He'd be better than that undead."

"...Commander. We're discussing what we should do if the King of Darkness is killed. At that point, it would be dangerous to go to the Nation of Darkness expecting further assistance."

"Maybe not." Ciriaco fingered his newly graying beard as he spoke. "One moment, Deputy Commander. The commander's idea is a bit risky, but it's not a terrible move. What if we told them Jaldabaoth was holding the king captive and asked for Momon to come?"

"With all due respect, that would be too dangerous. Even if Momon could defeat Jaldabaoth, the moment the lie came out, we could be at war all over again. In the best-case scenario, our kingdom's reputation would be worse than dirt. And the worst case could see Momon becoming a new Jaldabaoth and leading the Nation of Darkness's undead army against us."

"Exactly. Above all, we need to avoid giving the Nation of Darkness any valid reason to condemn us."

Hearing Caspond's explanation, Remedios cocked her head. "We're not bordering them or anything. Wouldn't we be fine?"

"...That's a dangerous way to think, Commander Custodio. I don't want to rely on any plan that could cause us trouble in the future... That said, I don't have any bright ideas. Do you?"

Both Ciriaco and Gustav admitted they did not.

For a time, silence ruled the room.

Eventually Caspond spoke up again. "For now...let's each think about it on our own. We won't have this problem if the King of Darkness defeats Jaldabaoth, after all." He clapped his hands together. "Now then, on to the next order of business. What's the report on the food the subhumans brought with them? Is it things we can eat? If so, how many meals can we get out of their supplies?"

Really, the King of Darkness had defeated the subhuman army, so the food belonged to him, but he promised he would hand it all over to them free of charge.

It was Gustav who answered as he was taking care of administrative odds and ends.

"There were a lot of things, like some sort of hardened bread, vegetables, and so on, that we can eat. The king's attack with the undead left it all pristine, so everything is in great condition. There are also some things we'll need to examine further, like a sour-smelling salad we found."

The Sacred Kingdom had its share of sour foods like anywhere. But some subhumans ate foods humans considered spoiled, so Gustav mentioned that they needed to figure out what exactly it was first.

"There's just one problem: the meat."

"By which you mean?"

Gustav turned to Caspond with a grim face. "Some of the dishes seem to contain human flesh. We're only guessing due to the shape, so we aren't certain. Eating some might tell us something, but I have absolutely no interest in trying it."

"How much meat is there?" Ciriaco asked with an offended expression.

"It appears many of the subhumans were carnivorous. There's quite a lot. Eyeballing it, I'd say about half the food they brought was meat."

"What?! The rations for forty thousand soldiers are half meat?!" It was only natural that Remedios's face twisted into a hateful expression.

If each subhuman ate two pounds of meat a day, that would be forty tons. Two weeks' worth would mean some 560 tons.

"So then"—the royal covered his face with his hands—"how much of that is human?"

"We aren't sure. It would take too long to investigate each individual piece, and for anything that has been processed…"

"It would be a shame to let food go to waste when we don't know what the future holds. If possible, I'd like to do our best to separate the human flesh from the other meat. Cleric Naranho, is there nothing that can be done with magic?"

"I'm terribly sorry, Master Caspond. I'm not capable of such a thing. And I believe the same goes for the paladins."

Watching Gustav nod once, Caspond heaved a sigh. "So magic isn't omnipotent, hmm? Then what about feeding it to the subhuman prisoners and having them tell us?"

"The dead should be allowed to rest in peace. If there is human flesh present, it should be returned to the earth."

"It's one thing to say that, Commander Custodio... What do you think, Deputy Commander Montagnés?"

"I agree with the commander on this one. Inspecting each piece of meat in the barrels would take more time than we could possibly get. There are more important things to put our minds to."

"Ah...I see. Then next up, how about their equipment?"

The King of Darkness was also giving them the military supplies free of charge. But if they appreciated it, he asked for it to be paid back eventually. So at some point, they would have to offer him something in return.

Caspond had mentioned before that if they could drive off Jaldabaoth or retake the royal capital, they could offer the royal family's treasure.

"First, we'll need time to strip the enemy corpses as well as bury them, so we don't have a detailed idea of what kind of quality we can expect yet... Cleric Naranho, if undead spawn there, will they be under the king's control?"

Locations where many lives had been taken had a greater tendency to spawn undead. A place where over ten thousand subhumans had been killed definitely fit that description.

Ciriaco looked incredibly troubled.

"I don't know. I truly cannot say for sure. But anything could happen, so we should take care of the bodies as soon as possible and purify the earth. We'll do our best on our own, but if the task proves overwhelming, it would be immensely helpful if the paladins could assist."

"Of course. We're actually quite used to handling undead."

"Wonderful. I knew I could count on you, Commander Custodio. If only the Holy Lady and Lady Kelart were here..."

Everyone fell silent as Ciriaco trailed off.

After what was almost like a silent moment of prayer, Caspond spoke.

"…Oh, that reminds me, Deputy Commander Montagnés. The King of Darkness said he would be taking the enchanted items, so please separate those from the rest. Of course, anything that obviously belongs to the Sacred Kingdom can be left out."

"Understood. The only thing I'd like to bring up is that while it's fairly easy to distinguish enchantments among our own objects, it's quite difficult for other items. We'll need help from someone knowledgeable about magic items."

"I know a bit about the items passed down in the royal family. And for faith items…" Ciriaco nodded when Caspond glanced at him. "For the rest, let's check among the people for someone who can help. I must admit, I never imagined this would happen. It's probably more accurate to say that this goes well beyond anything I had imagined. I suppose we should be thankful that the King of Darkness is so unfathomably powerful."

None of the others objected. Amid their silence, Caspond continued, as if speaking for them all.

"It was the King of Darkness's power that kept this city from falling."

At the audible teeth grinding, Caspond looked to Gustav for help.

"Later, representatives from the Paladin Order will need to go express our gratitude. I'd like you all to join us… At any rate, we're fortunate that we were able to win the battle thanks to the King of Darkness."

"It wouldn't have happened if we didn't give our all. Don't forget that."

The whole room seemed to freeze at Remedios's comment. No, only two people froze—Gustav and Ciriaco.

Gustav worked his mouth like a fish out of water. He was trying to think of a way to apologize for his superior's rude remark, but nothing came to mind.

"…Yes, of course, Commander Custodio. We couldn't have achieved victory without the desperate efforts of the paladins and the militiamen. That much is true." Seeing Remedios nod, Caspond continued. "And it's also true that without the King of Darkness, we would have been defeated. The fact is that he is the one who decided the battle. Am I wrong?"

Remedios ripped her helmet off and hurled it at the wall. It clanged loudly.

"Master! Did something happen?!" The door opened, and the paladin standing guard outside rushed in.

"Everything's fine. You can wait outside."

The paladin's eyes went back and forth between the helmet on the ground and the look on Remedios's face; it must have been obvious what was going on. Acknowledging the order, the guard quietly left the room.

"Commander Custodio. Please calm down. I need you to keep a level head."

"How can I be calm?! Almost every person I met on my way here was grateful to the King of Darkness and the King of Darkness only! It was as if he won the battle all by himself! But he only showed up partway through! How many people died for that victory?! Citizens, paladins, priests—young and old, men and women—so many sacrifices were made!" She glared at Caspond. "He didn't do this on his own!"

"Commander!"

Gustav could no longer hide his horror at how she was behaving in the presence of royalty. Remedios had never been the thinking type, but she understood who was her superior, if nothing else. But now she was different. She was like a wounded beast that had gone mad with pain.

"That bony bastard. Flying around trying to look cool! Is war just a game to him?"

"…Commander Custodio. The massive loss of life must be upsetting you. What if you rested for a while?"

Gustav shot Caspond a thankful look for handling the situation with such grace.

"Before that, there's something I've been thinking: I'm sure the King of Darkness and Jaldabaoth are working together."

The other three exchanged glances.

"If you're going to make such a claim, you'll need some proof, Commander." Ciriaco gave Remedios an icy stare. Given her recent behavior, a careful analysis could only appraise this assertion as an attempt to discredit the king she loathed so much—even though this was no time to be hypercritical.

"But isn't he the only one gaining anything? The subhumans and our people alike are dying in droves. He's culling our forces so that he—the Nation of Darkness—can take over the Sacred Kingdom and the hills. That's why he's here!"

"…I see. In terms of who benefits, it would be possible to see it that way. Do either of you have any thoughts?"

Caspond's question caused Gustav to furrow his brow. "The King of Darkness came to the Sacred Kingdom because we asked him to. Wasn't having the two of them fight your idea, Commander?"

"…That's true. Then the one with the mask from the Blue Roses is in on it, too. If she hadn't said anything, we wouldn't have gone to the Nation of Darkness. Without her advice, we would have turned to the Empire or the Theocracy. And besides, he might have come even without any word from us!"

Caspond sighed heavily. "Commander Custodio, all your inferences presume the answer you want to reach. It seems you're just lining up everything else accordingly. What do you make of the claim that the King of Darkness wants to acquire the demon maids?"

"…This isn't an appropriate comment for a cleric to make, but please forgive me. I hear those demon maids possess tremendous power. It's understandable why he would want them for himself. It's said that demons don't need to eat or drink and that they don't die, either. One powerful demon might be worth more than an entire army."

"So you could say that he volunteered to assist us because it would benefit him as well? That's a natural thing for the king of a country to do."

"But no one has even seen these demon maids!"

Remedios's emotional outburst was met with a glance from Caspond that he might have directed toward a pitiful child. "Commander Custodio, I wanted to discuss this logically, not clouded by emotions…but it seems you're a bit tired. Get some rest. That's an order."

Remedios blushed furiously and tried to shout something, but before she could, Caspond continued.

"And then go visit the wounded soldiers. You have your duties as front-line commander."

"...Fine."

Remedios picked up her helmet and left the room.

An indescribable sense of relief flooded the room. It was the atmosphere after a typhoon, the combined fatigue of having to clean up and the liberation of being past the storm.

But there was one man for whom it wasn't over yet.

"Master Caspond! My humble apologies for Commander Custodio's behavior!"

Gustav bowed his head low, and Caspond chuckled wryly.

"You've really got it rough. But you know, you should be thinking about the future, too. I can't fathom what will become of this country after the war. If we could find my little sister... Do you know what happened to the Holy Lady during the battle of Karinsha? Did you hear anything from Commander Custodio?"

Gustav was Remedios's aide. Naturally, he had heard the story from Remedios, and he had been present when she had explained it to Caspond.

If Caspond was asking again, it meant he suspected that he hadn't been told the truth.

"...Master Caspond, I heard the same story Commander Custodio told you when you first met her."

She had been thrown by an explosion, and when she came to, the Holy Lady and Remedios's little sister—Kelart Custodio—were nowhere to be found. The corpses of paladins, adventurers, and priests had been strewn everywhere, but the bodies of those two weren't there.

"I see. I guess I was overthinking things... And I doubt Commander Custodio is a very good actress. Well, I hope they've only been captured. If they've been killed...there will be problems surrounding succession."

Ciriaco seemed puzzled and asked, "Won't you become holy king, Master Caspond?"

"Is that flattery? Perhaps if my sister had died in an accident during peacetime, that's what would have happened. But not as things are now. The north is exhausted, and the south has an army. So it's very likely that someone the south chooses will be holy king. Frankly, it could even be one of the southern nobles."

"What?!"

Caspond smiled wryly in response to Ciriaco's surprise. "I don't think it's all that surprising… Anyhow, regarding Deputy Commander Montagnés's earlier comments, if things go according to plan, the first thing the southern nobles will demand is that Remedios Custodio be confined—to pin the responsibility on her."

"Why are you so certain that will happen?"

"Conversely, Deputy Commander Montagnés, why do you think it wouldn't? Isn't the paladin who failed to protect the Holy Lady the perfect target for their discontent? Of course, that's not the only reason. She can take a whole army on by herself. Isn't it a fundamental rule of battle to first defang your enemy?"

"Enemy?! Whose enemy?!"

"Whoever stands in the way of the southern nobles. In other words, the Holy Lady's faction. Remedios Custodio is the Holy Lady's aide. And I'm sure they feel the same about the Paladin Order she led."

"Then what about the priests Lady Kelart Custodio led?"

"It's possible that priests with connections to the southern nobles will be promoted…but I wonder. The magic the priests use is essential for daily life. I think everyone knows how foolish it is to put someone with no ability at the top, but people have a tendency to occasionally do things that anyone would recognize as foolish…"

"Master Caspond…what should we do?"

"What do you mean, Deputy Commander Montagnés? In order to keep her from being locked up? Or to prevent the rest of the paladins from meeting the same fate?"

"To secure a better future for the Sacred Kingdom."

"…We must find my sister. Then we need to achieve something that will allow us to say she saved the country so that the people will accept her wholeheartedly. Like if we could put an end to all this without relying on the south."

"That would be impossible… There's no way we can win without the King of Darkness." Gustav's grumble slipped out, and Caspond shrugged.

"And yet, we must. If we fail, we won't be able to withstand the pressure that will surely come from the south. Oh, right. The other thing would be to ensure that the south suffers as much damage as the north. As long as the balance of power remains the same, there won't be an issue." Caspond looked up at the ceiling. "If only friendly relations had been established before all this. My sister's approach to rule was too soft. I can understand why Commander Custodio was so irritated with her. The only one who gained any renown in this fight is the King of Darkness. In the worst case, he could become holy king."

Though the other two didn't think that could be possible, they found it impossible to deny, either.

"All right, then what should our plan be now? I wanted Commander Custodio to be here for this, but… Do you think she'll disobey orders?"

"…If the orders are aligned with justice for the kingdom, I don't think there will be a problem."

"I see… I think we should go around and liberate the prison camps. That is—"

Caspond began to explain.

The invading subhumans had numbered ten thousand.

There had been no reports that the subhumans facing the southern Sacred Kingdom were on the move, so it was possible to infer that the forty thousand in the army that had shown up outside the city must have been the majority of those left in the north to run the camps.

"I agree. We can raid the sparsely guarded camps and increase our own numbers while reducing theirs. This operation will kill two birds with one stone."

"I'm glad you approve, Deputy Commander Montagnés. How about you, Cleric Naranho?"

Ciriaco also agreed with Caspond's idea.

"With the King of Darkness around, the city should be safe. That being the case, I'd like the paladins to carry out the camp raids... Do you think that's possible? I'd also like you to leave Commander Custodio here. I think I'll assign her to be my personal guard."

"Thank you, Master Caspond!"

"I don't remember saying anything that warrants a thank-you, Deputy Commander Montagnés." Caspond smiled for a moment before his expression became grim. "Without the strongest paladin in the country, if you encounter a subhuman on par with the Mighty King at one of the camps, you could all be wiped out."

"Can we decide which camps to raid?"

"Of course. I'll leave that up to you. There's no need to go after the larger, more dangerous ones."

"Understood. Then we'll go on our own."

"Deputy Commander Montagnés, may we send a few priests who can fight along to assist?"

"Of course! That would be a great help."

"Very good. Then head out within the next couple of days."

•

Ainz had used Greater Teleportation to travel instantly in front of the log cabin situated on the surface of Nazarick. It was unclear how long they had been waiting for him, but Albedo, Demiurge, and Lupusregina were already outside.

Albedo and Demiurge were there because Ainz had asked to meet with them, while Lupusregina must have been on guard duty.

He had left the business of Carne up to Lupusregina, so logic dictated that she shouldn't have been on log cabin duty, but apparently that wasn't a given.

Maybe it had been someone else's shift, but something came up suddenly, so she was filling in on short notice. If so, that was wonderful. It meant that the system could fill any opening right away.

…But wait a second.

The Pleiades all had different roles, but their basic abilities as maids were mostly equal, so for a job like this, they could be swapped out easily.

But there were other people who couldn't be replaced. There could come a time when an NPC with completely specialized abilities—like a floor guardian or their captain—would need to have someone fill in for them. And Ainz had been meaning to adopt a vacation system for some time now.

Having only Pandora's Actor to cover any and all vacant posts was too risky.

What would happen in the extreme case that Ainz was gone? Like if he was captured or charmed. He didn't think they required his explicit approval to operate, but there was a good chance that Albedo and Demiurge didn't even consider such an event possible. He figured they would just say, *That would never happen to you, Lord Ainz.*

I need to put some serious thought into this—ASAP.

He put on his dignified voice and ordered the three who were bowing to raise their heads.

"It's been a while, Demiurge."

"My lord!"

Really, there was so much on his mind about the Sacred Kingdom that he was thinking about Demiurge every day, so it didn't feel like they'd been apart very long. But it actually had been quite some time since they had last seen each other.

"Now, you're probably both wondering why I did what I did. I'm going to tell you, but this is no place for a talk. Come with me."

Ainz led them into the log cabin.

There was a Gate mirror ready to transport them as a handy shortcut, but today he had no plans to use it.

In the center of the room was a table with two pairs of chairs facing one another across it. Ainz went for the most esteemed seat. He knew the trouble that would follow if he didn't. There had been a time when he would have needed to think carefully about which seat was meant for the highest-ranked person, but now he could choose it automatically.

When he stood next to the chair, Lupusregina immediately pulled it out for him.

Honestly, he felt perfectly capable of pulling out his own chair, but he had learned well while observing Jircniv that it was important for a ruler to put their subordinates to work. Nonetheless, as a member of the lower middle class, Ainz found it impossible to leave *every* last thing up to someone else.

Once Ainz had made it into his chair without issue, the others knelt instead of sitting. Lupusregina, who had circled around behind them, was doing the same.

"You may both be seated."

The two guardians declined in unison. It was only after he gave them permission a second time that they emitted a chorus of gratitude and sat down across from him. Lupusregina stood at attention behind them.

That took so long, and it's so much effort. Isn't there some other w…? Oops.

"Okay, now we can continue. I had said there was no one worth saving in the Sacred Kingdom, yet I saved some of them anyhow. You must find that quite puzzling."

"Not at all, my lord."

"………Huh? Wh-why not?"

Demiurge shook his head lightly as if he couldn't bear the admiration he felt.

"Everything you do is correct, Lord Ainz. If you did it, then it means there was some merit to the idea that I couldn't have imagined."

"I couldn't have said it better myself. If that's what you thought best, Lord Ainz, then it was the right thing to do."

—Wha—?

At Albedo's comment, Ainz's face froze completely. Not that his face could be considered expressive in any way, but…

The sight of the two guardians before him—the two smartest members of Nazarick—nodding to each other caused him panic and fear in every sense of the words.

"H-hold on. While… I mean, while it's true…" Ainz was flustered. The conversation had gone in an unexpected direction, which confused him; he couldn't remember what he was going to say. And yet— "It's true that normally, I behave as you might expect."

Er? Ainz was slightly embarrassed. He was so intent on getting his story together that he spoke without really thinking. Finding it strange that the two guardians were nodding deeply, he nonetheless pressed on, since he couldn't very well turn back now.

"But—yes, *but*—this time is different. I didn't have anything in mind when I made that move." Having managed to correct what he was saying, Ainz continued merrily. "This time I destroyed the plan without thinking."

"For whatever reason did you do that, Lord Ainz?"

"Mm," Ainz murmured as he leaned back in his seat—with the appropriate master attitude that he had practiced for a ruler. "Demiurge and Albedo. The two of you are wiser than me."

"Not at—"

Ainz held up his hands to stop them.

"I'm telling you that's what I think. Now, is there any element out of place in the plan you drafted, Demiurge? If we proceed according to your proposed operation, everything would go perfectly and we would reach a brilliant outcome."

That planning document was garbage, though, grumbled Ainz in his head. *Any plan that leaves the whole thing up to me is doomed to fail.*

"So I suddenly wondered, Demiurge, if your brain, capable of drafting such a wonderful plan, could continue to work when things didn't go according to it, if something changed drastically or went haywire. In other words, I wanted to know if your ability to adapt is equally outstanding."

"Ah, I see."

What? You already get it? He seems to understand the whole thing!

Witnessing how quick Demiurge's intellect was made him want to scream, *How can a genius like you think I'm smart? Are you bullying me?* but he managed to control himself.

"I'd expect nothing less… You really are brilliant, Demiurge."

"Thank you, Lord Ainz."

"S-so sorry to test you like this, but…"

"Not at all, my lord. I'm delighted that you are interested in learning more about my abilities. I'll be sure to achieve an outcome that will meet your expectations!"

"Good. I'm counting on you, Demiurge. So during this series of events in the Sacred Kingdom, I'll make the occasional mistake and request that you adjust the plan. That's all right with you?'

"Yes, my lord! Understood!"

Yeeeeeeees! Ainz was overjoyed. He got so happy, the emotion was immediately suppressed.

But there was still a lingering contentment.

Good, good, good. Now if I screw up, I can just say I did it on purpose! Of course, the idea is to not make mistakes, but…wow, I really should have told him this from the beginning.

He wasn't in the habit of celebrating the failure of his subordinates' plans, but it was possible he would somehow throw things off by accident. Now, instead of thinking, *Ainz must have done that for a reason,* Demiurge would automatically correct the error. For the first time in a while, Ainz felt a massive weight lift from his shoulders. It was so refreshing.

"…I understand your concerns, Lord Ainz. Would you like to investigate the capabilities of the other guardians and domain guardians at the same time?"

For a moment after hearing Albedo's question, he thought, *What in the world are you talking about?* But…

"That won't be necessary for now. Demiurge is doing the most work outside Nazarick—that's why it came to mind. For the others, we can do it as the need arises."

"I see…"

"Yes. And the next thing I wanted to talk about is… The plan was for me and my admirers in the Sacred Kingdom to go east to the Abellion Hills where the subhumans live, but I'm going to change part of that. I'm going to go alone, and I'm going to die."

For a moment, it was as if time had stopped. Then—

"What?! What are you saying, Lord Ainz?! How could the ever-lofty Lord Ainz perish?!"

It was Albedo criticizing the idea. She seemed so crushed that Ainz wondered if this was the most agitated he had ever seen her. Before Ainz could explain his intentions to Albedo, Demiurge spoke up.

"Albedo, surely Lord Ainz has a splendid objective in mind. I'm not sure you should be coming out against his proposal so emotionally."

"Demiurge, where do you get such a level head? If Lord Ulbert Alain Odle said the same, would you be so calm? Or…?"

"Ho-ho…Albedo. Would you mind telling me what you meant by that? What did you want to say after 'or'?"

One guardian glared with icy eyes while the other's blazed like a raging fire, creating an eerie vibe between them. It was the same suffocating sensation Ainz had felt fighting against Shalltear. Whether it was due to fear or anxiety, he could hear Lupusregina breathing harder.

"Cut it out!"

When Ainz shouted, the dangerous atmosphere dissipated instantaneously. The shift was so dramatic, it was as though the tense mood from a moment ago had been nothing but his imagination. But Lupusregina's irregular breathing told him it wasn't.

"Calm down, both of you. This is exactly why I have to die. This is an event called a safety drill. The idea is to prepare in advance for an emergency in order to be ready if it happens. So what would you do if I died? I'll ask you first, Albedo."

"My lord! After immediately subjecting the grave offender to every manner of suffering that exists in the world, I would resurrect you!"

"I see. Demiurge?"

"My lord! In parallel with preparation for your resurrection, I would strengthen Nazarick's defenses and collect intelligence on the one who committed the grave offense."

Albedo gave Demiurge a sidelong scowl.

"Collecting intelligence isn't enough. No matter what sort of being committed the offense, it was against a Supreme Being, so we must use every available resource to capture and torture them until their very sense of self breaks down."

"Albedo, everything you've said is quite right. But our opponent would be a being who killed Lord Ainz. We mustn't let our guard down. It's imperative that we collect data about their movements, strength, and so on. If the enemy is more powerful than expected, it will affect where Lord Ainz can be resurrected."

As Albedo's expression grew even more severe, Ainz struck the ground with the staff he had taken out. The *clack* had the effect of a dousing bucket of cold water, and the pair immediately composed themselves.

"I'm not even necessarily saying someone killed me. For instance, I could die in…some kind of unimaginable natural disaster."

Honestly, he couldn't imagine anything like that killing him, so his example ended up being very vague.

"But I see that there's a slight difference in opinion between our two sharpest minds. We can't have that. That's why we'll have a drill—to make sure that if it actually came to pass, there wouldn't be any issues."

The guardians bowed.

"Of course, this isn't just about me. Demiurge, you're in charge of defense in the event Nazarick is attacked, but what if you're killed somehow? Will Nazarick still function?"

"Yes, my lord! All the arrangements have been made. I believe I gave you a report on the matter."

Ainz thought, *Huh? Did I get a report about that?* for a moment, but he trusted Demiurge's memory more than his own.

"Hmm, but that was only on paper, right? Have you tested it to see if it works?"

"My humblest of apologies, my lord! No, we have not." Demiurge's voice trembled as he replied with pangs of deep regret.

"I-I'm terribly sorry, Lord Ainz! I'm also a fool for merely signing the document and not suggesting that we run a test!"

Albedo bowed her head with the same look of remorse on her face.

Ainz was suddenly tormented by guilt. If anyone was to blame, it was him. If he had been more attentive, neither of these two would have had to apologize. *A boss who makes his subordinates apologize for his own errors is the worst—just a shitty piece of trash.*

"You don't need to apologize. I'm the one who didn't explain well enough. I should have noticed that the test hadn't been run. It's all my fault." Ainz bowed till he could place his forehead on the table. "Please forgive this reprehensible error."

"Wh—?! Lord Ainz!"

"P-please don't!"

Both guardians immediately begged him to stop bowing. But Ainz didn't raise his head. He couldn't—because he was embarrassed at how shamelessly he had lied even while apologizing.

"L-Lupusregina! Get Lord Ainz to stop bowing!"

"Eh? Me? F-forgive me, but I can't possibly force Lord Ainz to raise his head!"

""""P-please raise your head!""""

The three of them—especially Demiurge—seemed so out of sorts that Ainz hurriedly returned to a normal posture. There were three audible sighs.

"…I appreciate you accepting my apology. So while I'm doing what I need to do in the Abellion Hills, please begin a drill that assumes I'm dead. Ah. This is a good chance, so maybe you should train for more than just that. Maybe you could assume that both Demiurge and I have been killed…"

Having said that much, Ainz was suddenly nervous about his proposal.

"That said, it's not as if my plan is the perfect training program. If you have a better idea, do that. Also, you don't need to ask me for permission. Right? Because I'm dead."

The pair winced.

"For us to act like you've disappeared during the planning stages of the drill…"

"Demiurge has a point, Lord Ainz."

""""Ha-ha-ha-ha."""" The log cabin filled with the laughter of three people.

Two were laughing genuinely; one was faking.

"I should add that you don't have to get too serious. The goal isn't to cause discord in Nazarick, like what happened between you two earlier. Going forward, I'd like to run a variety of drills, so I want you to gain some experience from this and share it with the other guardians... But you're both brilliant, so I don't need to tell you that. Do whatever you deem necessary. I'm counting on you two. Got it?"

Thinking back, he realized that Satoru Suzuki was never the type to take disaster prevention training seriously. As such, Ainz couldn't very well ask them to put everything they had into the drill, so he made sure to tell them not to stress about it.

Upon confirming their sober bows, Ainz said, "On a different topic..."

You got this!

He had built flowcharts and simulated how he would persuade them any number of times. It was all for this moment.

"I want you to halt all plans for the giant statue of me."

"Understood. I'll make sure of it."

With a single remark from Albedo, the conversation appeared to have ended.

Huh? It puzzled him, so he boldly inquired into what he wanted to cautiously ask about.

"...Is that okay? You wanted to build it, right, Albedo?"

"Who could object to something the Supreme One decided? If you say black is white, Lord Ainz, it is white."

Ainz swallowed hard, though he had no spit or throat. *That way of thinking is actually terrifying, you know.* He shuddered.

"...I'm not fond of that argument, Albedo. It's the same as ceasing to think. There are definitely times that even I will be wrong."

If he was being honest, it felt like he was always wrong.

"If someone takes control of me, we'll be done for. The ones who brainwashed Shalltear are still out there, after all. You don't need to ask my objective every time I speak, but if something comes to mind when I make a suggestion, you should tell me."

"Understood."

Albedo and Demiurge exchanged quick glances.

"In that case, why are you halting construction of the statue? The aim was to inform the world of your supremacy…"

"Hmm." Ainz grinned with nihilism in his head. "My greatness shouldn't be conveyed via some object." He thought of Neia's face; she had understood him with that single comment.

Perfect.

"Isn't conveying it through an object a good idea? Fools can only understand things they can see with their foolish eyes."

Albedo's remark caught him off guard. It was as if the pitcher had thrown the ball, and instead of hitting it, the batter had caught it and thrown it back as hard as they could.

"…I see. You have a point, Albedo. But…" Impressed that his voice wasn't shaking, Ainz frantically whipped his mind into action. When he didn't think of anything, he was about to give up and shrug, but he couldn't break his character as a ruler in front of his subordinates.

"Ah, never mind. You must have thought of more pros than the five cons I came up with. In that case, I don't have any complaints."

"F-five, my lord?! …Demiurge, I need to talk to you later. Let me borrow a bit of your wisdom."

"O-of course. A-and you're brilliant as usual, Lord Ainz. It's so modest of you to claim that we're smarter…"

The two of them seemed flustered, and Albedo bowed low.

"M-my apologies, Lord Ainz. We went so far as to secure your permission, but I'm very sorry; we'll suspend construction for now."

"M-mm. Well, that's fine. Please do, Albedo."

He had thrown the number out without thinking very hard, but the two of them were terribly shaken. He even heard Lupusregina murmur, "Wow," behind them.

Feeling guilty for befuddling them again with his arbitrary pronouncements, Ainz looked down slightly. But he was genuinely happy that the plans for the giant Ainz statue were being halted.

Next, I need to do something about the Thanks to the King of Darkness festival; the Happy Birthday, King of Darkness festival; and the other two events with my name in them. But I guess if the giant statue is being canceled, then it can't walk around for the Thanks to the King of Darkness festival, so that's one down! I would've been perfectly happy with normal festivals!

It had actually been Ainz who had casually suggested a festival. But the result was the establishment of a bizarre, embarrassing festival committee. He sighed heavily in his head and turned to Demiurge.

"So what's left is our next steps, Demiurge. The plan is to have a demon summoned by you—Jaldabaoth—attack the city, right?"

"Yes, that is correct."

"Then…I have two favors to ask. One is a plan I've been working on personally that isn't going very well; I'd like your help. Oh, but it doesn't have to be flashy or anything. Secondly, can you order the demon you summon to fight me for real?"

•

Neia shut the door to the King of Darkness's quarters, turned on her heel—and trembled.

Smacking her slightly flushed cheeks, she pulled herself together and schooled her expression. One reason was that she knew how much her relaxed face put others on guard, but even more than that, grinning like a fool would be embarrassing.

She didn't want to strut around outside with a goofy look on her face. She was on her way to meet people, so she wanted to look a little more dignified.

On top of that, Neia Baraja was attendant to the King of Darkness. Embarrassing herself could harm the king's reputation.

Really, I'm only serving him temporarily, so my missteps should reflect on the Sacred Kingdom if anything, but…

She knew those who felt hostile toward him would not see it that way. Hatred, especially, clouded one's eyes. Perhaps the saying "Hate the sword, hate the blacksmith" was more apt.

Okay!

Neia didn't want the king to regret choosing her as his attendant, either. That just meant she had to do a good job.

She headed for the meeting place. On her way, she ruminated on how compassionate the King of Darkness was.

…Ah, I see. So that's what happened. A sad state of affairs.

When he said those words, she had detected the intense disappointment and regret. He wasn't just saying them for show.

…His Majesty is just so kind.

She couldn't think of any other king—of course, Neia didn't know any other kings, so she could only compare with imaginary ones—who would mourn another country's war dead as his own like the King of Darkness did.

If they could have held out just a little longer, they would have surely been saved just like Neia was. Even the man who lost his son would have probably survived.

Neia didn't think anything about the fact that the rescue had come late. The King of Darkness said he needed to conserve mana for the fight with Jaldabaoth, so she thought it was good fortune he came at all. Besides, she heard from someone in Remedios's unit that before the king had rescued her, he had faced powerful subhumans right in front of the west gate.

Two who could kill a paladin in one hit and another who fought at the level of the Sacred Kingdom's strongest.

The militiaman hadn't been able to contain himself and gushed about the events that unfolded there. "If the King of Darkness hadn't shown up, we would've been dead."

That's right. Neia felt a warmth in her chest.

Before saving Neia and those near her, he had been helping others elsewhere.

She felt a little sad that he hadn't prioritized her, but it was wrong to think that way. Defense of the wall was certainly important, but if the gate—the entrance to the city—had fallen, that would have been a disaster. If the subhumans had flooded the city, it would have been the start of a merciless massacre.

For anyone thinking straight, it was natural to prioritize the gate in order to save more lives.

People who don't get swept up in emotions, but instead act according to logic, are the most trustworthy.

I'd expect nothing less from the King of Darkness!

She recalled the strongest paladin of her own country.

Even comparing them is an insult to His Majesty!

And after the initial battle, the King of Darkness slaughtered the few subhumans that had gotten into the city. Many people said he saved their lives. *And actually…*

"Oh! If it isn't His Majesty's attendant! Did you give him my message?"

Apparently, she had been so absorbed in her thoughts, she had reached the meeting place without realizing it.

In a part of town that still had the air of a battlefield, six men were gathered on the road. They called out to her as if they had been eagerly awaiting her arrival—in fact, they probably really had been that eager.

"Yes, I extended all your gratitude to His Majesty."

Under Neia's gaze, the men braced themselves, but they thanked her, wearing smiles.

"Ahhh, good. It would be awkward to thank the king of a different country. Well, it'd be hard to face the Holy Lady, too."

"Yeah, but there's no way royalty would agree to meet you in the first place."

The ages ranged from quite young men to those who were approaching their twilight years, but they were all around platoon leader rank. Some of them had been career soldiers, servicemen.

None of them was put off by the fact that the king was an undead.

Certainly, some people were still wary of him for that reason—more so in the general population than among the paladins and priests. There were those among their ranks who often claimed that he was only being kind so that he could betray them when the timing was right.

But Neia figured they felt that way because they didn't know the King of Darkness. It was all conjecture based on their negative impression of normal undead. Why? The proof was these men standing here. Once people got to know the king, many changed their minds.

"Ah, you don't need to worry about it. I simply told him thank you from you all. Oh, and he told me he was happy to hear it."

The militia representatives looked bashful. "Awww, geez, we're the ones who are happy…"

"Really. What a kind ruler. It's embarrassing that we used to be afraid of him just because he's an undead."

"His Majesty truly is so kind. But he also said, *I don't want them to assume that luck will hold. I used a tremendous amount of mana in that fight. Next time, I really won't be able to save them.*"

The men's expressions grew meek.

"He won't be able to save us again…? We're in trouble."

"…Lots of people will be frightened when they hear we won't be able to get his help again, especially my group."

"Not only yours. Mine is the same… We can't tell them."

Neia spoke softly to the shaken militiamen. "There's something I've learned, everyone, and that is that it's bad to be weak."

The men seemed puzzled, so she continued slowly. "Look, if we were strong, then this never would have happened. We would have been able to save our own parents, children, wives, friends, and so on. His Majesty once said that you're the only one who values your loved ones as highly as you do. The King of Darkness isn't the ruler of this country. He only came to lend a helping hand."

Neia inhaled.

She wanted the citizens hurrying down the road with a glance at their group as they passed to hear this, too. She raised her voice slightly before continuing.

"…What will we do if we're attacked by subhumans again after His Majesty defeats Jaldabaoth and goes home? Will we run crying to the king of another country again and ask him to save us? He might not do it a second time. This is extraordinary. Have you ever heard of a king helping another country this much?"

No one answered—because there was no precedent of such a thing, no matter how far back they searched.

"Maybe it's offensive to be lectured like this by a girl. But our only choice is to protect what we care about ourselves. That's why I'm going to get stronger. I'll get stronger so I won't need to ask His Majesty the King of Darkness for help defending what's important to me."

"Yeah. That makes sense. You're right. I'll train, too!"

"Me too. Next time, I'll be the one to protect my wife and kids."

"…I'll do the same. When I got drafted, I hated it so much, but…now I'm glad."

"But wow, the King of Darkness has a way with words. No one values my loved ones as much as I do, huh—it's true."

"If anyone valued my wife more than I do, I'd have to kill him."

"…Um, I don't think that's what the King of Darkness was talking about."

"…Hey, I was only joking."

"Didn't sound like a joke to me!"

As they laughed, Neia made a suggestion. "Would you all like to train with me? I can't teach swordsmanship, but I might be able to show you a thing or two with a bow."

Weakness is wickedness. Being a burden to the king was wrong. That meant she would simply have to get stronger. As his attendant, the proper course of action was to make sure she didn't cause trouble for him so he could focus on his duel with Jaldabaoth in the next fight.

"That's not a bad idea."

"I definitely gotta train some. I need to protect my family myself."

"—What are you all doing out here? Having a meeting or something?"

"Oh, Commander."

When Neia turned around in response to the sudden question, there was Remedios Custodio standing there. She had heard the footsteps but never guessed it would be her commander.

Of all the people to show up, thought Neia, but she did her best not to let her feelings show on her face. The militia representatives seemed confused.

"You're not going to answer my question?"

"Ma'am! I was just telling them how I conveyed their gratitude to the King of Darkness."

"To that jerk?"

"…I'm not sure it's a good idea to call a foreign king a jerk…"

Remedios glowered at her.

"Isn't it only natural for the strong to protect the weak?"

"…I don't know if it's natural or not, but I think that's something for the strong to say, not the weak."

"What?! Are you calling me weak?!"

"Yes!" Neia shot back immediately. "Compared to His Majesty the King of Darkness, you're weak… Do you think I'm wrong, Commander?"

Neia replied to Remedios's glare by glaring right back.

"Hmph. It's fine for you to be friends with him and all, but he's an undead, you know. He's a monster not from the world you and I live in."

"Yes, I'm aware of that."

"I'm saying this because I'm worried about you, but it doesn't seem to be getting through."

Her expression was one of regret, but it reeked of insincerity to Neia. The paladin before her didn't seem to think it was all that tragic.

"Commander, I know you're busy, so I would feel guilty taking up any more of your time. We're going to talk a little more, so maybe it would be better for you to be on your way to your meeting."

"…I'll do that. Remember, everyone, it was only natural that the King of Darkness save you. You don't have to read so much into it."

With that, Remedios walked off. Watching her go, one of the militiamen murmured, "Woof… She's really something… So that's the Sacred Kingdom's strongest paladin…"

"Yes. That's what she's like."

Neia sympathized with the honest remark. And all the militia representatives covered their faces with their hands. They seemed to be fairly shocked.

It wasn't as if Neia had done anything wrong, but she still felt guilty.

"I-it's not as if all the paladins are like that. She's a bit special, you could say, er...you know. Something like that. Yeah."

"Must be tough being a squire. If you drank, I'd be buying."

"I'll manage with the sentiment alone, thanks. Um, where were we again? Oh, right. Training together. I know a way for us to get a space and borrow some gear. Can I contact you all again once I have a plan?"

"Sure thing." The men answered in the affirmative. "We'll be waiting to hear."

2

Neia smoothly drew her bowstring.

With her sharp eyes fixed on the target, she saw the white of her quiet breath dissipate in her peripheral vision. Spring was near, but it would still be chilly for a while.

Burying her extraneous thoughts, she cleared her mind and carefully took aim.

She had learned quite well during the fight to defend the city that there was no time to aim on the battlefield, but this was an exercise in accuracy, not speed.

And then she let go.

Leaving a whistle in its wake, the arrow flew straight ahead until it struck the target right where she intended.

Phew, Neia exhaled.

In ten shots, she had missed none.

It was an excellent bull's-eye rate, but Neia wasn't happy.

Previously, it would have been impossible for her, but now she could even hit the nock of the previous arrow she'd sent downrange; of course, she didn't do that because the arrow would break.

She had been capable of feats like that only since the battle. It wasn't merely her bow skills that had improved; she could also draw upon holy energy now. But what struck her as a bit strange was that, as far as she had heard, it seemed to be a different sort of energy from what the other paladins were tapping into. Well, paladins generally poured it into their weapons for close-quarters combat, and she was using it for her ranged weapon.

She wasn't sure what it meant, but when she asked the King of Darkness, he was mightily intrigued. But even he had said, *It's hard to tell from just that. Report back when you've awakened more of your powers.*

At the sound of clapping, Neia smiled awkwardly. It was embarrassing.

"Wow, Baraja, you're amazing."

"Seriously. I've never seen someone so good with a bow. There was nobody like that in my village."

"No kidding. I've been a hunter all these years, and I know a few, but none of them has the archery skills you do, Baraja."

The compliments came from the people sweating it out with her on the training range. Many of them hadn't been around during the battle three weeks prior.

The city's population was rapidly increasing as a result of the influx of people freed from nearby camps. The ones with an aptitude for archery or experience with a bow were sent to train under Neia to be part of the archer unit.

Common sense would dictate that most would be opposed to having a girl, a mere squire, commanding men (and some women) old enough to be her parents. But no one complained.

The reasons were mainly that no one was willing to dissent when she looked at them with her terrifying eyes, that they were impressed by her prowess with a bow, that she was the attendant to the King of Darkness, and that they knew others were grateful to her.

Some were frightened after learning she was the king's attendant because of their fear of the undead, but they didn't all react that way. Because during those three weeks, the Paladin Order had been out liberating prison camps, but so had Neia and the King of Darkness.

When the king proposed the idea, a surprising number of people objected. But when the king suggested that *With fewer soldiers, the subhuman alliance will realize they can't manage the camps and begin killing off the prisoners. We need to save them as fast as possible,* Caspond allowed them to go.

The King of Darkness was supposed to be conserving mana for his fight with Jaldabaoth. Neia wanted to say as much. But the reason she respected him and sensed justice within him was that he was the kind of person who would leap into action to protect another country's people. There was no way she could stop him.

That was how Neia and the king set off to rescue a huge number of prisoners before leading them to the city. Several of her new subordinates gladly joined her unit because of that.

"Ahhh, we need to be more like Baraja."

"Uh-huh. She's truly an inspiration. And when she uses that bow she borrowed from His Majesty, Ultimate Shooting Star: Super, she's even more powerful, right?"

"Ultimate Shooting Star: Super… It's a magnificent bow…"

Everyone's gaze shifted to Ultimate Shooting Star: Super, which was strapped to Neia's back.

Though she felt it might be best to train with it, too, she didn't want to rely solely on her weapon, so she refrained.

"Yeah. It was thanks to Ultimate Shooting Star: Super that I was able to hold out in the battle on the wall until the King of Darkness arrived… No, that's not right. It wasn't only Ultimate Shooting Star: Super but the armor and other items His Majesty lent me…"

Neia stroked Mighty King Buser's armor.

"That was originally owned by a named subhuman, right? It's unbelievably gorgeous …"

"She let me touch it once. That armor is insanely hard. I couldn't even nick it when I slashed at it with my sword."

"Seriously? That's crazy."

The discussion about her gear was heating up, but she clapped her hands to get everyone's attention.

"Please cut the chatter for now and get back to training. His Majesty says Jaldabaoth's forces are probably nearly ready to move. We don't have a moment to lose."

Everyone acknowledged her order.

"You've done enough observation. Please get started."

As Neia watched her subordinates—though she still felt a bit embarrassed and arrogant thinking of them that way—disperse, she removed the item covering half her face, also borrowed from the king.

The Mirror Shade was a visor that allowed her to use the skill Snake Shot once every three minutes. Its effect made her arrow leap up in front of her opponent like a serpent attacking its prey.

She had never shot it at anyone, so she didn't know for sure, but she figured that someone would have to be awfully nimble to evade it.

For Neia, whose main weapon was a bow, it was an extremely handy item, but even more wonderful was that it allowed her to conceal her eyes. Without the item, she probably never could have gotten so close to these people.

Neia put her visor back on and took aim.

The ones training under her had experience; she didn't need to instruct them in the basics. Even for quick shooting, a brief explanation was enough. For the most part, she just had them practice till their fingers hurt. The most important thing was to shoot as many arrows as possible.

I need to request healing from the priests as usual, she thought as she loosed her arrow.

Just then, her keen ears picked up a buzz.

It was coming from outside. She fought the urge to smile. It might not be who she thought, and even if it was, it was possible he was simply passing by.

But the one who appeared in the entrance to the training grounds with his bony visage was none other than the great ruler, the King of Darkness.

Some people were still frightened of the undead, but there were also many whom he had personally rescued from a camp or saved on the defensive lines. The whispers of awe and gratitude merged into a buzz announcing the coming of the king.

But no one stopped training. Normally, they would prostrate themselves before him, but the king himself had put a stop to that.

He did say that wasn't necessary, since it wasn't a public place and he was just poking his head in.

That should have been an unforgivable act of disrespect not only for a king but also a hero who had saved their country.

But he himself had asked them to not do it.

What incredible power…

Neia marveled with a sigh and trotted over to the king. She made a conscious effort to keep her mouth from relaxing into a grin.

She kept her visor on—because His Majesty had told her she should always be combat ready, it was fine not to take it off.

He probably wanted her to get so used to the magic items that they felt like parts of her body while making sure she was taking precautions against whatever kind of unexpected circumstances might arise. Neia admired his foresight.

She felt his eyes shift from his hands to her as she ran over; she was happy to notice the usual pattern in his behavior.

Knowing little personal quirks about someone so extraordinary made her smile.

"Your Majesty! Thank you for coming to our humble training range!"

Even charged with leading the archer unit, she was still his attendant. That said, she had left him to go train with her bow and made him walk all this way alone on top of that, so she couldn't claim to be doing a very good job.

Neia preferred to prioritize her attendant role, but since she didn't want to hold him back again, she accepted things as they were. And there was another reason, one she hadn't told anybody.

The king had told Caspond right in front of her that he didn't want another attendant, only Neia.

The population of the town was growing steadily. There were plenty of people more impressive or charming than the girl with the sinister eyes. Yet, he said Neia was the one he wanted. The one she considered to be the embodiment of justice had chosen her.

Could there be any greater joy?

"Mm. I can appreciate the desire to be modest, but there's no need to call it 'humble.' This is where you're preparing for battle."

"Th-thank you, Your Majesty!"

When she glanced aside (normally it would be rude to do that while speaking with the king, but with her visor on, no one could really tell), she noticed the men listening nearby were blushing so hard, even their ears had gone red. Maybe it was because of the added stress of doing their best, the trainees weren't doing as well as they had been a moment ago, which was vexing.

That said, she could feel her own ears growing fairly warm as well.

"...Miss Baraja. Your troops seem to have progressed quite a lot since the last time I saw them. It must be because they have you as their leader."

Slightly flustered by the flattery, Neia fretted about how to respond.

It's a bit embarrassing if I tell him they're underperforming because they're nervous he's here—that probably goes for them, too.

She decided to let it be. But—

"No, not at all. I've hardly taught them anything. They were this capable from the start."

"Really? Well, if you say so."

If you say so, which meant he didn't think so. He had a very high opinion of Neia.

She raised her voice slightly to distract herself from the feeling of wanting to skip for joy. "S-so, Your Majesty. If you're here, does that mean your meetings are over?"

"Yes, for today. That said, it's not as if I really contributed much."

The city was facing a mountain of problems at present, and all of them stemmed from the population surge. Previously, this small city, Roytz, had been home to less than twenty thousand people. But now, because of the people they'd pulled from the camps, there were over one hundred fifty thousand residing within its walls.

One overpopulation issue was that due to the abundance of nutrition, the slimes that processed the city's sewage had caused a disturbance by reproducing so much that they overflowed from the sewers.

Sometimes slimes had to be culled with fire when there were too many, but this time their numbers had increased with such unimaginable speed that there wasn't enough time to thin them out, leading to a number of people getting attacked.

When the slimes surrounded them, garbage-eating monsters called fecudesses appeared out of the sewer to rescue them.

Fecudesses were much more intelligent than they looked, and these creatures were fully aware it was the humans who kept them fed. With their resistance to acid, they were able to save the people accosted by slimes.

But no one thanked the fecudesses: While sanitation slimes were bacteria-free, fecudesses were conglomerations of germs, so anyone who came in contact with their tentacles got horribly sick. The cases of encephalitis were particularly awful.

Other issues included a dearth of wood and other fuel for burning, since it was winter, and the slow rate of housing expansion; they hadn't had a problem feeding all the extra mouths, but it was liable to become a problem in the near future.

The King of Darkness had been invited to meetings nonstop that week. Everyone must have expected him to have lots of advice on how to best respond.

The king himself claimed he didn't have much wisdom to offer and was merely listening in, but those in charge wouldn't repeatedly invite him if that was the case.

Neia respected him even more for maintaining a humble attitude as the leader of a nation.

"So what will you do now?"

"I think I'm going to go check to make sure the logging is going well. You…must be busy training? Or would you like to go together?"

To solve the housing and fuel shortages, the King of Darkness had summoned undead horses to transport felled trees from a distant forest. At first, many people were averse to using undead horses, but now more and more people were openly impressed by them.

"Yes, allow me to accompany you! I'm your attendant after all." It had been a while since she had done work for him, so the idea of going somewhere with just the two of them made her so happy, she spoke quickly and a bit louder than necessary.

She blushed.

"A-ah, okay. Well then, let's get going."

"Yes, le—!"

Neia was interrupted by a roaring burst of flame a short distance away, so intense it seemed liable to scorch the sky.

For a moment, she wondered what had caught on fire.

But that wasn't what had happened. No, it was something else entirely. Nothing like that would occur naturally.

The fire was surrounding the city. In other words, a wall of fire; Neia immediately remembered what the Blue Roses had described.

"Your Majesty, that's—!"

"Yes, it must be. I heard the story from Momon... So the time has finally come. It's Jaldabaoth. He's here to attack. Miss Baraja, I've got to go."

He must have anticipated this moment. His levelheadedness helped Neia stay calm, too. No, just his presence as an absolute ruler was a relief.

"Where?"

"Er, so...we don't know what Jaldabaoth is after. And, uh, it could be that he's here to commit indiscriminate slaughter. But if he has a target, it could be me or the Sacred Kingdom's leadership. That means I should regroup with them. Have your troops prepare for combat and then lead them somewhere safe."

"What?!"

"If Jaldabaoth is here, they won't be any use in that fight. I'd rather have them deal with the demons he may summon. The city will probably get too chaotic, so if you're going to form up, it might be better to do it outside."

At first, he wasn't being very clear, but as he went on, his thoughts seemed to become more organized. The rest of his instructions flowed smoothly.

"Okay! Thank you, Your Majesty! All right, everyone!"

They had a plan for if Jaldabaoth appeared leading an army, but they hadn't anticipated a wall of flames. Or rather, the problem was that they had no idea how many enemies they were up against.

Neia instructed her troops. They were only one unit, so she couldn't do anything too drastic, but until new orders arrived, it was her duty to have them do what seemed best to her as their leader.

The orders were as follows.

They were to take their families and head for the east gate (because if enemies were attacking, they would most likely show up at the west gate). There they would get into formation, and if there were demons outside the east gate, they would go up on the wall and attack from there. Until Neia arrived, her second-in-command would play things by ear.

Neia's troops moved swiftly to carry out her orders.

"Your Majesty!"

After directing her troops, she turned around to find him looking at one of his hands, hovering at about the height of her head with a flight spell.

"Your Majesty! I'm going with you!"

Did she surprise him by calling out like that? He balled his hand up suddenly. She heard a slight noise from inside his fist.

"Mm…sure, that's fine."

He cast a flight spell on her. That instant, she found she knew exactly how to fly, proving once again how fantastic magic was.

Neia and the king glided across the earth. When they came upon a jumble of confused people, they flew over them, but otherwise they hugged the ground. Flying higher with no cover would have made them stick out, and if there were demons around, they could have been attacked from any direction.

Neia realized she was a liability and bit her lip. A demon's magic was probably nothing to the King of Darkness. She figured he was avoiding the straightest route for her sake.

Eventually they reached headquarters—in other words, Caspond's quarters and command post.

Two paladins were busy handling all the people who had rushed to the entrance.

"Miss Baraja, we're going up!"

"Yes, Your Majesty!"

Seeing that it would be difficult to get in the front door, they floated up. When they landed on the balcony, the window opened.

"Your Majesty! We've been expecting you."

It was a paladin.

"Is everyone here?"

"No, Your Majesty. The priests are still gathering. Deputy Commander Montagnés is out liberating a camp and wasn't planning to be back today, so we only have Commander Custodio and Master Caspond."

"Oh. Well, if those two are here, this'll be quick. Take me to them."

"Right away!"

The paladin led them to Caspond's quarters. There were voices arguing behind the door. The disagreement sounded quite complex.

When the paladin opened the door, they were met with ten pairs of bloodshot eyes.

"Sorry I'm late. We probably don't have much time. What's the plan?"

Everyone inside the room exchanged glances. Caspond spoke as their representative. "We haven't spotted Jaldabaoth yet. Your Majesty, do you think another demon or some enchanted item could produce these flames?"

"I'm not sure. Though I know that I sure can't."

That alarmed everyone. There was no telling how many different spells the King of Darkness could use. So how powerful was this demon Jaldabaoth if he could cast a spell that even the king couldn't?

"So…what are the effects of this fire? The Blue Roses said they could walk through it like it wasn't even there, but can an ordinary person do that?"

The King of Darkness turned to Remedios to answer her question. "Yes, that's no trouble. There were a variety of opinions about what it does: boosting the abilities of demons within the fire circle, boosting spells that are strengthened by negative karma points, raising the drop rate, and so on, but the survey team discovered none of those effects. There are still those who believe it bestows some other advantage, however."

"So it's possible to pass right through it, then?"

"Hmm? The first thing I said was that it would be fine."

"If that's the case, then if there are no subhumans or demons outside, we should have the people evacuate the city and form ranks—because in the attack on Re-Estize, demons appeared within the flames. Come up with a plan along those lines." Caspond gave that order to the paladins and then turned back to the King of Darkness to ask another question. "Is there a way for you to check if Jaldabaoth is nearby, Your Majesty?"

"If I could do that, there wouldn't have been any need for me to remain in this city all this time."

"Fair."

As the king was responding to question after question, Neia heard something—a bizarre, ominous creaking.

At first, it was so quiet, the commotion in the room drowned it out, but it grew louder. One person after another noticed it and fell silent, and before long the only sound in the room was the creaking.

As everyone was looking around uneasily, Neia noticed something strange about the wall connected to the outside. "Ah!" she gasped.

The wall had a crack in it. As everyone watched, cracks radiated outward, and the wall began to bulge inward. Then—

"Watch out!"

Just as Remedios shouted, the King of Darkness moved in front of Neia.

The wall loudly burst open, scattering bricks into the room like buckshot. A few people groaned. They'd been struck by the flying bricks.

If the King of Darkness hadn't shielded her, Neia might have been screaming with the rest of them.

"Th-thank y—"

She tried to thank him, but he raised a hand to stop her. He was pointing at the billowing smoke.

A shadow was visible in the blazing flames.

"I appreciate you coming to meet me, humans."

A deep, heavy voice.

As if parting the cloud of dust, the figure stepped through the gaping hole in the wall and slowly showed himself.

It was…a demon.

He was so large, he had to bend over slightly to fit in the room. He definitely looked a bit ridiculous, but this was no time to laugh. Neia's throat wasn't working properly, and when she tried to swallow the suddenly very noticeable spit in her mouth, it wouldn't go down.

Here was a mass of overwhelming power.

Neia had never been all that good at perceiving the power gap between her and her enemies, but this one she understood. No matter how many tens of thousands of Neias there were, it wouldn't be enough to win. In the face of a presence as overwhelming as that of the King of Darkness with his ring off, Neia couldn't so much as lift a finger.

At this point, she knew who it was.

Th-that's Jaldabaoth… Evil Emperor Jaldabaoth…

A furious face, crimson wings, flaming hands…and he was holding something in one of his hands. Neia blinked.

She didn't want to believe it, but it appeared to be the lower body of a human. There was a strange smell coming from it; the body was putrefied.

"Yeeeeeeeeegh!"

A battle cry. Or maybe a bizarre scream. From behind her, she heard the sort of scream humans emit when they've lost control and gone mad.

A shiver ran up Neia's spine. It was Remedios's voice.

Holding her Holy Sword in front of her, Remedios charged at Jaldabaoth as if she had absolutely no sense of self-preservation.

It was reckless. Even Neia, who wasn't that skilled with a sword, could tell it was foolish.

"—You're in the way."

The heavy, quiet voice was accompanied by a wet slap. At the same time, Remedios hurtled straight into the wall, crashing with a noise so loud that it seemed like the building might've taken damage. After bouncing off like a ball, she lay weakly crumpled on the floor.

Jaldabaoth had smacked her away with the remains he held.

The blow probably would have killed Neia, but as might be expected of the strongest paladin in the kingdom, Remedios seemed to have survived.

Not that it was the reason her life had been spared, but a pungent, nauseating stench soon filled the air.

The rotting flesh in Jaldabaoth's hand had come apart and spattered the entire room when he hit Remedios.

"Oh dear...what a pity. First, allow me to apologize for making a mess of your room. If that woman wouldn't have thoughtlessly come charging at me, this wouldn't have happened, but...that's just an excuse, isn't it? I hope you'll forgive me."

Jaldabaoth slowly bowed his head. Horrifyingly, his regret felt genuine.

Then he took the charred ankle bones from the corpse still in his hand and tossed them carelessly onto the floor.

"Sheesh, I was swinging it around so carelessly, the top half went flying off somewhere. It was filthy, so I had been waiting for a chance to dispose of it quickly. Using up every last bit proves what a considerate demon I am, don't you think? I'm sure she's thanking you in the next world," Jaldabaoth said to no one in particular.

"Ahhhhhhhh!"

A scream went up. Blood dribbling from the corners of her mouth, Remedios had sat up slightly and was moving her hands over her body. No, she was collecting the bits of flesh sticking to it. *What's she doing? Has she gone insane?* thought Neia.

No, there had to be a reason for her strange behavior.

Could that corpse have been...? No...

The half a body had been clad in the beat-up husk of some armor, but it appeared to be female. Then there were two people it could have been.

If so...

"A beautiful tone." Jaldabaoth waved one arm as if conducting. "Now, then. I believe this is the first time I've had the pleasure of making your acquaintance, King of Darkness, Sir Ainz Ooal Gown. Or do you prefer Lord?"

"That's not necessary. So you came here to fight me, is that correct?"

"Indeed. There's no point in wasting time on weaklings no matter how many there are. That much is plain to see."

"I agree with you there. I have no interest in incurring pointless sacrifices."

The king turned pointedly to Remedios, who was sniffling.

"King of Darkness, you are strong. Even stronger than Momon. That's why I'm going to make sure I win."

When Jaldabaoth raised a hand, faces peeked in from the other side of the hole in the wall.

They were masked women in maid uniforms—two of them.

"Don't tell me you're a coward now."

"Hmm. This is…hmm… Hmmmm."

The king seemed anxious. That was only natural.

Surely, he wasn't surprised that he would be fighting Jaldabaoth as well as two maids. No—

That can't be. He's so wise. I'm sure he realized ahead of time. So then why? It must be because the rest of us are here. He might be worried that he won't be able to save us!

"Your Majesty, please don't worry about us!"

"Eh?" He emitted a little surprised noise.

She knew. She knew the maids could kill everyone else in that room with no trouble, and that even if she told him not to worry, it's not as if he could trust her to put up a decent fight. Compared to the King of Darkness, Neia and probably even Remedios were so weak they couldn't even be measured on the same scale.

If they were just going to be in the way, it was fine even if they died.

She had heard His Majesty's servants were prepared to die if they were taken hostage. He had mentioned it as a problem, but at this moment, Neia understood very well how they felt. She wasn't here to be a burden to the one she respected.

"Ha-ha-ha-ha! Relax, humans. I'll slowly torture you to death later. We'll be waiting at the fountain in the center of town. Of course, King of Darkness, you're free to flee with them if you wish!"

"I offer you the very same chance, Jaldabaoth."

Then Jaldabaoth turned to go—and Remedios, clenching her sword, jumped up and set off sprinting.

The arc of the faintly glowing blade looked almost like a ribbon of light.

"Dieeee!"

And she stabbed Jaldabaoth in the back.

"Huh? What's this? …Are you satisfied now?"

An icy voice.

"Wh……wh-why……? That was a clean hit…and you're evil, so…?"

Remedios looked so small.

"I dunno. Why? What do you mean, 'Why?' It did sting a little bit. If you're satisfied with that, then could you get out of the way? I have no intention of killing you here. You come after the king."

Jaldabaoth paid Remedios no further mind and spread his fiery wings. Blown back by the force of the motion, Remedios tumbled and rolled.

Without a single glance at Remedios pathetically crawling on the floor, Jaldabaoth took off. The demon maids followed.

"…Okay. I'll be on my way as well. You guys should take shelter so you don't get caught up in the fight. I doubt it'll happen, but please forgive me if half the city gets destroyed in the battle."

"Your Majesty, will you be all right?" Caspond asked as he rose from the floor where he had dived to avoid the flying debris. His eyes were on Remedios's slumped shoulders; she wasn't even trying to get up.

"It'll be no problem…unless it is. But this is a good chance. If he had brought some subhumans as a shield, it would have been a much trickier situation, but it appears he's still underestimating me. And it's an opportunity to bring those maids under my control, too."

"It's okay. We're still okay. There's my sister, Kelart. If we have her, then even Lady Calca can be…" Remedios mumbled, slapping her face as she hopped to her feet. "King of Darkness! I'm going with you! Lend me a weapon that can hurt him! I'll be your sword, if only temporarily!"

In response to Remedios's bloodshot, hatred-filled eyes, the king shook his head. "…No. You'll only be in the way."

"What?!"

"Do you not understand the difference in power? Or do you understand it but refuse to accept it? Allow me to be clear: You'll be deadweight."

Remedios glared at him as if he was her mortal enemy.

Certainly, what the king said was harsh. But it was also the truth. On further thought, it was probably because it was precisely the truth that she couldn't accept it.

"Commander Custodio! I have another role for you! Lead the evacuation of the city!" Caspond ordered in a dignified tone.

"You agreed that we would have His Majesty the King of Darkness take on Jaldabaoth from the beginning, didn't you?"

"...Yeah, fine," Remedios fairly spat, biting her lip. "Make sure you kill that scum."

"Understood."

"Paladins, gather up that corpse. Don't leave a single trace."

"Commander... This body is—?" a paladin who had a sneaking suspicion asked in a trembling voice, but Remedios cut him off.

"Don't forget: It could be some sort of demonic deception."

Remedios headed out without turning back. Some of them followed her looking half-frightened.

"Your Majesty, I'm truly sorry about her attitude... Not that I think apologizing makes it forgivable." Caspond bowed. "But I do hope you'll forgive the transgression."

"...I accept your apology. So please hurry the evacuation along. If we make them wait too long, that demon may not stick to what he said. I'll go over there and buy some time. But I want you to assume that we don't have more than thirty minutes."

"Understood. You heard him! Let's move!"

Several priests and paladins followed Caspond.

Then the only ones left in the room were the King of Darkness, Neia, and the handful of paladins and priests cleaning up the body.

"Your Majesty, may I go with you?!"

She heard audible gasps around them, but Neia ignored those outsiders. She took off her Mirror Shade and looked the king in the eyes.

"…Mm. No, I can't allow that. He made a lot of claims, but in the end, he's a demon. If he felt pressured, he might show his true colors and take you hostage."

"But if that happened, you would kill me with zero hesitation, wouldn't you, Your Majesty?"

"When you say that with such a serious look on your face, it makes me sound like a pretty horrible guy. But, well, if I couldn't save you, I would cast a spell that would attack you both."

"Then—"

"—It's not…! It's not as if I enjoy killing captives!"

"Ah! I'm sorry…"

Of course not. He only did it because he knew it was the greatest good. He was a kind person who would choose the better option if there was one. And he thought the best option in this case was to not have Neia accompany him.

"But…in order to liberate this city, you used a lot of magic—and magic items—which expended your mana. I'm worried that as a caster, you might have lost a significant amount of your power. Will you be all right?"

"Hmph! It may be dangerous, but I came here to slay Jaldabaoth. If he's here now, that's convenient. I'll destroy him and take his maids. Though it makes me sound like an old perv when I say I want maids…"

Grinning wryly at the king as he made such a poor joke under these circumstances, Neia was about to reply, but he held up a hand to stop her.

"Besides, if I ran now, I'd be a laughingstock." He shrugged and played it as a joke.

But Neia couldn't take it seriously and found herself shouting at him. "Your Majesty! Let those who would be so foolish laugh as much as they want! I humbly propose you fight him once you're at full power! You only came here in order to defeat Jaldabaoth. You already spent a vast amount of mana for the sake of the Sacred Kingdom. That's not what the original deal was, so if we explained that to the people, I'm sure…!"

"You're right. But you humans believe what you want. Even if you spread the word, surely no one would believe it."

"I don't think…! But in that case, I'll testify! And…"

Neia quieted down and gave the paladins and priests listening to their conversation a sidelong glance. They would probably corroborate her claims.

"…Neia Baraja. I appreciate it. But it's not necessary. I still intend to fight Jaldabaoth now."

"But…why?"

"It's simple: Because I gave my word as a king."

Neia was speechless. What could she say to that? It would surely be impossible for someone of no rank like her to change the mind of a ruler.

From around them, she heard murmurs of admiration. *That's right. This great, proud being—this is His Majesty the King of Darkness, Ainz Ooal Gown.*

Neia wanted to sing his praises with all her heart because she respected this king so much.

"Your Majesty, I realize it's rude of me to say so, but I insist. If you feel you're in danger, please run!"

It surely offended him that she would mention the possibility of him losing. Even so, she had to say it.

"…Of course. Only a complete fool would enter a fight with no plan for escape. Even if you lose one battle, surviving means accumulating knowledge that can be used to your advantage in the next. I don't mind ceding the first round."

"Brilliant as usual, Your Majesty."

Ultimately, if the objective was to defeat Jaldabaoth, the important thing was the final victory. His way of thinking, not as a warrior but a king, made Neia shiver with excitement.

"Then I'll be off."

•

Ainz walked toward the location Jaldabaoth had specified. Along the way, he Messaged the two Hanzos he had brought with him to make sure no one was following him or observing from a distance.

Having confirmed it was all clear, he was about to end the Message when the Hanzos hesitantly informed him that the Pleiades were present.

Ainz said he was aware and cut off the spell.

…No sign of any players or people with World Items this time, either, huh? At this point, maybe it's just… But then what the heck happened with Shalltear? Some kind of crazy coincidence? It seemed like a World Item attack, but was it just some other weird ability they had to begin with?

Detecting nothing despite the extreme vigilance made it seem, conversely, like a trap. Was someone waiting for him to lower his guard?

This is ridiculous… I guess it is what it is. You can never be too careful.

Ainz sent a Message to a separate Hanzo team. Then he made sure he was ready and had given everyone adequate instructions.

Okay. I'm all set. Of course, all I have to do now is follow the plan Demiurge drafted, so it'll be a piece of cake—especially since I already arranged it so that if I screw up it's because I'm testing him!

Amazing.

Ainz was impressed by how light he felt on his feet. It might have been the freest he'd felt since coming to this world. He was floating on air.

Then he arrived at the not terribly large square.

There was a time when this was a place where fountains would spray at certain intervals, a place where the city's inhabitants could relax. But now there was no water to feed the mechanism, and the subhumans had broken the fountains to boot. There were no plans to fix them, leaving the area hopelessly forlorn.

A single demon stood there.

A giant being with wings of fire and fists the color of flame.

It was an Evil Lord Wrath, like they had in Nazarick. But this one had been summoned by Demiurge via an ability he could use once every fifty hours to call upon an evil lord, so if it was killed, there would be no loss to Nazarick.

It was level 84.

Of all the evil lords, it boasted particularly powerful physical attacks and fairly high HP as well. It was a pure warrior-type monster.

The most troublesome skill evil lords had was their ability to summon other monsters—either one other evil lord or multiple lower-level demons. However, summoned monsters were unable to summon monsters of their own, so the evil lord Demiurge had conjured couldn't bring another evil lord into the fight.

If it had been a create or make spell, the summoned creature wouldn't have the same restrictions, so an Evil Lord Sloth would keep summoning demons and undead until it was defeated—an absolute pain.

The other tricky thing about Evil Lord Wraths was aggro management.

Their aggro rose more easily than that of other evil lords, and Ainz had heard from tanks that managing enemy attack priorities got very hectic when facing a mixed group of evil lords.

On top of everything else, they had special abilities that gave them more powerful attacks or higher defense as their aggro increased. Still, he didn't have to worry too much.

The only thing he was a bit scared of was Soul for a Miracle because there was no telling what might happen.

The spells the demon could use were:

Tier ten: Meteorfall, Stop Time, Field of Unclean

Tier nine: Greater Rejection, Vermillion Nova

Tier eight: Distorted Morals, Insanity, Astral Smite, Wave of Pain

Tier seven: Napalm, Hell Flame, Greater Curse, Greater Teleportation, Blasphemy

Tier six: Flame Wings, Wall of Hell

Tier three: Fireball, Slow

The number of spells a *Yggdrasil* monster could use varied widely depending on level and type, but the standard was eight. Meanwhile, elite monsters like dragons, demons, and angels could use a number that completely disregarded whatever standard there might have been.

But since Evil Lord Wraths were pure warriors, their spells weren't so worrisome.

They didn't have skills that would boost the power of their magic, and they had low magic-related stats. Plus, Evil Lord Wraths' magic attacks were primarily fire based. While the undead were innately weak against fire, Ainz had long since learned the importance of defending against it and no longer had to even consider it consciously. Psychic spells wouldn't work on him, since he was undead, and since he had negative karma, Distorted Morals wouldn't have any effect, either.

For someone with negative karma like Ainz, an angel posed more of a challenge than a demon.

Recalling the evil lord's stats, he glanced at the two maids behind it. He would talk to them afterward.

"So you know the deal?"

"Of course, Lord Ainz."

The same deep, heavy voice made not Ainz but Satoru Suzuki smile. It wasn't just this demon— Who had decided all the demon voices in Nazarick?

Was it the admins or the devs who had designed them? Then who dreamed up the adorable voice of the Lip Bug before it had eaten anyone's vocal cords? Was it the mental voice actress that Peroroncino had mentioned?

Nah, that couldn't be.

Pandora's Actor was a good example. It was impossible to say that the creator's intent had been fully realized. Besides, Ainz didn't even have vocal cords, yet he could speak. Perhaps it was more sensible simply to be surprised by the laws of this magical world.

"If you're using that name and that tone, you must have cleaned up this area, right?"

"Yes, that is correct."

"Then here is the most important question of all. You can come at me for real—like you actually mean to kill me, okay?"

"Yes, that is what I was ordered to do."

Ainz nodded in response to the evil lord's reply.

Something had been on his mind for a while now: He hadn't done much combat against powerful enemies. He was concerned that there hadn't been any chance to fight all out like he had in his battle with Shalltear.

By training in close-quarters combat, Momonga's body had gained decent mobility, and his fighting ability was comparable to a level-33 warrior.

But it remained to be seen whether he could practically utilize those skills in high-level combat.

As such, he wanted to face powerful enemies and work on making full use of his combat abilities. Unfortunately, he hadn't encountered any powerful monsters recently.

That was why he told Demiurge to order the summoned evil lord to kill him.

The idea was to defeat his murderous attacker in order to strengthen himself.

Saying it was simple, but he had to spend a lot of time persuading the two who were vehemently against it. In his mentally fatigued state, Ainz couldn't help but think, *I thought if I said black was white, it was white…*

In the end, after making a bunch of compromises and swallowing lots of demands, he was finally able to arrange this life-and-death duel.

The thought that he might die made something cold ooze out inside him. When he had fought Shalltear, there were other emotions that were stronger. This time he was unnecessarily risking his life, so it was quite different.

But…

I did a fair amount of PvP in my Yggdrasil days. Still, as I realized during the fight with Shalltear, this world isn't a game. If I end up having to face a level-100 player with experience here, I had better make sure I'm just as seasoned, or I'll lose. Hesitating here will lead to future defeat.

Ainz was thankful he was undead—because he could mostly stifle the fear of dying. If he were human, he may very well have called off the fight.

"Now then, Yuri," he spoke to one of the maids behind the evil lord. "I can assume you and Lupusregina are there to fight me alongside the evil lord, right? The others aren't here?"

Looking around, he didn't see Solution, Entoma, or Shizu anywhere. These two had been the only ones to show up before, so were the others busy somewhere else?

"We are the only ones here. It will be us sisters and the evil lord facing you. We came because Mistress Albedo said it wouldn't be a bad idea to show the people of this country the demon maids and because she thought you wouldn't be satisfied by the demon alone, my lord."

Certainly, a single level-80 demon wasn't much of a challenge for Ainz. Then again, even with Yuri and Lupusregina added, it wasn't exactly intimidating.

That said, sometimes just making the effort can be all the difference. Only an idiot would underestimate the odds and get smacked down. I need to stay on my toes.

"Just to confirm, Lord Ainz, since we were ordered to do so by Mistress Albedo, you agree to the condition that if you lose, you won't leave Nazarick for a year?"

"Yeah, that was one of the conditions I used to persuade Albedo. If I'm defeated, I'll spend a year working inside Nazarick. With Albedo. In the same room… You're not going to confirm Demiurge's conditions?" He looked at the evil lord, but the demon didn't answer. Had he figured there was no need to confirm, or had he simply not been given those orders?

"Thank you." Yuri bowed.

Okay. Ainz was forced to change his plan. At the same time, he was mentally sweating in response to how intense things had gotten.

It would be extremely easy to kill Yuri and Lupusregina. The gap between him and them was that large. But Ainz Ooal Gown wouldn't allow that. Killing NPCs for training purposes was out of the question.

In other words…

I need to keep Yuri and Lupusregina from getting hurt but also kill the evil lord.

He burst out laughing in spite of himself. This was quite the difficulty setting. But it would be good training.

"Is somethin' wrong, Lord Ainz?"

"No, don't worry. It's nothing."

"Then I should mention that Master Cocytus has a request. He'd like us to record the fight, so everyone in Nazarick can watch it later. Is that okay with you?"

It would be extremely embarrassing, and he hated the idea, but back in *Yggdrasil*, it was common to make combat logs. He figured he should just think of this as the same thing and accept.

"Sure. But I'm pretty sure any recording measures get caught in countersurveillance attack walls. Should I turn mine off?"

"You're just runnin' the kind that detects surveillance, not the one that actively attacks, right, Lord Ainz?"

"Yeah, that's what I'm using. I can't have someone from Nazarick searching for my location and end up setting off an attack."

If he was using an active defense that automatically triggered an offensive countermeasure like he used to, the moment someone from Nazarick cast a spell to look for him, they would sustain major damage. Back when there was no friendly fire, he could simply leave it on all the time, but now, that would be pretty dangerous.

Of course, with the protection of the World Item Nazarick was under, even if the attack activated, the victim probably wouldn't be terribly hurt. The only thing was that activating the Nazarick defense system would cost money. If he wasn't careful, the expenditure would hurt.

"Then it should be fine."

"Nah, I'll cancel it. Attack walls can only activate once before you have to recast them anyhow, so it's no big deal to turn it off."

"Oh? Then please do."

Ainz disabled his attack wall.

"Okay. So please record the fight. Who will it be focused on? I don't mind if it's me."

"For now, it's gonna be me."

That was fine with Ainz. He didn't much care who would be the focus of the recording.

Somehow, it all reminded him of training with his old friends—he was starting to have fun.

Sparring with friends was standard after devising new tactics or equipping new gear.

He had often fought with Touch Me, but Ainz didn't count those, so he didn't include them as part of his PvP experience—mostly because he never won against Touch Me, which meant his victory ratio would have dropped. His excuse was always that he only did it for training, knowing that he would lose, so he hadn't been taking it seriously.

"Then should we get started? You guys should come at me with everything you've got as well. I don't have any intention of killing you, but still."

"Oh, we don't mind if you kill us."

Before Ainz could say he didn't want to, Yuri was explaining the reason.

"Lord Ainz, we aren't the Pleiades. We're greater doppelgängers."

"What?! Really?!"

"We're members of the Erich String Orchestra under Master Chakmol—one of the Five Worst despite being a musician. Mistress Albedo ordered us to transform into the Pleiades."

"I see."

He took a hard look but really couldn't tell they weren't Yuri and Lupusregina. He wondered if they were lying in order to allow him to fight them to the death.

Or maybe one of them was real? He had heard somewhere that the best lies contained some truth.

Ainz wasn't able to see through doppelgänger transformations. He had a spell that allowed him to detransform them, but as a side effect, it would prevent them from transforming for a set amount of time. That would defeat the purpose of the disguise. If he had a more basic version of the spell, he could have cast it…

Eh…

"Lupusregina, you're talking differently from usual. What's that about?"

Lupusregina gave him a blank look. "I'm talking strangely, my lord?"

The Lupusregina doppelgänger changed the way it spoke. This must have been the base speech pattern.

"Yeah, you don't sound like she usually does."

"With me, she always talked like that…"

The closer you were to a person, the harder it was to see through a doppelgänger transformed into them. Why? Because the doppelgänger would use mind control abilities to read the shallow thoughts of the person they were interacting with and the people nearby to gain information about the one they were impersonating and incorporate this into their act. At least, that's what the monster description had said.

Pandora's Actor said it was possible to use that ability in the reality of this world.

But it could only be used to glean the reactions a transformation's source was likely to make, so it wouldn't work for collecting intel by peeking into someone's private thoughts.

And the ability was ultimately a type of psychic attack, so it wouldn't work on undead like Ainz, nor would it be very difficult to resist unless there was a considerable level gap between the user and the target. So the doppelgänger had basically been exposed by failing to read Ainz's mind.

Incidentally, the more people to interface with, the greater the chances of exposure due to everyone's different perceptions of the source.

Hmm, why does Lupusregina speak like that in front of these people? Ohhh, I see. She must have done it so I would notice something was off. Maybe she wanted to give me a hint. That's cute…

"…Hmm? Sorry. I have one question unrelated to our fight. You said you have orders from Albedo, but if I was to tell you to cancel that order, whose order would take precedence?"

"Naturally, your order as the Supreme One would be prioritized, Lord Ainz. But apologies, the highest priority is given to the one who summoned us, Lord Dark Melody."

"…Hmm? Who's that?"

Did we have an NPC by that name? Ainz wondered, but the flames in his eye sockets brightened at Yuri Doppel's next words.

"Lord Temperance."

"Huh? Temperance? Dark? Ah…I guess he did look like that, but… Dark Melody?"

"Yes. Lord Temperance called himself that, so Master Chakmol instructed us all to do the same."

"...When we get back to Nazarick, I reallllly want to hear more about this. Dark Melody, huh...?"

This nickname was news to Ainz.

Hearing that his old friend had given himself a secret sobriquet made him laugh. And lowering his will to fight right before battle— What a setup.

Whoops, can't have that. No falling into Dark Melody's trap! Heh, heh-heh...

Though he knew the timing was bad, he couldn't help but remember his guildmate.

What was he feeling? What kind of look was on his face when he gave himself that name?

Ainz smiled at the fond memories, but when he saw Yuri Doppel cock her head, puzzled by his response, he realized he had lowered his guard too much.

He could think about his friend later. For now, he needed to analyze the doppelgängers' story.

And I want to survey the other minions and NPCs. I wonder what else everyone kept hidden away. Ho-ho-ho. But now I'm curious about something.

Without direct orders, minions such as doppelgängers would apparently follow the NPC master above them. So what would happen if an NPC from Nazarick, bent on killing him, gathered a ton of high-level minions and ordered them to use their most powerful moves to beat him up? If he didn't figure out the plot and stop it in time...

Would the orders be carried out? Or would they refuse orders like that?

"...And you're going to come at me with the intent to kill, correct?"

"Yes. Those were our orders, and we understand that we have your permission to do so."

Yuri Doppel's response caused Ainz to furrow his nonexistent brow.

...Is this dangerous? At some point, I should really test where the line is.

It was highly probable that if it was something Ainz was thinking about, Albedo had already looked into it, but it was obviously a good idea to confirm. He couldn't just leave a security hole unchecked.

"…Yes. For this one battle, I permit you to fight with all your might to kill me. Then I'd like to have you swear on the name Ainz Ooal Gown that your identities are as you stated a moment ago."

"We promise on your name, O Supreme One."

Yuri and Lupusregina changed just their hands into something else.

"Ah!"

"What? What is it, Yuri Doppel?"

"Lord Ainz, I forgot one thing. We borrowed this gear from the Pleiades. So if you kill us, could you please make sure to recover it?"

Doppelgängers could copy clothing and equipment perfectly but only in appearance; they couldn't reproduce the performance of the gear. Having resistance or not made a night and day difference when fighting a caster like Ainz, so they must have had to borrow the gear from the real maids.

Greater doppelgängers can transform into beings up to level 60. And unlike when you make them as NPCs, they can copy abilities up to 90 percent. Even if their gear is the same as the Pleiades', they still don't pose much threat to me. Killing them would be quite a waste—especially since it costs money to summon mercenary minions. Yeah, I'd rather leave it at incapacitation. I guess I should make that a rule.

"Okay! I'm changing the rules. If you doppelgängers are about to die, you're out. I'll monitor your life energy with Life Essence. I'm pretty sure you're masking your strength, right?" Seeing Yuri give the affirmative, Ainz nodded. "Then suppress that power for the time being. When I judge that you've gotten to the point that a nudge would kill you, I'll call your name, and that means you're out. You count as a corpse. Get out of the combat zone as fast as you can. And if either I or the Evil Lord Wrath declare victory, then the fight is over. Got it?"

The Evil Lord Wrath and the two doppelgängers signaled that they understood.

"All right, we'll start by coin drop… It's been about twenty-five minutes, so I doubt anyone would complain if we got started."

Ainz activated Life Essence and took out a gold piece. Of course, it wasn't a *Yggdrasil* gold piece but the currency from this world.

"You don't need to cast any buffs?"

"Making time to cast buffs is part of the combat training," Ainz answered Lupusregina Doppel and distanced himself a little before flipping the coin so that it would land between them.

The moment the coin hit the ground, he leaped back, thrust his hands forward, and shouted, "Perfect Invincible Wall!"

He could see that the Evil Lord Wrath and the doppelgängers had frozen. But they charged soon enough.

Of course. That was the right thing to do.

Ainz's action just now had been meaningless. There was no such move as Perfect Invisible Wall in *Yggdrasil*—or at least there shouldn't have been. Not one that he knew of anyhow. He had shouted it even so as a feint, yes, but there was another reason.

Ah, I feel like they're moving slowly. Are they worried I did something to them? Well, when you think your opponent may have set a trap, it's normal to want to avoid rushing right into it.

The fear that perhaps in this world that move did exist put a limit on what they could do. In other words, caution of the unknown had worked as a feint.

And it wasn't merely unknown. Ainz's Create Undead was a good example of this.

Back in the game, it wasn't possible to make unlimited undead using corpses with no time constraints. But in this world, the power had changed. There could very well be other altered moves still waiting to be discovered. No, it would be stranger to think there weren't any.

In other words, it was extremely dangerous to make decisions based only on *Yggdrasil*-era knowledge.

I should talk to Albedo…and probably Cocytus about this sort of thing.

Having silently cast Fly, something occurred to Ainz as he retreated to get some space.

Albedo was saying it would take two years of prep to destroy the Re-Estize

Kingdom. Should I be spending my days gathering intelligence that whole time? Developing your country means more contact with the outside world… I should probably ask Albedo and Demiurge their thoughts on that, too. Hmm…illusions might be stronger than I thought. Maybe I need to be more careful. Someone smart could probably do incredible things with them. I'd like to find someone who excels at illusions and win them over with preferential treatment. Fluder is— Whoops.

The evil lord was running toward Ainz faster than he was flying. Unfortunately, Fly didn't provide much speed.

"Ngh!"

Taking a hit from the evil lord's hammer-like fist, Ainz felt pain, though it was immediately suppressed. He had had the same thought fighting Shalltear, but he was truly grateful for this body that suppressed pain. This body was the reason Ainz could fight.

He had been knocked back, and the evil lord was closing in.

For Ainz, that was the worst.

So Yuri will come around behind me? I'll be pincered between these two who deal blunt damage, my weakness? And Lupusregina is casting from a distance? Buffs, I see. Well, that's the right thing to do against a caster. Is this how the evil lord is programmed to fight? Or are these moves that wise Demiurge chose? Well, whatever.

If they wouldn't let him gain any distance, he would just have to acquire it by force.

Greater Teleportation.

His field of vision opened up all at once, and he saw the city spread out below. Usually, you needed to know where you were teleporting to or it wouldn't work, but if the destination was within view, there was no problem. Having teleported over half a mile into the air, Ainz cast another spell.

Body of Effulgent Beryl.

Both Yuri and the evil lord were coming at him with bludgeoning attacks, so this would be a very effective spell.

"Of course, that's not all," Ainz murmured as he looked down at the surface. "Man, if BubblingTeapot or Variable Talisman were here, the rear guard would never get hit."

When playing as a team, a tank with good aggro management skills would never make the mistake of allowing a caster to get punched.

Even once his guildmates stopped logging in—during the period when Ainz was earning Nazarick's upkeep fees by himself—he would employ some mercenary NPCs to be safe. He hadn't been in a serious fight alone since that time with Shalltear. Maybe that was why he was grumbling.

At this distance, he couldn't tell where the evil lord was, but he could make out the square. Carpet-bombing it from his current location would be a good strategy, but there wouldn't be much point in doing that this time. His objective now was to slug it out in a proper showdown.

Widen Magic: Delay Teleportation.

That reminds me, back when I hired mercenary NPCs, I was bothered by their sloppy aggro management. Maybe the admins were telling us they wanted players to work together...

Ainz took note of the large figure—the evil lord—teleporting above him into the range of Delay Teleportation. Due to the delay, the demon wouldn't be appearing in this world for another couple of moments. In other words, the two vulnerable enemies had lost their shield.

In order to chip away at his enemy's fighting power, it was best to dispatch the two weaker ones first. Ainz gave himself up to gravity and then used Fly to accelerate further.

That combined with his falling speed was some serious velocity. The air roared into his face and past him. Ainz kept his eyes open all the while, staring at the square.

Ainz mumbled as he targeted Lupusregina, who was standing out in the open. "You should probably hide in a building..."

Yuri was a short distance away. She could see him but showed no signs of engaging. Having the healer stand by herself was brow-furrow-inducing, but if they were concerned about area-of-effect attacks, then Yuri's behavior wasn't a mistake.

Stopping just before the ground—though he could have slammed into it and not taken any damage—Ainz cast a spell.

He chose the tier-ten spell with the most destructive power, Reality

Slash. At the same time, he activated a skill that would strengthen its effects. If he tripled it, he could deal a ton of damage at once, but he figured that was dangerous when he didn't know how much the doppelgängers could take. He wanted to avoid accidentally killing them in one hit.

"Maximize Magic—"

The moment he raised his arm, it was hit by an incoming projectile, and the spell dispersed. The mana he'd planned to use on it was wasted.

What?! Shooting to disrupt a spell? Is that a skill?

Whether it was due to his being an undead or his capability as a seasoned player, he was confused for only a split second. He immediately set about analyzing the attack he had taken.

Neither the evil lord nor Yuri nor Lupusregina had a power like this.

It could be the World Item wielder who brainwashed Shalltear, but…

If the Hanzos missed someone…

The one who would use projectiles was…

And she had skills that could obstruct spells…

"They tricked me!" Ainz shouted once he had the answer.

Yuri was closing in to punch, but he had magically raised his defense, so he didn't need to be too careful about it. There was something more problematic he had to take care of.

So it was all a trap?! No, Yuri— Oh! When she said "here," she meant the square! And the Hanzo said the Pleiades were here, too! Shit! I thought it was a weird way to put it if there were only two of them!

The realization came together in an instant.

It was Shizu who had just attacked him.

It wasn't just Lupusregina and Yuri. Shizu was on this battleground as well. And probably Solution and Entoma. This city had a full set of Pleiades Doppels inside it.

Okay, okay, calm down. The Shizu doppelgänger just got lucky there. With our different levels and the gap in our abilities, it won't be hard to resist. She just got lucky this time—and I was unlucky.

"Greater Curse."

He had no trouble resisting the spell cast by the evil lord who belatedly arrived on the scene. What frightened him was close-quarters combat; as long as they were at a distance, he would be fine.

Ainz ignored the evil lord in the sky, and he also ignored Yuri, who had been chipping at him with small blips of damage for a while. Then he charged at Lupusregina.

That instant…

An insect-shaped shot came from somewhere off to the side. It had to be Entoma.

He doesn't even need to block it with Greater Physical Damage Immunity. Any projectile attacks that weren't enchanted had no effect on Ainz.

The Pleiades' gear had large data capacities, so they would probably come prepared for all of Ainz's areas of resistance. Yuri's and Shizu's previous attacks were good examples. But some special abilities were dependent on the character's level. Entoma, especially, had a lot of moves tied to her level.

At level 50, Entoma couldn't do anything to Ainz. And if the damage was completely blocked, the secondary effects wouldn't work, either.

It would be safe to shift his attention away from her.

Solution must have been hiding, determined not to get crushed by Ainz, who hadn't given Entoma so much as a glance— She pushed up out of the ground in front of Lupusregina. There wasn't much point to coming out before an area-of-effect attack, but she had no choice when it came to protecting their healer.

But Solution made one fatal mistake. Ainz was a caster. There was absolutely no reason he needed to make it a close-quarters fight. He could launch attack magic from a distance. She should have thought about why someone like that would be charging straight for Lupusregina.

Ainz had a single objective: to make clear who he was fighting and get all the cards on the table.

Narberal isn't here?

He wasn't sure. She hadn't been in the group that had attacked in the royal capital. But since she was a member of the Pleiades, there was nothing to guarantee she wasn't present. It was possible she would continue hiding until the last possible second. But now that he had figured out what kind of hand his opponents were playing with, there was no reason to fight from right in the middle of them all.

"Greater Teleportation."

With no obstruction from Shizu, he successfully teleported to the roof of a building in sight.

I need to remember what they can all do. Who should I take out first? Yeah, the healer, Lupusregina. I need to be wary of Shizu, too, but…I don't know where she is… The rest I can worry about later. And the evil lord will take the longest, so he's last.

He could see Lupusregina casting a spell on Solution. There was no disadvantage to them if he took his time. That must have been why no one was following him. No, it was probably because they knew that if they chased around Ainz, who could teleport wherever he felt like at will, they would be picked off one by one after getting split up. Of course, that was what Ainz was hoping for.

But even if they saw through his scheme, that was no problem.

He could harass them with magic attacks at range and still pick them off. Shizu was in her element in a ranged battle, but attacking continuously would reveal her position. So it seemed like she would only fire when she had a perfect shot. If so, then he didn't have to be too worried about her. Or…?

"I don't see her here, so are you taking her place?" he asked under his breath to the evil lord who landed dramatically back on the ground.

Ainz smiled wryly in spite of himself.

"Ha-ha. You've gotten massive, Narberal. Maybe I should call you Gorillal. And the attributes you use have changed considerably as well. Well, isn't that funny. If the Pleiades Doppels are my opponents…" He fluttered his mantle—not that it meant anything. He just wanted to try striking a kingly pose. "…Then I guess I should be a bit serious about this."

"Twin Maximize Magic: Re—"

As he was trying to send a spell flying at Lupusregina, another bullet went through his arm. And the spell became pointless once again.

"Huh?"

This was impossible.

Even if once was possible, he couldn't get his magic canceled twice. The level gap between him and Shizu was enormous.

Could he really be so unlucky as to have his resistance fail twice in a row? What were the odds of that happening? Or was this not luck but the natural outcome? For example, if his opponent wasn't Shizu?

The Evil Lord Wrath spread his flaming wings and approached. Yuri flew right, and Entoma took off on a wide arc to the left.

Why? How? Is this another change that happened since coming to this world? Or did Garnet give Shizu something? Or is it not Shizu? What did Yuri say? She said sisters, but if they're doppel... Pando— Aaaah!

The Evil Lord Wrath had come within hand-to-hand distance and was winding up for a full-powered punch.

Shit! I hate when they just get in close and hit me! If you're here as a stand-in for Narberal, you should be using magic, Gorillal!

Well, if he did use magic, it would all be completely blocked, so that would be sort of boring...

Without hesitating, Ainz charged forward to close the gap entirely.

The evil lord reacted slowly, probably because he had expected him to run away. The idea had most likely been to pincer him in coordination with Yuri.

And that was why Ainz was able to duck under the blow (intended as a feint) from the demon's great fiery arm.

The arm went past his ear with surprising speed, and the wind it whipped up sounded like a scream.

A pure caster had dodged a warrior monster's attack.

He wondered if he could have pulled that off in *Yggdrasil*, but this wasn't luck. As previously mentioned, the evil lord didn't expect Ainz to come forward, so he hadn't put all his strength behind the blow. And the other reason was Ainz had trained.

This ducking and weaving in close quarters was a move he had practiced hundreds of times with Cocytus. The result was that one out of ten times, he was able to dodge Cocytus's not-at-all-serious attack.

Cocytus told me that a good warrior would never attack in such an easy, exaggerated way, so I couldn't let my guard down, but…it seems like I can actually use this in combat.

From there, Ainz put a hand against the evil lord's thick chest—and cast a touch-triggered spell.

Spells all had an effective range, and some had a range of essentially zero. Those required the caster to be touching their target, so only people who had acquired both a magic class and a warrior class could use them properly. Because the spells were so inconvenient, they were more powerful than others on the same tier and, in fact, closer to the strength of a spell from the next highest one.

Ainz used a tier-eight spell from his specialty, ghost magic, called Energy Drain. It temporarily drained levels from the target and gave the caster benefits proportional to the number of levels lowered. And he boosted it. Penetrating the evil lord's resistance, the spell stole his levels. As a result, the wound Ainz had gotten from Yuri was mostly healed. Of course, the healing this spell provided was only an auxiliary effect.

All of Ainz's abilities were temporarily strengthened. And he also got a special buff for a short time. Meanwhile, the evil lord received a special debuff that reduced his level and wouldn't disappear over time.

This time it was the evil lord who backed away.

His face twisted in rage had another note to it.

Surprise? Or perhaps admiration?

Ainz was filled with the urge to pat himself on the back for managing to get around that blow. That said, the main factor was that he had caught his opponent off guard. Just as a magic trick that had been spoiled would be boring, he figured that move wouldn't work again.

"Well, only a fool puts an ingenious strategy on repeat. Right, Pleiades? Aureole Omega!"

*   *   *

That's what it was.

In this fight, there were five doppelgängers and an Evil Lord Wrath, plus a level-100 NPC.

Did Albedo come up with this plan in order to defeat me? I can't believe she's using Aureole Omega.

The littlest Pleiades sister, Aureole Omega, was a domain guardian on level eight, a level-100 NPC specialized in commander classes. When she gave orders as a commander, her teammates all received various buffs. That was probably why Shizu's skill had been overcoming the level gap.

Ainz wasn't sure what sort of skills Aureole had, but he knew she fell outside the typical categories of melee DPS, magic DPS, healer, and so on—she was a wild card. Nothing she did would be a surprise.

What kinds of stuff did Squishy Moe usually do?

The commander classes never fought directly against their opponents in PvP, so Ainz didn't know very much about them.

There's no way she would have left the eighth level to come here without my permission. So the Doppels must have just gotten some buffs before they came, and she figured anything too elaborate wouldn't work, so... No, is an Aureole doppelgänger here?

Stop. He didn't have time for extraneous thoughts. Only one thing was important: His magic could be completely disrupted—indefinitely.

Skills in *Yggdrasil* came in two types. One required a cooldown period after use. The other was allowing a set number of uses within a certain time period. And some were a combination of the two.

The stronger the skill, the fewer uses or the longer the cooldown. Ainz's ace move, the Goal of All Life Is Death, could only be used once every hundred hours, for example.

So which were Shizu's magic nullifying shots?

For such a handy move, it seemed to have hardly any cooldown time at all. So then it probably had a limited number of uses. But he had no way of knowing the recovery time. He wanted to believe that once she used the power-up, it wouldn't come back again this fight.

I should really save tier-ten spells for finishing moves, but…

Ainz quickly confirmed the locations of the Pleiades and the evil lord. The evil lord was right in front of him. Behind him was Yuri—but she had just closed in to punch him. Imbued with chi, her fist could break iron, but at Ainz's level, it didn't cause much damage. *The dangerous one really is the evil lord*, he confirmed and then checked on everyone else.

Entoma was in a building on the left side of the square. Lupusregina was in the square. Solution was defending her from the front. Shizu's location was unknown.

Not knowing the sniper's location was the worst of the worst. On the other hand, having the enemies all spread out was the best.

"Heh," Ainz laughed in spite of himself.

He knew it was no time to laugh, but he couldn't hold back.

This is so fun!

"Enjoy your flight. Maximize Magic: Nuclear Blast."

"Ngh!"

Right before Ainz's eyes: A flash of light between him and the evil lord expanded, swallowing up everything in an instant. It was only natural for Yuri to be surprised—because Ainz was caught up in the blast, too.

The tier-nine spell Nuclear Blast was only so-so as attack magic. It dealt both fire and battering types, but the total amount was low for the ninth tier.

Against an Evil Lord Wrath, who had an ability that gave him fire immunity, it shouldn't have been an option. Of course, there was a reason Ainz used it despite that.

First, it had a large area-of-effect, and of all the spells in existence, it was up there with the best. It also delivered the negative status effects of poison, blindness, hearing loss, and more, but he didn't expect much out of those. At the evil lord's level, most of them would be resisted, and the Pleiades had gear that would block them. The main reason Ainz chose this spell was its powerful knock-back effect.

The resulting damage affected Ainz as well, of course. In *Yggdrasil*, there hadn't been any friendly fire, so it was possible to use it in this reckless way without issue, but now it was a type of self-harm. No matter how high his magic defense was, there was no need to take damage himself in order to use this; if he was going to self-destruct, he should have chosen a different spell.

But Ainz had already thought that through.

If he could block the blunt damage completely by activating Body of Effulgent Beryl, he would be fine, since the fire damage would be nullified as a matter of course. And as an undead, the negative statuses couldn't affect him.

In other words, Ainz would take no damage.

And if he blocked it completely, the knock-back effect was also canceled. Ainz stood alone unfazed in the blast zone.

"Ha-ha."

Ainz laughed. As one would expect, it felt great to have things go according to plan.

Blow the enemies away and ruin their formation—that was his aim.

His guildmates—who had taught him so many things, including these sorts of tactics—briefly crossed his mind.

Just like before, recalling his *Yggdrasil* days made things fun, even in this life-and-death situation.

I've thought this before but… I don't remember being addicted to combat or anything…

"That's not all. I'm just getting warmed up. Watch how well you all trained me."

As a result of the raging tier-nine spell, the buildings in the area had been blown away, making the square suddenly much larger.

Well, it was out of his hands. This town's role ended here, in any case.

He wanted to make sure he got Shizu in the blast, but he was hesitant to boost the spell's power any higher than that because he didn't want to cause too much destruction; that may have been a mistake.

Well, it's fine. All that's left is…

He stared in the direction Lupusregina should have been. The enemy encirclement was completely broken.

Even with Aureole's buffs, they couldn't escape the effects of the explosion. He saw them all scrambling to get to their feet.

They didn't lose much strength from Nuclear Blast, so…

Flying toward Lupusregina, Ainz cast Reality Slash.

This time there was no disruption from Shizu, and blood spurted from Lupusregina's body.

"Widen Magic: Shark Cyclone."

He created an extra-large tornado and sent it to the rear where it would catch Yuri and the evil lord. He could use it to buy time, since it would obstruct their view while creating a disturbance. He had come up with the plan to create the tornado before using Nuclear Blast to cut off Shizu's line of fire and take out Yuri first, but he figured the evil lord would have no trouble getting through it. He judged this timing, when everyone was confused, to be most effective.

Out of the corner of his eye, he saw Entoma moving a crumbling pillar out of her way as she stood up.

It was unclear what had happened to Shizu, whom he hadn't managed to spot yet. If she was trapped under some rubble, that would be great.

"He's over here! Stop him!" Solution yelled from in front of Lupusregina, but Yuri and the evil lord couldn't hear her over the roar of the wind. Yuri was on the move, desperate to avoid being blown away by the tornado. Some classes could use magic or skills to teleport or go incorporeal and escape with no trouble, but Yuri didn't seem to have any of those abilities.

Of course, that meant she had strengths in other areas.

After this battle, we'll all learn what sort of equipment changes and preparations we should make. No…

The real Pleiades might have handled everything like experts. These were only doppelgängers who had copied their abilities. Their combat prowess had to be inferior to the real combat maids.

When Ainz tried to close the distance and use Reality Slash, a bug dropped in front of him. It was a large transport bug with no combat ability. He was sure it was only there to obstruct his attack vector.

In *Yggdrasil*, this usage would have been impossible. That Entoma—the doppelgänger—had done it anyhow impressed Ainz a lot even as he was casting his next spell.

"Greater Teleportation."

Evading the bug by teleporting skyward, he aimed Twin Maximize Magic: Reality Slash at Lupusregina.

Even if Shizu had been targeting him, he should have been able to shake her off by abruptly teleporting up into the sky. Humanoids were weak when it came to following sudden vertical motions with their eyes.

That said, an archer with a wealth of experience like Peroroncino could predict an enemy's movements and handle vertical motion as well, so there was a chance that teleporting wouldn't help him.

Peroroncino has led his targets so well, it seemed like he was locked on. Shizu needs to work hard so she makes it to that level.

Feeling nostalgic, he shouted, "Lupusregina, you're out!"

It was pretty hard to fight while keeping a close eye on his opponents' HP. It could even be considered a handicap. For that reason, he wasn't entirely sure if she was really out or not, but he wanted to avoid accidentally killing her.

As a doppelgänger, she's weaker than normal with less HP than the real Lupusregina. Now that I've crushed the caster, I'm going to get sneaky. Perfect Unknowable.

There were ways to find someone using Perfect Unknowable, but he was pretty sure the only one of the Pleiades who could do so without using an item was Lupusregina, and it was likely the evil lord didn't have that power. In other words, he could assume they had no way to cope with his stealth attacks.

I knocked out their source of healing, so maybe it's time to hunt for Shizu. They wouldn't use consumables, would they?

Ainz wouldn't forgive them for wasting Nazarick's resources on a fight like this.

"Where is he?"

"He disappearrrred! Invisibility?"

"If it was Invisibility, I could find him! But I don't see him anywhere!"

"Then another type of concealmennnnt?"

He could hear the two in their confusion.

"You dummies! It's Perfect Unknowable!"

"Lupusregina! That's against the rules!" Ainz shouted, but no one could hear him because of Perfect Unknowable. "Ahhh, geez…" He scratched his head self-consciously.

The evil lord and Yuri must have made it past the tornado, because Ainz saw them searching for him. Following up with another Nuclear Blast would have been a good plan except for the possibility of killing Lupusregina. He quickly gave up on that idea and estimated his distance from Yuri as he dove into a free fall. Then he compared the others' HP loss, made sure that they had all taken fire damage in addition to battering in his previous attack, and…

"Triplet Maximize Magic: Vermillion Nova."

He launched his most powerful single-target fire attack spell—not counting the super tier—at Yuri.

Of course, there were attack spells on tier ten that dealt fire damage.

Like Stream of Lava and Uriel. But there were issues with Ainz using them.

For starters, he couldn't cast Stream of Lava. That was a faith spell for druids like Mare.

Uriel could be acquired by casters of any type as long as they fulfilled the conditions, but it only dealt the listed damage if the caster's karma was as high as it could go. Any lower and the damage dealt began to decrease, so for Ainz it would be less powerful than a tier-one attack spell.

In the sense that this spell was simple to use, as it was Ainz's only choice.

It took a huge dent out of Yuri's health. Then…

"Perfect Unknowable."

"He's gone again!"

"No faaaair."

"I wish he'd fight fair and square!"

Nah, it's your fault for not having a way to cope.

"Really, though, I still don't know where Shizu is, and you three hid the fact that you were here! So who's really being unfair?!" He knew they couldn't hear him, but he shouted anyhow.

The next thing he knew, the evil lord was charging toward his previous position.

"Sorry, better luck next time!"

He was already on the move, but Ainz was no longer there. Just as Ainz was thinking that the evil lord was in range for an area-of-effect spell, he suddenly changed course and headed straight for Ainz.

"Huh?"

He shouldn't be able to see me! The confusion was erased by the ensuing pain.

The evil lord's punch sent him flying. Since it was a more serious blow than the last, it was impossible to evade or defend. No, more than that, he was off guard, so the idea of dodging hadn't even occurred to him.

Using Fly, he was able to stabilize his posture, so he managed to avoid falling. Just like in the fight with Shalltear.

The evil lord flew after Ainz. The demon's gaze was definitely tracking him.

An Evil Lord Wrath with a detection ability...? Oh, he used it! He used his ace move, Soul for a Miracle!

Based on the fables where demons would make wishes come true in exchange for someone's soul, this ability manifested a miracle. Ainz wasn't sure how the data were handled internally, but in *Yggdrasil*, it allowed the user to cast any spell tier eight or lower.

Evil lords generally used it to cast a healing spell. But this time, he must have used it to see through Perfect Unknowable.

Though Ainz was thankful to know the power he feared the most was out of the way, he was forced to reformulate his plan.

Slugged again by the evil lord dogging him, Ainz felt irritated and impatient.

There was a large level gap. He still had plenty of leeway, but that didn't mean it was okay to continue getting hit.

"Tch, right back at you. Triplet Maximize Magic: Call Greater Thunder."

Elite demons had high resistance to elemental magic. Which attributes that applied to were usually all over the place, but electric tended to be one that worked. Suffering a triple max damage dose of effective magic, the evil lord staggered.

Then Ainz cast again.

"Perfect Unknowable."

"You're playin' dirty, Lord Ainz! So dirty!"

"Aaaagh! Aaaagh!"

Entoma was stomping her feet, and Lupusregina was rolling around on the ground. Only Solution kept her eyes sharp and scanned the area.

Mercenary minions should have all been the same, so did the differences in their personalities stem from the fact that they were imitating the Pleiades? Or were their personalities differentiating over time? The evil lord before his eyes stayed on his tail and shouted.

"He's here! Use an area-of-effect attack! Take me out with him!"

Without missing a beat, Entoma vomited up a black cloud.

It was her ace move, Fly Breath.

But it wouldn't work on Ainz. More specifically, it was counted as a piercing attack. Besides, how were flies supposed to eat away at a body that was nothing but bone? Only the evil lord seemed to be having trouble.

"Hey! It's not working! Or more like, it's only working on me!"

"Whaaaat?!"

Being able to copy a power was different from being able to use it competently. The real Entoma never would have made a mistake like that.

"I don't have any area-of-effect attacks! Do you, Mistress Yuri?"

"This'll do!"

A light appeared in Yuri's hand.

Chi Palm Blast. On contact, it targeted a single enemy, while if it was touching no one, it radiated a shock wave over its area of effect. Of course, the move was meant to be used by touch, so the diffused version was very weak. Monks were specialized in contact moves and had very few—really as good as zero—reliable area-of-effect attacks, so that was just how it was.

"There! He's on the move!"

"Here?!"

Yuri did a Chi Palm Blast in the direction of where Ainz had been a moment ago. Furrowing his nonexistent brow at her, he thrust his arms out.

"…No, you should be focused on healing." Ainz was pretty sure Yuri could heal using chi. After snarking, he cast another spell. Of course, it was one that he already learned was effective. "Twin Maximize Magic: Vermillion Nova." Having revealed his position by casting, he told the flame-engulfed maid in a cold tone, "Yuri, you're out. Perfect Unknowable."

Now I really have to find Shizu, decided Ainz. Still wary of the evil lord, he took a spin around the area.

3

Standing on the wall among a crowd of other people, Neia watched the fight.

Many of the spectators had been saved by and revered the King of Darkness, but not all.

Paladins were present, too, as were priests. Neia couldn't see her through the wall of people, but even Remedios was so close by, she could hear her voice.

Of the leadership, it seemed only Gustav and Caspond were absent.

No one watching said any— No. There simply were no words for this fight.

They knew.

The Blue Roses had said Jaldabaoth's difficulty level was over 200. So this was essentially a fight with a dragon shaped like a man. Simply having it take place in the human world guaranteed disaster.

They were probably lucky only one part of town had been destroyed. A few buildings were burning, sending up plumes of white smoke, but there were next to no human casualties.

As the people watched, a tornado, fire, lightning—a storm of powers beyond human comprehension was unleashed. Any one of them would have been enough to take scores of lives.

Especially…

"That was beautiful…"

What moved Neia was the white sphere of light that occurred twice.

A power that swallowed everything up and cleanly erased it. Neia sensed good in it. She wasn't sure if it was a sacred power or not. The utter destruction left behind after the light faded was actually frightening, but her admiration of the immense force won out.

It seems like the fight is still going. If His Majesty can use such powerful magic and things still aren't finished…Jaldabaoth really is strong.

She had heard tell, and she had seen with her own eyes, but she had apparently still been underestimating him. She would certainly never do that again.

The king she had been serving, if only while he was in the Sacred Kingdom, was fighting. Neia felt it was her duty to bear witness to his heroism, which is why she was watching. *And in the case that…*

…Neia clenched her hand around her bow.

She could tell multiple opponents besides Jaldabaoth were challenging the king—the demon maids, said to be difficulty level 150. Even fighting all those powerful enemies at once, he was holding his own; Neia couldn't help but be awed by his might.

She was sure now that she was envious of the Nation of Darkness's people, who were protected by such justice. A country with a king like that had to be such a happy place.

"Weakness is a sin, so I have to get stronger. Either that or I should reverently accept the justice of one like His Majesty the King of Darkness." Neia murmured what was always on her mind of late. Having repeated this so many times, it had come to resemble a prayer.

Suddenly a meteorite fell, causing a huge explosion.

The wreckage of buildings went flying and then rained down mixed with dirt and dust.

"Commander… Isn't Jaldabaoth…impossibly terrible?"

"Yeah."

"The King of Darkness—His Majesty—is also so strong. If he ends up our country's enemy in the future…er, what do you think would happen to us?"

"Yeah."

"Commander?"

"Yeah."

Neia could hear Remedios talking with three other paladins.

The three asking her questions must not have seen her unleashing the power of her Holy Sword from behind only to be spurned like a child.

Yeah, maybe they didn't see it. Anyone who had seen that fight would know that the King of Darkness and Jaldabaoth possessed unimaginable power. It was too late to ponder those things now. No…

If His Majesty took over this country, the subhumans would never be able to attack again.

Neia was surprised at what a perfect idea she had come up with. It was so perfect, it was a little scary.

We could have him absorb the Sacred Kingdom… If he was a horrible tyrant, I wouldn't think that. But that's not who His Majesty is. He is justice. So I should rally the people who agree with me!

Neia considered her plan.

The number of people who respected and adored the king was on the rise: people who were attracted by his overwhelming power, people he had rescued from their abject suffering, people who hated subhumans so much that they were happy to have him avenge them, and so on.

Among those people, she would find the ones who wanted the kingdom to stay peaceful forever and tell them her idea.

Neia knew she was young and still lacked life experience. But if a conscientious adult thought she was wrong, she was sure they would stop her.

I'll look for the first few among the archers I'm in charge of.

She figured a good starting place would be people who had lost someone close to them and people harboring deep-seated hatred—because she could understand their feelings.

When she had thought that far—*booooooooom*—an explosion larger than the others up until now went off.

And a tall building awfully far away began to collapse.

The King of Darkness would never destroy it for no reason. Neia squinted but couldn't make out what it was through the cloud of dust as the building fell.

As if to follow that up, a thick column of lightning flashed down from the sky.

Yes, it seemed like he had an objective.

Magic spells continued to hammer that part of the city for a little while.

Neia grew anxious.

It went without saying that all these spells were fantastic, but would the king's mana last?

Neia shook her head and cleared out her anxieties and fears.

It's okay! I'm sure His Majesty has already considered that. He used a bunch of his precious mana for our sake, but he's still…!

But if Jaldabaoth did win, there would be no saving this world—only despair would remain. What could she do in that situation?

I believe in you, Your Majesty!

As if Neia's wish had been heard, two things flew into the sky.

The first thing left pitch-black darkness in its wake. The other beat its fiery, crimson wings trailing flames.

The maids didn't seem to be in pursuit. That told Neia one thing. The king had dispatched those difficulty level–150 monsters among monsters while fighting Jaldabaoth.

Wow! Neia trembled with emotion. *His Majesty is stronger than Jaldabaoth!*

Yes. There was no other way to look at it.

Jaldabaoth was lower ranking than the King of Darkness, and the demon maids were lower still. That must have been why His Majesty could handle Jaldabaoth while fighting off the maids.

Neia tensed up to contain the joy that realization gave her. Being able to see the one she respected in all his greatness right before her eyes made her feel like she was going to explode with happiness.

Her heart was beating so hard, it hurt.

She was sure they were witnessing a heroic moment that bards would sing of for generations to come.

No…that's not it.

Renewed combat had broken out in the sky.

Balls of flames and balls of light were formed.

The crisscrossing spells were probably enough to blow away another neighborhood, but they were so far away, they looked charming.

Still, it was an exchange of energies that humans could never come close to.

This is…

She could see with a sidelong look that everyone on the wall watching with bated breath understood. They followed the battle in the sky in sober silence.

Someone folded their hands. The person next to them followed suit. Everyone on the wall pressed their hands together and gazed up at the sky.

Whatever it was resembled worship.

…This is mythical.

Neia had no idea how much time had passed. Eventually—a commotion erupted.

Everyone saw a single speck fall across the eastern sky—and disappear.

Victory had been decided.

As they all looked on, the sole remaining speck descended slowly. With better vision than anyone else, Neia was the first to clamp her hand over her mouth in shock.

As the crimson flames became visible to the others, a grave quiet enveloped the wall. But no one tried to run. Anyone who saw that battle knew running was pointless.

Flapping his flaming wings, the victor showed himself.

He looked too wretched to have won.

His entire body was covered in scorches from the lightning that had coursed through it, and half his face was caved in. Bright-red gore gushed from a deep wound. It must have been hot, because the blood made a hissing noise when it hit the wall—a hiss that didn't stop for so much as a second.

His condition spoke louder than words, showing exactly how fierce the battle had been.

"It can't be…"

A dignified yet pained voice rang out over the entire wall, drowning out Neia's murmur.

"…He was strong. I haven't fought anyone that strong since Momon. I underestimated him. That was foolish. Leading the subhumans nearly became pointless but—yes—he's dead."

Neia didn't want to believe it, so she screamed, "You're lying!"

Jaldabaoth's good eye looked at Neia. Under the gaze of a being on another level, Neia still didn't waver. She could be brave because passionate emotion had taken over her mind—there was no room for fear.

"It's not a lie."

"His Majesty has a horrible sense of humor… It's a lie, isn't it?"

"It's not a lie."

Jaldabaoth's repeated words made Neia feel like her chest was being crushed.

The world swayed.

Without even thinking, she knew why the King of Darkness had lost.

Evileye of the Blue Roses. And Nabe of Raven Black. Because those two, who were capable of stopping the demon maids, weren't in this country.

And one more reason.

"If that undead had been fully rested, I might have been defeated. He wasted mana on you humans—to think he was such a fool who failed to prioritize. I'm grateful to you all."

I knew it. I knew weakness was wickedness.

Neia was absolute in her conviction.

"So I'll grant you a reward. Your lives."

"…What do you mean?"

Jaldabaoth sneered in amusement at the question someone had asked. "I'll spare your lives. This time anyhow."

Someone breathed a sigh of relief—but Neia was furious.

"Don't you dare play these games with me! Don't you dare! It's all lies! Everything you say is a lie! Who would believe what a demon says?!"

"If you can't accept reality, then you've gone mad, human. Poor thing." Jaldabaoth pointed a finger at Neia, said, "Be go— Aha!" and then immediately lowered his hand.

"What, Jaldabaoth?!"

"You wanted to provoke me, to prove I was a liar, hmm…? At least giving up your life would have had meaning? It's beyond my comprehension, but that seems to be the case."

Neia clenched her teeth so hard, they made a sound.

Jaldabaoth had to be lying.

He had to be a liar to tell such a huge lie, like that the King of Darkness had died.

"I won't let you do that. I already said I would spare your lives. Anyhow, I'm leaving for now. I've sustained enough wounds that I must rest for a time. In the meantime, feel free to cry as you drown in your despair."

The moment Jaldabaoth flapped his wings and took off, Neia's hands moved on their own.

Her bow was aimed, and she let it fly.

It was a perfect attack from behind. No extraneous motion.

And yet, Jaldabaoth turned around that instant and caught the arrow. Even with his horrible wounds, he was quick.

Jaldabaoth glared straight at Neia, and his eyes shifted to her bow, Ultimate Shooting Star: Super. Something changed slightly in his furious expression.

"Oh?! Ah! Wh-what an amazing weapon! It's been quite some time since I saw a weapon this splendid! You nearly got me. That was close."

Jaldabaoth spoke rapidly. He had seemed plenty calm, but perhaps he had actually panicked?

"Where'd this weapon come from? How did you make it?"

"As if I'd tell you!"

What is this guy thinking? Molten hatred flared in Neia's breast.

There was no way she would tell this deceiver the precious things she had learned from the King of Darkness.

"Why would I tell a great big liar like you?!"

"Mnrgh. Ah, c-could it be that it was made using rune technology?"

When he guessed the truth, Neia's heart throbbed. She was feeling a bit more composed, but when her memories of the kind king came to mind, her anger reignited.

"No!" Neia spat, and Jaldabaoth snarled. Recognizing it as an opening, Neia loosed another arrow.

This time she aimed at his leg, which would be hard for his hand to reach.

He's on guard! Maybe this bow…

Jaldabaoth could take a Holy Sword in the back like it was nothing, so if he jumped to evade, what explanation could there be aside from that her bow could hurt him?

Neia was assailed by regret, and tears blurred her vision.

She knew she would have been killed all too easily had she joined that fight. But if Ultimate Shooting Star: Super could reach Jaldabaoth, then maybe she should have tried to act as the king's shield. If she had, then maybe…

Neia shot another arrow.

He moved his head, and her arrow flew on and on.

"Hit him!"

Another.

Another.

But none of them connected. Even though he was so huge, even though he was so terribly wounded, he was so nimble that he could dodge Neia's attacks.

"Runes—"

"Shut up!"

Neia interrupted him with another arrow.

But as expected, that one didn't strike him, either.

Why? Why isn't anyone else attacking him?

She realized that since he was flying, they didn't have the means. But did they think it was fine to just let this evil liar go? He said he killed the king they were all indebted to!

"Mrgh… I suppose I have no choice… Greater Teleportation."

And with that, Jaldabaoth disappeared.

"You're running?!"

Neia scanned the area.

All she saw were the faces of people surprised by her reaction. Jaldabaoth was nowhere to be found.

"Shit! He's gone!"

"Calm down!" Remedios snapped. The voice of the strong woman carried a physical weight. Normally it would have brought Neia back to her senses, even causing her to stiffen up. But now it was no different from plain noise.

"How can I be calm?!"

"Squire Neia Baraja! You borrowed that weapon from the King of Darkness, right? Why was the demon so interested in it?"

"Please don't come at me with questions that don't matter! We have to go find His Majesty! I saw him fall in the east! We should mount a rescue party at once!"

"That guy's probably dead."

"He can't be dead! His Majesty wouldn't just die!"

Neia grabbed at her without thinking, but Remedios easily brushed her off, sending her tumbling across the top of the wall.

"Simmer down. He couldn't have fallen from so high and lived."

"What? Why do you believe that demon? Did you sell your soul to him or something?!"

Remedios's expression changed. Then she flew at Neia.

"Squire! There are some things you can say and some things you can't!"

The grip on her lapel was so tight, it was hard to breathe.

"Both of you, calm down! Please calm down!"

Paladins, priests, and servicemen rushed between Remedios and Neia to pull them apart.

Breathing rough and hard, Neia shouted, "Dispatch a unit to rescue the king—now!"

"We don't have the troops to waste on a pointless exercise!"

"Pointless?!" Neia stepped forward to slug Remedios, but because of the people between them, she couldn't. "It's no use talking to you!" Having composed herself somewhat, she addressed the people holding her back. "Would you mind releasing me? I have somewhere I need to go."

"Where?!"

Neia eyed Remedios with absolute incredulity.

"What's that look for? Is that any way for a squire to look at a paladin?!"

"Ha," Neia scoffed. "First, I'm going to request that the Holy Lady's brother dispatch a rescue party for the King of Darkness. Then I'm going straight to the Nation of Darkness to tell them the truth of what happened and request their cooperation in the search."

Going to the Nation of Darkness under these circumstances didn't bode well for her. Still, she had to fulfill her role as the king's attendant.

She wasn't even sure if she would make the journey safely. Still, she had to go, even if it was the last thing she would do.

"Oh, Baraja, if you're headed to the Nation of Darkness, I'll go with you!" The older man who spoke up was a retired serviceman living as a hunter. Commended for his skill with a bow, he belonged to Neia's archer unit. "You don't have to worry about me. I've lived this long. This old body doesn't have too many more years in it anyhow."

"Bardem!"

He had spoken with the knowledge of what sort of fate likely awaited them even if they reached the Nation of Darkness.

"Oh, Neia. Don't forget me!"

"You too, Codina?"

"Count me in. I wouldn't leave for you, really, but if it's for the King of Darkness, then I pretty much have to."

"Even you, Mena?"

The most skilled members of Neia's unit took the initiative and stepped up to join her. With them on her side, they would surely be able to reach the Nation of Darkness safely. The only thing was…

"Thank you. But would you do me a favor and join the rescue party instead?"

"Where do you get off making plans like that?! You were all gathered here in order to liberate the people of the Sacred Kingdom from their suffering under the demon! Don't get your priorities mixed up!"

"With all due respect, Commander, what are you talking about?! What could possibly be more important than rescuing the King of Darkness?!"

"That should be obvious! How many people are being tortured this very moment in the hell the subhumans have created?! What could be higher priority than them?!"

"I'll tell you! The—"

"What in blazes is going on here?! Why are you all screaming at one another?!"

Suddenly, someone intruded on their quarrel. It was Caspond.

"Commander Custodio. Weren't you supposed to come straight back? Where is His Majesty? What happened to Jaldabaoth? What happened…? Someone give me an explanation."

Caspond was at his wit's end, and his voice sounded awfully awkward in the oppressive silence.

•

In addition to the paladins and priests, the nobles, who had been prisoners until just the other day, and honorary knights had been invited, so the meeting room was feeling rather cramped. Still, the room Caspond had originally been using had been damaged by Jaldabaoth, and there was no other more suitable location.

Upon receiving a report from a paladin, Caspond had called this emergency meeting and instructed the participants to gather here.

Caspond hastened into the room, accompanied by Remedios, moments after everyone else had arrived.

With the appearance of the Holy Lady's brother, many of the attendees bowed. Neia was one of them. It wasn't as if she had anything against Caspond.

Remaining standing before them all, Caspond began to speak.

"I appreciate you all gathering here. I'd like to discuss what to do next."

He could say he wanted to discuss it, but to Neia, there was only one thing they needed to do. And she was confident in her answer. She moved to speak, but Caspond held up a hand to stop her.

"I'm sure everyone has their views, but first I want you to listen to what I have to say." He slowly scanned the room. "I believe many of you have confirmed with your own eyes that Jaldabaoth's power is beyond all imagination... Yes, unfortunately, we must admit the truth—that there is no one in this country who can defeat him."

Several people glanced at the strongest paladin in the kingdom, Remedios, who remained sullenly silent. Upon learning that she agreed with him, fear and despair became faintly visible on their faces.

"But it's too soon to succumb to pessimism. We'll drive him off indirectly instead of directly." Caspond waited a few seconds for what he was trying to say to sink into the heads of those listening before giving his conclusion. "We'll kill every last one of the subhumans he's leading."

"Why will that work?"

Caspond responded to the question. "Jaldabaoth once went on a rampage in the Re-Estize Kingdom. He fought in single combat with a warrior there and ended up fleeing in defeat. That time, he was leading demon forces, but there was no subhuman army. Doesn't that mean he decided to lead the subhumans because he was defeated?" Caspond looked around to make sure everyone understood. "Doesn't it seem like he is using the subhumans as a shield to avoid single combat with that warrior...? When he was fighting the King of Darkness, he even said, 'Leading the subhumans nearly became pointless.'"

That was true.

At the time, Neia hadn't understood, but now that it had been laid out so clearly, it was hard to imagine it could mean anything else.

"In other words, to Jaldabaoth, the subhumans are his armor and strength for the next time he has to face that warrior. So then what would happen if he lost them? Would he press on without his armor and strength? Even though the warrior who defeated him could appear at any time? Or do you think he would run?"

"I see... So you think we should abandon this city, attack the subhuman army in the south, and coordinate with our own southern allies to drive the enemy off?"

A liberated noble answered the priest's question. "That would be good. The King of Darkness killed around forty thousand of the subhumans here. That's a massive chunk of their forces! The rest of them are facing off against our forces in the south. If all the liberated people in this city maneuver to pincer them, we should be able to annihilate their army. Then we could join forces with the southern army to take back our country's territory!"

There were murmurs of approval, but Caspond shook his head, and the silence reigned once more.

"No, we'll do the opposite and move west to retake the vital hub of the north, Karinsha."

"Why?"

"Yes, what is the reasoning behind that decision? The major cities in the west—Karinsha, Prato, Limun, and the capital, Jobans—will all be difficult fights. Many sacrifices will be made. So wouldn't wearing down the subhuman army in the south be more along the lines of what you're thinking, Master Caspond?"

"Ah. I see what you mean. I'm thankful that so many wise people are gathered here. But will everyone understand that?"

Most of the people in the room wore expressions that said they didn't see what he was getting at.

"Listen. Going south now would be the same as leaving behind—

abandoning—if only temporarily, the people who are still imprisoned. Do you think the masses will accept that?"

"W-well…it's more logical and would give them a better chance of being rescued!"

"You're a baron, correct?" It was a man in his prime who asked.

"Y-yes, I've had the honor of making your acquaintance once before."

"Oh, huh. So have all the people of your domain been saved?"

"N-no, not yet. I was imprisoned while fighting under Her Majesty the Holy Lady, so I don't know what has happened to my land…"

"Ah. So if you joined the southern army to get it back, you might be accused of fleeing to the south."

The noble's face stiffened.

Rationally speaking, what the noble was saying was correct. But that didn't mean all the people, some in very difficult situations, would accept noble logic. It was possible the blade of the people's hatred would be turned on them. Neia had seen some make comments like, *Why didn't you rescue us sooner? My family was killed by the subhumans.*

But no one from the camps liberated by the King of Darkness said that. Given his overpowering magic (a single spell could scatter a moat) and that he was the king of a foreign country, who was bold enough to take their personal anger out on him?

"Additionally, I had intended to talk to those of you with land after this, but I might as well say it now… How do you think the southern nobles will treat us when we're weak and exhausted? What do they think they would do to us, especially if the masses think we have abandoned our lands?"

The air took on the muddy stench of politics and power.

Neia couldn't believe it, but the nobles nodded as if they understood.

"Our land would be…"

"I won't ask you to spell it out. It's not as if I can promise you anything, after all. But it's clear that the power of the southern nobles will increase dramatically. That's why we need to consider the postwar scenario to choose the best course of action."

"Wait!" A paladin raised his voice. "We have no desire to spill extra blood over a courtly feud!"

"Hear, hear!" Ciriaco boomed in his voice trained by delivering sermons. "What's important is what will save the most people!"

"…This won't end just because we get rid of the subhumans. If the southern army makes off with all the spoils, it'll be a struggle to reject any demands they make after the war. It could even mean more heavy taxes levied on the already weary people."

"…If a new holy king is chosen on the advice of the southern nobles following the death of the Holy Lady, that would be the worst. But we've made it this far, so…"

Opinion began to split down the middle.

There was a faction of nobles and a faction of paladins and priests.

Their views clashed. Remedios was getting Caspond's plan broken down for her by the other paladins.

Neia didn't join either side, instead merely watching the proceedings in silence. Really, she already knew what she needed to do, so she didn't care what outcome they reached. She just wanted to make her proposal and be on her way already.

That said, if I suddenly start talking about something completely unrelated, everyone might get annoyed with me to the point that even those who would have cooperated might refuse to help me…

She listened, though it all bored her, and eventually everyone got tired of arguing past one another and threw it back at Caspond.

"Master Caspond, you were the one who brought this up. Why don't you tell us the rest of your idea first?"

"Of course. As I said, my plan is to retake Karinsha. This will benefit us militarily. Honestly, our current city is small, and much of it has been destroyed. It has become difficult to live here. I want us to have a resilient base of operations with ample room. And taking back one large city should also give us some leverage against the southern nobles. Karinsha was designated as a bastion to stem enemy invasions, so it should have a decent stockpile of military equipment, if it hasn't already been raided."

"…It *would* be nice to have a better base."

"Yes, with the city in this state, sanitation is a concern. And many people are shivering in the cold."

"But we also want to avoid huge losses."

"Of course. Which is why we act now. Now is the perfect time to attack the enemy garrison. Moving while Jaldabaoth is out of commission is key."

No one knew how long it would take Jaldabaoth's wounds to heal. But it probably wouldn't take any longer than it would for them to get rid of the subhuman army.

That said, he probably wouldn't come out if he hadn't recovered at all yet. It was hard to imagine him making a move when he knew that his nemesis Momon could appear. Surely, he would wait until he was mostly healed to attack again.

And no matter how many forces the Sacred Kingdom mustered, they wouldn't be able to do anything once Jaldabaoth returned, so it was best to capture the base now.

"Now, there's one thing you're all dissatisfied with. The number of casualties. So can I take that to mean that if we're able to avoid a massive amount of casualties, you agree to my plan?"

Everyone besides Remedios nodded. Neia didn't care, but given the way things were going, she felt it would look bad to be the only one not nodding, so she assented along with the rest.

A few people glanced at Remedios and decided from her expression that she had no particular reason for not nodding, so she was ignored.

"Okay. Then let's come up with a plan for taking Karinsha later on. Next—" Caspond heaved a sigh and looked straight at Neia. "Regarding the death of the King of Darkness…"

"Forgive me for contradicting you, Master Caspond, but we don't know for sure that the King of Darkness is dead. That's merely what Jaldabaoth told us. Taking a demon's words at face value would be incredibly foolish." Neia continued with a glance at Remedios. "I believe there's a good chance that he's deceiving us."

"Then why hasn't the king returned? He can use teleportation magic."

"He might be wounded and unable to move. He might be low on mana. I can think of any number of reasons."

Remedios had no further questions.

"Right, then I'd like to hear your opinion, everyone. What do you think we should do?"

"It's not even a question!" Neia roared and then, gritting her teeth, forced herself to speak more levelly. "…We must dispatch a rescue party. And we need to inform the Nation of Darkness about what has happened. If it's all right with you, I'll be the messenger."

"I see. So that's Squire Baraja's opinion. Anyone else?"

Caspond's gaze floated over the group gathered there. A noble spoke.

"I have a thought. The theory that he fell in the east is persuasive, but if we're sending a rescue party into subhuman territory, we should have more concrete information…"

"That would be too late." Neia could rebut that argument immediately. "The longer it takes, the more danger His Majesty will be in. I propose sending a party immediately."

Many people nodded in agreement. There was nothing wrong with the rationale of Neia's idea.

"Then we should send a messenger to the Nation of Darkness at the same time that we send out the search and rescue party, right?"

"…I'd like to ask you as His Majesty's attendant: Do you think he told someone in the Nation of Darkness that he was coming here?"

Neia searched her memories. "My apologies. I don't know. But I wouldn't be surprised if he had—because he sometimes teleported back."

"Then, Master Caspond, I don't think we should send a messenger."

"Why not?!" Neia glared at the noble who had been opposing her the entire time. Withering under her gaze, he went pale and backed up a couple of steps, and those around him moved away slightly.

"I—I mean…I'd like you to keep a cool head and listen to what I have to say. It's because it'll cause trouble. Wait! Calm down and listen! If you think about it, isn't it possible that his undead army would want revenge? Simple retaliation would be one thing, but we might even be annexed. And…the other thing…is that who can say that isn't what the king was after the whole time?"

"You think he would do that?!" Neia was so angry, she was dizzy. "Then allow me to ask you this! If His Majesty had teleported back to the Nation of Darkness, what would he think of the Sacred Kingdom if we didn't send a messenger to inform his country of the situation?!"

She could see many of the people were nodding in agreement. Then Remedios spoke.

"But what could we do? We're strapped as it is. We can just apologize when this is all over."

"So then—"

Neia was about to snap back when someone loudly clapped their hands several times. She saw it was Caspond. If the Holy Lady's brother wanted to speak, Neia had no choice but to let him.

"Squire Baraja, I'll choose a messenger to send to the Nation of Darkness. How about that? Don't you think they would feel we're looking down on them if we sent a mere squire as a messenger?"

"Th-that's true, but…"

He had a point, and she knew it. A messenger sent by the government or a squire who borrowed a bow from the king? Officially, the former was undoubtedly more proper. Honestly, she wondered if they would really send someone, but it would be problematic to act as if she didn't trust the Holy Lady's brother.

"I'm glad you seem to understand."

"Then please let me take a group to the east."

"Sure. I'd like you to do that. But first, we don't actually know where he fell. It could be five miles to the east or fifty. If we're unlucky, he might have fallen in the Abellion Hills as previously pointed out. Do you have some way to search for the King of Darkness in those unexplored lands?"

Neia wasn't sure what to say.

There was no way she could search for him in unfamiliar lands populated by subhumans. It was clear that the rescue party would only meet with disaster and be wiped out.

"The skills to survive in the hills. The skills to evade subhuman surveillance. The skills to gather intelligence." Caspond counted on his fingers. "If you go without preparing any of those, it's a roundabout way to suicide. What's the point of a rescue party doomed to fail?"

"Th-then do you have any better ideas?!"

"I do."

"Huh?"

She never imagined that he would, so her eyes widened at how simply he replied. Caspond braced himself slightly and told her what it was.

"You just need to find someone who knows the hills."

He smiled wryly at Neia as she blinked in confusion.

"Got it? Capture a subhuman and make them lead you. With a subhuman as your guide, you should be much safer out there."

"Oh."

That made sense. Venturing into those lands came with too many risks for humans, but with a subhuman guide, it was a different story.

There was just one problem that couldn't be ignored.

Even if the subhuman could be coerced into leading the party, if they decided to stop following orders and turned against them, the rescue party would just be journeying to their deaths again. The orcs from the other day seemed like exactly the type who would exercise that sort of life-and-death courage.

They needed a subhuman they could trust. But where could they find one of those?

Neia felt Caspond's plan was impossible, but she didn't have any better ideas.

What kind of subhuman would guide them, and what would she have to do to strike the deal?

Neia racked her brain. Still, all she could think of was the horde of enemies charging with bloodshot eyes; none of them seemed open to negotiating their defection.

No, the orcs and Mighty King Buser seemed sort of humanlike. Oh, maybe it'd be possible if we took their family hostage? Hrrrm…or if we could take a king like Buser hostage, then we might be able to get an entire race to follow orders.

But it was easy to imagine a furious uprising instead, and in the first place, where and how was she supposed to capture a subhuman king?

As Neia was getting lost in the maze of her inconclusive thoughts, the door flew open, and a paladin rushed in.

Panting, he scanned the room and headed not for Remedios but Caspond.

He must not have wanted the others in the room to hear, because he pulled him into a corner and whispered into his ear, but Neia's sharp hearing could pick up a word here and there. The ones that interested her the most were *demon maids.*

"Everyone, I have an urgent matter to attend to. Apologies, but this meeting is adjourned. I want you to draw up a plan for taking Karinsha. Commander Custodio, come with me."

Intermission

Jircniv had been doing well.

Very well.

In any case, well.

The stomach pains he had suffered since visiting the magnificent nightmare that was Nazarick were long gone, and the drawer he had once stocked with potions now held only paperwork as it was meant to. He had been liberated from every sort of distress, and he didn't have to stare in shock at the collection of hairs he had been pulling off his pillow.

It felt wonderful.

It felt nice.

It felt comfortable.

It was quite possibly the first time in his life he had ever felt so free. He nearly expected to sprout wings and go soaring into the air.

He kept his genuine smile put away in his heart and faced his subordinates. His unattractive consort told him he had been smiling more recently, but he couldn't do it here. There was a base level of dignity he had to maintain.

And so the meeting of the Imperial Court began.

Jircniv had several secretaries, but the one before him now was the absolutely outstanding Reaunet Vermilion.

The man's transfer to a sinecure after he had returned from the King of Darkness's palace, in order to make sure nothing had been done to him there, was ancient history; he was now appointed head secretary. Certainly, it hadn't been done because they were sure he was free of undue influence but to show the Nation of Darkness that they suspected no secrets. And it was the truth that Reaunet was outstanding.

Glancing over the documents Reaunet had handed him, Jircniv couldn't help but laugh at how ridiculous they were.

"They really write the silliest things. What do you think about the report that His Majesty the King of Darkness has died?"

"For one thing, it is, without a doubt, a complete and total whopper of a lie."

Jircniv was in utmost agreement.

"Yeah, it's certainly a fabrication. It's unthinkable that His Majesty the King of Darkness would lose or die."

This was the caster who had turned an army of two hundred thousand into rubble with a single spell and could hold his own in hand-to-hand combat against the martial king, the strongest warrior in the Empire. Jircniv could declare with confidence that no one could possibly kill him.

Of course, the king couldn't be poisoned and wouldn't die of sickness or old age, either. The report was more likely to be a bad joke with the punch line that he was dead to begin with.

"Well, he's probably trying to sniff out discontents. But there's one problem."

"Which is?"

"Would the terrifyingly wise King of Darkness choose a plan like this that anybody could see through? Perhaps there's some other... Yes, perhaps there is some plot that even I cannot fathom lurking further down."

Who could claim with certainty that there wasn't? No, this was a plan by the same intellectual monster who could read Jircniv's every move. He was sure this was only the tip of the iceberg. The fact that Jircniv was even thinking these sorts of things could have been part of the king's aim for whatever reason.

But what if this was intrigue cooked up not by the king but by one of the king's subordinates—for example, that stupid-looking frog monster?

"...I don't know. That said, if I don't know, I have no choice but to give up and accept my ignorance. My only job in the first place is to follow orders from the prime minister, Lady Albedo. As long as I obediently perform my role, we won't have any problems. As someone in charge of a vassal state, being moderately incompetent will make me less likely to get purged."

"I think you're right, Your Majesty." Reaunet shrugged. He never used to do that, but experience must have taught him well. Perhaps it's better to say he had been emboldened.

Whether the King of Darkness was dead or alive, the Empire would be fine as long as it didn't lose its status as a vassal of the Nation of Darkness. That way, Jircniv could stay clear of whatever intrigue would play out. Loyalty was the best defense. If he did all that and was still killed, he could die laughing at how narrow-minded they were.

"Is that it for today's work, then?"

Since becoming a vassal, Jircniv was about half as busy as usual, but even so, he was surprised by the lack of duties.

"No, Your Majesty. There's more. This arrived first thing this morning. It's from the knights."

Sadly, that wasn't the end.

Jircniv accepted the paper with a sardonic smile.

A quick glance revealed it to be complaints about the reorganization of the orders.

At one time, it had been necessary to pay the knights a certain degree of consideration. Frankly, Jircniv had a lot of nobles who opposed him, so he couldn't afford to make enemies of the country's martial powers as well. But now things were different.

"Tell them they can complain to His Majesty the King of Darkness themselves. What a waste of paper."

The paper that reports and the like were written on was made with daily-life magic, and it cost a lot no matter what tier of spell was used. Someone of Jircniv's status could toss sheafs of the stuff after one use, but he had no intention of tacitly advocating the abuse of expenses.

The paper created with tier-zero daily-life magic was coarse, thick, and tinged with color.

The paper created with tier-one daily-life magic was thinner and whiter. This type could be made with paper manufacturing technology as well. But due to low production at this level, it fetched a high price.

The paper created with tier-two daily-life magic was remarkably thin and pure white. Of course, with magic, it was possible to make nearly any color of paper one desired, but since this tier could make the silky smooth, high-quality "noble paper," all production capacity was entirely devoted to churning that out.

"I can't say that I fail to understand their resistance to leaving our national security up to another country…"

"And like I'm always telling you, direct those sorts of complaints to Lady Albedo, not me. Besides, we're not leaving it completely up to them."

This was about instructions from Prime Minister Albedo of the Nation of Darkness to fill out a portion of the Empire's military power with the Nation of Darkness's undead soldiers.

Jircniv's response to this direction, which seemed like part of the overarching vassal-state plan, was going to be to have some of their knights retire and disband two of their eight armies.

Many of their troops were mentally drained after the recent massacre, so it didn't strike him as a bad idea; the poor reaction must have been protesting the fewer number of positions to go around.

"They'll still have a place in the military. This is just a reshuffle…"

"They must be upset about reduced pay and anxious about doing jobs they've never done before."

"All I can say about the latter is that they'll have to work at it, but the former is simply a matter of course. Who would pay people simply performing manual labor the same as people risking their lives?" Jircniv sniffed disdainfully and decided to ignore the message.

Before, he would have had to put some thought into how to lead them, but not anymore.

Jircniv was backed by an absolute power, the King of Darkness. If there were any problems, he could just say, *Talk to the king*, and shut down any discontent immediately.

There was no one in the Empire who would dare complain to the one who had perpetrated *that* slaughter, who was skilled enough in martial arts to defeat the martial king.

Previously, their dissatisfaction would have been directed at Jircniv, but now that they lived under the King of Darkness's umbrella, he was secure. No, the king was feared, so Jircniv was more than secure.

And in the first place, there was surprisingly little discontent in the Empire at being made a vassal to the Nation of Darkness.

That was because the Nation of Darkness made very few demands. There were some small things—mainly two.

One was to amend some of the Empire's laws to include a preamble about the absolute supremacy of the King of Darkness and his aides.

The second was to hand over criminals sentenced to death. That was surprising in a different way. Jircniv had expected them to be brutalized, but one had even been returned to the Empire as falsely charged.

The people's daily lives hadn't changed much at all.

"Now then, I need to finish this work so I can welcome my friend."

Today a new, true friend was scheduled to come. The preparations had all been made, so Jircniv just had to get through his tasks.

After about thirty minutes of administrative odds and ends, one of his subordinates arrived, and the guards and Jircniv allowed him in.

"Your Majesty, the guest you're expecting has arr—"

"Ohhh! Show him right in!"

He wasn't done with his work yet. But what did that matter? What could possibly be more important than greeting his friend?

The friend was ushered in.

Jircniv stood with a huge smile and spread his arms in welcome.

The friend was a subhuman that looked like a stout little mole. The enchanted pendant Jircniv had gifted him jangled around his neck.

"Ohhh! So good of you to come, my true friend Riyuro!" Jircniv didn't hesitate to clasp his arms around Riyuro.

"Ahhh, Jircniv, my comrade in pain! My deepest gratitude for the invitation!"

Riyuro hugged Jircniv back. He had claws, so he took care not to injure the emperor with them, which Jircniv could tell from how gentle the motion was.

After embracing for a time, the two naturally separated in a mutual way.

"What are you talking about? You know my gate is always open to you, Riyuro!"

Riyuro grinned.

Since he was a subhuman, his grin looked downright ferocious, but Jircniv understood he was smiling. Their relationship was that close.

Jircniv found it somewhat funny.

From the time he was born, he had been raised as a candidate for emperor, and his peers had only viewed him as the crown prince. Thus, he was never able to build any meaningful relationships. Still, to think his first friend would be a subhuman…

Heh-heh. Me of ten or fifteen years ago would never believe it… This is one thing I really do owe to that undead.

They had met in the waiting room when he had gone to visit the King of Darkness.

At the time, he had only wondered where the subhuman was from and how far the King of Darkness's rule had expanded.

After that, they met once more, so they talked, each angling to draw information out of the other—only to unexpectedly hit it off. One minute together felt as rich as a month's worth of time spent with anyone else, and thus this best of friendships was formed.

They didn't bother with stiff terms and titles, but not because they were both rulers.

No, they had something else in common.

The two of them suffered under the same abuser; they were both victims.

"Come, your jaw will hit the floor at the sight of the sumptuous feast we have prepared. Today we can take a load off and appreciate each other's struggles."

"Yes, I look forward to it, Jircniv. And I brought you a bunch of those mushrooms you liked. Please eat them later."

"Oh! You shouldn't have, Riyuro!"

The mushrooms Riyuro prepared as a gift were an incredibly fragrant, precious variety known as black jewels.

They left the room shoulder to shoulder.

Jircniv had been anxious when he heard that in the Nation of Darkness, subhumans were treated the same as humans.

But with a glance at Riyuro next to him, only one thought came to mind.

There's nothing wrong with subhumans.

Not compared to undead, not compared to the King of Darkness.

"By the way, did you hear the news, Riyuro? Apparently, the King of Darkness has passed away."

Riyuro exhaled hard through his nose. That was a laugh.

"Jircniv, that can't be true. Th-the king wouldn't simply *die*."

"Yeah. I agree. But…I wonder which country's people he's torturing this time."

"Hmm…"

Riyuro stared into space like Jircniv.

Their eyes contained sorrow—as the pair grieved the tragedy that was no doubt occurring in some far-off place. And they felt pity for those who would surely become their new friends.

•

"Ahhhhhhhhhhhhhhh!"

The scream that abruptly filled the room caused the man to freeze. He was a member of the underground organization known as the Eight Fingers, and he had seen a lot of shocking things. But he had never witnessed such an explosion of deep, dark emotions as this. This was true hatred, a genuine curse.

He wouldn't have been so surprised if it had come from an

enemy. He surely would have even been able to crack a smile if that had been the case. But the voice came from his friend with whom he had shared identical pain and strife.

Until now, even members of the same organization would have held one another back, struggled for power, and exploited one another's weaknesses on the daily. If two people's interests clashed, there would have been blood on the ground.

But now things were different.

If one person was gone, everyone else had to work harder, and the chances that they failed increased. When that happened, they were held jointly responsible and dragged off to an unspeakable hell. Being reprimanded once had given them nightmares and made it impossible to keep solid food down. Who knew what the next hell might contain.

The thought alone was enough to make them all pitch in if someone fell behind in their work and to be considerate of one another's physical and mental health—out of desperation.

They were all in the same boat, a community with a common destiny—true friends.

And it was one of those friends who was howling and rolling around on the cold marble floor. The fear that if he didn't learn the cause he would soon end up the same spurred the man into action.

"Wh-what is it, Hilma? What happened?"

The screaming woman stopped her flailing, and her motion was almost an oozing as she looked up at him. "I can't! Trade spots with me! My stomach hurts! I can't watch this idiot anymore! What is wrong with him?! Even if he isn't stupid, he must be completely devoid of intelligence!"

There was only one man among them who got called an idiot. Before, the word *idiot* had been used in various ways, but this guy was a *true* idiot, making it impossible to throw the term around lightly any longer.

"...What happened? The idiot's up to his usual stupidity?"

It was as if Hilma was spewing out all her pent-up anger as she began to talk a blue streak.

"Yes, exactly! You heard about how His Majesty the King of Darkness died, right?"

He would have liked to ask her to slow down a bit, but half the point of listening was to relieve her stress, so he decided to bear with her. "Yeah, of course."

The Eight Fingers had spread the news. Which meant, of course, that they spread it throughout the Re-Estize Kingdom via merchants they had no direct connections with.

"And what do you suppose he said when he heard that?!"

This guy was an idiot. That had to be kept in mind when replying. But he could only think of normal things. Realizing it would be impossible to know what a true idiot would say, he gave up and offered something commonplace.

"...Something about a funeral?"

"If that were all, my stomach wouldn't be killing me like this!

He's saying that if he marries Lady Albedo, maybe he'll be able to gain control of the Nation of Darkness!"

"Eeegh!" Emitting a hoarse yelp in spite of himself, the man hastily scanned the area.

He couldn't sense them, but he was sure there were observers from the Nation of Darkness present. Confirming that they weren't coming for him, he breathed a sigh of relief.

They had been ordered to find an idiot, but he was not about to be thrown into that hell for turning in someone too idiotic.

"Hey, hey, hey! We were ordered to get an idiot, but maybe we should do away with that guy and find one who's a little more normal!"

"Is there anyone else we can get?"

The man's answer made Hilma scream and flail again. "Aaaaaaah!" The hem of her dress flew up, exposing her thighs.

The man pitied the woman for being reduced to this shameful state, utterly devoid of any charm or appeal, despite her past renown as a beautiful, high-class prostitute—because he knew that if it were him in her place, he would surely be screaming and rolling around on the floor, too.

"Hilma, please hang in there a little longer."

She froze again and cast an envious glare at him. "You could manipulate the guy...or rather, warn him not to do anything stupid."

"But shouldn't that idiot be easy to handle given how you're a woman?"

His question had Hilma rolling around, screaming "Aaaaaaaaaah!" again. That was her answer.

"It won't be that long. Two or three more years and we'll be able to make our move. Make him an even bigger idiot by then. I'll help you build the idiot faction."

"Two years is way too looooooong!"

"But those are our orders. Control the intel so that no matter what they do, it doesn't matter, and create a faction that acts in an increasingly stupid manner."

"I know that, but c'mooooooon!"

Hilma froze and sat up. "You're so lucky. All you did was use traders to tell the second prince that the King of Darkness—His Majesty, yes, His Majesty, is dead!"

You say that like it's nothing, he thought.

He had never thought of that prince as clever. But recently it hit him that he had been putting on an act because of his elder brother.

Since the recipient was no slouch, he had to take careful pains before handing over any information. It couldn't come out that they were working for the King of Darkness.

"…My job isn't a walk in the park, either, you know."

"…Yeah, sorry. I know you have it rough, too… How's tonight look?" Hilma mimed drinking.

"Not bad. Let's do it somewhere no intel will leak even if we get trashed."

They couldn't handle solids, but drinks were a different story.

"Ha-ha." A wan smile appeared on Hilma's face. "We'll be fine. Our supervisor will handle it."

"Ha-ha." He matched her laugh. "I suppose...you're right..."

"I do wonder where the lucky fellow is..."

There was only one lucky fellow among them.

"Coccodor? He lost all his authority during that mess. He must still be locked up...lucky bastard."

"Uh-huh...seriously..."

Chapter 6   **Gunner and Archer**

Chapter 6 | Gunner and Archer

1

Neia left Caspond's room and headed straight for the archery range. The unit members who had been waiting for her return promptly gathered around.

Surrounded by her comrades asking questions like, "Miss Baraja, how did the meeting turn out?" and saying, "We're ready to go anytime," she told them about the meeting.

She told them everything: what had happened, what they had spoken about, and what conclusion they reached.

Many of them made their livings as hunters, so they had advanced survival capabilities. But though frustrated, even they had to agree with Caspond's decision. Apparently, it really would be a challenge to mount a search and rescue operation in the hills.

If that was the case, then sending a rescue party right away would be impossible. But they would at least search the Sacred Kingdom's territory in the east, up to the fortress line. They didn't know where the king had landed; it was possible he was inside their borders.

A few with ranger skills came forward.

Neia wanted to participate, but she had next to no ranger skills. If she went along, she would only be a burden.

Not being able to assist in the rescue of the just king, who had offered aid to a foreign country, made Neia, as his attendant, feel so disloyal that it was as if her heart were being gouged out.

She wanted to scream like Remedios had that one time. But even if she did, it would change nothing.

She told everyone that she had gotten permission to search their country's territory, but she wouldn't be accompanying them.

"You can count on us, Miss Baraja."

"Yeah, we owe His Majesty a huge debt, so we'll keep our eyes peeled and be sure not to miss a thing."

"Thank you, everyone. Once we get the okay from Master Caspond, I'll be entrusting everything to you." Neia bobbed her head.

"So, Miss Baraja, what should the rest of us do? How can we be of use to His Majesty?"

Seeing their passionate gazes, Neia felt happy.

Even after witnessing what they had, not a single one of them believed the King of Darkness was dead.

That's right! There's no way His Majesty would die! He must be waiting for us to rescue him…right?

She couldn't imagine such an absolute power waiting for their rescue. It seemed more likely that when they found him, he would be sipping a glass of wine in front of a giant heap of subhuman and demon corpses.

"Okay! Then, the rest of you, let's get training! Weakness is wickedness, you know!"

Yes. That was all Neia was capable of at the moment. She had to get stronger so that she would be able to help more next time. If they had been strong to begin with, the embodiment of justice never would have been put in such a situation.

"Yeah!" came the spirited cheer in reply. They all understood Neia's words: *His Majesty the King of Darkness is justice, and weakness is wickedness.* More than a few had been on board from the beginning, but others had grown to understand as they heard it repeated over and over.

"All right, then I'm going to go meet with Master Caspond!"

*   *   *

When she went to discuss directly with Caspond, she immediately received permission to dispatch a search party. The group left that day, and it had been three days since then.

She had been worried that if people with differing opinions were in charge of selecting the search party members, it would be a big mess. But luckily, she was allowed to select the members, and they were able to make a speedy departure.

As for those three days, despite the rumor of retaking Karinsha going around, the liberation army wasn't moving, and—though Neia's unit continued their diligent training, and the number of people who accepted the King of Darkness as justice was growing—time passed meaninglessly.

Neia scowled in irritation as she loosed an arrow into her target.

Perhaps her impatience and anger had caused her hand to slip. The arrow struck slightly off-center.

Usually, someone would crack a joke, but now no one dared comment.

It was because of her face.

Her vexation at not being able to do anything for the King of Darkness, combined with the lack of information coming in, kept her from sleeping, so huge dark circles had formed under her drooping eyelids; that plus the creases in her brow made her face a sorry sight. She was always hiding her expression with her Mirror Shade, so it was quite a shock to see her whenever she took it off.

Neia's subordinates understood plenty well what she was thinking. But they still couldn't approach her.

—ty the King of Darkness, His Majesty the King of Darkness, His Majesty the King of Darkness, His Majesty the King of Darkness, His Majesty the King of Darkness, His Majesty the King of Darkness, His Majesty the King of Darkness, His Majesty the King of Darkness, His Majesty the King of Darkness, His Majesty the King of Darkness, His Majesty the King of Darkness, His Majesty the King of Darkness, His Majesty the King of Darkness, His Majesty the King of Darkness, His Majesty the King of Darkness, His Majesty the King of Darkness, His Majesty the King of Darkness, His Majesty the King of Darkness, His Majesty the King of Darkness, His Majesty the King of Darkness, His

Majesty the King of Darkness, His Majesty the King of Darkness, His Majesty the King of Darkness, His Ma—

The words swirled around and around in Neia's head.

"Agh, I just—"

She knew the shoulders of the people drawing their bows nearby flinched whenever she grumbled.

—Darkness. This is no good. I have to calm down. Calm down. It's only been three days! Even just the Sacred Kingdom's territory east of here is huge! You don't want to frighten everyone, do you?

Neia removed her Mirror Shade—she heard someone who happened to be looking her way emit a tiny shriek—and massaged her temples, trying to loosen up her rigid face.

Just then, she picked up the sound of two sets of feet rushing across the training range toward her. From the jangle of mail shirts, she gathered it wasn't militiamen who had come to practice. Paladins wore plate armor, so it wasn't them, either. It was probably either high-ranking servicemen or their adjutants.

"Squire Neia Baraja!"

When she looked in the direction of the interruption, the two men backpedaled and screamed.

"Wh-what?! Do you need something?!"

You're the ones who came to talk to me, thought Neia as she replied. "Ah, haven't seen you guys in a while. Thanks for the usual reacti— Or I guess it was a bit more dramatic than usual?"

They were two squires Neia had studied with. That said, she had never really talked with them, so she didn't know what their personalities were like. Still, she remembered their names and faces.

If she knew them, that meant they knew her. They should have been used to her serial killer eyes. So was her face really that horrifying right now?

Oh, right, she recalled. They had been liberated from one of the prison camps.

"O-oh. You're not usually so— Your eyes don't always make you seem to hate the whole world...quite so much. Or maybe they do?"

Neia rubbed her face. Maybe it was better not to take the Mirror Shade off.

"……Uhhh, sorry. So could you tell me why you're here?"

"Oh, er, Master Caspond is summoning you. He wants you to come right away."

"Master Caspond?"

She had some ideas why he might summon her, but she couldn't think of any reason that made sense. She hoped it was good news.

"Got it. Please tell him I'm on my way."

Even after she replied, they didn't seem to be going anywhere. Neia found that puzzling.

"What? Is there something else?"

"No, just— Not your expression but something about you overall—the vibes you give off have changed a bit. I can't really describe it, but…"

"If you mean that in a good way, I'm glad, but…people change. We've all been through so much."

"Yeah, hmm. You're right. That makes sense, Baraja."

The two smiled weakly and must have been satisfied, because they said, "Let's talk more later," and left.

Neia addressed the subordinates looking her way and told them she was going to see Caspond, then left immediately.

The house Caspond was living in was the same, but she was shown into a different chamber because of the huge hole Jaldabaoth had opened in the wall of the room he had been using up until last time.

Even with her Mirror Shade on, she could pass freely through to his chamber.

Was the reason she didn't have to check her bow with a guard because they trusted her? Or was it because the item had been borrowed from the King of Darkness?

"Squire Neia Baraja reporting in, Master Caspond."

In the room were Caspond, seated, and two standing paladins: Remedios and Gustav. Neia immediately took a knee.

"Thank you for coming. We were waiting for you. Oh, don't worry about kneeling on ceremony. Stand up."

Rising as instructed, Neia replied, "My apologies for keeping you waiting. What may I do for you?"

"First, Squire Neia Baraja, remove that item covering your face."

Gustav said something utterly obvious. From a commonsense standpoint, he was entirely correct.

"Yes, sir! Please excuse the oversight!"

When Neia removed the Mirror Shade, Gustav's eyes bulged slightly.

"…Oh, are you not feeling well? Maybe you should have a priest take a look?"

"No, I'm doing all right." It would have been a pain to explain, so she moved the conversation along. "So could you tell me what this is about?"

"About that… There's one more person I want to join our discussion. I'm going to invite them in now, so please don't be alarmed."

Out of the corner of her eye, Neia saw Remedios make a sour face. If her commander was grumpy about the person, they probably had something to do with Jaldabaoth. The words *demon maids* came to mind again.

Gustav opened the door to the next room as instructed by Caspond and called inside.

The one who came out was a grotesque. Neia knew what race, too.

A zerun.

It was a race with glistening skin, but contrary to what one might expect given their appearance, there was no foul smell—only a bloody scent so faint as to go practically unnoticed.

What's a subhuman doing here? Perhaps sensing Neia's question, Caspond spoke.

"We've received a messenger."

Does that mean this is a messenger from Jaldabaoth? The zerun braced themself as Neia unconsciously projected hostility.

"Wait, Squire Neia. You seem to be misunderstanding. This isn't Jaldabaoth's messenger. Just the opposite. This zerun is one of the ones trying to rise up against him."

"Huh?"

Neia's murmur seemed to be just what Caspond was waiting for, and he grinned. "You seem surprised. Well of course you are. You probably didn't imagine anyone was rebelling against the ruler of the subhumans, did you? But there is resistance. According to what the messenger has told us, not all the subhumans are faithful followers of Jaldabaoth. There are other races like the zerun, whose ruling class—equivalent to our royal family—was taken hostage, so they're forced to obey. And they want us to rescue those hostages, right?"

"That's right."

Neia was surprised to hear a new woman's voice and glanced around the room. Her gaze landed, as unlikely as it seemed to be, on the zerun. She wouldn't have been surprised to be told it was the voice of a human.

From where in this repulsive body did a human voice come from?

Was it one of the zerun's racial abilities? Or was it a magical power?

"Our cherished leader is being held captive in the city five days southwest from here that you humans call Karinsha. We're requesting a rescue operation."

Neia pictured the map of the Sacred Kingdom in her mind.

It seemed that the zerun was indeed speaking of Karinsha. She wondered if it wasn't more southwest by west or if it would really take five days to get there, but that all felt within the margin of error.

But there was one thing she didn't understand: *Why are they coming to me with this topic?*

Before she could think more about it, Caspond said something that startled her. "So, Miss Baraja. We've decided to join forces to resist Jaldabaoth."

Huh? Neia doubted her ears. *Can we really trust this monsterlike race? We can't even tell what expressions they're making!*

"We bowed before Jaldabaoth's immense power and invaded this land as one wing of his grand army, but we received word that our king, who was left behind in the hills as a hostage, has been killed by demons. So if you will save the other symbol of our subordination, our imprisoned prince—well, he's already the king now that our previous king has been killed—we'll cooperate with you."

Had they killed him because they decided they didn't need two hostages? Or was there a more demonic reason? Neia wasn't sure, but the important thing was surely that their king had been killed.

"That said, we intend to have the new king flee to somewhere Jaldabaoth won't be able to reach him, so his elite guards won't be able to participate. But the other three thousand soldiers brought here by Jaldabaoth will probably fight on your side. With at least the king and one female, our race can survive, so you can grind the army into nothing if necessary."

"So that's the deal. You know the conditions I believe in for victory against Jaldabaoth, but turning subhumans against him will result in fewer losses than reducing their numbers in battle. Additionally, they've volunteered some valuable intelligence, which we've just finished verifying and following up on." Caspond grinned as he continued. "We've confirmed that this leak isn't a trap from Jaldabaoth's side, so it becomes something to hold over the zerun. If Jaldabaoth finds out, they'll be purged, and their prince—their new king—might even be killed." Caspond threateningly suggested what might happen if the zerun betrayed them.

Maybe it was a normal precaution for a leader to take, but Neia was a bit frightened to see Caspond calmly exhibiting such heartlessness.

But as she regained her composure, a question bubbled up. *Why is he giving me all this background?*

If he wanted her to carry out the rescue, he could simply order her to do it. Sure, she led the archer unit, but at the end of the day, she was merely a squire who was handy with a bow. She didn't need to know all the details about the operation. Yet, here they were…

…Oh, is he still treating me as His Majesty's attendant? Since I have one foot in the Nation of Darkness?

Maybe the idea was to be able to say that he had intended to have her listen along with the King of Darkness. Or maybe he wanted her to explain the situation to him the next time she saw him.

Yes. Neia was still the king's attendant.

When Neia stood up straighter, she noticed Caspond look puzzled at the change in her.

"Any...how. We've decided that it would be nearly impossible to get the prince out during the chaos of our raid on Karinsha."

"That's right," said the zerun, taking over from Caspond. "First, let us explain where the prince is being held. Deputy Commander, please fill in details as necessary."

The zerun explained their reasoning with some extra commentary about Karinsha Castle from Gustav.

First, the major city of Karinsha was a city governed directly by the royal family and located in an area covered with low hills, surrounded by a thick defensive wall. Its large castle stood on the highest spot, in the west.

Since it was situated in such a way as to block a subhuman invasion that had broken through the country's fortress wall, and the trade junction with a route to the south was also nearby, it was the most fortified city in the entire Sacred Kingdom.

And Karinsha Castle—which was almost never used and only built for siege battles—was just as tough.

The problem was the prince was being held in one of the spires of that castle. It was the spire farthest back, meant to be the site of final resistance, and was thus the most impenetrable place in the entire Sacred Kingdom.

In order to avoid invasions by flight, the spire had no windows; it was only accessible via an aerial walkway that stretched out from the main castle.

The spire currently had a powerful guard—of a race thought to be a close relative to ogres, the va-um, who could use water powers—and zerun weren't allowed to go anywhere near it, so there was no telling what would happen to the prince if they did.

But if the betrayal happened in a way that kept the true actors secret, if they saw a human with no connection to the zerun, there was no way they would hurt the prince; on the contrary, might they not protect him? That was the zerun way of thinking on the matter and the reason they wanted help from the humans.

"Naturally, if a major battle began while the prince was still imprisoned, we would have to fight you to the death, just like all the others who were brought to these lands for that purpose. And then..."

The zerun faded out, but Neia knew the rest without it being said.

It would be too late.

It was only because the zerun had the humans as an enemy that flipping sides and saving the prince had value. If the zerun were wiped out, there would no longer be any reason to save the prince.

"Once fighting breaks out, it will be too late to send a rescue party. So sending in an elite group to work in secret now would be the safest way to save the prince and have the highest chance of success. Squire Neia Baraja, I want you to lead the operation."

"I can't. There's no way." Her response to Caspond's order was instantaneous.

Objecting to her commander's order was both against military regulation and generally unacceptable socially, but the appeal was to common sense because the order went against it in the first place. It was too great a challenge.

"I thought you might say that. But, Miss Baraja, this is a very good deal for you." Caspond smiled. "They'll tell us everything they know about the hills and introduce us to a reliable guide."

Neia's breath caught slightly.

She wanted to bite her lip, but she restrained herself, choosing to keep her emotions hidden.

"…How far can we trust what they say?"

"If we save the prince, the zerun will coordinate with our attack and revolt internally. That should make it much easier to take back Karinsha. We should be able to capture many more prisoners than we would in an ordinary siege. The zerun have also said they'll tell us which of the prisoners have information that you're looking for."

"We don't know the details," the zerun chimed in, "but we heard you want to go to the Abellion Hills. If you save the prince, our entire race will be indebted to you. We wouldn't hesitate to share our knowledge with such a person. It's not as if it's particular, special knowledge that we need to keep secret."

It was an argument that made complete and utter sense.

Refusing this would be disloyal to His Majesty. I can't just hang around twiddling my thumbs because I don't want to die when I have a chance to be of use to the king.

Thinking more calmly, Neia felt like this was the best chance she would get. Still, she didn't feel like committing suicide.

"Who would join me on the team to rescue the prince?"

Neia glanced at Remedios, who had remained silent the whole time.

"I'm not going. Stealth isn't my forte."

That goes for me, too, though, thought Neia, but she said nothing and turned to Caspond.

"…I've been telling her she has to go with you, but she won't have it. So we're sending you with a prisoner…no, a cooperator."

"Hmph. You can just call her a prisoner."

"…Commander."

"It's fine, Deputy Commander Montagnés. Will you bring her in?"

Gustav left with a "yes, sir." The zerun messenger left at the same time. Neia figured they wanted the identity of their cooperator to be on a need-to-know basis only.

Gustav returned right away, but he wasn't alone. He was leading a girl in chains whom Neia had never seen before. She was smaller and more delicate, and judging by her face, she seemed younger than Neia, too.

She wore a scarf with a complex, distinctive pattern of dark green and ocher paired with an unusual maid uniform. Looks-wise she had the complete package; even with one eye covered, her beauty was unmistakable.

Recalling what Evileye of the Blue Roses had said, Neia could make a confident guess as to who this was, but she asked just to make sure.

"Master Caspond, who is this?"

"…Haven't you guessed? She's one of Jaldabaoth's maids who appeared in the city."

Neia froze. Even though she had imagined that to be the case, it was a surprise. Difficulty level 150. In other words, a monster among monsters. A being a human couldn't hope to defeat was standing before her eyes.

But there was still something else surprising her—that she could still harbor such intense hatred in the face of an unbeatable enemy.

They were creatures on completely different levels, so if Neia could feel that way, was it because the maid wasn't scattering fear? Or did it stem from her devotion to the King of Darkness?

Regardless, Neia banished the hatred to the depths of her heart so it wouldn't be visible.

If she wasn't careful, she would openly curse this maid for being one of the reasons the King of Darkness had been defeated by Jaldabaoth. But neither Gustav nor Caspond seemed to be worried about Remedios putting her hand to her Holy Sword.

They must have decided there was no immediate danger. Otherwise, they would never let her appear somewhere with the Holy Lady's brother.

"……I'm a killer. You don't need to be afraid. I'm loyal to Lord Ainz now, not Jaldabaoth. I won't attack you."

"I can't believe that," Neia spat, irritated at the way she called him "Lord Ainz." But the maid replied in a steady tone.

"……You don't have to believe me. I merely stated the truth."

"Miss Baraja, it appears that during that battle, His Majesty the King of Darkness somehow managed to steal control of her from Jaldabaoth."

Neia's eyes widened slightly.

So even though he was surrounded and outnumbered, he was fighting with the goal of flipping the maids, not killing them?

Neia didn't know much about magic, so she wasn't sure how much of a challenge that would be. Would it be similar to stealing a powerful opponent's equipment mid-duel? If so, it was a feat only the King of Darkness was capable of.

Neia fiercely admired him.

But two questions came to mind.

She had no problem believing that the King of Darkness was capable of such a thing, but was this maid really under his control? Could she simply be pretending to side with the king on orders from Jaldabaoth?

And the other question was…

"…I understand that you'll be faithful to the King of Darkness. But why are you here? Because you're in chains?"

"……No."

The maid flexed, and the thick chains began to make awful creaking noises.

"Don't!" Remedios boomed murderously, and the noise stopped.

"……Even I can break normal, unenchanted chains."

"Then why? Why don't you leave here and join the King of Darkness?"

Neia wondered if maybe the maid had some sort of demonic intuition or an ability as a demon under the king's control that would allow her to find him. When she asked in a roundabout way, the maid gave her a matter-of-fact reply.

"……Because I have orders. The last order he gave me was to cooperate with you. So I'll do everything I can without dying."

"What?!"

Neia was shocked.

…His Majesty came here in order to take control of the demon maids, to gain their powers and strengthen the Nation of Darkness. So he should have ordered her to go to the Nation of Darkness. Yet, he… How kind of him… Could there possibly be another king so generous and compassionate toward people from another country? No, it's impossible. The King of Darkness is special. He truly is justice! Amazing! Nothing I've been thinking is wrong!

Neia felt like something hot was starting to pool in her eyes, but she pushed through the feeling.

"…Uh, without dying?"

"……I'm not going to fight Jaldabaoth. If you face him, it will be difficult to escape."

Ah. Neia understood. Caspond must have looked into the truth of her story. He wouldn't have brought her here otherwise.

"So you want me to take this demon with me."

"That's right. The other option would be to send her to the Nation of Darkness as a messenger, but instead, uh, after the other thing, once we get some help and acquire some information, uh, we'll send a rescue party over there, and it would be better to have her be part of that—because it's a dangerous mission… Since the people you sent out to search our lands haven't found anything, he must have fallen on the other side."

For some reason, Caspond was being awfully vague.

Neia glanced over and saw that the maid's expression wasn't so much as twitching. She didn't even seem worried.

Of course, it was possible this maid didn't know what had happened to the King of Darkness; maybe she hadn't imagined that he could be in danger. But her expressionless face offended Neia.

And was she even allowed to be so casual with him—"Lord Ainz"?

No, there's no way she has permission to do that! decided Neia. *Even I'm not that friendly with him!*

"—Miss Baraja?"

"Er, yes?"

Crap. She blushed slightly. She had gotten too absorbed in her annoyance at the maid.

"What is it? Is something bothering you?"

"Oh, it's nothing! Only three days have passed since the search set out. I think it might be a little soon to conclude that he didn't fall in our territory…"

"I see. That's true. But we should probably be prepared just in case."

"Yes, of course."

"Good. Then Miss Demon Maid. This is our third time speaking. We talked the day we found you, yesterday, and today, right?"

The maid said nothing and just stared at Caspond.

"If I told you I wanted you to infiltrate a major city and rescue a prisoner being held there, would you agree to cooperate?"

"……As I said yesterday, I will cooperate."

"Oh, I see. Got it. Then sorry, but would you mind going back into the other room? Deputy Commander Montagnés, please see her out."

After taking the maid out, Gustav returned alone, and the conversation started back up.

"Miss Baraja, I don't know if it's necessary to tell you this much or not, but if we send you into Karinsha, it's possible the success of the operation will depend on what you know or don't. For that purpose, let me explain a few things. First, about Jaldabaoth."

Caspond relayed what they had heard from the demon maid.

There hadn't been much about Jaldabaoth. Or more like, next to nothing. She didn't even know what sort of abilities he had or what attacks he was vulnerable to. She didn't know what he was currently doing or what his aims were, either.

The only thing she said was that if he was seriously injured, it would take a while for him to recover. Apparently, it was similar to how the bigger a vessel was, the longer it would take to refill if drained of its contents.

After being told things about Jaldabaoth, the subhumans, and other demons in this way, Neia's first question to Caspond was, "How far can we trust her?"

"We can't. Killing her would be safer." That was Remedios.

Neia wanted to ask, *Can you defeat a difficulty level–150 demon?* But she held it back and waited for Caspond's response.

"It's tricky. It could be part of Jaldabaoth's plot. She might be a spy on the lookout for Momon or someone else who could resist against him."

That was why he had the zerun leave before bringing the maid in and also the reason he was putting things in such vague terms.

"I told you. We should kill her. Then we don't have to worry about any of that."

"I see, Commander Custodio. That would be one way of doing things. But there's a good chance it's true that she's under the King of Darkness's control. She's not just spewing lies about Jaldabaoth but instead telling us she doesn't know. However, the fact that she hasn't heard anything about the King of Darkness is… Hmm. And you made a pact with the King of Darkness that we would turn over the demon maids, right? So if we killed her, we would be known as a country that doesn't follow through on its promises. If that happens, there might not be any countries who would help us if we need it."

"But Jaldabaoth killed that guy."

At Remedios's remark, Neia lowered her gaze and focused on containing her rage. Thanks to this woman, she actually felt like she had gotten better at controlling her emotions.

"We haven't confirmed that. That's why I'd like to test her by using her in the rescue of the prince. If she betrays us by leaking intelligence, all that will happen is the zerun will be purged, which means fewer subhumans to deal with. And we can get rid of the rat trying to smuggle itself in here, so there are two benefits. Or if it works out instead, we can just be happy."

I hope you don't forget the life of the person you're sending on this stealth mission…, grumbled Neia in her head.

"You don't know what the maid's weakness is? If I'm supposed to travel with her, it'd be nice to have a way to handle her if she betrays me."

"No, I couldn't very well ask that."

He smiled awkwardly, and Neia wore the same expression.

Even if she answered, how could they verify it? They wouldn't be able to tell by looking, and it would be impossible to test.

"Well, it's not as if we have control of her. She's just cooperating with us because the King of Darkness ordered her to." Gustav stated the obvious; both Caspond and Neia were aware of that. There was only one who didn't get it.

"So the infiltration team will be the maid and me. Who else?"

"About that. If you have no one else to recommend, I'd like it to be just the two of you."

For a moment, she was sure he was joking, but when she looked at him, his expression was serious.

"To add to what Master Caspond has said, it's better for an infiltration mission to have fewer people, right? You can't have anyone getting in your way. So we don't recommend anyone else."

Gustav offered a sensible reason, but Neia knew it wasn't the only one.

That was simply the position Neia Baraja was in.

If the rescue operation went well, it would be great for everyone. If it failed, it would just mean the deaths of a troublesome squire who was close to the King of Darkness and the King of Darkness's subordinate. And if the maid betrayed them, they would sacrifice next to nothing. It could be called a perfect plan.

So then was the story about telling Remedios to go with her a lie? Or was it possible they really did just decide that this way would risk fewer losses?

Neia exhaled with a "phew." Either way, there was only one thing to do. This was a good chance to demonstrate her loyalty to the King of Darkness.

"Understood. She"—*That's a she, right?* she thought—"and I will go on our own."

"Ohhh, fantastic. We're counting on you."

"Yes, sir."

"We're having Deputy Commander Montagnés draw up a plan of the castle. It should be ready by the time you depart. And if one of Jaldabaoth's aides is there, avoid combat."

According to what they'd heard from the maid and the zerun, Jaldabaoth was served by three great demon aides.

One ruled the Abellion Hills where the subhumans lived.

One commanded the army invading the southern Sacred Kingdom.

And one managed three major cities, moving among Karinsha, Limun, and Prato.

That was the story anyhow.

So if they were unlucky, they might run into the one managing the cities.

Apparently, this manager demon was headless and had a body like a dead tree. No wings or tail and a height of around six and a half feet. It had claws, and its slim body was far stronger than it looked. Despite not having a head, it was fully aware of its surroundings and could even read.

Well, expect the demonic when you're dealing with demons.

Incidentally, the capital, Jobans, was under Jaldabaoth's direct control, which is why there was no aide managing it.

"Who is stronger, the maid or that aide?"

"She told us she isn't sure."

Neia wanted that maid to show her what she could do. Not knowing what sort of weapons she specialized in or what kind of special abilities she had could result in unexpected failures.

"The three great demons are all generals and landlords. But perhaps because they don't consider subhumans capable of using their heads, they are building dictatorships. That means the great demons do much of the administration themselves without appointing successors or deputies. By defeating them, we could ruin the better part of the subhuman alliance army's coordination and supply chain."

"Which would satisfy your conditions for victory, Master Caspond."

"Yes. Well, if Jaldabaoth's wounds heal, he may step in and take command…but I doubt he would push his luck by showing up now. If we rip off his arms and legs, we may not even need to crush the head to win. That said, our priority right now is the rescue."

"Understood."

"So…when will we initiate the rescue mission?"

"I'd like to set off as soon as we're ready, but may I first please talk to the demon maid some more?"

"Very well. Then how about you leave in two days?"

Neia agreed and left the room after getting permission to speak to the maid again.

The responsibility weighed heavy on her shoulders, but her steps were firm and her expression brimmed with determination. The wild flame that seemed to have lost its purpose of late gained new direction and provided a faint light illuminating her path forward.

There was something for her to do, and what lay ahead was that Supreme Being. With that in mind, what did it matter if she had to travel with a dangerous demon?

•

The demon maid was in a mansion with a garden—well, it wasn't really big enough to call a mansion, but neither was it small. It seemed like one of the wealthier residents of the city must have lived there at one time. Some of the lavish ornamentation it had before the tyrannical occupation by the subhumans was broken, and what must have been a statue had been smashed. Still, the bones of the house had remained intact, and it didn't seem likely to let in the cold winter air.

But it might as well have been a poorly built shack. Every last window had been boarded up as if someone was so paranoid, they didn't want to let even a tiny bit of air in—or out.

In essence, it was a cage, or perhaps it would be better to call it an isolation cell. Accommodating this monster lackey of either an undead or a demon, who was also the subordinate of the hero king ostensibly visiting from his country to rescue the Sacred Kingdom, the place was an interweaving of various speculations: the sense of crisis, the urge to steer clear, and more.

It was unclear what exactly the purpose of wrapping her in chains was at that point, but perhaps it was difficult to show the demon maid proper hospitality when she hadn't received an official introduction from the King of Darkness.

The wall around the mansion had been repaired in a hurry, but the all-important portcullis was missing. It must have been requisitioned during an iron shortage.

Meant perhaps as a replacement, there was a hastily built hovel of a guardhouse out front. Sturdy men equipped with armor occupied it, as well as one paladin who was there as a commanding officer. Neia handed him the parchment Caspond had prepared for her.

After looking it over, the paladin handed it back and gave her a candlestick; the candle was lit.

She was visiting during daylight hours, but since there was no way for the sun to reach inside through the boards and the demon maid didn't require light, the interior was pitch-dark.

Neia passed through the gate and crossed the overgrown garden. The brick path leading to the entrance was crumbling in places; when she reached the door, she took a deep breath.

She used the knocker. There was no answer. After hesitating a moment, she turned the knob. The door wasn't locked. Darkness peeked out from the narrow opening. She couldn't hear the slightest sound. It was as quiet as a mausoleum.

Neia braced herself and went inside. There were no lights and no

servants. The only people in the house at this moment were Neia and a difficulty level–150 demon.

Cold sweat dripped down her back. The candle in her hand flickered
feebly. Beyond the glow of the flame existed the darkness as it had been,
ready to swallow everything up.

"It's Neia Baraja! I've come to visit! Where are you?" she called into the
dark, but there was no answer.

Was she sleeping?

She tried calling again, more loudly this time, but as expected, nothing.

Neia walked forward, determined.

This was a two-story house. It probably had a fair number of rooms,
but it wouldn't take very long to check them all. And maybe with her
keen sense of hearing, she would pick up a sound before that even became
necessary.

The search began with the first floor.

Just as she was about to proceed—

"—Boo!"

Someone shouted from right next to her, and a face appeared in the
light.

"Eeegh!"

Her shoulders jerked, and she instinctively recoiled from the face.

Bam—her back hit a wall.

She couldn't have overlooked it. If she didn't know better, she would've
sworn the face had come through the wall.

"……Nice reaction."

When Neia looked with her tear-filled eyes, it was the demon maid
who was looking back at Neia's panic with no expression.

"Stupid demon…," Neia grumbled resentfully without thinking.

It seemed her Crown of Psychic Defense wouldn't protect her from
surprise; her heart was beating an alarm bell and felt like it was about to
burst. Maybe that had been the demon's aim in the first place…?

Nah, that couldn't be, could it…?

"……So why are you here?"

"I wanted to talk to you. In two days, we'll be…" She didn't know how far she could trust this maid. Maybe it was dangerous to discuss the details of the plan. "…going on a mission together."

"……Okay."

"So I thought it would be good to exchange info and find out what each other can do."

"……It's important to exchange info. Understood."

Whether Neia would really share anything depended on how their talk went.

"……Then come this way."

The demon maid walked off at a brisk pace. It didn't seem to matter if there was light where she was going or not. So the paladin had been telling the truth.

Following after her, Neia observed the maid from behind.

Delicate limbs, regular features—she was a pretty little girl who would stimulate anyone's desire to protect.

But to Neia, who knew her true identity, it all seemed like a ruse.

Here, the maid wasn't bound by the chains she had been wrapped in when she visited Caspond's chamber. Well, the chains served no purpose in the first place. This demon only took the form of a little girl; she was actually a monster stronger than a dragon.

Thinking about how even being lightly patted might kill her gave Neia stomach pains.

"I'm squishy, so please be gentle with me…"

In reaction to that murmur, the demon maid stopped, turned only her head, and said, "I know." Even with her exceptional eyesight, Neia couldn't detect any change in the maid's expression. Not knowing what she was thinking made her a little anxious.

She was led into a sitting room.

The only light was a single candle.

"……Sit." Neia sat in the opposite chair as the maid's gesture indicated. "……A drink."

A bottle filled with a tea-colored liquid appeared. She had produced it in the same way the King of Darkness sometimes took things out of nowhere.

While she was still marveling, the maid took the lid off and put a straw inside. It was made out of a material that seemed somehow both hard and soft.

The liquid was syrupy, but Neia wanted to believe it wasn't poison. There would be serious issues if the demon suffered some lapse and forgot which drinks were harmful to humans.

But when she thought that this maid might actually be in the service of His Majesty, she couldn't refuse, so she made up her mind to take a sip.

Putting some in her mouth, she rolled it around on her tongue. There was no shocking bitterness, no sharp stimulation...

It's sweet?! What is this?

Neia had another sip and then another. It took a little doing to suck up the thick liquid, but it was freezing cold and delicious.

"......It's chocolate flavored. A bit high calorie...about two thousand. But don't worry about that. One of the great ones once said that growing fat on delicious food is every woman's true wish."

She was talking a bit differently, so Neia looked at her face, but her expression hadn't changed a bit.

"Great one" made Neia think of the king, but she seemed to be talking about someone else.

"......Would you like to have another?"

"May I?"

She had drunk it so fast, she was sad it was gone, and the maid must have noticed. She produced another one.

Neia was like many other women—despite the orcs' uncertainty—in that she didn't want to partake if it meant gaining weight, but the drink's container wasn't very big, so the portion wasn't very large. It only made sense that if you ate a lot you would get fat, so she figured she could cancel it out later with a light dinner.

I don't know what "high calorie" means or if two thousand is a lot, but she said "a bit" so it's probably fine.

This time she decided to savor the sweetness that was distinct from the taste of fruit or honey.

She took a sip…

"Oh! Wait. This is getting me all mixed up. I came here to talk."

"……Mm-hmm." With the straw in her mouth, sipping in the same way Neia was, the demon maid signaled with her eyes that she should continue.

"Um, first, if you have a name, could you tell me what it is? My name is Neia Baraja. Please call me whatever you like."

She had heard from Evileye of the Blue Roses that the maids all had different appearances and equipment. And in reality, the two maids who had appeared in Caspond's room had been completely different from this one. Maybe they were like goblins and hobgoblins in that different types of demon maids had different names.

There wasn't really any need to know her individual or group name, but if this was really a subordinate of the King of Darkness, then it was natural for Neia, as his attendant, to treat her with that much courtesy.

"……Pwahhh. You can call me Shizu. I'll call you Neia."

"Shizu?"

Neia had expected to be called "human," so she was somewhat surprised.

So this demon maid's name is Shizu? Or is that her type? Well, it doesn't really matter, but…

"Is that your individual name?"

"……Individual name? What a wild question. Yes. It's my name."

"Oh, I beg your pardon. I don't know much about demons…"

"……Nrgh. Demon…? That's…nrgh…"

Shizu was grumbling under her breath. Of course, with Neia's hearing, she could make out what was being said, but it sounded like Shizu was talking to herself, so she didn't press her on it.

"So, Shizu. What can you do? And it seems like there were a few demon maids, so why did His Majesty the King of Darkness choose you?"

"……I'm good at attacking from a distance. And I was the best."

"The best? Oh, I see. Because you were the hardest to handle during the fight?"

Shizu chuckled triumphantly, "Eh-heh." And it probably looked like her expression didn't change at all. But Neia, with her excellent eyesight, could tell.

It was an extremely small change, but the maid's face looked slightly proud.

At the same time, Neia was relieved. This maid hadn't been chosen because she was the weakest.

"I can use projectiles a bit. But I'm not as good at close-quarters combat... We don't have anyone to be our front line, huh?"

Shizu said nothing and just sipped her drink.

"Do you have any good ideas?"

"......What is the mission?"

"We need to sneak into a city and rescue a VIP." Neia refrained from saying the word *zerun*.

"......Then what we need are stealth abilities. It's better not to have a noisy vanguard."

"Yeah. Hmm. You're right."

"......Can you operate quietly, Neia?"

"I've trained a bit, so I think I've improved. But if you asked whether I feel perfectly confident, I'd be hard-pressed to say yes."

"......You don't have any spells like Invisibility? No enchanted items?"

Neia shook her head.

"......Oh. Then do your best."

"Yes. I will. So..."

Can I really trust her—and believe that she works for the King of Darkness?

If she was only feigning loyalty to the King of Darkness in order to spy for Jaldabaoth, it would be bad to tell her about His Majesty's situation. But Neia felt there was a good chance the King of Darkness really could have stolen the maid away from Jaldabaoth. In that case, if she didn't trust her, it would be like throwing away a secret weapon.

So she hesitantly began to explain.

"In our lands, I was the attendant to His Majesty."

Shizu's almost artificially beautiful face didn't move.

"……I've heard. About your nasty eyes. And that he lent you a bow. A rune bow. Let me see it."

Jaldabaoth was interested in it, too, Neia thought in a corner of her mind, but if this maid was serving the King of Darkness, she couldn't say no.

Neia handed over the bow, and Shizu examined it. After a quick look, she gave it right back.

"This is splendid. You should show it off to more people."

The maid spoke so calmly, Neia couldn't help but feel she was reading prepared lines. Or maybe it was only her imagination—because she didn't get the feeling the maid had been looking at the bow with real interest. Or maybe she talked like that because this was their first time meeting.

"Thank you… Oh, right. And when we're done with the mission…"

Shizu put a hand up to interrupt. "You should show it off to more people."

Why is she repeating that? Perhaps the question showed on her face, because Shizu continued.

"You should let everyone know that Lord Ainz is the kind of great being who can lend out a splendid rune bow like that."

Hearing "Ainz" made Neia flinch. This was something she had to address urgently. "His Majesty the King of Darkness."

From Shizu's lack of expression, she gathered that she hadn't explained well enough, so she continued.

"It's 'His Majesty the King of Darkness.' Isn't calling him 'Lord Ainz' a bit overly familiar?"

This time Shizu's face flinched. No, at a glance, she was expressionless. But Neia was sure she had seen some movement.

"It's not overly familiar at all."

"No, it is. Normally, you call someone like that by their exalted title, not their name. You've only just started working for him and haven't even been of any use yet… What's that look for?"

"Nothing. But I'm calling him Lord Ainz, not His Majesty the King of Darkness."

Was the faint emotion on her face pity? Or was she gloating? Neia wasn't sure, but it irritated her. It was incredibly offensive that this new-comer could appear out of nowhere and speak the name of the one she worshipped like they were close.

It was time to take the mask off. As the king's attendant and a repre-sentative of the Sacred Kingdom, she had intended to treat her with respect, but she was over it now. It didn't matter that this maid was a matchless terror. She had to be made to understand.

"Listen, you—"

"I was told to call Lord Ainz Ooal Gown 'Lord Ainz.'"

"Huh?"

"So I can call him Lord Ainz. *I'm* allowed to."

The shock of the implication—*but you aren't*—made Neia light-headed.

Then again, this was a demon magically controlled by the King of Darkness. Maybe this attitude was to be expected.

"N-no, that can't be. Y-you're lying. How natural for a demon to lie. He wouldn't have had time to specify little things like that…"

Shizu sighed and shook her head in an *oh, brother* way. "Unfortunately, for you, it's the truth. Well, I understand what a shock it must be. I really do. But that's simply your status right now. If you work hard for him, though, someday you'll be able to call him Lord Ainz, too. It requires devotion."

"—Shizu."

"……Neia. Those who come before are tasked with leading those who come after."

That was a grand statement to make for someone who had come after. Although if she was allowed to call him Lord Ainz, then maybe she was in the superior position here. There was still something that didn't sit right with Neia, but for the moment…

"For now, I'll go ahead and say thanks."

"……It's nothing. We should be compassionate toward anyone who comprehends Lord Ainz's greatness."

Neia's eyes bulged in surprise. How had he gained her respect so fully in such a short time? No, it didn't need further explanation. The King of Darkness was simply that amazing.

"Yeah. Of course I know how great His Majesty is."

After Neia answered, they stared at each other for a little while.

Shizu was the first to move.

She extended her right hand. Neia responded without hesitation.

It did bother her that Shizu kept her gloves on, but they shook hands across the table.

If she reveres His Majesty that much, she must be under his control. If she wasn't, she wouldn't call him Lord Ainz—that would be suspect. She would call him His Majesty the King of Darkness like me.

Was she being naive? Neia was firmly convinced that Shizu's allegiance was real. Something seemed to click into place; they were able to understand each other like two worshippers of the same god.

"……We get along surprisingly well. You have some admirable qualities for a human."

"I admit I have complex feelings about getting along with a demon. We only get along because what you're saying is correct. It's just because you think the King of Darkness is wonderful—that's all."

Shizu nodded, thinking over Neia's argument.

"……Before, I didn't care what would happen to you, but I'll get you back here safely. I promise."

"Thanks."

Her gratitude was genuine. Difficulty level 150. She would be protected by a demon even the Blue Roses were forced to admit they had little chance of defeating. That deserved a thank-you. Doubly so when said by a subordinate of the King of Darkness. But she wanted to confirm one thing.

"…Do you swear on His Majesty's name?"

Shizu raised a hand, like a student getting called on by a teacher.

"I swear on the name of the ever sacred Supreme One, Ainz Ooal Gown… But if you die and I revive you, that counts, right?"

"As safe…? Er, not quite…"

They exchanged looks.

Neia felt that dying and being resurrected were far from safe, but she stated the compromise she was willing to make. "Maybe if I'm revived as a human and not an undead or a demon…it can count…"

"……Then there's no issue…… Good."

Shizu had been speaking in a monotone this whole time, but her tone changed slightly. It was like she had added some emphasis.

"……You're not cute, but you can have this."

She took something out and came next to Neia. Then she stuck the thing to Neia's forehead.

"Huh?! What?! What is this thing?!"

Startled by the weirdness of the act, Neia tried to pull the thing off, but it was stuck. It was stuck fast. Neia was terrified.

"What the heck! Huh? Wait! This is so freaky!"

"……You're fine. It doesn't hurt, and it's not scary. Here."

Shizu showed her an item that had the number one and some other symbol—maybe a letter—written on it. It was extremely glossy paper, and the thing on her forehead felt slick to the touch as well. Neia had heard of talismans before, so was this a contact art using one of those? Whatever it was, surely she wouldn't give it to her for no reason, so was it enchanted? That's what gave Neia the creeps. *Is this going to be stuck to my head my whole life?*

"Why did you stick it to my forehead?! Couldn't you have put it somewhere else?"

"……Ngh, you're like my little sister."

"Huh?!" She felt like she had heard something unexpected, but there were higher-priority matters at hand. "More importantly, get it off! At least stick it somewhere else, like on my clothes!"

"……What a hassle."

Shizu took out a little bottle and dripped something on Neia's head. The thing peeled off so simply, it was as if it had never been firmly stuck in place. She looked at it and saw it was indeed the same thing Shizu had showed her.

"……It's a sticker. You're supposed to put it somewhere you can see it."

Apparently, she had to put it somewhere. Making Shizu mad wouldn't help Neia. Her only choice was to do as the maid said.

"Okay…"

"……Are we done talking?"

"Huh? Oh, no, I also…wanted to talk about, uh, searching for the King of Darkness—that is, going to get him…"

"……I'll go, too…… There is lots of prep to do, but once it's done…"

"Really?"

"……I promise. But I want you to take time to help finish the subhuman map of the hills."

"Right. Huh? Subhuman?"

For a moment after agreeing, she felt strange. She hadn't said anything yet. So why did the maid mention subhumans?

Maybe…she heard from Master Caspond that the king might have fallen in the hills?

"……What's wrong?"

"Um… Okay. I'll talk to my superiors."

"……Thanks, Neia."

"Thank *you*, Shizu."

The sticker was still on her mind, but she held out her hand, and Shizu took it. They shook again.

"You don't believe His Majesty is dead, either, right?"

Shizu's eyes went round. "……What are you talking about?"

"He fell in the east, and we haven't heard from him since then… Considering he still hasn't come back even though he can use teleportation magic, some kind of accident might have happened… So…maybe he's…"

It hurt too much to say the rest. She hesitated, because it felt like if she put it into words, it would be true.

Shizu responded with what was probably annoyance.

"……He's fine. He's not dead. The fact that I'm under his control is proof of that. Huh? ……What are you crying about?"

The tears fell on their own.

The King of Darkness was really alive.

She had believed that he wasn't dead. But there were nights she couldn't sleep when worry would consume her mind. All sorts of people had told her he was fine. But their comments all sounded like consolations only said to assuage everyone's fears, not something they actually believed.

Just now, however, Shizu's confident words, brimming with conviction, and her presence as proof of the King of Darkness's survival, gave Neia peace of mind.

As relieved as a lost child who had finally found her parent again, she couldn't stop crying.

Shizu pressed some cloth—the same fabric as her scarf, probably a handkerchief—against Neia's cheeks. Then she rubbed. It was more unpracticed than violent, but for the one getting her tears wiped away, it hurt nonetheless.

When the handkerchief moved, a string of mucus went with it, forming a bridge.

"……There's snot on it… That's quite a shock."

Hearing Shizu's clearly scandalized voice, Neia wasn't sure what expression to make.

So she dug in her pocket and broke the slimy bridge with her own handkerchief.

"I'll wash it."

"……Mm."

2

Getting into Karinsha Castle was simple.

All they had to do was hide in barrels and get transported in as cargo. Of course, there would be an inspection, but there were other barrels—eight in all—so one of those could be opened. The reason such lax security went unchecked stemmed from the fact that the subhuman alliance was such a diverse gathering of races.

It was a group of people with different common sense due to their varying cultures. If they had a common value, it was that combat strength was absolute. So if someone strong pushed for something, it would be granted even if it required bending the rules. For subhumans, strength was like a peerage based on violence. Lower-ranked beings had no choice but to submit.

In other words, if a strong zerun gave a hard stare, the inspection would be abbreviated to the greatest extent possible.

Eventually the barrels were placed on the floor with a *thunk*.

Then there was a knock on the top—*bam*.

That was the sign that they had reached the designated location. Neia followed their plan and counted out three minutes. During that time, through the barrel staves, she heard the zerun who had brought them there open the door and go somewhere.

After the three minutes were up, Neia pressed up on the inner lid. It slanted, and though the big slab of raw meat stuck to it didn't fall on her, smaller chunks rained down. This barrel had two bottoms: Neia was in the lower compartment, and the raw meat was above her.

The reason they had used raw meat instead of wheat or vegetables was to mask the body odors of Neia and Shizu in case of a subhuman guard with a keen sense of smell.

She was probably lucky that their preparations had been unnecessary. Except the part where she was covered in blood and other raw juices.

Slowly removing the barrel's lid, she looked outside.

Having scanned the room—it was dark, but there was a small magic-seeming light—and confirmed that no one else was around, she stepped out of the barrel. The room was a pantry. The shelves were lined with various foodstuffs and jars, and there were other barrels besides those just brought in.

It took some doing, but once she was out, she stood the inner lid up inside the barrel to make it easy to get back in when she returned.

Depending on how things went with the prince's rescue, she would be traveling out again in this same barrel.

Neia wondered about her co-infiltrator and saw that Shizu was coming out of her barrel, too. She was shorter than Neia, so she had a bit of trouble exiting the large barrel, but the maid had more physical strength than Neia or even Remedios. Before Neia could offer assistance, she was out.

"Miss Shizu."

"......Hmm?"

"You have some meat in your hair."

Shizu was miffed. Her expression may not have changed, but that didn't mean she lacked emotions. Whether it was thanks to her efforts to see Shizu frequently before they left or that she had trained her powers of perception on the King of Darkness's skull expressions, Neia had come to have at least a vague grasp of what sort of mood the maid was in.

Shizu tried to pluck the bit of meat from the back of her head, but it was really stuck.

I was always taught that short hair was better in combat because your enemy might pull longer hair, but now I see there are other advantages to keeping it short...

Neia went over to Shizu, took all the meat out of her hair, and tossed it into the barrel.

"......Thank you...... I'm never infiltrating anywhere like this ever again."

"We still have to escape."

"......"

Shizu shot a glance of disgust at her and then took a towel out of nowhere to wipe her hands. Then she gave one to Neia.

The moist towel was softer than any Neia had ever touched and so silky. It had to have been awfully valuable. How did she get ahold of an item like that? Were there lots of similar things in the demon world?

Her questions were endless, but she wiped the meaty stickiness from her hands and then used the clean part of the towel to wipe off Shizu's hair. It wasn't much more than a symbolic gesture, but it still probably felt better than nothing.

"......Thanks."

"You're welcome."

While Neia was doing that, Shizu took out her weapon.

It was an unusually shaped projectile weapon called a Mana Gun. It used magic power to shoot bullet-like arrows, so it was sort of similar to a crossbow. Shizu also explained that there was no combustion reaction like with something called gunpowder, but Neia didn't understand what she was talking about, so she let it go in one ear and out the other.

She had wanted to see how it worked, but Shizu hadn't been authorized to go outside, so her combat ability was a mystery. Still, if she was difficulty level 150, then Neia probably didn't need to worry.

"......Nn."

In the same way, she took Ultimate Shooting Star: Super and Neia's quiver out of space and handed them over. And Neia returned the dirty towel.

At first, they had debated how to sneak Neia's bow in. Between its length and all the ornamentation that would get caught on things, they also wouldn't be able to get the inner lid on if they put it in a barrel. So if the barrel was opened, that would have been the end of it.

Another idea had been to have the transporting zerun equip it, but it was such a splendid piece of gear that it was likely to stick in people's minds. If the rescue failed, the bow would then link the zerun to the attempt, so they rejected the plan.

Finally, it was starting to look like she might just leave it behind, when Shizu had said she could carry it for her by storing it in the mysterious space where she kept her own weapon.

She was both anxious to be carrying the precious item she borrowed from the King of Darkness into a dangerous situation and relieved to not have to part with it. Amid those swirling emotions, Neia expressed her deepest gratitude to Shizu for her kindness. Apparently, that was the moment she really became the junior of the duo, and after that, Shizu often emphasized her seniority.

The "Miss" Neia had to add before her name was part of that. If she left it off, Shizu's mood noticeably soured. Pretty Shizu's annoyed face—which looked no different compared to her usual expression at a glance, but Neia could tell—was actually more adorable than anything else, but Neia refrained from telling her that.

After readying their weapons, they set off with Shizu in the lead.

At the door, they listened for any sounds outside, but there didn't seem to be anyone.

"……Okay, let's go."

They didn't have much time, so Neia nodded.

Rather, the liberation army was approaching Karinsha in coordination with their infiltration and rescue operation. The capture of Karinsha would begin soon.

The plan was for Neia and Shizu to sneak into Karinsha Castle and rescue the zerun prince.

Then the liberation army would approach Karinsha and attack when the moment was right.

If the rescue was a success, the zerun would cooperate from the inside.

If the rescue failed, the guidance and gate opening the zerun would have helped with fell to Neia and Shizu. But there were a lot of things, so whatever they could manage would be good enough.

That was the rough outline of the operation.

The fact that once they rescued the prince, even if they were forced to hole up somewhere, they could count on help from the liberation army and the zerun was major. It benefited the zerun, too. If things went well, they would be able to get the prince out of the city to keep him even safer.

In other words, a smooth retaking of Karinsha depended entirely on the prince's rescue succeeding.

With the sudden weight on her shoulders, her stomach pained her; the whole thing made Neia groan.

But that was why they didn't have time. Once the battle started or the liberation army was spotted, security would tighten up.

As they had planned, Shizu took something like a perfume bottle out of space and spritzed herself and Neia. It was a consumable with the same effect as the tier-one spell Odorless. Apparently, it needed to be conserved because she didn't have many.

She cracked the door open, peeked out, and then slipped through.

They had referred to the castle plans to decide a route and discussed ahead of time how to handle various scenarios and how they would divide up the tasks involved.

When Neia went out, she closed the door behind her, taking care not to make any noise. Then she ran after Shizu.

I'm not going to be any help at all.

To be frank, Neia could only think of herself as a burden in her current circumstances. One glance at Shizu's gait was enough to convince her. Her steps were as soft, or even softer, than those of Neia's father moving through the forest. She had skills.

She has humanlike skills even though she's a demon... I guess it's just scary that you can't tell what she is from looking...

Really, everything could have been left to Shizu, but in addition to having Neia there to supervise, the Sacred Kingdom probably also felt it looked good to have one representative from their country along with the representative from the Nation of Darkness (assuming Shizu was really under the king's control).

The corridor was dark. It was nighttime. Moonlight filtered through the windows. Or perhaps, "There was only moonlight" was more accurate. In other words, there were no torches or magic lights in the corridor.

Most subhumans weren't bothered by the dark. But apparently, some had better night vision than others. Some could see perfectly, but others could just make things out decently enough. So Neia and Shizu avoided the moonlight and raced along from shadow to shadow.

As a human, Neia really had to keep her wits about her. Not only was it so dark that she couldn't see, but the guards on patrol didn't carry lights, either, so it was impossible to spot them from a distance.

The reason for the light in the pantry wasn't clear, but it might have been for one of the races that couldn't see in the dark.

The pair ran as fast as they could, keeping their footsteps noiseless.

The pace got Neia breathing hard, but for Shizu, who had physical strength far surpassing that of Remedios, it probably didn't even count as a jog.

Sometimes they came upon a guard and had to wait with bated breath until the subhuman had passed. They couldn't kill anyone. It would have taken too much effort to deal with the body and erase any traces. They were in the middle of enemy territory, so the best-case scenario would be if no one noticed they were there until after the rescue was complete.

Thankfully, they were able to proceed without anyone discovering them.

The reason the castle was so sparsely protected was that guards were also needed for the wall, the lookout towers, and the prison camp inside the city. The zerun had explained that since the King of Darkness had killed so many subhumans, they weren't able to properly staff the perimeter, and security at the castle wasn't very tight.

Thanks to that research performed ahead of time by the zerun and the perfect arrangements they had made, things were going smoothly, but Neia was anxious.

There were two hurdles in the operation.

One was the long corridor on the way to the spire.

The other was the walkway leading to the spire—the skybridge.

There wouldn't be anywhere to hide in either place, and the areas would most certainly be guarded. And it wasn't just one guard but multiple; apparently, they had one standing away from any lines of fire in case of ranged attacks.

They had discussed as a group Gustav's sketch of the castle plans, but these two critical junctures simply had to be overcome.

Using Invisibility to take care of sight and the Silence spell priests can use to take care of sound would allow us to infiltrate perfectly... I see why adventurers who can form versatile teams are so valuable...

Eventually the pair reached their destination.

Their first hurdle was the long corridor, and if they simply walked straight down it, the guards would spot them before they managed to get very far. They needed to move into a position from which they could line up their shots before being discovered.

To do that, they had come to the room directly above the guards' position in the corridor. From there, they would rappel down the outer wall using a rope, creating a bypass.

"......Here?"

Neia compared their position to the map in her head and nodded that it was the right spot.

"......Mm-hmm. Nice work."

Momentarily praising her junior as the senior member of the duo, Shizu put her ear to the door, then swiftly opened it without a sound.

The room was filled with miscellaneous items, and it seemed like it hadn't been used in a long time; there was a thick layer of dust on the floor, only disturbed by the zerun who had come to investigate. The tracks moved between the window and the huge shelving unit.

Shizu reached into her mystery pocket and took out a rope the same color as the outer wall.

Then she attached it to the shelving unit. In order to test if it would support their body weight, she yanked on the rope with all her might, and there was no sign of the shelves moving or breaking.

It was less thanks to the size—which came with the weight of the shelving unit itself—and more the spider nest–like object plastered to it. The zerun who visited the room had glued it in place using some sticky thread from a spidan.

The window opened easily. Shizu stared down at the wall and made sure there were no guards patrolling in view, then slung her weapon over her shoulder and said, "I'll go first."

She went out the opening and slid down the rope to the window below. Supporting her weight with one hand, she pushed at the window with the other, and it swung open with no trouble. That had also been prepared in advance by the zerun.

Shizu slipped inside. The whole feat took only a few seconds.

After confirming the safety of the room below, she poked her head out and waved to Neia.

Neia grabbed the rope and leaned out the window.

The window was only a little over ten feet below, but her current position was a few hundred feet above the ground. If she fell, she would definitely die. No, it would be worse if she somehow survived. She would be tortured for sure, and after they extracted what intelligence they could from her, her tormentors would kill her. It would be better to die on impact.

The rope had knots every so often for handholds, and in the practice runs she had done, there hadn't been any problems. But the real thing was completely different from training.

Ahhh, I don't wanna go…

Nevertheless, she had to use the rope to get to the floor below. If there had been a balcony, she could have just jumped, but alas…

Gripping the rope tightly, she pulled her entire body outside. She didn't forget to cross her legs around the rope.

All she had to do now was inch her way down.

The surface is just below me. The surface is just below me.

Putting that idea in her head, she descended without looking down.

Her weight shifted from her right hand to her left, just as she had practiced. But her body swayed in the wind. It was blowing much harder than it had during her training.

C'mon, you can do it! Go, me! I'm sure Shizu was even more frightened!

The room's window had been unlocked thanks to the zerun.

But if someone had gone in afterward and locked it again, Shizu would have been forced to climb back up the rope. Compared to that, knowing she had to only make a one-way trip made it easier on Neia.

Eventually she reached the window. Shizu reached out to grab her and used her incredible strength to pull her inside.

"Th-thanks."

"……Mm. But you took too long.…… I'm going to clean up. One sec."

Shizu leaned out the window and aimed her Mana Gun. When Neia held the rope as instructed, there was a sound like escaping air—*psht*—and some tension on the line. Shizu had cut the rope with her weapon.

They recovered the severed rope and tossed it into a corner. They had taken it down because they wouldn't be using this route to return, but there were pros and cons to that plan.

The pro was that they would avoid being detected by the subhumans patrolling outside. The con was that if for some reason their retreat plan had to be changed, returning here to climb up a floor was no longer an option.

In the end, they had decided that con outweighed the pro.

"All done, Miss Shizu. So now we're about to clear our first hurdle…"

"……Mm. We go…… And kill for sure. Can you do it?"

"Yes, I think so."

When they exited this room, they would be perfectly positioned with a direct line of sight to the guard.

Unless they could kill him in a single blow before he could cause a disturbance, the whole plan would fall apart. Neia took her bow, nocked an arrow, and drew the string back. Shizu held her Mana Gun up, too.

"I'll go left. You go right, Miss Shizu."

Shizu made an okay sign with her fingers.

Then they looked each other in the eye, and…Shizu pushed open the door.

Their eyes met those of a subhuman right nearby, not even five yards away. He had no idea what was going on or who they were. He wasn't even surprised, just uncomprehending. Neia loosed her arrow.

Schpuck. The arrow pierced his forehead easily.

Got him!

Neia had skills, but she owed much of the success to Ultimate Shooting Star: Super.

Thank you, Your Majesty!

While Neia was skewering one subhuman's head, Shizu was blowing half of another's away with her Mana Gun.

The guards collapsed, causing a louder clamor than expected. Dismayed, Neia listened hard for any subsequent sounds. Fortunately, she didn't hear anyone rushing their way. It seemed like no one had noticed what had happened yet.

"……Hurry."

They had divided up the work ahead of time. While Shizu was shutting the bodies up in the room where they had left the rope, Neia used an Odorless item she had borrowed from Shizu. Then she splashed the strong alcohol she had put in her water pouch and washed away the blood, flesh, and brains. By the time the corridor reeked of alcohol, Shizu had come out of the room. She reached into thin air for an empty wineskin, poured some of the liquid from Neia's water pouch inside, quietly broke it, and then left it on the floor.

"......Let's go."

"Okay."

They had set up their little strategy, but when it came time for the guard to change, the new arrivals were likely to be suspicious. If they could have stuffed the corpses into Shizu's mystery space, that would have made things easier, but Shizu refused to do that, so they had to leave them in that room. Of course, that room had been set up in another way, but it didn't guarantee that the bodies wouldn't be found.

It was best to assume they were on borrowed time.

Eventually they reached the second hurdle. The mission was going as well as they could have hoped. They still had time, and they hadn't been discovered.

"......Now it's a fight against time."

"I know. If I slip or something, you can ignore me."

The walkway stretching from the castle to the spire was only the width of about two humans. There were no walls—it was completely exposed. Apparently, a handful of people had fallen, and looking at it now, Neia could see why.

This skybridge was the final choke point for enemy invaders in a siege.

A large army couldn't pass, so it neutralized any invading force's numerical superiority, and it introduced the danger of falling to one's death. With sentries wielding shields and spears holding the other end, the exposed walkway was a truly loathsome obstacle for the attacking side. It was probably only possible to brute force one's way through with a caster who could use Fireball or some similar attack spell.

Chipping away at the enemies with projectiles was a disadvantage due to their limited time and the fact that they would have to be stealthy about it. That was why they needed to charge, even though the enemy would probably respond with ranged attacks, and do away with the sentries at close quarters where they wouldn't have the benefit of cover.

For that reason, they needed to close the distance as much as they could before being spotted by the guards in the lookout post. But when they took a closer look at the path, they found that the surface had been made uneven to slow people down, and in some places, it seemed like it was purposely built to cause invaders to trip and fall.

Wow, this isn't safe at all… And if the enemies knock us back or cling onto us…we'll fall to our deaths… I have to be careful!

Having steeled her resolve, Neia realized Shizu was watching her. Being stared at by Shizu with her pretty, doll-like features made her feel bashful even though they were both girls.

"Wh-what?"

"……I'll use it…… Neia, you wait here."

"Huh?"

"……I'll take care of the guards at the entrance. Don't come out no matter what happens."

"Wait, what?!"

Before she could even respond, Shizu was gone.

She had disappeared. It didn't seem as if she had sped off somewhere. It was more like the Shizu who had been standing there dissolved into the air like a mirage.

Neia was terribly confused. But Shizu had told her to stay put, so all she could really do was wait.

Hiding near the entrance of the walkway, Neia focused her hearing to see if she could pick up any disturbances either toward the spire or behind her—back the way they came.

After a few seconds, it seemed like something had happened at the lookout post. She could hear screams and the thuds of guards collapsing.

When she looked over to see what was going on, she saw Shizu's face poke out of the lookout post. Shizu waved her over.

Seeming annoyed at Neia standing there, still overwhelmed by wondering what had just happened, Shizu's waving grew more exaggerated until she was flailing her whole body around.

At that point, she realized she had better go over there.

It was pretty terrifying to cross the windy walkway, but Neia kept her body low and her eyes on her feet.

When she arrived, the lookout post was emitting the stench of blood. Several expired subhumans were lying strewn about. In the middle of it all stood Shizu with her usual blank expression. Her right hand was clasped around a sharp-looking knife stained with blood. In her left hand was her Mana Gun.

"……Clear. We move on."

"O-okay."

"……I can't disappear anymore today. We need to be careful."

"Understood."

Neia could tell Shizu didn't feel like explaining, so she followed her without questions.

That's a demon maid for you, thought Neia.

She never would have made it this far without Shizu.

I owe this to His Majesty the King of Darkness for ordering her to help us.

Even when he was absent, her respect for him only grew.

The fact that he was undead was really such a trivial issue.

I really have to let everyone know how great he is!

The spire was made almost entirely out of stone and only had narrow windows, so it was even gloomier than the main castle. The corridor was fairly broad, so Neia and Shizu could walk side by side. It was built in a spiral that led up along the wall.

Their object, the zerun prince, was supposedly being kept somewhere near the top, so they only listened for sounds on the other sides of the doors they passed on their way higher and higher.

About two loops up, Shizu raised her hand in a signal to stop at about the same time that Neia heard the footsteps of a creature.

It appeared to be wearing armor, as the sound was metal clanking against stone.

"Just one, Miss Shizu."

"……Yes, but……those footsteps are heavy."

Neia wasn't sure, but if Shizu said so, then it must have been true. She must have meant it was bigger than a human.

"What…should we do? Should we go back and hide inside one of the rooms we passed?"

"……We've come this far. We kill it."

"Okay."

Following Shizu's lead, Neia readied her bow. She was prepared to shoot as soon as the creature showed itself. They had been told that the zerun prince was the size of a human child. And he wouldn't be wearing metal armor.

As soon as the hulking form appeared around the bend, Neia and Shizu both attacked without hesitating.

The arrow and mana bullet appeared to sink into the giant body.

"Gahhhh!"

The large creature staggered and then began to retreat up the path. All it had to do was backtrack slightly to break Neia's and Shizu's lines of sight.

If this subhuman could take the pair's attacks—especially Shizu's—and still be alive, it had to be quite strong.

"Who are you people?!" A scream came from up the corridor.

"What should we do, Miss Shizu?"

"……Twiddling our thumbs here won't do us any good… Let's close in and attack before our opponent summons all the guards in this spire."

"Got it."

Neia and Shizu sprinted forward.

Since their opponent had been able to weather their surprise attack, Neia figured it was safe to assume it was the guard—the va-um—because all ogre types had not only excellent combat ability but impressive physical strength.

As they ran, Neia felt almost as if the amount of moisture in the air was increasing; it smelled like rain.

"Gooooahhh! What are humans doing here?!"

When they closed in, they had a full view of the huge subhuman.

He had an air of violence similar to an ogre but appeared to be much more intelligent.

His skin was a pale blue, but rather than looking unwell, it gave the being an evil impression.

His forehead had one horn sprouting out of it. In his hands was a mace larger than Neia.

With that appearance, he certainly resembled a va-um.

Even if he wasn't quite on Buser's level, he would be a difficult opponent. The magic bullet and arrow from their previous attack had been direct hits, yet he had no visible injuries. And Neia didn't smell any blood, which meant he probably wasn't concealing any with illusions.

How had he neutralized their attacks—especially Shizu's?

"You came here to kill me?! Seems like even some humans are in the know!"

He seemed thrilled.

Then maybe it was best to let him think tha—

"……No," Shizu said, firing her gun.

Something shot out with a *psht* of escaping air. Part of the va-um's body dispersed, and the bullet flew right through it.

"……Mngh."

"Hoo-ha-ha-ha-ha! Projectiles won't work on me!"

Neia loosed an arrow at his brow, but sure enough, his head turned to mist, and the arrow stuck into the wall behind him.

"It's futile! Futile, I say! Fear me, the mortal enemy of any sharpshooter, and die!"

"……So you have perfect resistance to all projectiles? At that strength?" Shizu grumbled to herself. "There must be something else going on."

Neia looked to Shizu and shook her head. Unfortunately, the zerun didn't know the details of the va-um's powers.

"What are you blathering about?"

"Fall back!"

The va-um closed in. He was so much larger than a human that Neia felt like her sense of distance had been completely ruined.

She wouldn't be able to take a single hit from this guy, so she accepted Shizu's kindness and backed up.

The va-um swung the massive mace at Shizu, who remained in front. It was like a gale-force wind, but she evaded it with elegance.

To wield a weapon as big as Shizu with one hand, he had to be extraordinarily strong. When the mace hit the floor, cracks radiated from the point of impact, and chips of stone went flying. It almost felt as if the huge tower had shaken.

"Tch!"

Neia shot an arrow.

Though he was in close combat with Shizu, he was so much larger than her that if she aimed for his upper body, Neia could target him without hitting her.

The arrow sliced through the air, but just as before, he turned to mist and evaded it.

"It's no good! It's pointless! I'm telling you, arrows won't work on me! You foolish— Uoagh!"

He was going to keep shouting at her, but Shizu interrupted.

Shizu's prowess as a shooter far surpassed Neia's, but she didn't appear to be very skilled in hand-to-hand combat, and unfortunately, the va-um blocked her attack with his mace.

Neia drew her bow again.

Next, she aimed for the hand holding the mace. It was possible that he wouldn't drop his weapon even when he turned to mist, but she had decided that if there was even a slight chance, it was worth trying.

And the result…

…was that his arm turned to mist, but he didn't drop the mace.

"Give it up, human!" He thrust his free hand out at Neia. "Water Splash!"

A liquid missile flew at Neia.

It struck her right shoulder, knocking her back so hard, she went sprawling.

It hurt as much as if she had been punched with full force. Bones were possibly broken.

Carefully attempting to move her right arm, she found herself able to without any issues. But pain zapped from her shoulder through the rest of her body. When she put a hand to the wound, she felt sopping wetness. At first, she was worried it was a massive amount of blood, but a moment later, she realized it was just water.

"Hmph! Making me use a wimpy spell like that!" the va-um fairly spat, brandishing his mace.

The gust of death that would've broken Neia to pieces, Shizu nimbly dodged as she muttered, "......Why her? Why attack someone who posed no threat to you? It's incomprehensible."

"Hmph! You fool! Don't get—"

"Are they actually effective? Is there a limit to how many times you can use that power?"

The va-um's expression changed. In other words, that was the answer.

"Neia!!"

"Yep!"

Neia loosed an arrow. The va-um turned to mist and evaded. Then she shot another—and this time it hit him.

The va-um yelped in pain, and Shizu said, "......I see. So you can avoid projectiles seven times. Is that...in one day? Or in one hour? ......It doesn't matter now. You will......die here."

Realizing he wouldn't be able to take Shizu out because of her brilliant evasion—seeing, in other words, that he would be one-sidedly attacked and killed—the va-um's face stiffened.

"Wh-why, you! Fog Cloud!"

Fog billowed up.

It was even thicker than the fog Neia had seen in the Nation of Darkness; she couldn't even tell where she was standing. She couldn't see Shizu's back ahead of her, yet she heard her Mana Gun going *psht, psht.*

When she thought about it, the situation was actually quite simple.

Even if he created fog in the middle of the corridor, he was still in the same place as a moment ago. She could just shoot at that area. Neia followed Shizu's lead and loosed an arrow. She was a bit nervous, so she aimed higher up to make sure she didn't hit Shizu.

The arrow disappeared into the fog immediately, and then she heard it strike the wall. Apparently, she had missed.

"He's behind you now."

The remark from Shizu made Neia think, *What?!*

Considering the width of the corridor, the huge va-um wouldn't have been able to get around them without them noticing. But having traveled with her this long, Neia knew that Shizu was a trustworthy demon. Or perhaps it was less that she trusted Shizu and more that she trusted the King of Darkness commanding her.

Neia spun around, and sure enough, the fog was thick there, too, but she took a shot.

The arrow hit the wall just like the previous time.

"Where...where is he?!"

".....Mm. He's in the direction you're facing. He must be trying to escape. Get down!"

Hearing what was a forceful voice for Shizu, Neia promptly got out of her way.

".....I'll switch bullets and......Full Burst."

There was a high-pitched ring, and then a *boom*, so loud Neia had to plug her ears, filled the corridor.

Neia heard a *blorgh* sound like vomiting and the crash of a large body crumpling. Then the fog dispersed, and the fallen va-um came into view up ahead in the curving corridor.

Parts of his body had been blasted away, and there were marks on the walls. How was it possible to wield such a power?

The subhuman tasked with guarding this place was supposed to be quite strong. And in reality, Neia hadn't seen any way to defeat him. Meanwhile, Shizu had killed him the instant her weapon specialty became effective. She really was a difficulty level–150 demon maid.

"How...did you...? Well, I suppose with magic you can do anything."

Neia moved the shoulder that had taken the attack spell. The heat of battle had caused her to forget about the pain, but it was starting to hurt more now.

".....Are you all right?"

"Yeah. But it hurts to draw my bow, so my aim won't be very good."

".....Do you have a healing potion?"

"No, but I have a healing item His Majesty lent to me."

In the battle back then, she had been able to use it only once, but now she felt like maybe she could use it a little more. Still, she couldn't waste mana. It could end up that she would need to heal Shizu at some point.

"It's okay. All that's left is to rescue the hostage and escape."

"......Mm. If you say so."

Neia nodded and ran onward with Shizu. They had beaten the va-um who was supposed to have been so tough.

All that was left was to collect the prince and make it back to the pantry they had started in.

3

"......We're here."

"Yes."

Upon reaching the top floor, Neia and Shizu exchanged glances. There was a single door. This had to be their destination. They nodded at each other and kicked it in.

They were no longer in the mood to enter quietly. This was after their battle with the va-um. But they did move to either side of the door to be ready in case an attack came lashing out.

But their caution was for nothing. So they rushed in, with Neia, her shoulder hurting, taking the left side and Shizu taking the right.

The first thing Neia saw when she entered the room was a bed with a canopy. What had surely been originally snow white was stained with age. There was also a simple dresser and a plain wooden wardrobe as tall as a human. All the furnishings befitting a noble were old and banged up; they seemed less like antiques and more like secondhand acquisitions.

At first glance, there didn't seem to be a subhuman in the room.

When Shizu gestured with her jaw, Neia approached the wardrobe and opened the door. Of course, she stood off to one side so she would be safe whatever happened, and Shizu trained her Mana Gun on the inside.

"......There's no one."

Then they looked at the bed.

After peering underneath to make sure no one was hiding there, Neia went over to it.

There was a little lump.

When she looked to Shizu, they nodded at each other, and Neia pulled the sheets down.

There was a shiny, purple, almost attractive chunk of meat. No, perhaps it would be better described as a large maggot. It was about three feet long and had protrusions that couldn't quite be called legs.

Shizu pointed her gun immediately, but Neia rushed to stop her.

"Wait! This is the zerun prince we're here to rescue!"

"……This thing is?"

That's what they had heard from the zerun messenger. But she could understand Shizu's doubt. She had been pretty confused when she heard the description, too.

The zerun was a race of subhumans in which the royal family differed greatly in appearance from the others. Not only that, but perhaps there were also significant male and female differences?

"Um, can you speak, zerun prince?"

"Sure I can. You don't seem to be my food…"

It was a boy's voice. When she took a closer look to see how he was speaking, she saw a little maggot-like mouth flapping.

"That is correct. We were asked to come rescue you. First, we'll get you out of this room."

He may have looked like a maggot, but he was a prince. Neia had to treat him with the proper respect. They would also need his race's assistance when searching for the King of Darkness. She needed to make them feel indebted, not offend them.

"By my fellow spawn? Who? Who asked you to do it?"

"It was a zerun called Beebeebee. Is that someone you know?'

"Beebeebee? Ah yes. Mm… But if I leave this place, Jalda— Er, Emperor Jaldabaoth will be upset. That would put many zerun and our king in danger."

"I don't know all the details, but the reason we were asked to break you out was that the king has died, and they want to at least save you."

"No!"

It was absolutely impossible for Neia, a human, to read the emotions of this giant maggot prince. But she could hear the grief clearly in his voice.

"My one and only father... I see—that Jaldabaoth... In that case...is it possible to escape here safely?"

"Your aides have made arrangements, so please consider it doable."

"I see... This is a rather shameless request to make of the human heroes who have come all this way to rescue me, but could we pretend that you dragged me out of here against my will?"

He must have meant if it came to that.

"Understood. That's what we'll say."

"I appreciate it."

The prince raised his head. He was like a maggot rearing up, but that must have been a gesture of thanks for his race.

Neia wrapped him in a sheet and put him on her back like one would a baby (although she had only done it a couple of times because the babies would cry without fail).

She tied the ends of the sheet fast in front of her so that even vigorous movement wouldn't loosen the sling.

The weight on her shoulder hurt. Wiping the sweat that had oozed from her forehead, she cast a spell.

That instant, her wounds were completely healed. Now she would have no trouble running while carrying the prince.

"Do you feel all right? Please let me know straight away if anything hurts."

"I feel fine, but... You sure smell good. I'm starving."

The words spoken into the nape of her neck made Neia shiver.

"......What do zerun eat?"

Shizu asked the question Neia would rather she hadn't.

"The bodily fluids of living things, alive or dead."

A chill went up Neia's spine.

"……I'll be mad if you pull anything weird with my protégé."

"Don't worry. I'm not so hungry that I'd do something like that to a hero who came to rescue me. I haven't been allowed outside even once since coming here, but they have been feeding me properly."

Neia felt like if she heard what kind of food he'd been eating she might want to hurl him to the ground, so she plugged her ears. Luckily, Shizu didn't ask any more questions.

"……All right, time to go."

"Yes, ma'am."

"Thanks."

With that brief exchange, the two—three—of them were on their way. It wasn't as if they had time to stand around chatting while they were on a stealth mission.

Fortunately, they made it back to the pantry with no trouble. Then Shizu raised a hand.

"……There's someone in there."

"Please take care of them."

Shizu readied her Mana Gun and threw the door open.

Then she froze. She turned around.

"……I don't know who they are, but there are zerun in there. A lot of them."

Perhaps it was the recovery team? More specifically, the group that was supposed to guide them outside. If they were already there, it must have meant that Neia and Shizu were running late.

When they went inside, the five zerun turned to look at once. Neia couldn't read the grotesques' expressions even a bit, but when they all made the same motion in her direction, a wave of something that wasn't quite fear or disgust came over her.

Neia undid the sheet and showed them the prince.

"Oh! Our prince!"

It was Beebeebee. Without hearing their voices, it was impossible to tell them apart. They looked so different from the prince that it was impossible to even tell they were the same race.

"My kindred. I heard my father has died. I've realized that Jalda-baoth doesn't intend to keep his promise to us. But where can we run to if we betray him? He has taken over our territory completely, and one of his demons now governs it... Wouldn't escaping from here merely be going down the path to destruction?"

"You're quite right to be concerned, Your Highness. But he only sees zerun as slaves or livestock. Our valiant Boobeebee lost some shoulder flesh for being slightly late to a gathering once."

"What?! He did that to Boobeebee?!"

Neia gathered from the prince's shock that Boobeebee must have been quite the zerun.

"When this is all over, will there be a place for us under Jaldabaoth? We think not. Prince, there's no time. Let's disc—"

"—You fool. Could we do it after we flee? This is a borderline. Once we cross it, we'll have no choice but to follow through on that plan. There'll be no turning back. Tell me now. How are we going to return to our nest, to the hills, and survive?"

"Well...the land is vast. I think we can find somewhere to hide."

"You think? You're leading our entire race down a path of destruction based on such a fuzzy prospect? Come up with something more realistic and concrete!"

"W-well, not everyone is devoted to Jaldabaoth. We could create a rebel army and—"

"Idiot. It would just be annihilated by his aides. One ant might be over-looked, but an infestation can't be missed."

Rebutted at every turn by the prince, Beebeebee fell silent. Things were looking bad. They had come all this dangerous way to cooperate on this mission, but if the prince declared he didn't want to go, their efforts would be for nothing.

Then Neia thought of a way to resolve the prince's worries.

"Then what if all the zerun went to the Nation of Darkness?"

"The Nation of Darkness? What in the world is that?"

It wasn't only the zerun who turned to look at her—Shizu did, too.

"The hero who repelled Jaldabaoth back in the Re-Estize Kingdom, Momon, is there."

She had the feeling the zerun were staring at her, but she didn't know what sort of emotion was contained in their gazes. There was no way for a human to tell what a zerun was feeling.

"Is that true?"

That one remark made her realize what the zerun's silence was about. They must not have believed her. But that made sense. The more one learned about Jaldabaoth, the more impossible it seemed to drive him off.

"It is. I was told so by someone I trust. Actually, Miss Shizu?"

"……Yes. What Neia says is true."

"And so…" This was the hard part. Neia psyched herself up. "If you all went to the Nation of Darkness, I'm sure they would accept you as refugees."

"Refugees…?" There was a definite sourness in the prince's tone.

"But if you brought them news of their ruler, His Majesty the King of Darkness, I'm sure no one would look down on you."

"Wait, wait. News of their own king would make them happy? What's that supposed to mean?"

"The king is… Well…he's currently missing…"

"That won't work, then. He could very well be dead."

"Please wait. It's impossible for the king to be dead. We have proof of that."

When Neia explained how he might have fallen in the hills and they wanted the zerun's help, the prince fell silent. *So that wasn't good enough?* she thought, but she had already taken her best shot, so she didn't say any more. It was in the prince's court now.

Still, even if direct assistance was impossible, they would surely fulfill their promise of sharing knowledge.

"…I see. If we make them owe us…but will they accept subhumans? The Nation of Darkness is a human country, no?"

"No, it's not. It's ruled by an undead."

"An undead?!" The prince yelped in shock, as did all the other zerun. "You would have us go somewhere so dangerous?!"

Every race had a strong aversion to undead. Neia had been no exception before she met the King of Darkness. Being confronted with herself from only a short while ago made her a bit emotional.

"Please wait. He may be an undead, but he's a wonderful person, and I saw humans and subhumans living in his country in harmony."

"An undead a wonderful person? What do you take—?"

"—Enough. Please bear with my rude retainer. But is this King of Darkness really as wonderful as you say?"

"Yes," Neia answered confidently, standing proud.

"...We can't understand human facial expressions at all. But you're brave enough to infiltrate deep into enemy territory to rescue me, so if you say it with such steady conviction, then I can understand. I will believe in this undead king...in whom you place such trust. Let's turn to him for help."

An "Ohhh!" of happiness rose from the zerun.

"That's settled, then. Please flee to the Kingdom of Darkness as fast as you can, Your Highness. One problem is that one of Jaldabaoth's great demon aides has arrived. I thought he would be visiting a few days later... There will be trouble if he spots you. Hurry!"

Most zerun were female. Males were exceedingly rare. Really just the king and the prince. If all the males in a tribe were wiped out—though females sometimes changed sex—the tribe would basically go extinct.

They suggested the prince run first because they absolutely needed to get him somewhere safe—to the Kingdom of Darkness.

"One of Jaldabaoth's aides? Here?" There was no way to overlook those words.

"Yes. You didn't see him? He has three demon aides. It's one of those."

"......We'll defeat him here."

At Shizu's sudden remark, the prince flip-flopped on the floor. "Don't be ridiculous! If you two could save me, you must be quite strong. But that doesn't mean you can beat this demon."

The only strong one was Shizu, but Neia didn't want to interrupt.

"......We heard that he teleports among different cities...... If he's here now, it's a great chance. If we let it go by, the next one might not come so easily."

"What you say is true…"

"Prince!"

"Let's be sensible. If we kill one of Jaldabaoth's aides, there will be a disturbance in the chain of command, so it would probably be difficult for them to detect us if we went straight from here to the Kingdom of Darkness… But is it really possible to defeat him?"

"……I don't know. But this is our chance."

"…Then I'll make the wager—on your strength that killed the va-um!" said the prince, who had been astonished to see the corpse on their way over. "Okay, everyone? We're going to cooperate with these two and kill Jaldabaoth's aide!"

"Yes, Your Highness!"

"Two humans. Six of us. Eight who were enemies until a few days ago unite against a more powerful enemy. Sounds like a saga in the making."

Huh? thought Neia and counted the zerun in the room once more to make sure she wasn't mistaken before hurriedly interjecting, "Hold on. Please wait. Don't make the prince fight. We're here to save him."

And more importantly, even if he did participate, what could he do? Putting it as kindly as possible, he was still just a big maggot on the floor. If he meant to go along as a figurehead, she would rather he spared them the trouble.

"You consider your job done as long as I escape? Aha, I see. But! I think with my help it will be a bit easier to defeat Jaldabaoth's aide. No—without me, it would be quite difficult, even for heroes who beat a va-um."

It was Shizu who had beaten the va-um; Neia couldn't claim any part in it, so it felt shameful to be counted as a hero.

"Uh, do you mean without all of you zerun?"

The prince emitted a strange cry. "No, no, hero. I may not look like it, but I can use tier-four psychic magic."

"Tier four?"

Neia was amazed. Tier four was what a human with genius-level aptitude could just barely reach if they devoted everything they had to the pursuit. In the Sacred Kingdom, only the high priest Kelart Custodio and Holy Lady Calca Bessarez were capable of it.

Neia turned, thinking to share her shock, but Shizu had her usual blank expression on. Perhaps, as might be expected from a difficulty level–150 demon maid, tier-four magic wasn't very surprising.

"U-uh…are zerun all that powerful?"

With another strange cry, the prince flopped around again like a fish out of water. "I'm special!"

"Yes. That's why he's the prince."

Ohhh. Hearing the pride in his voice, Neia remembered something from a class she had taken long ago. *Right, some other races have royalty that are so different from the common people that they are practically a different race.*

"But I have a weakness. I'm…er, not very quick."

Yeah, thought Neia. That was clear at a glance.

"If he closes in on me, I'll die helplessly. So I hate to ask, but will you carry me? Then I can use magic on your signal."

"I see. I understand what you're asking, but couldn't the other zerun—your guards—carry you?"

"Unlike the prince, we excel at close-quarters combat. You fight at range, correct?"

"That's…true. I suppose Shizu or I should ca… Wait, we're getting off topic. If we take His Highness into battle and he dies, that would be a huge problem."

"……Neia. There's a point to him being there…… That's why he's suggesting he go."

"Heh-heh-heh. That's right. Are you familiar with this aide of his? The demon like a dead tree decorated with trophy heads."

"……There are several types of demons like that. In order of power: silk hat, crown, circlet, corolla." She counted on four fingers. "……The aide has to be one of those. But…if it's a silk hat, we should run for it. I can't beat those."

"You knew that?!"

Neia was surprised, and then anger began to smolder. She had said during their prep meetings that she didn't know anything about the aide.

Was that a lie?

If she was purposely avoiding giving intelligence on Jaldabaoth to troops under the Sacred Kingdom, that would mean she was never under the King of Darkness's control. Which also meant that Shizu's mere presence would no longer be enough to calm her worries about His Majesty's safety!

"…You went and gave me hope! But it was all just to make me feel better?!"

Together with her outburst, she grabbed Shizu's shoulders. So hard. But it didn't seem like the demon maid sensed any pain. Not because she was expressionless—because she actually didn't feel any.

Neia felt so pathetic, she nearly began to cry. *What a fool I was, thinking we had managed to grow a little closer.* She couldn't help but criticize herself.

Shizu remained expressionless as usual. Still, there was something subtle there that only Neia could detect.

Hesitation, thought, or perhaps regret.

"……I'm sorry."

The words Shizu forced out after a long silence were those. It was an apology so lacking in explanation that it only fueled the anger of the person it was meant for. But Shizu seemed somehow uneasy in that moment, which helped calm Neia down a little.

"……I thought that if you knew how powerful his aides were, you would all decide not to take on this mission. But in order for Lord Ainz to achieve victory……this mission has to succeed. That's why I lied."

Carefully selecting each word in turn, she took great pains to express her thoughts. But she was also sincere, and her unshakable faith made her reliable.

Neia didn't have a technique for seeing through lies. And when she was talking to a demon—or really any girl with such a blank face—there was no way she could know what was the truth.

But if Shizu really was a spy for Jaldabaoth or was secretly working to destroy the Sacred Kingdom military from the inside out, then her actions up to this point didn't make sense. She should have been able to integrate herself more skillfully.

And regardless of the logic, Neia wanted to believe Shizu. Not only was she pointing the way to the King of Darkness, but the strange affinity they had for each other felt like something one of a kind to Neia.

"...I see. I believe you. But don't misjudge me again. I would brave any danger for His Majesty the King of Darkness."

Shizu was visibly relieved. *She couldn't possibly be a spy. She's simply not cut out for it.* The thought brought a natural smile back to Neia's face.

"Okay, so can I keep our earlier conversation going? If you know so much, then do you know about his powers, too?"

"These demons all have the same general type of powers, and they aren't that strong to begin with. They become an issue when they acquire the head of someone intelligent...a caster's head."

According to Shizu, this branch of demons could accessorize with casters' heads and use their powers. Silk hats could equip up to four; crowns, three; circlets, two; and corollas, one. If the heads they wore belonged to accomplished casters, the danger these demons posed ramped up very quickly.

"Corollas can only use up to tier-three spells no matter what kind of head they use. Silk hats can use up to tier ten, and—"

"Wait!"

"Hold on!"

It was the prince and Neia. Shizu fell silent at the sound of their voices.

Neia exchanged a glance with the bouncing prince. Though she couldn't read his expression, she was sure they were both thinking the same thing.

"......Go ahead."

"Ahem... What's this 'tier ten' you mention? Isn't five the highest?"

Exactly. Neia had heard that tier five was the upper limit. That was why she guessed that the King of Darkness could maybe use tier six.

Shizu shook her head as if she was about to sigh and say *here we go...* "......There are ten tiers of magic. The spell Jaldabaoth used to drop a meteor from the sky was from tier ten."

"B-but there's no way we can win against— Hmm? Huh? So if His Majesty was fighting on an equal level with Jaldabaoth, does that mean…?"

As Neia discovered something astounding, the prince shivered in amazement.

"Tier ten? Huh? Nah. That can't be true, can it? Tier ten… Really…? And here I was proud of being able to use tier four…"

Tier four was plenty commendable; he could definitely be proud of that. Only a handful of casters ever became that accomplished.

"Shizu…I'm just wondering… But can His Majesty also use tier-ten spells?"

"……Duh." Her tone was obviously annoyed at being asked something so basic. It was perhaps the clearest Shizu's emotions had ever come through during all the time they had spent together so far.

The prince, as a caster himself, seemed to be jiggling in shock.

"Huh? What? The undead king of the country I'm about to flee to is that awe-inspiring? Tier ten… That means twice as strong as me?"

"……Hahhh," Shizu sighed. "His Majesty."

"Huh?"

"……You should call the king His Majesty."

"Oh yes, of course. His Majesty the King of Darkness is so awe-inspiring…"

Shizu was being pretty pushy considering this was a prince of an entire race they were dealing with, but what she said was correct, and Neia approved wholeheartedly.

"That's right, Your Highness. His Majesty the King of Darkness is indeed awe-inspiring."

"Ah, yes."

"……Prince, wouldn't it be great if you could get someone so amazing to owe you?"

"Y-yes, you're right! Okay! We pledge our full support in the search for His Majesty in the hills."

Neia clasped her hands and squeezed. "Thank you so much, Your Highness. So, Shizu, can you explain the rest?"

"……About how amazing Lord Ainz is?"

"Right now, we need to hear about Jaldabaoth's aide. Oh, but I want to hear about His Majesty, too, so will you tell me after we get back?"

"……Mm…… Demons who equip multiple heads can use all of them together to cast several spells at one time. But there are limitations. One is that the same head can't cast two spells at once. The other is that there's a max cumulative tier restriction. For example, silk hats can cast spells that add up to fifteen tiers—"

"Fifteen tiers?! Are there actually tier-fifteen spells?!"

"……No, obviously not. I said it's cumulative."

The prince wriggled in relief.

Neia was a bit freaked out by the way she had learned to read the prince's emotions based on how he bounced around.

"……Moving on. The important thing is how many heads the demon has."

"Two. One is subhuman. One is human like you two."

Neia had a bad feeling. The body Jaldabaoth was carrying around… Its top half was missing. "…What was the human head like?"

"Sorry, but I'm no good at telling apart people from outside my race. The other one I know, though. It's the queen of the pandexes, Grand Mother."

The words *pandex* and *Grand Mother* piqued her curiosity, but there were other things she had to ask at the moment. "I'd like to inquire about the human head. What color is the hair?"

"Hair is the furry part at the top of a human head, right? It's light black."

"Black? So it's not someone from the Sacred Kingdom?"

That provided her some slight relief. She had been worried for a moment that it would be the Holy Lady. Being able to rule that out put her mind at ease. She also realized it might be a hint for this puzzle.

She had heard that black hair was common of people in the south. *Aha*, thought Neia—because she presumed that was where Jaldabaoth had come from.

There were no human-majority countries south of the Sacred King-dom. Less than half of the people were human, and even if there were humans, many of them were mixed with other races. She had heard that the only countries led by a purely human royal family were Sacred Kingdom Roebel, Baharuth Empire, and Re-Estize Kingdom. There were no royal families in the Theocracy or the city-state alliance.

Perhaps that was why news of Jaldabaoth hadn't reached this majority human country.

"......Incidentally, demons that accessorize with heads can't use the abilities of non-caster heads. Wearing a warrior's head won't give them warrior powers. There are different monsters who can do that."

"Then that subhuman head... Your Highness, could you tell us about the Grand Mother?"

"Sure. That's what I'm on your side for. Pandexes eat moss and look similar to us in both face and body."

So like maggots.

Neia trembled for a second, thinking how creepy a demon would be to wear a head like that.

"...Was she a psychic caster?"

"Yes, while I can manipulate the five elements of yin, she could manipulate the five elements of yang. Yin and yang are in a bipolar relationship; they can neutralize and interfere with each other."

"......I see." Shizu nodded. "Having you with us will increase our chances of winning."

"I'm glad you understand. I, too, find the demon using the Grand Mother in this way disgusting. Yes, because she was my first love."

"Prince!"

"What?! You fell for a member of a different race?!"

"Oh, it was just a little crush in my youth! I'm different now!"

It must have been a bittersweet tale, but to Neia, the first crush of a maggot was just unpleasant.

"S-so if our opponent has two heads, we can guess that it's a circlet. What's the cumulative number of magic tiers it can cast?"

"......The max would be six. Incidentally, a crown can do ten."

"So if I used a tier-four spell, they would have two tiers left to use. Of course, that assumes the demon is aiming to neutralize my powers, so we need to be careful..."

"......Then we need to think about that human head. We don't have enough information. Neia?"

"Sorry. I wish I knew about people with black hair, but I don't. I'm a bit surprised, though. I thought you might go to battle without worrying about it."

"......Lord Ainz said collecting intelligence is important."

"Oh! I'd expect nothing less from His Majesty. It's a brilliant idea!"

In response, Shizu stretched out her hand. Neia took it unhesitatingly and shook up and down.

"......You really get it. I should have given you a cuter sticker. You should grow fluffy hair."

"...Sticker? Oh, if you mean the thing you stuck on me from before, I don't need another. Please give it to someone else you like."

"......Mrf. You're the first person who has ever disliked my stickers."

"Huh?"

Hearing she was the first surprised Neia. But then she wondered how many humans this demon had really hung out with. And there was also the possibility that everyone hated them in secret but wouldn't dare tell a demon. She wanted to point those things out, but she couldn't be so cold to a fellow devotee of the Great One. In the end, she settled for just wincing.

"...If I remember correctly, humans, like zerun, don't grow fur. That's why they live in buildings like this. Digging a hole and living in it like we do isn't bad, either!"

"Prince, we're getting off topic. We don't have much time. Everything needs to be finished by the point the humans come to attack the city."

"......Mm. Conclusion: The prince should come with us."

No one disagreed. Well, Neia had been the only dissenter in the first place.

"In terms of tactics, we'll take the lead, but what should we do if a guard blocks our way? Leaving an opponent with casting abilities to roam freely would be quite dangerous…"

"……I'll fight them at close quarters."

No one asked if she could. One of the people who had defeated the va-um—though it had been all Shizu, really—was saying so. No one would doubt her.

"Okay. Let's do that, then. Carry us in the barrels to near where the demon aide is located. If you say the demon ordered you to bring food, it'll probably work out."

"Us" meant the prince, Neia, and Shizu. As long as those three weren't discovered—if they could proceed in secret, meaning that the zerun's betrayal wasn't found out—this would be doable.

Shizu and Neia went back into the barrels they had been carried to the castle in.

"…How lucky, Miss Shizu, right?"

Shizu poked her head out of her barrel. "……What is?"

"I mean, everything is going so well. Thanks to the zerun rebelling, we were able to come save the prince, and Jaldabaoth's aide just happens to be here at the perfect time. If we defeat this demon, it'll be a great accomplishment, you know? No one'll be able to argue with us anymore. It'll make it easy to form the search party for His Majesty."

"That's just a coincidence."

Shizu's unusually forceful tone of voice weighed on Neia.

"Huh? Uh, y-yeah. It's a coincidence, which is why it's lucky… Well, considering how powerful His Majesty the King of Darkness is and him making you belong to him, maybe it's not a coincidence."

"Belong to……Lord Ainz……?"

"Oops, did I make you sound like an object?"

"……It's fine. Neia."

"Huh?"

"……You're my favorite…… You're not cute, but I think you're worth giving another sticker."

It stings when you keep saying I'm not cute, though, ya know..., Neia thought as she declined the stickers and disappeared into her barrel.

4

Though the zerun were stopped multiple times by other subhumans as they carried the barrels containing Neia, Shizu, and the prince, they managed to make it to a location near the great demon's office without a single barrel being opened.

Neia and the others finally emerged from their barrels.

Neia had been watching from inside for a while, and there was no sign of tightened security. It didn't seem like their infiltration and rescue of the prince had been discovered yet.

Neia put the prince on her back, and while she strapped him into place and made other preparations, one of the other zerun requested an audience with the great demon aide—for reconnaissance purposes.

Around the time everyone was ready to charge in, the zerun returned.

"He's alone. No guards."

Neia frowned.

With Jaldabaoth seriously injured, would one of his only three aides really not boost his security? Or had they lowered their guard because they thought the King of Darkness was dead?

She had a lot of ideas, but the prince's next comment said it all.

"Then that makes it easier to kill him. Let's go."

Everyone took that as the signal to proceed.

When one of the zerun opened the door, Neia, who was standing right in the center of the group, could see clearly into the room.

The office had a high ceiling—at least fifteen feet—and was extremely spacious. Finely furnished, it was the classic image of a luxurious chamber.

Behind a dark, massive desk, a grotesque monster raised its voice.

"A human? Ze—?" He started to say something. But Neia and her squad had no intention of chitchatting.

The prince on Neia's back immediately fired off a spell. "Yin Wu Xing: Raging Fireball!"

Just barely missing Neia, a small, feeble blaze shot into the room. On their way here, the prince had boasted about the power of tier-four attack spells. The fireball would explode on impact, so the idea was to get one off before they entered the room. But then—

"Yang Wu Xing: Raging Fireball!"

The fire disappeared in midair as if it had been blown out in the wind.

"As I thought...," the prince murmured bitterly.

He didn't attack again. The first had been a test. If it hadn't been neutralized, he would have continued, but unfortunately that didn't work out. In order to not waste mana, it was probably best to use his magic to attack in coordination with the others.

"...Is the one on the human's back a zerun? It doesn't look like you caught the humans and dragged them here... Khuh-ha-ha-ha! A rebellion, then? How fun."

The demon who slowly stood looked like a human caricature straight out of a nightmare.

First, he wasn't wearing any clothes, so his arms—long enough that they reached his knees—his legs, and his skin-and-bone body were all exposed.

His withered frame was so thin that even Neia felt like she would be able to snap him in two, no problem.

There wasn't anything that seemed like a head that she could see. From his shoulders came another set of shoulders. No, there was an awfully thin—thinner than a woman's wrist—neck that rose up like a branch and carried two fruits. Was that his head?

"Huh? Oh!" Neia yelped. The shock was so great, that was all she could say at first.

Shizu had mentioned that circlets had two heads.

One of them was grotesque, like a big maggot. It looked a lot like the prince, just as described. That had to be the Grand Mother. The issue was the other one.

It was the head of a woman whose half-open eyes showed only the whites and whose mouth hung partially agape. But though her face was pale, not only had she not decomposed, but her blond hair had even maintained its luster. Red flesh peeked out from the stump of her neck, and it looked so fresh, Neia practically expected blood to start gushing out. The fact that it seemed to have been recently ripped from its body could only be described as strange, but it was also the reason Neia knew who it was immediately.

"Lady Kelart Custodio…"

She had only seen it from a distance, but there was no mistaking the highest-ranking priest in the Sacred Kingdom.

Doubts swirled in Neia's mind.

What did it mean? Was the zerun lying, then? Did they think that Neia and Shizu would run away if they found out it was Kelart?

"I see, I see, I see. Well, zerun, are you saying you don't care what happens to your king or the others living in your homeland? I'll give you one last chance. If you apprehend those two, I'll let you off with a light punishment."

The heads hung there immobile, like two strange fruits. And eyeballs showing only whites were the same. It was as if they really were nothing more than decoration. Then where did his voice come from?

Having no answer for Neia's silent questions, the prince shouted at the great demon.

"Hmph! It's a bit late for that! Why would we believe your nonsense when you already killed the king?!"

"The king? Really?"

Neia could hear the uncertainty in his voice. Since this demon didn't have his own head, he didn't have facial expressions, which, yes, was a pain. They wouldn't be able to tell from his face whether a blow was effective or not. In that sense, zerun were also tricky opponents for humans.

"My job is to rule this land, so that place isn't my jurisdiction, but… hmm. So he was killed? That just means you had a fool for a king."

"How dare you!"

"Tsk, tsk, tsk. You traitors didn't come here to talk, did you? You came because you thought you could defeat me, right? So then what's your trump card? That human?"

A nearly two-foot claw extending from the tip of the finger of his slender hand pointed at Neia.

"As if we would tell you!"

The demon replied calmly to the prince's shout. "You don't have to. Shadow Demons."

The great demon's shadow stretched.

Then it puffed up and went from two to three dimensions. What appeared was a pair of demons, typical in appearance except that they looked as if they'd been doused in black paint.

This must have been why he didn't have any subhuman guards.

"You two, kill the zerun aside from the prince. I'm going to capture him… Human, if you turn on them, I'll free a number of people important to you trapped in the camps equal to the number of fingers on your hands."

The demon proposed the deal Shizu had anticipated he would.

Impressed with that foresight, Neia asked a question to put their opponent off guard. "Really?" She spoke timidly, testing his mood, and he sounded delighted.

"What! You'll betray us?!" When the zerun shouted, all the demon's attention fell on Neia.

"Shut up, shut up, shut up. I'm talking to her… I keep my promises. Count out who you'd like to protect and rescue. If you don't have enough fingers, we can negotiate…"

Unprotected, as if he'd forgotten the words *on guard*, the great demon's stance was full of openings.

Shizu, the ace up their sleeve, didn't fail to notice that. Springing from the shadows, she aimed her Mana Gun.

When the gun spat fire, the great demon clasped a hand over his shoulder.

Shizu had been standing by outside, so this was a total sneak attack. And it was the attack that kicked off the fight.

The talk of negotiations that they had used to distract their enemy was over. The zerun attacked the shadow demons. At the same time, Shizu, who had burst into the room at tremendous speed, didn't slow down for an instant as she employed lightning-quick footwork to bypass the forward fighters of both sides and close in on the great demon.

"What?! Aren't y—?"

"……I don't owe you an explanation."

Shizu used a knife to make a wide slash, but the great demon brushed the attack away with his claws.

Neia knew there was no time for it now that the battle had begun, but she still complained to the zerun on her back. "What do you mean her hair is black? It's blond!"

"Blond? What is? Clearly her hair's light black."

"What?"

He didn't seem to be bluffing. *Could it be that zerun perceive colors differently from humans?*

She had heard that some races who could see through any darkness were color-blind and only saw in black and white. Or that some could only distinguish colors in the light.

The lighting in the pantry had been like that, geared for multiple races—probably so they could distinguish the colors of the foods.

"We can talk later! Yin Wood: Lightning Claw!"

"Tch! Yang Wu Xing: Lightning Claw!"

Lightning coursed through the air like the swipe of a beast's claws but disappeared midway.

There were also the spells Wu Xing: Gentle Metal to lower defensive power and Wu Xing: Metal Strength to increase attack power, and Wu Xing: Summon Lightning Storm, but there was always the possibility that instead of canceling them out, the great demon would use a powerful spell of his own.

To avoid that, the prince only cast attack spells that couldn't be ignored. He narrowed it down further to lightning, which he surmised was the great demon's weakness, and boosted its power with a wood element skill. A normal Wu Xing spell might have been perfectly neutralized, but the prince's strengthened version could deal a tiny bit of damage that would add up.

The Grand Mother should have had the same strengthening powers as the prince, but now she was an accessory for the great demon. He didn't have skills to boost spells, so the power of the prince's magic kept the pressure on.

Since Neia was leaving the vanguard to Shizu, she needed to make sure she pulled her weight as the rear guard. Against such a tough enemy, she couldn't merely act as the prince's feet. She took aim with Ultimate Shooting Star: Super and let an arrow fly.

Though her aim was extremely precise, the great demon had no trouble slapping the arrow away with one hand.

"What a pest. Shock Wave."

Kelart's face—her mouth—moved, and the tier-two spell flew at Shizu. The invisible shock wave took her slightly off her feet, but there was no sign she had taken any damage, such as sluggish movement. One would hardly expect less from a difficulty level–150 demon maid.

"Yin Wood: Lightning Claw!"

"Yang Wu Xing: Lightning Claw!"

They cast the same spells again, and a small amount of electricity coursed through the demon aide's body.

"Open Wounds."

The counterattack was a spell that worsened wounds. The target was, naturally, Shizu, who was the most exposed to the demon's claws.

Neia could only see Shizu's back, but she didn't seem to be losing even a bit of her agility.

A drop of sweat ran down Neia's spine.

Neia was the only one in the party who could heal. That meant she was also in charge of healing, but regardless of how well one could sense their own body, it was extremely difficult to tell how injured someone else was without a wealth of experience.

Especially with someone like Shizu, who didn't show emotions on her

face, Neia was worried the maid would push past her limits before she realized it and collapse. That's why she was keeping an eye on how both Shizu and the prince were moving, but it made her busy in the complicated way of someone ambidextrous.

Nonetheless, she had to do it.

The prince continued firing off spells, and Shizu slashed at the demon with her knife while being slashed at in return. Everyone was performing their roles perfectly, so there was no way Neia could be the only one to complain that she couldn't handle it.

"Heavy Recovery."

Having judged that Shizu's wounds had started adding up, Neia activated the item from the King of Darkness to use the tier-three healing spell on her.

"Aha!"

Neia sensed that the faceless great demon's gaze was directed at her.

His exclamation must have meant that he had discovered the healer—that is, the one he should take out first. And then he really did use the magic he was still allotted after countering the prince's spells to attack her.

"Shock Wave."

An invisible impact hit as if she'd been clobbered with a war hammer.

A nauseating creak reverberated inside her body, and the pain coursing through her made her want to writhe. This hurt a lot more than the magic the va-um used. She couldn't believe Shizu had weathered this like it was nothing. It was a powerful blow—no wonder Kelart Custodio was known as a genius.

"Nnnngh!" A hoarse scream escaped between the gaps in her gritted teeth.

"Are you okay?!"

"I-I'm fine!" Neia replied to the concerned prince.

"Next, I'll get the zerun along wi—"

"—No. I'm protecting Neia." Shizu spread her arms and stood in front of Neia to shield her.

The great demon was tall; Shizu, in contrast, was short. She could stand there, but he probably still had a direct line of sight. Nevertheless, the sentiment made Neia so happy.

"What? Ahhh!" the great demon cried hoarsely.

Shizu's action must have done something to him.

Did she use some kind of special ability? Or a spell?

Neia had no idea what Shizu had done, but the great demon's urge to kill seemed to have weakened. Of course, it was probably just her imagination. There was no reason his hostility should have dropped at this moment.

Neia felt she would be able to withstand one more spell like the attack earlier. Well, she wanted to believe she could anyhow.

She had regained the mana she consumed in the battle with the va-um, but she wasn't sure how many times she would need to use Heavy Recovery, so she wanted to conserve it to the extent possible. That said, if she pushed herself to the brink, one little mistake could send her over. It was an extremely difficult thing to make out.

"And her weapon is a bow that Lord Ainz lent to her!" Shizu stated in a voice that was loud for her. She must have wanted to talk up the King of Darkness? Neia wanted to remind her they were in the middle of a battle, but maybe there was some reason behind it if the most experienced, most powerful person here was saying it.

"What?! That King of Darkness?" the demon aide shouted in surprise. The King of Darkness really was amazing. Jaldabaoth must have told this demon to be on guard against him.

"Yes! A bow made with runes!"

Unable to ignore what was just said, Neia admonished her, "Don't give away our secrets!"

"Oh?! It's a weapon made with lost rune technology? With a weapon like that, you might be able to kill me!"

Why does he seem to be explaining everything so conveniently? thought Neia before feeling ashamed of herself. They were in the middle of a life-and-death battle with a powerful enemy. A weakling like her had it hard enough already. She couldn't afford to waste even a tiny corner of her brain on idle thoughts like that.

"Runes, you say? Marvelous!" The demon aide spoke again, sounding extremely cautious. Maybe the idea was to distract Neia, breaking her focus. And in reality…

"Runes?" she heard the prince asking from her back.

So she said, "No! It's not that kind of weapon!"

Neia felt both Shizu and the great demon freeze. *Oh, that, right.* She figured they were locked motionless, faced with the realization that they were evenly matched.

"Runes…"

"No!" she fairly spat.

"Grm…," the demon aid groaned. "I see… Well, then… Blindness."

Suddenly Neia's field of vision went black. That must have been his way of disabling the healer.

The magic item Neia had borrowed could only cast Heavy Recovery, not any spells that would cure a status like blindness. If their party included a priest or other faith caster, it could have been healed easily enough. Unfortunately, things wouldn't be that simple.

It was unclear how long this enchanted darkness would continue, but if she wanted to heal Shizu, she would have to approach within touching distance…

"I can't see!" It's important to communicate with one's teammates. "Shizu! If you get hurt, let me know!"

"……Mm."

"Sorry! I don't have a spell that can cure a status like that, either!"

"Don't worry about it!" Replying to the apology that came from her back, Neia drew her bow. A body that large she would be able to shoot at from memory. She had learned a bit about fighting sizable opponents from their clash with the va-um. The bowstring twanged.

"Gwaaaooohhh!" The demon aide howled in pain.

"Nice! He tried to evade it but dodged the wrong way! A perfect shot!"

Hearing the prince's commentary, Neia prayed to the King of Darkness. *How lucky was that?*

"……Let's maintain this momentum and take him down."

"Yeah!"

"Right!"

It was difficult to hear through the sounds of the zerun fighting the shadow demons nearby, but focusing every fiber of her being, Neia sensed how Shizu was doing, as well as the demon aide's position, and continued attacking.

Perhaps the demon had realized that he needed to crush Shizu first or he would lose; all his attacks were aimed at her. And many of the spells were the disabling type, like Blindness that he had cast on Neia, so pretty much everything was neutralized.

At that point, all they had to do was keep pushing.

By the time the prince's mana had run out, they had won almost as if it had been a matter of course. His joyous shouts at that moment were borderline obnoxious.

The zerun had lost some members but also won their battle.

The only thing was that the spell on Neia still hadn't lifted. Her field of vision remained pitch-black. But it shouldn't have been a spell that would rob her of the light forever; she was sure it would wear off soon. It was lasting so long because Kelart Custodio was just that powerful of a caster.

She couldn't see, but from the feel and sounds, she could tell the zerun had gathered around her.

"Prince! We're so glad you're safe."

"Yes… Please partake respectfully of the Grand Mother's corpse."

You're gonna eat her? Neia quipped in her head.

But he had said "respectfully," so she could only assume that it was some sort of zerun mourning ritual.

"Neia, what will you do with the human's head? Do you eat it?"

"N-no, that's not how we humans dispose of our dead. I'll bring it back to the castle."

"I see. Human funeral rites are quite puzzling. Well, you must feel the same about ours. I suppose that's what they call a cultural difference. Still, I can't thank you both enough. We never could have—"

"—Wait. We don't have time to chitchat here. We need to get moving."

A disturbance was audible in the distance. Either the liberation army was advancing toward them, or they'd been discovered by the subhuman alliance. It could also be some guards rushing toward them upon hearing the battle noises. No matter what it was, they couldn't stand around dawdling.

"You're right, Miss Shizu. As promised, please assist the liberation army with the capture of Karinsha."

"Yes, of course! Hey, you!"

"Sir! We'll get started right away. Would you and the humans please get into the barrels, Prince? We'll carry you out of the castle."

Neia couldn't see so she wasn't sure, but she got the sense that Shizu, next to her, was hesitating about something. She understood why. She must have hated the barrels. Neia felt the same way.

"......I'll assist."

"I will, too, after my blindness gets cured."

The prince flailed on Neia's back like a freshly caught fish. It was trembles of delight. The fact that she knew that, her adaptability, was a bit stupefying.

"If my sisters-in-arms are off to battle, then so am I. Of course, I used up most of my mana, so I can't rely on any fancy spells, but I can cast some strengthening magic on you."

"Your Highness!"

"Don't make a fuss. Are you telling me to be the kind of male who lets those who fought beside me battle on alone?!"

"......That's about enough. Time to go." Shizu urged them to depart— as if she wanted to be done with the barrels as soon as possible.

"Let's take the barrels to a place where many of my fellow spawn are gathered. Please get in."

Chapter 7 The Hero Who Saves the Country

Chapter 7 | The Hero Who Saves the Country

1

The liberation of Karinsha was surprisingly simple.

The betrayal of the zerun, the absence of the great demon aide, and the lack of subhuman soldiers compared with the size of the city combined to work in their favor. Of course, both sides incurred numerous losses, but the damage to the Sacred Kingdom Liberation Army was surprisingly light in exchange for retaking such a large city.

One reason for that was Neia leading the way with Ultimate Shooting Star: Super.

Though part of the reason she stood out was that Shizu had entered the shadows, and equipped with the splendid, gleaming bow, Neia possessed a dignity that inspired the people.

And now, she was standing on a dais in public giving an impassioned speech to an audience.

Telling them how there was no more wonderful king in this world than the King of Darkness.

The first thing she did after the retaking of Karinsha was seek support for a search party for the king.

Though she had gathered information about the Abellion Hills with the zerun's assistance and also by interrogating subhuman prisoners, she was still lacking the supplies, intelligence, and experience required.

If there were unlimited chances, it would have been one thing, but sending a search and rescue party into enemy territory was a challenge. In other words, she had to succeed in one shot. That meant that it was impossible to overprepare. So she took advantage of the fact that they had retaken Karinsha and saved a lot of people to appeal to a variety of powers.

But just because she asked for help didn't mean she could get it immediately. They may have recaptured Karinsha, but other cities were still occupied, and many people were imprisoned, too. Some people had no idea where their families were. In order to move the hearts of those people, Neia had laid out the benefits of rescuing the King of Darkness.

As the number of supporters increased, however, the content of her talks began to change.

The ones who came to her wanting to hear about the King of Darkness were those who had been saved by him. These were people who had tasted agony and clung to the powerful being as solace for their mental wounds that wouldn't heal.

Those who knew the greatness of the King of Darkness had a sense of belonging.

So it was only natural for Neia to tell them comforting stories of how wonderful he was.

Gradually, people who didn't know the king began to attend. People who had been saved by him invited their acquaintances. Word of mouth had spread to the point that now her audience was a crowd of unrelated listeners.

Neia in her Mirror Shade smoothly related the retaking of the city and the battle with Jaldabaoth and described all the King of Darkness's wondrous traits.

A few weeks ago, she wouldn't have been able to speak so confidently like this. She got nervous in front of so many people and wasn't sure what to say; her mind had blanked like that any number of times. But as she continued speaking, she realized she didn't have to put on any airs. Explaining her experiences of the king's wonderfulness was enough, and she gradually grew more eloquent.

Yes, and then she was called a faceless preacher.

Which was why…

"As you see, His Majesty the King of Darkness is like no other! Has anyone ever cared so much for the common people?! I know what you want to say! And Holy Lady Calca Bessarez is also a wonderful leader. But have you ever heard of someone who has done this much to save the people of another nation? Have you?" Neia pointed at one of the people listening at the front of the crowd. "Have you ever heard of a king who went out on his own because the people of another country were suffering?!"

"Uh, er, well, no, I haven't."

With so many eyes on him, the singled-out man shrank.

"Wonderful! Exactly!"

As Neia praised him, the people on either side of her on the dais, who shared her views, gave the man a round of applause.

He was clearly embarrassed.

"We actually did the research to see if we could find another king like that. But there aren't any! There has never been a king like that anywhere! His Majesty the King of Darkness is the only one!"

There were kings who had led soldiers to a neighboring country as aid, but it was true that no other king had ever gone well and truly alone.

"The king of a nation thought nothing of the danger and assisted the common people of a foreign country. That hasn't happened before! His Majesty is the only one!" After a pause, she repeated herself. "His Majesty is the only one! That's the kind of ruler we can call a king of justice, wouldn't you say?!"

"We're supposed to believe that?! He's an undead!"

The question shot at her from the audience was one Neia could answer with a gentle smile. She had felt the same way at first. In other words, this man was her past self. He was simply ignorant; he didn't have the knowledge.

She wanted to open his eyes—no, the eyes of everyone who felt that way—just as her own had been opened. That was her motivation for speaking to the people.

"It's true! His Majesty is an undead! It's only natural to be wary! It's also true that undead are terrifying monsters. I have absolutely no intention of saying all undead are good. Most undead are undoubtedly evil beings that despise the living."

Grasping from the atmosphere of the venue that all the people listening were following her every word, Neia drove her point home.

"But! There's an exception to every rule. Just as there is a warm day even in the most freezing winter. Like a single bud on a withered old tree. Like the sudden flare of a shooting star in the dead of night. His Majesty... is an undead who helps the living! Some of you probably want to hear from people who have been saved by him. Some of you might have been saved yourselves. Those stories will prove that what I say is true."

Confirming that no one was objecting, Neia spoke in a heavy, dark tone.

"...Our sturdy fortress line had been broken, and the subhumans flooded in. Is this the only time such a tragedy will occur? Do you think we're safe from a second invasion?"

The silence of the audience spoke volumes.

They wanted to think they were, but they couldn't believe it.

"I understand your fears very well. Perhaps we and the generation of your children will be all right. We witnessed the tragedy with our own eyes, so we won't drop our guard... However!" She spoke more forcefully. "Your children's children, your grandchildren's grandchildren—it's impossible to say that they'll be safe! Who can say that history won't repeat?! So we have to be prepared. We have to make sure our fortresses are never breached again."

"Yes! She's right!" shouted voices in the crowd.

"It seems quite a few of you agree with me, but will your children's children and your grandchildren's grandchildren, who will only know of this tragedy as a story, maintain the necessary military power? Do you think they'll have two or three times the army we had on the fortress line?"

Military expenses strain a country's budget, but it's difficult to see the deterrent effects of fighting power.

"I believe some of you were drafted and stationed in a fortress. So please recall something for me. If we needed three times the amount of food in your memories as a regular expense, wouldn't that be a painful burden on our kingdom's coffers? Do you think the royalty of future generations, who know of this tragedy only as a memory, will continue to pay it?"

Neia waited until this had sunk in for her audience before giving her conclusion.

"That's why we need the protection of His Majesty the King of Darkness!"

"Why?! Why from some undead?!"

It was the same man as before.

A single man had been arguing this whole time. Having someone like that in the audience actually made things easier for Neia. It was much harder when no one reacted at all. When that happened, she worried they didn't understand or might not even be listening.

Her collaborators thought maybe they should plant a few people into each crowd on purpose, but Neia refused. She was similarly against fake opposition, too.

"It's precisely because he's undead that we want his protection. His Majesty the King of Darkness is strong and, above all, undying. He'll be there for your children's children and your grandchildren's grandchildren."

"B-but I heard he was defeated and killed."

"That is both true and false. Sadly, the former part is true. In order to help us in our powerlessness, His Majesty used a great deal of magic, consumed a huge quantity of mana, and lost to Jaldabaoth as a result. But the latter part is false. His Majesty the King of Darkness is not dead. Shizu's presence is proof of that."

She was one of those known to have played a critical role in the retaking of Karinsha. Shizu appeared from one wing of the stage when the time was ripe.

Admiring gasps and worshipful "It's Lady Shizu"'s rose from the audience.

"……Mm."

Shizu stood tall.

"This is a demon maid who was once under Jaldabaoth's control. Yet, she was our steadfast ally in the battle to retake Karinsha. Why? Because His Majesty the King of Darkness wrested control of her away from Jaldabaoth."

Many people had seen Shizu hunting and killing subhumans by the dozens during the battle. Those who addressed her as "Lady" had probably been saved by her personally.

Shizu was very popular. Though people knew she was a demon maid who used to obey Jaldabaoth, she was beautiful and retained a certain childishness that endeared her to the masses. In a nutshell, it was hard to be hostile toward her.

Neia had once asked if the King of Darkness had taken that into account when choosing her, and Shizu had answered, "It's possible."

"Shizu is magically controlled by His Majesty the King of Darkness. That control holds as long as he is alive. In other words, her presence here proves that His Majesty is not dead!"

The audience erupted in chatter, and Neia spread her arms to calm everyone. She wasn't finished talking.

"You must wonder why he doesn't show himself. I don't know the answer to that question any more than you. But I can't imagine that merciful being would abandon us! Something must have happened to prevent him from returning right away! We don't know if it's his own decision or if he's in danger. And that's why"—her voice echoed over the silent crowd—"that's why I'm asking for your help! I need your help to go look for His Majesty the King of Darkness. Even if we travel through the hills under subhuman rule and find him, that doesn't mean the Sacred Kingdom has repaid its debts. Because, as I said before, despite the fact that he only came here to fight Jaldabaoth, we were so weak that he was forced to fight subhumans, and since he had used up his power on that, he was defeated!" Neia spoke even louder. "And so—everyone! We must repay the one who came to our rescue! I don't want to be the kind of person who wouldn't go help my savior when he was in need just because he's an undead! Anyone who wants to repay the debt we owe His Majesty, I have a favor to ask of you."

She paused for effect before raising her voice.

"I'm seeking people who will help me aid His Majesty the King of Darkness! You don't have to actually go on the journey! Your technology, your knowledge—anything is welcome! Please lend me your strength! I beg for your assistance!"

When Neia bowed, Shizu next to her also gave a shallow bow.

The audience sent up cries of approval.

Upon straightening, Neia had one last thing to say.

"...I'm sure some of you have listened to what I had to say and still don't believe me. So will you listen to someone who was part of the liberation army even before the battle for Karinsha? Then I think you'll see that I haven't been lying to you."

●

When she got back to her room, Neia flopped heavily into a chair.

"Welcome back, Lady Baraja."

The one welcoming her was a quiet-seeming, heavyhearted woman.

No more than twenty, her most distinctive features were her ample bosom, which would have likely caught Neia's attention if she were a man, and short hair. She said she used to have long hair, but it had been cut in the prison camp.

The woman was a member of the support organization Neia had created. Because those working with her wanted to give it a name, it was called the King of Darkness Rescue Team.

She assisted Neia, who had suddenly become incredibly busy.

It had been a couple of weeks since they had met, and her presence had become essential. She performed her tasks—cleaning, washing, cooking—so perfectly.

"Th-thank you."

She wiped her face with the moist towel the woman handed her. The coolness felt good on her warm cheeks.

"Oof." She emitted a noise like a middle-aged man as she put the towel on the table and then looked to the woman, who immediately picked it up.

"Um, like I always say, I wish you wouldn't call me 'Lady.' I'm no one so important as that."

"How can you say that? You're the representative of His Majesty the King of Darkness in this country. It would be ill-mannered not to show the proper respect to someone taking the initiative to work for His Majesty."

She wasn't sure how to respond when a woman older than her said that.

It seemed like a common worry for anyone not used to being in a superior position.

And in the first place, Neia didn't speak for the king. Or rather, how had she ended up in such a position?

Shizu, who was looking on absentmindedly from where she lay on a sofa, seemed a better choice.

Really, anyone should have been able to recognize the King of Darkness's greatness just by looking objectively. It seemed absurd to be called a spokesperson when she was only stating the obvious. It wasn't as if she was explaining the organization's beliefs and opinions or something.

She had been the first to move, but she didn't expect this to happen.

"All right, I'll be going now. Oh, and Beltrán Moro would like to see you."

"Okay. Would you have him come? Thanks for your help today."

Her assistant left with a bow, and a man came in as if to take her place. The woman who helped her had an aversion to and fear of men, so being in the same room with them made her feel sick. For that reason, they always took turns.

"Lady Baraja, apologies for calling on you when you could use a rest. May I have a bit of your time?"

Beltrán Moro…

He was a thickly built man in his midforties with noticeably thinning hair.

The Moro family was originally a house of rather high rank and had been butlers for generations; Beltrán himself had previously worked as a butler. To take advantage of his skills, she made use of him as something like a secretary in the organization.

She was lucky to have met someone like him right as she was establishing the organization. If she hadn't, she would surely have gray hair already despite being so young.

"Oh, I don't mind. What's going on?"

"Thank you. Then I'll get right to it. Currently the organization has over thirty thousand members."

"Wow, that's amazing! To think so many people grasp how wonderful His Majesty the King of Darkness is! Well, no, it's a matter of course, isn't it? His Majesty truly is an awesome being."

Shizu nodded.

Their organization now had enough members to populate a small city. There were 3.5 million people living in the northern Sacred Kingdom, so almost 1 percent of the population was on board.

"Those supporters are saying they would like some kind of symbol that shows they are a member."

"I...see... Yeah, that...might be good."

"Yes. Having something that indicates their belonging puts people's hearts at ease and gives them a sense of solidarity."

Neia nodded, *hmm*ing. Belonging—something associated with the King of Darkness would make them happiest. Even Neia wanted something like that.

"Then, uh, please come up with whatever you think is best. But don't distinguish between different amounts of financial support."

"......Unoff...an...lub..."

Neia heard something that even she with her sharp ears couldn't make out completely.

"Miss Shizu, did you say something?" she asked.

"......Nope."

"...Oh. Well, if I say something wrong regarding His Majesty, please let me know." Neia turned back to Beltrán. She was happy that more people were unfazed by her gaze of late. "You can proceed with manufacturing. And…can you tell me what the schedule is looking like today?"

"Of course, Lady Neia. In about two hours, there will be a supporter event titled With Thanks to His Majesty the King of Darkness. Your participation and a speech about His Majesty's feats would be most appreciated."

"Got it."

Neia was a little excited. She had an affinity for these supporters, her comrades, who understood the notion she had discovered, that His Majesty the King of Darkness was justice. She loved talking with people who shared her feelings.

"And there's been a request for a drill inspection. You're very busy right now. Shall I refuse?"

They had created the Supporters Guard and were training hard. Neia sometimes joined, and Shizu popped in now and then, too.

To Neia, who knew she was only deadweight to the king because she was weak, it was only natural to train and get stronger. If her participation would inspire them to keep at it, then she felt she should definitely go.

"No. I'll go."

"Everyone will be delighted to hear that! And…that was everything I had to report for now. Factoring in prep time for the event, you have about an hour, so please rest well."

Beltrán exited with a bow. After watching him go, Neia stood from her chair and walked over to Shizu on the sofa. Then she lay down and squashed Shizu in an embrace.

"……There, there."

Shizu was shorter than her, but the maid rubbed her back like a mother would for a small child.

"I wonder when we'll be able to go look for His Majesty. It's already been a month…"

The group that searched the eastern part of the Sacred Kingdom didn't find the king. They couldn't rule out the possibility that they simply missed him, but Neia was sure that he must have fallen in subhuman territory, the

Abellion Hills. That was why they needed to prepare so much, but even so, it was taking too long.

Of the three thousand zerun that betrayed Jaldabaoth, two thousand eight hundred had gone with the prince to the Nation of Darkness, and the other two hundred had headed to the hills on an intelligence-gathering mission, but Neia hadn't heard anything yet.

"……Failure isn't an option."

"I know! But—but…"

Neia hugged Shizu even tighter, clinging. Shizu smelled like tea, so she inhaled.

Shizu was the only one who could make Neia feel better—because as long as Shizu was around, it meant the King of Darkness was alive.

"……Don't worry. Lord Ainz is a generous master."

"Yes, you're right, Miss Shizu."

"……So we should increase our supporters and build a plan that will definitely succeed."

"Yes, you're right, Miss Shizu."

"……That will make Lord Ainz happy."

"Yes, you're right, Miss Shizu."

"……Neia, you really are one of my favorites. Once you get used to it, your face definitely has its own flavor."

"…Flavor… By the way, it must be a drag to be cooped up in here. Would you like to go somewhere together sometime?"

Shizu attracted lots of attention with her unusual, almost handcrafted beauty. But when people learned she was a demon maid, their gazes filled with fear and suspicion. Often, they became convinced she was after their souls or something. That was because of the demons of legend who transformed into a beautiful woman and struck contracts to rob people of their souls, but Neia felt like even that demon probably had standards for her targets.

And in the first place, why would a difficulty level–150 demon maid, serving the generous, merciful King of Darkness, want some random townsperson's soul?

Still, they wanted to avoid any trouble, and if any harm came to Shizu, Neia would never be able to face the king. Of course, she realized that Shizu was so powerful, it would be impossible for anyone to hurt her.

In any case, Neia had her stay indoors. Still, now that their supporters had grown, she figured going out in areas where they gathered wouldn't be a problem.

"......That's not a bad idea. I'll go as practice."

"Then let's get ready. That maid uniform will stick out... Do you think you could change into regular clothes?"

"......The professor......ahem. I'd like you to lend me some. I'll leave the look up to you."

"...Sorry. I don't have anyone to go out with, and I'm not interested in clothes, so I don't have much confidence when it comes to planning outfits."

Shizu patted her shoulder gently. At a glance, she appeared emotionless, but Neia noticed something motherly in her kindness. Then Shizu pointed a thumb at herself. "......Leave it to me."

"Really?"

It was after this that she realized Shizu had unexpectedly decent taste.

•

After the recapture of Karinsha, the amount of work on Caspond's plate suddenly increased. With all the newly liberated people, he had a lot of organization-building tasks to do. And because of the influx in information he had to deal with, confirming everything and delegating also took considerable time.

Guarding him during this busy time was a single paladin.

It was reckless, but he couldn't use a paladin with superior skills in maintaining public safety who could read, write, do arithmetic, and manage events as a mere bodyguard. In that sense, it would probably have been most efficient to have Remedios paired with him, but given her mental state, he was having her train with some other paladins.

Her fit of rage when Neia and Shizu had returned with Kelart Custodio's head was so great that he worried there would be casualties. She had calmed down but was still treated as if she was liable to go off at any moment.

Honestly, he wouldn't have been able to do this alone. *I really owe it to all the people who have lent me their wisdom*, thought Caspond, his respect only growing for them, as he got down to work with his pen.

It was practice for the future, yes, but still annoying work. Caspond kept his complaints to himself, but a paladin who either couldn't take a hint or was really that distressed spoke to him.

"Master Caspond, what about Neia Baraja?"

Realizing what the question implied, he answered without looking up from his paperwork, an exhausted smile on his face. "There's nothing we can do. Leave her alone. And 'Master' is plenty title for me."

"Thank you. But what do you mean, there's nothing we can do?"

The paladin didn't seem to get it, so Caspond looked up from his work and made eye contact. "If we pressured her to stop, what do you think would happen?"

"I don't think anything would happen, sir. Her activities will destabilize the country if they keep going on."

"I see. Have you ever listened to her teachings? Although I'm not sure that's the right word. It doesn't seem like it, so you must have read a summary? Let me ask you something: Were there any lies in them?"

The paladin seemed to be searching his memory, so Caspond gave the answer.

"She's not lying, but it would be better if she were. Anyone with a little knowledge can corroborate almost everything—that the King of Darkness is a hero who liberated the people and single-handedly recaptured a city." He took a sip from the cup of water on the table before continuing. "And Neia Baraja is a hero who contributed to the liberation of Karinsha. We made that public. We introduced the demon maid, the King of Darkness's servant, and went a little overboard praising Neia so that the king wouldn't get much more profile. She even looks like a hero with that equipment of hers." With the splendid bow she borrowed from the King of Darkness and Mighty King Buser's breastplate, what did she appear to be if not a hero?

"So back to my question. What would we look like if we put pressure on her? Don't you think it would go something like, *What she's saying is inconvenient for the Sacred Kingdom, so they're trying to silence the hero?*"

"That would never…" The paladin mumbled a denial, but the look on his face spoke louder than words: He had realized that was how it would go.

"A rising hero or a falling royal family? Which do you think the people would belie—?"

"Master Caspond, please don't talk like that!"

"Sorry… Anyhow, what do you think the demon maid would do if we tried to interfere with Neia's teachings?"

"Urk…"

The paladin's face scrunched up, and Caspond put on a devious expression.

"Heh-heh. Being protected by that maid means she has the most powerful military force in the whole city! It's too dangerous to try to subdue her head-on. That's why she's being left alone. I understand your fears. But there are no good moves available to us."

There came a knock at the door, and the serviceman from outside entered.

"Master Caspond, the deputy commander of the paladins requests an audience."

"Show him in right away."

Gustav must have heard him from where he was standing by outside, because he came right in. His slightly hard breathing indicated that he had rushed over.

"Apologies for the interruption, Master Caspond!"

Gustav had even more work to do than Caspond, so he was very busy. For that reason, he didn't come in person very often, so Caspond knew something was wrong. It had to be some kind of problem that he couldn't solve on his own.

"I tell you every time, you don't have to worry about it. And it's just us—there's no need to bow so low. It seems like you came in a hurry, so what's going on?"

"A lookout spotted an army of fifty thousand flying the crest of a southern noble. It's headed this way."

"I see… Did the southern army defeat Jaldabaoth's subhumans, then? In any case, prepare for combat. There's no guarantee that they aren't being manipulated by Jaldabaoth."

"Yes, sir!"

"Make sure no one attacks unless the other side does first. If they want to talk, bring them here. And"—Caspond turned to the paladin—"you take point on welcoming our guests. If my hunch is right, we'll be entertaining a number of high-ranking nobles. We need to have food and drink they'll enjoy."

"Yes, sir!" the two of them acknowledged and left the room.

Watching them go, Caspond murmured, "So…has the time come?"

•

"I do so appreciate you coming, Marquis Bodipo, Count Coen, Count Dominguez, Count Granero, Count Landaluze, Viscount Sants."

"Oh, we're just glad you're safe, Master Caspond."

"Indeed! Indeed! We were ever so worried!"

After a toast, once the southern nobles had quenched their thirst with a sip of wine, Caspond celebrated everyone's safety and continued to trade smiling greetings.

The nobles told him what had been going on, how they had struggled. Caspond spent all his time listening; they were relating their suffering to show him how devoted they were to the Sacred Kingdom.

After speaking at length, Count Coen seemed to realize something and asked, "Hmm? Master Caspond, has something about you changed?"

"Yes, of course. You've heard that Jaldabaoth has been traveling around the north? I've changed a great deal on the inside as a result of that. Not only that, I think I've changed in places you can't see as well… Look here, don't I seem thinner?"

Caspond indicated his belly with a merry smile and got the response,

"It does look like that, doesn't it!" At the same time, a faint yet sharp glint appeared in the nobles' eyes.

Caspond didn't miss it—he knew that they were comparing him now to the way he was before.

They cleverly concealed the fact right away, but he was certain they were continuing to appraise him.

He didn't want them to think anything had changed. His main goal was to avoid allowing anyone to meddle in the royal family's affairs after the war.

"…How can I ever thank all you heads of houses for sallying forth to fight in this battle to save the Sacred Kingdom?"

"What are you saying, Master Caspond? It's only natural that we would do so as servants of the royal family. Any able-bodied noble who wouldn't fight for the future of our kingdom isn't fit for the rank!"

All the nobles nodded. In other words, there were heads of households who didn't go to battle, and they were these men's political rivals.

Unfortunately, Caspond wasn't familiar with which nobles got on poorly with whom. It could be counted as an unfortunate lapse of knowledge.

He needed to avoid making promises, but at the same time, not giving these men preferential treatment would be problematic. Flitting from side to side was frowned upon.

"Your devotion to the Sacred Kingdom must be known far and wide. I should say it even deserves to go down in history."

The one who appeared the most delighted, if only for a moment, was the eldest among them, the graying blond-haired Marquis Bodipo.

It was because he already had rank and influence that he was interested in glory. The others were probably still more interested in rewards. Of course, they had brought a large army. It was only natural they would want to be compensated.

As he was flattering the marquis, who was refraining only from speaking much, Viscount Sants, looking peaked, awkwardly spoke up. "Master Caspond, there's something I'd like to ask you… What in the world happened to the Holy Lady? We heard she passed away, but…"

"That is the truth."

His ready response left Viscount Sants blinking, and the man asked a further question. "A-and where is her holy body?"

"It was in such poor condition that we cremated her. Normally, we would have used Preservation and held a royal funeral after driving off Jaldabaoth, but..." Caspond's pained face indicated that he couldn't say any more. "The death of high cleric Kelart Custodio has also been confirmed..."

"I see..."

The nobles trailed off, affording Caspond the time to sip his wine.

A substitute for the Holy Lady was seated before them, but the most advanced faith caster in the kingdom couldn't be replaced so easily. They were probably thinking about how to best take advantage of her death.

When no one had spoken up after his second sip of wine, he volunteered more information. "We cremated her as well. The condition of her body was simply too horrible to consider any other option."

The nobles frowned. Had something occurred to them, hearing that the two most honorable people in the country had died awful deaths? This was a life-and-death battle—losing meant dying. Perhaps they had finally realized there was no paying a ransom to go free if they were taken prisoner, and it scared them.

"And what happened to Commander Remedios?"

"Did you want to speak with her? Do you mind waiting a moment?"

"Oh, she's alive? Even though the Holy Lady and high cleric are dead?" the splendidly bearded Count Landaluze remarked nastily, and the others sneered. Caspond opened the door and had the guard standing by call Remedios.

By the time his cup was empty, she was entering the room.

When Count Landaluze saw her, his eyes went wide. "What?! You're Commander Remedios Custodio?!"

Instead of disdain, his voice contained shock. Surely, every noble in the Sacred Kingdom knew her face. And that went for Count Landaluze as well. That was why he was so surprised: the gap between his memory and the woman before him.

Remedios Custodio was almost like a ghost.

Sunken orbits, hollow cheeks. But in contrast, her eyes shone bright.

"You called me, didn't you? Who else did you think would come?"

"What! You impu...dent..." His voice trailed off—because she glared at him.

Frankly, Remedios as she had become was terrifying. It was impossible to know what was on her mind, and there was no telling what she might do. That was why Caspond couldn't keep her with him. And they were even taking pains not to let any information about Neia's activities reach her.

"What do you need?"

Everyone in this country knew that Remedios was its strongest paladin. She had achieved a pinnacle of martial prowess.

Authority was no use against berserker violence. The most robust armor that could protect a noble was like paper to Remedios. In the past, there had always been someone nearby who could rein her in, and her mental state had been such that a little sarcasm wouldn't set her off. But now things were different.

It was because they realized that that none of the nobles said a word. Remedios snorted with a shrug. "...Master Caspond, can I leave? They don't seem to want anything."

"Yeah, thanks."

Once Remedios had left, the nobles finally twisted up their faces in disgust.

"She was so discourteous to you, yet you allow it?"

"She may be the commander of the paladins, but that attitude was too much. Someone who clearly lacks devotion to the royal family shouldn't be left to command any longer."

Caspond stayed the eruption of discontent with a raised hand. "We're currently at war. Her skill with a sword is useful. The next king can decide what happens after that."

How many people had actually been offended by her attitude? Certainly, there were those who concealed their fear with anger, but Caspond smiled wanly in his mind knowing that they had a different agenda.

Remedios was the previous ruler's military might and a fine weapon. There had to be those who didn't want to see that weapon passed on to the next holy king. Or perhaps that was true of all these nobles.

"Ohhh! That's an excellent point! We're at war! But we can't keep fighting the subhumans forever!"

"Yes, it's as the count says! I believe our messenger summarized the situation for you, but we were able to come all this way because the subhuman forces have retreated! Master Caspond! We should capitalize on this momentum and attack!"

"Hear! Hear! Now is the time to rout them and thus increase your renown!"

"I see, I see. And…what happened to Elder Purple?"

The nobles exchanged glances, and Marquis Bodipo spoke as their representative.

"He seems to be in poor health and was not able to come with us."

The oldest marquis, who was in his eighties, was called "Elder," and he was also one of the Nine Colors. A great noble in the south, he had been awarded the color for his faithful service to the royal family.

So it was that not all the Nine Colors were given strictly for strength; sometimes they were given for outstanding deeds. The famous artist wife of a certain duke who held the Indigo title was another example.

Reading the momentary emotion that Bodipo couldn't conceal as he answered the question, Caspond mentally smiled. He had already been aware, but confirming it with his own eyes produced that reaction.

"…Ah. Gentlemen, your opinion aligns with my thoughts on the matter." Caspond told them about his idea to stall Jaldabaoth's plan by eradicating the subhumans. "…But what will we do if Jaldabaoth shows up?"

"Is this Jaldabaoth demon really so powerful as all that? We've heard that commander of yours wasn't able to protect you."

Count Granero was able to ask such a naive question because he had never faced the demon, and Caspond responded gravely, "He's terribly powerful. We invited the King of Darkness to face him, and the fight was extraordinary."

OVERLORD 13 The Paladin of the Sacred Kingdom Part II
3 2 0

"The King of Darkness? You mean that undead?!"

It was only natural that they would react in surprise.

"Oh? You haven't heard about that? Huh…"

"You went to another nation for military support, Master Caspond? That's unacceptable!"

"Not the military, the king—just the king."

"Eh?" The nobles all froze. It took a little while for them to thaw out.

"Just the king? A ruler, the leader of a country, came on his own?"

Caspond nodded at Count Landaluze that that was the case.

"But that can't be true! Who has ever heard of such a king? Perhaps his army was stationed nearby?"

They all murmured in turn that it went against common sense, that it might be some sort of plot. But Caspond shut all their opinions down.

"In any case, it's the truth, so that's that. And if his army had been nearby, it surely would have sprung into action the moment he was defeated in the duel."

"He lost? …I don't quite follow. We've heard he's an undead, so did his brains rot through? And…isn't this extremely bad?"

"Indeed. And Remedios was one of the messengers who invited him. We'll need some sort of diplomatic maneuver, like sending her to request forgiveness."

"You think we'll get off that easily…? That said, the Nation of Darkness is situated on Re-Estize land. It would be difficult to cross through enemy territory to reach us. If the Re-Estize Kingdom falls, I suppose we'll need to watch out."

The nobles were all frustratingly confused. It was like trying to decide what to do about the sun suddenly rising in the west. Thus, they seemed to have decided it would be best to think about it later.

"Setting that aside, what are you planning to do now, Master Caspond?"

"I want to retake the royal capital—and as soon as possible."

"If that's your intention, you have our support!"

"You can be the hero who saves the country from Jaldabaoth!"

"A subhuman army of a hundred thousand invaded. So far, we've probably reduced them down to just over thirty thousand. I'm sure by combining the forces in this city with those that we've brought, defeating them will be a simple matter!"

"It seems like the time has come to call you 'Your Majesty,' Master Caspond!"

Hearing all the nobles say the things he wanted to hear, he purposely put on an expression that said things were going exactly as he wished. "Right, and it's only possible with your cooperation. I won't forget to extend my gratitude."

"Whatever are you talking about?! We're only acting out of loyalty to the Sacred Kingdom and the royal family!"

In his mind, Caspond smiled a different smile.

"Good. Now then, gentlemen, let's set about retaking the capital, shall we?"

2

One week after combining forces with the army the nobles had led up from the south, preparations were complete, and a new offensive was launched.

The next objective was Prato, a large city to the west of Karinsha.

Swaying along with the motion of her horse, Neia was unable to conceal her displeasure.

Her mind agreed with the plan to seize this chance—Jaldabaoth healing his wounds—and eradicate the subhumans. But her heart found it unforgivable. She wanted to increase the number of people who understood her feelings and put her efforts into preparing a perfect search and rescue party for the King of Darkness.

That said, Neia knew from watching Remedios that having an edgy, irritated commander affected a unit's morale. It was awful the way she took her stress out on her reports.

When Neia took a deep breath to calm down, chilly, refreshing air filled her lungs. Though spring was near, the cold of winter still lingered a bit in the atmosphere.

Having composed herself, Neia turned her attention to the massive advancing army.

There were around ninety-five thousand soldiers streaming endlessly forward. Of those, roughly thirty thousand came from the south under the command of the newly arrived nobles, and sixty-five thousand were from the liberation army. Incidentally, of the remaining twenty thousand of the nobles' forces, ten thousand set off for home, and ten thousand were resting in Karinsha.

Neia was leading an archer unit of two thousand. They were all members of the support organization.

Meanwhile, the remainder of the subhuman army was estimated at thirty thousand, so there was an overwhelming numerical disparity.

But individual subhumans were stronger than humans, and above all, there was still the lingering fear of Jaldabaoth, so they couldn't rest easy even when outnumbering their enemies.

This operation was premised on the assumption that Jaldabaoth, injured as he was, wouldn't make a move. If the demon's wounds had healed, it was clear that this would be a death march.

Neia's heart began to pound.

She fell into the loop of worrying that they should have prioritized the rescue party.

"—Lady Baraja. Do you require any information from the other units our members are stationed in?"

The question from Beltrán, riding next to her, was confusing. She didn't understand what he was getting at.

After thinking for a moment and catching his drift, she quickly waved him off with the hand that wasn't holding the reins.

"N-no, there's no need to act like spies. We're all working together toward the same objective here."

"Ohhh, I'd expect nothing less from Lady Baraja, representative of His Majesty the King of Darkness. You're so kind."

"……But her face is scary." It was Shizu who mumbled that following Beltrán's praise. She was riding behind Neia with her arms around her waist because she couldn't ride herself.

Shizu always, always had to comment like that, and despite the fact that Neia respected her for her experience, the verbal jab stung.

Maybe I should make her walk…

Of course, Shizu was stronger in her legs and in general than an average human. The reason Neia let her ride with her was that she figured it would be rude to force a servant of His Majesty to walk.

Beltrán was listening, but he didn't stick up for her. He neither confirmed nor denied it. In all likelihood, he simply found it awkward to disagree with a servant of the king and more that the comment was the undeniable truth.

Yeah, I'm sure it's impossible to argue… I mean, if it weren't true, I wouldn't have to wear the Mirror Shade …

But Neia was a woman nonetheless. Being told how frightening her face was all the time—even if it was the truth, even if she was used to it—still hurt her feelings a little.

"So, Lady Baraja, a message has arrived from the main force. The scouts have spotted the subhuman army. We've been told their estimate was thirty thousand, and it seems we're going to camp here for the moment. The messenger only told me that much before returning to the main force, but did you need him?"

"It's fine. If it didn't bother you, then it's no problem."

Beltrán made a fantastic adjutant.

"But do the subhumans want a field battle…?"

The subhuman alliance forces were only a third of the size of the Sacred Kingdom's. Though they were superior one-on-one, they seemed to have no hope of victory in a battle with formations on an open plain. If, instead, they holed up in a city, they could use those defenses to ameliorate the numerical disparity.

Either way, if Jaldabaoth was healed up, a Sacred Kingdom victory would be a long shot. Buying time was the subhumans' best option.

Or perhaps they meant to have a localized fight somewhere horses couldn't go.

"The site of the battle would seem to be flat, right?"

"Yes, that's correct. There is no forest or any other cover where they could conceal forces. And there aren't any hills, either, so there will probably be some dispute over where precisely to camp."

"……Why would they choose a place like that?"

"My guess is"—Beltrán prefaced his answer to Shizu's question—"they mean to run."

"Run?"

"Yes, Lady Baraja. Similar to the zerun, who switched sides, not all the subhumans are enamored with Jaldabaoth. If they want to flee and survive, even if that means betraying him, they would choose a field battle over a siege. It would be difficult to escape during a siege battle."

A dark emotion glinted in Beltrán's eyes.

Neia wondered if she needed to exercise her newly acquired power, but the darkness gradually dissipated, and the usual gleam soon returned. The reality of the impending battle must have quelled his hatred for the time being.

"……I see."

Beltrán replied to Shizu's admiring nod with, "It was nothing."

What he had said certainly made sense.

And it would probably be difficult for Jaldabaoth to tell who died in battle and who tried to flee. *In that case, waiting until night to attack would give them a chance to run, which could reduce the number of needless deaths.*

That's what Neia thought, but she couldn't say it aloud.

The subhumans had caused the people of this country too much suffering.

Apparently, subhumans who serve His Majesty the King of Darkness are just barely allowable, but the rest have to die…

It was rumored that people who called for reconciliation with the sub-humans or allied with them were being secretly lynched.

And when she had liberated prison camps with the subhumans, they had found corpses that seemed to have been lynched. They appeared to be the bodies of those who had tried to collaborate with the subhumans.

"Lady Baraja, I don't know what the higher-ups are thinking or how we will be positioned, but shall I gather the leaders of each squad?"

"No, you can do that once you figure out where we're going. I think everyone knows what to do no matter where they get stationed."

Neia figured that where they would be positioned would depend on how the higher-ups wanted to use Shizu.

If there were powerful subhumans among their enemies, they would probably be sent to the front lines in order to make use of Shizu. If they were going to be used as normal archers, they would probably be put somewhere in the army's center or wherever the other archers were. If the leaders were concerned about being shown up by a servant of the King of Darkness, they would probably be sent to the rear.

Neia expected that they would be in the follow-up wave until a first attack had been launched.

And three hours later, she learned that she had been correct.

•

Facing the subhumans, who were lumped into a single wedge-like formation, the humans were broadly split in two. The thirty thousand troops of the nobles' army plus ten thousand from the liberation army made up the forty-thousand-strong left wing, and the remaining fifty-five thousand from the liberation army were in a sort of flying wedge on the right.

Since the humans intended to eradicate the subhumans in this battle, they began to enact a gradual encirclement.

Whether they meant to break through and flee or turn the fight into a melee and kill as many humans as possible, the subhumans had chosen a formation built for penetration.

In the end, Neia and her unit were stationed on their own, somewhat removed from the battlefield, guarding the military engineers constructing the camp.

Rather than an order from Caspond, it had been a request, and they were practically allowed to operate as they pleased. It didn't matter if they ignored the engineers' security. The current top of the Sacred Kingdom gave those instructions, seeming to forfeit his authority.

The reason was, unsurprisingly, the presence of Shizu.

Neia was the commander of the unit, but Caspond probably felt they couldn't order around Shizu, who accompanied her; she was basically a resident of the Nation of Darkness. The Sacred Kingdom's royal family giving commands to a subject of the King of Darkness could cause trouble in the future.

It made Neia wonder why now, after the maid had worked so hard during the capture of Karinsha, but it seemed her treatment had changed somewhat with the arrival of the southern nobles. Perhaps it was because they had to think about the future now, not just the present.

Neia and her unit organized themselves into ranks, gazing at the battlefield in the distance.

That said, since they were so far away, there was none of the usual battlefield tension. The seething energy didn't reach them. The sound, coming from behind the unit, of the engineers hammering posts into the ground with their wooden mallets was so peaceful.

"......Are they still just staring at one another? When will it start?"

"Any time that passes works against us. I think we'll be the ones to make the first move, but..."

It was Beltrán who answered Shizu's question.

Darkness was an ally to subhumans. On an open plain like this, moonlight would allow the humans to see clearly, but the sky was overcast. If the enemy attacked during the night, it would definitely mean trouble. Their position wasn't terribly solid at the moment.

So surely, the human side would attack before nightfall.

And they had overwhelming numerical superiority, so it would be a total victory—if they took out the majority of the subhumans, it might also thwart Jaldabaoth's plan. In other words, the Sacred Kingdom would finally be rescued from this long period of suffering. There was no reason to sit on their hands.

Neia, too, hoped that with this battle it would all be over. Then there would be nothing to hold her back. She would be able to put all her energy into searching for the King of Darkness.

She raised her head.

A battle cry went up, and she could hear with her sharp ears the thudding of a vast number of feet. Beltrán must have heard it a beat later. "So it's begun," he murmured.

From where they were situated, it was difficult to tell how the two armies, over a hundred thousand troops in total, were maneuvering or how the clash would happen.

The subhumans had chosen to wait for them on such flat land that there were no vantage points from which one could take in the entire battlefield.

That was a job for a watchtower, but the engineers were in the middle of assembling it inside the camp.

"……What should we do?"

"Our role is to stay here and guard these guys. Let's do a proper job."

She couldn't imagine that the outnumbered subhuman army would break through the human forces to reach them. Positioning Shizu, with her immense power, in the rear may have been the best move politically, but in a military sense, it could be said to be an awful idea.

Simply by putting her on the front lines, the Sacred Kingdom Liberation Army's casualties would fall dramatically.

Everyone understood that, yet they still refused. They wanted to avoid her becoming any more famous than she already was.

These deaths will be pointless, thought Neia, but there was no way she could say that.

Thirty minutes or more later, she heard a cheer go up on the right wing. It wasn't her superior ears that picked it up—the roar was loud enough to reach her entire unit. If they could hear it all the way where they were, someone must have achieved something fantastic.

It was ten minutes later that a messenger arrived on horseback to shout the news.

"Paladin Commander Remedios Custodio has slain the scale demon, which was both aide to Jaldabaoth and commander of the enemy army!"

With that, he rode off.

Neia wondered if that was really true.

Well, it was probably true that Remedios slayed a demon. But was it really one of Jaldabaoth's great demon aides?

Neia knew how strong the aides were from fighting that one with Shizu in Karinsha.

She hardly thought Remedios would be a match for a demon like that.

Has she gotten strong enough to defeat that thing? Or…could it have been a body double? I need to ask Shizu.

"Miss Shizu, I have a question. How strong is a scale demon?"

"……Just weak enough that the commander could beat one."

"But I thought circlets were stronger than that."

"……Some demons are strong, and some are weak. Scale demons are weak."

"I see…"

Neia was relieved. This meant they had defeated the two great demons who had invaded. The only one left was the one in the hills, so it wouldn't do any good to worry about it now.

"Now our country can be saved… The enemy commander is dead. The subhuman army will surely collapse as a result. According to Master Caspond's calculations, this should be the end of it…"

Beltrán must have seemed disappointed because they had lost the opportunity to get revenge.

"……There will still be the job of hunting down the defeated remnants."

"Right! Of course, Lady Shizu!"

But Beltrán's delighted expression as he replied immediately stiffened.

A column of flames had gone up in what appeared to be the center of the left wing—the nobles' forces. The hellish fire, tall enough that they could see it from a distance, seemed as though it was trying to burn the very heavens.

Neia looked to Shizu in a panic.

There was only one being capable of something like that. And Shizu confirmed her fears.

"……Not good…… It's Jaldabaoth."

•

"Paladin Commander Remedios Custodio has slain the scale demon, which was both aide to Jaldabaoth and commander of the enemy army!"

When they heard the news from the messenger sent by Caspond on the right wing, a cheer went up. Marquis Bodipo broke into a smile.

"Mwa-ha-ha-ha! We did it! I can't believe she got the commander! That woman may not have much of a head on her shoulders, but her arms sure know what they're doing. Now the enemy will lose heart. Tell them to keep pushing and crush the subhumans so that not a single one escapes!"

"Yes, your lordship!"

Having taken the marquis's orders, the soldiers scattered.

"So we've done it, your lordship. It's extremely fortunate that we were participating in this battle where we were able to take out the enemy's commander," Count Coen said, all smiles. The marquis rather favored this member of his faction.

"Right you are, Count. Now we're a step ahead of them."

The commander of the army that the forces of the southern nobles' alliance had been skirmishing with for ages had been slain. This was a major achievement, and it was sure to be a useful card to play against the other southern nobles.

It was less their interactions with Remedios Custodio than her younger sister, Kelart, that had left a bitter aftertaste, but this feat was enough to make them forget that grudge.

And this would give Caspond some prestige. Frankly, if he survived to the end, he was almost certain to be the next holy king. Even the southern nobles who still had power remaining wouldn't be able to complain, and if Bodipo backed him with everything he had, there were not likely to be any issues.

If he was anxious about anything, it was what had happened to the other members of the royal family, but if they were dead, that problem solved itself. He had no intention of getting his hands dirty, however, so regarding that matter, he could only pray.

He cheerfully pictured the future map of influence in noble society.

He couldn't stumble in these critical moments if he wanted to become the most powerful noble in the Sacred Kingdom. Everything had gone perfectly so far. All that was left was to keep it up.

"Count, do you think it's possible to drive the subhumans south?"

"Forgive my ignorance, but why would we want to do that?" the count asked with a shocked look on his face. He sounded utterly confused.

The marquis inwardly chuckled at him.

There was no way he didn't understand. The marquis didn't remember appointing anyone so inept to such a high position. He was feigning surprise after surmising what the marquis was thinking.

The idea must have been to pretend that the great marquis was plotting something he could never have come up with. A hollow bit of flattery.

But the marquis played along. If the count was convinced he had Bodipo in the palm of his hand, Bodipo would have an easier time manipulating him.

"Look, don't you think the subhumans would make an excellent tool for weakening the nobles from the other factions down there?" He pointed a finger and played the role of the old man who was terribly eager to explain. "With the northern nobles weakened, the balance with the south has been lost. At this rate, it's unavoidable for the voices of the southern nobles to grow more prominent, but that would be an issue for the royal family—the royal family we support, you see?"

"You're always so smart, your lordship. I'm amazed you're able to think so far ahead!"

It was blatant brownnosing, but the marquis spoke louder, seeming pleased.

"Yes, there would be nothing better than to have the territory of the unhelpful nobles ransacked."

Seeing the way the count glanced around nervously, the marquis fingered his beard—thinking what a good actor the man was.

"Relax, Count. These are all my men; we can trust them. This conversation won't be leaking anywhere. And who would believe it anyhow?"

"I—I see. But simply allowing them to escape to the south entails too many variables. What if instead of driving them off, we signed a secret agreement with them…?"

"Employ the subhumans, hmm? Not a bad idea."

The count sounded and appeared to loathe the idea of utilizing the subhumans, but that was probably more acting. He was the type to take advantage of whatever could be used.

Part of the reason the marquis inducted this outstanding man into his faction was to keep an eye on him.

In fact, he had installed several people in the count's house. He cleverly employed members of other factions in order to avoid being found out even if Charm spells were used.

"Count, if we get a chance to make a deal with the subhumans, will you come with me?"

The marquis could tell many calculations were being made behind the count's eyes.

"I-I'd rather not, but if you're going, I shall humbly accompany you."

Was the count's intention to keep the fact that they had had this conversation as a card against him? But if he accompanied him, they would be in the same boat. It wouldn't be a very strong card at that point.

"…You will? Then I suppose I should speak to Master Caspond and request that he suspend the attack? I can say there's no need to suffer more casualties by continuing to fight and that we can finish this sitting down."

"Yes, that sounds appropriate to me, your lordship. The other counts seem to be attacking all out, so the sooner we can stop them, the better."

"Hmm."

He felt bad stopping them when they were concerned with achieving as much as possible on the battlefield, but with an eye on the future, having them finish up at this point was the better option.

The marquis was delighted to find himself more and more in a position to think about the future of the Sacred Kingdom. Of course, he didn't let that show.

"I'll contact the other cou—"

A sudden column of rising flames cut off the marquis mid-sentence.

He wasn't completely ignorant of magic. Though they couldn't wield it, having some knowledge of faith magic was standard for Sacred Kingdom nobles. Still, that only went as far as tier two, and they knew nothing of the other types.

That said, even he could tell that the column of fire was an incredibly powerful spell.

"What in the—? Could that be tier-four magic? Kelart Custodio and the Holy Lady were said to be able to use such spells."

"I—I don't know. What shall we do, your lordship?"

"Uh, hmm. I'm not sure, but for now, let's fall back and move somewhere safe."

3

Robby, a serviceman, was twenty-four years old. He hadn't been able to receive a satisfactory education, but he was wise enough to understand that there was a mountain of things in this world that he didn't know.

Which was why—

"Humans. I have returned. It appears that while I was out healing my wounds from the fight with the King of Darkness, you've been having your way."

—when the roar that reverberated in the pit of his stomach hit him, Robby pissed himself.

But he didn't even feel his wet pants clinging to his skin.

Since he intuitively grasped the immense power of the monster before him and sensed imminent death, his survival instincts were out of control. All noncritical senses were shut out as he quickly searched for a path to continued existence.

But before he could locate one, Jaldabaoth unleashed his powers.

"Perish. Burn in the fires of my rage until there's nothing left of your life."

Flames roared upward, and the heat wave hit Robby in the face. The terrible hotness dried out his eyeballs instantly, causing intense pain. The air entering his lungs through his throat felt like it was burning the inside of his body. No, that was simply the truth of it.

His skin burst, and the moisture it contained began evaporating. First, his epidermis was burning; next his subcutaneous fat, muscle, and nerves caught fire. The muscles and nerves of his arms and other areas with less fat heated up immediately. That caused the muscles to contract, and his body was about to assume a strange pose—but his skin stuck to the scalding hot metal of his armor, preventing it.

Once his clothes, skin, muscles, and fat had gone, his still pristine intestines fell out of his torso.

Human bodies are mostly water. For that reason, it takes a long time for the insides to char. In a fire, there is time for the insides to burn, but this magic heat created by Jaldabaoth's flame aura moved with the demon, so it was already fading.

That was why the entrails came out perfectly pink, hardly changing color in the heat. A heap of burned corpses and sickeningly bright-colored innards floating in a sea of blood was enough to make anyone who laid eyes on the sight ready to vomit. It was truly a vision of hell abruptly made manifest in this world.

Leaving behind the charred corpses of Robby and the fifty-odd others who had spilled their fresh entrails, Jaldabaoth strode forward.

Jaldabaoth—a newly summoned Evil Lord Wrath—walked. That alone was enough to envelop the humans in his Aura of Fire and kill them.

*   *   *

"Move! You're in my way!"

There were a number of similar shouts, but the first was the militiaman Francesc.

Day after day, he had lamented his misfortune. Because the Sacred Kingdom used a draft system, everyone had to belong to the military.

Yes. Even someone like him, the son of a rather successful merchant whose future was guaranteed. Though he had been assigned to a comparatively comfortable unit, thanks to his father's donation money, life as a soldier was nothing but suffering for him.

And just as he was thinking the pain was nearing its end, this war had happened.

Not a day went by that he didn't gripe about how unfair it all was. Still, he had thought that soon everything would be over, and he would be able to return to his job at the giant store multiplying his beloved money.

Everything was supposed to have been over soon.

Only a little longer.

But now he was running for his life from that monster.

If he was chased, he would definitely die.

He seemed liable to trip from the fear, but he frantically pumped his legs.

All around him, everyone was fleeing. As a result, though he was in a hurry, he was having trouble getting anywhere.

Especially obnoxious was the chubby man in front of him.

So Francesc shoved him—so he would be able to get even a single step farther away from that monster. For the enjoyable future that awaited him.

But there was someone else in front of that man.

There is a good chance that if a person crashes into someone in front of them, it will cause a whole slew of people to fall like dominoes. And that's exactly what was happening in front of Francesc.

If it had been a single person, he probably could have dodged. Maybe he could have leaped over.

But Francesc wasn't athletic enough to avoid this clump of fallen runners.

He sprawled over the pile.

He was going to struggle to stand—but he wasn't given the time.

The aura of flames with Jaldabaoth at the center had caught up to them.

Francesc wasn't even able to scream.

Why do I have to…? The thought was erased instantaneously from his brain by the agony; he could only writhe in the pain enveloping him.

Francesc was fortunate. Why? Because he was able to die quickly.

Jaldabaoth didn't stop. Crushing blackened human corpses underfoot, he strode across the field as if it were deserted.

"Run! Run for it!"

One man was stating the obvious. He was a serviceman called Gorka, and he had some confidence in his swordsmanship.

That was why, even facing Jaldabaoth, he had the courage to shout like that.

But it was recklessly brave of him. Why? Because Jaldabaoth turned to walk toward him. He wasn't sure whether he had caught the demon's interest or it was simply a coincidence.

To the ones who had been about to be caught, he was a servant of God; to those now in the path of destruction, he was an agent of the devil.

Judging that it would be impossible to escape from the monster in the chaos, he held up his sword.

The monster's gaze landed on him for a single second and then shifted behind him.

That was Gorka's worth in the monster's eyes.

He was worth exactly one glance.

With a roar, Gorka charged against the current.

The people collapsing as charred corpses drawing nearer frightened him, but he also had the hope that maybe he could be the one—maybe he could reach Jaldabaoth.

Gorka learned the answer physically.

Violent pain coursed through him.

It was impossible to approach the monster.

Gorka was broiled in flames at the same distance as those servicemen who were weaker than him.

That was when he realized—that to the monster, there was no difference between him and the civilians around him.

His regret of not fleeing was forgotten in the searing pain shooting through every nerve in his body, and he collapsed with an incoherent shriek—looking just like all the other bodies scattered around him.

Jaldabaoth walked with no destination. Humans were running, so he chased them; that was all.

"Stay baaaaack!"

She ran.

Viviana, who was serving in this battle as a faith caster, ran.

Her long blond hair disheveled, she ran.

She didn't have the composure to wipe away the tears and snot.

There was no way they could win against that monster.

Someone was saying something.

But what did she care?

If she could just get a little farther from the monster, that's all she wanted. She ran with that single-minded purpose.

It was no good to shove the person ahead of her forward. She cut around the side and ran.

You're in my way.

You're in my way.

You're in my way.

Why are there so many people in my way?

I don't care who dies as long as it's not me. I need to make sure I survive.

That was all Viviana thought as she ran.

Though she was fleeing, everyone around her was, too, in a panicked tumult. Even someone with above-average strength like Viviana was moving at a turtle's pace, unable to gain distance from the demon.

A frizzling heat tickled her hair flowing behind her.

"Nooooo!"

It brought to mind the repulsive sight of people dying.

"I don't wanna diiiiie!"

It was an utterly natural thing to scream.

Anyone would agree.

It's hard to face death calmly and accept it. And it only gets harder the more unexpected it is.

"Owwww!"

The heat was so great that she could only perceive it as an all-encompassing hurt. Sensing a pain her brain couldn't endure, she realized she was going to die. *No, I don't wanna die.* That was Viviana's only thought as she burned to death.

Jaldabaoth was bored as he silently continued his advance.

"Don't run! Fight!" a brave man on a horse barked.

Leoncio was the second son of a retainer of the marquis. He was participating in this battle in the hopes of being promoted based on his swordsmanship. Those around him were all skilled swordsmen he had borrowed from his father.

He wanted to leave behind the bodies that died in agonized contortions and run away from the demon plodding toward him. But if he ran now, he wouldn't have much to look forward to. If he wanted a bright future, he had to bet it on this moment.

Having made up his mind about that, he screamed again, "Don't run!"

But his horse had other ideas. It knew instinctively that the demon approaching was a horrifying monster and tried to flee.

What happens if a horse bolts in a chaotic mob?

That's simple.

It falls, taking some people with it. Those crushed beneath the panicked animal wailed in pain. No, some of them died outright.

And Leoncio, who had been seated atop it, was thrown a great distance and sprawled over the ground.

Luckily, he was thrown over the others who were fleeing, so he managed to escape being trampled.

But when he tried to stand, a sharp pain coursed through his arm. He must have sprained it in his fall.

And his sword had gone somewhere in the impact.

He was about to go look for it when—that instant—his entire body was assailed by a pain that made him forget everything. It was the first time Leoncio had felt such a pain in his life.

The agony robbed him of all thoughts.

Only one bobbed among those ripped to shreds by the horrible pain: *Why me…?*

"……Mm."

Standing alone before a mountain of burned corpses, the evil lord given the role of Jaldabaoth gazed out at the routed humans.

He was a bit bored.

Aura of Fire wasn't a very fancy ability. All it did was deal fire damage to an area around him; casting a spell that boosted fire resistance would block most of it. Of course, he had been informed that the rank-and-file soldiers in this country were incapable of that.

He may have been a demon, but it didn't mean he was a fan of bullying the weak. He was the type that preferred toying with weaklings who were convinced they were strong. So he had been hoping to encounter an idiot who would put on courageous airs and try to challenge him, but sadly there didn't seem to be any.

The Evil Lord Wrath brought his foot down on a blackened corpse.

Succumbing to the pressure, the intestines splurted out and instantly caught fire.

There had been detritus inside, so a foul smell filled the air.

The Evil Lord Wrath turned on his heel.

If I had been more serious and flown after them, countless more humans would have died, but do they realize that? he wondered as he went.

Everyone watched in silence, stupefied, as the demon confidently turned his back on them and returned to the subhuman camp.

What is that monster? No one asked that question. And there was no need to. Even the biggest fool knew.

Evil Emperor Jaldabaoth…

The being who had overrun the Sacred Kingdom and visited suffering upon vast numbers of its people.

The demon who had rampaged through two countries had demonstrated that no human would be able to defeat him and returned to plunge people hopeful of victory back into grief and despair.

4

Who knew silence could be this heavy? Neia marveled, as the air was so grim inside the tent she was summoned to.

The faces of the southern nobles seated around the splendid table they had gone out of their way to bring out were pale. No, not only them; the same went for the leaders of the liberation army.

Their reaction was only natural.

What human wouldn't be shocked upon receiving a demonstration of Jaldabaoth's overwhelming power? Well, Neia hadn't been very surprised. But in Neia's case, the shock of losing the great King of Darkness ranked highest. And it was possible that everything she had witnessed so far had dulled her reaction.

But the southern nobles, who hadn't participated directly in the fierce fight, were utterly astonished. How could they have imagined that just by the demon walking, people would drop like flies, their tragic corpses exposed?

And on top of that, nearly a hundred thousand soldiers were terrified of a single demon and on their way to collapse.

"What? What is it?! What *is* that monster?!" Count Dominguez's voice grew louder with each shout.

In response, Caspond, who was familiar with Jaldabaoth's unconditional power, casually shrugged. "That's Jaldabaoth... I'm fairly certain I gave you a realistic description of him, Count Dominguez."

"You never told us he had an ability that allowed him to kill people simply by walking!"

"That's true. His fight with the King of Darkness—His Majesty—took place inside the city, so we were unable to get a complete view. But I did tell you how powerful he was. Knowing that, it's not so strange to find he has a power like this, is it?"

"B-but still!"

"Count, I understand what you're trying to say. Seeing truly is believing."

It was the marquis who spoke. It could only be said that no one expected any less from him—he was far calmer than any of the others.

"...But if we discuss that now, we won't get anywhere. Why don't we talk about what to do about it?"

"Quite right, your lordship. What shall we do?" Viscount Sants piped up quickly. Having realized one's position isn't safe, it's surely natural to be in a hurry.

From the southern nobles' point of view, this was supposed to be a quick matter where they could become heroes and saviors of the country by defeating an inferior force with their overwhelming numbers. But that clearly wasn't going to happen. Now they found themselves hunted instead of hunting.

The marquis had crossed his arms and fallen silent, so Caspond replied instead. "We still have the number advantage on our side. The issue is that

Jaldabaoth makes up for it on his own. Brother of the Holy Lady, I ask you: How do you think we can attain victory under these circumstances?"

After a short pause, the marquis spoke, bursting with the absolute confidence that this was the only option they had. "Master Caspond, you said that Jaldabaoth may retreat if we eradicate the subhumans, correct? Then there is no other way."

"Your lordship! You mean to continue fighting?"

"That I do, Count Landaluze. Do you really think we could get away if we fled now anyhow?"

"…Your lordship, it may be impossible for everyone to flee at once, but I should think a handful of people may be able to escape."

"Ha." Remedios scoffed in response to Count Coen's idea. "That's just what I'd expect an inept who can't even grasp Lady Calca's philosophy to think."

"Wha—?!"

"You plan to run, survive, and then what? Hide terrified in a barn under the straw? There's no doubt you're a noble, huh? Then how about at least saying you'll sacrifice yourself for the people!"

"You're one to talk, Commander Custodio. You're a paladin with a Holy Sword, yet you can't defeat a single demon?" It was Count Landaluze who erupted at her.

With gleaming eyes, the ghostlike woman turned to him. "That's right. I can't win. The only one who could face him in a proper fight was that undead. But if you want me to buy time so the people can survive even one second longer, I'll fight him and perish! So how about you?"

A warrior resolved to die versus nobles fleeing death—it's clear who would win in a face-off.

Count Landaluze averted his eyes, and Remedios snorted snarkily. "Master Caspond, I'd like to order the paladins to their deaths now. Are we done here?"

"It's important to have them prepare themselves, but…well, will you? You don't mind if Deputy Commander Montagnés stays behind, do you?"

"All right. Then the rest here is up to you, Gustav."

Having said that, Remedios swayed out of the tent—with one last glare at Shizu, who was spacing out next to Neia.

"Everyone, I apologize for our commander's behavior." Seeing the nobles eye him with glares that said, *You had better*, he continued. "Nonetheless, that is our consensus. We paladins are prepared to die shielding the people. We need you, at the highest ranks, to be prepared to do the same. We can't have our superiors running away in a fight."

"Why, I—!"

Before Neia could even figure out which noble had shouted, Marquis Bodipo raised his voice.

"Could we leave it at that...? We aren't here planning an operation in order to die beautiful deaths. We're here to achieve victory, no? Master Caspond?"

"To be sure, your lordship. We don't have long before Jaldabaoth seizes complete control. We need to find a way to win before—"

"There's no way for us to win! Have you seen what that demon can do?!" Count Granero jumped to his feet, shouting. "If he had used magic or attacked, there may have been ways to prevent him from doing that! But all he did was walk! Walking is all it takes for his surroundings to turn into a fiery hell!"

"Count Granero...I believe you are familiar with magic, yes? Is there...?"

"I didn't learn anything about a spell like that."

"I see... There are only about ten thousand subhumans left. Would it be possible, for example, to eradicate them while fleeing Jaldabaoth?"

The marquis solemnly agreed with Caspond's suggestion. "It seems like that's all we can do... It will be awfully difficult, but defeating Jaldabaoth would be even harder."

"One moment." It was Count Coen who held up a hand. "I object. Maybe Jaldabaoth will leave if the subhumans are defeated. But it's possible that he'll kill everyone here as a parting shot before doing so."

That was true. Naturally, Caspond had a question.

"Then what are we supposed to do?"

"Negotiate."

A number of people couldn't help but laugh at the count's earnest proposal.

Being laughed at, Count Coen blushed, but Caspond spoke up before he could say anything.

"Count, what kind of deal are you going to make with that demon?"

"W-well. Maybe we could give him something in exchange for letting us go…"

"Give him what? Wouldn't it be easier for him to kill us and steal it? Or do you mean something that isn't here? Like what?"

"Master Caspond, please wait! I'm trying to say that fighting isn't our only option! I'm simply proposing negotiation as something to try."

"Your idea seems a bit, yes, optimistic. In the first place, who would negotiate…? By the way, about His Majesty the King of Darkness taking control of a demon maid and her power being of great utility in the taking of Karinsha, couldn't we do something with her?" Count Granero eyed Shizu.

"……I can't defeat Jaldabaoth. It would be practically impossible to even buy time."

"But wouldn't you be able to buy a little more if you were fighting alongside Commander Custodio?"

He was on to something. They would need to slow down Jaldabaoth even just a little bit if they hoped to carry out Caspond's plan.

"……Nn." Shizu cocked her head and then looked at the ceiling. "…… Dang."

"Well? It would strengthen the ties between Sacred Kingdom Roebel and the Nation of Darkness, too."

"……Nn. Ngh!"

What's the right thing for me to say in this case? Neia was still thinking when Shizu answered.

"……I refuse."

"M-may I ask why?"

"……No particular reason."

"N-no particular reason?" Count Dominguez asked, taken aback, but Shizu just nodded. "Are you scared of Jaldabaoth?!"

"……Hmm? …Fine, that's the reason. I'm scared, so I'm not doing it."

"Guh…" Count Dominguez was lost for words. There was no way to respond to that. He would be stuck if she replied with something like, *If you're not scared, then why don't you go buy time.* If she had some logical reason, then all he would have to do is overturn her logic, but an emotional reason was tricky.

In the silent tent, one of the leaders of the liberation army, those thousands of service and militiamen, suddenly spoke up.

"What if we just ran away before Jaldabaoth gained full control? I doubt we can beat him. Before, maybe when we had the King of Darkness, but he's not here now… Does anyone have any ideas of who could beat him? You don't, right? If we flee to the south…"

A commander next to the one who had spoken muttered, "…There's nothing to say that Jaldabaoth won't chase us to the south."

Bang! The one who spoke earlier pounded the table and barked, "Then Master Caspond's proposal of killing all the subhumans is the only way! If we can't run, then that's our only option—we fight! Simple."

"Yeah. That's the only path to survival. I'm not about to bow down and experience that hell again. For now, let's speed up the construction on our—"

The tent flap whooshed open, and a serviceman reporting directly to Caspond rushed in. "Master Caspond! The subhuman army is on the move! They're getting into formation!"

In the previous clash, there had been nothing even worth calling a formation. This development must have been the result of Jaldabaoth taking charge.

"I see. Gentlemen…it appears the enemy is about to attack. We need to be prepared to fight!"

With Caspond's words, everyone stood at once. That included Neia and Shizu.

They all raced to be first out of the tent, knowing there was no time to lose.

Neia and Shizu were the last to leave. Neia's unit was ready to go, so there was no need for extra preparations at this point.

She wondered about the awfully severe expression on the face of the messenger who had burst into the tent, but there was nothing she could do about it, so she and Shizu returned to the unit.

"So it seems like there is more bad news."

"Yes, Master Caspond. Is it all right that everyone left?"

"I'll decide that after I've heard your report."

He had told his men not to discuss anything in the presence of a third party that wasn't already common knowledge. That must have been why he waited until everyone else had gone.

"…Subhuman forces are approaching from the west. At this rate, we estimate they'll arrive in an hour or so."

"…Of all the ridiculous…" Caspond was about to shout but forced himself to hold back. He couldn't have anyone outside the tent overhear this discussion. "Karinsha is in the west. We haven't heard anything from them! Even if they took a wide detour, how could they get past the patrols…? Is it a small group?"

"No, it seems to be over ten thousand… What should we do?"

Even if ten thousand were added to the remnants of the subhuman army, the Sacred Kingdom outnumbered them. But the fact that they were coming from the west was no good. Being pincered by small amounts of troops would normally just call for the larger force to defeat the divided enemy in detail, but Jaldabaoth was in this fight.

This essentially meant that their escape route was cut off.

"…Then listen to me. Do not under any circumstances let anyone else find out." The lookout was surprised, and Caspond continued icily. "That information is too dangerous. If it spread throughout the entire army, the troops' will to fight will crumble, we'll lose even the battle we might have won, and we'll incur a huge number of casualties. In order to maintain solidarity, those facts cannot be known."

"But…"

"…What? We just have to win in under an hour. Don't worry so much."

"…Understood."

"And to the extent possible, keep the lookouts from checking on the west. If the intel leaks in a haphazard way, that alone will cause divisions, and our units will be picked off one by one. Keep the truth hidden until it's not possible any longer, got it?"

"Yes, Master Caspond!"

The messenger didn't seem convinced as he was leaving, but he apparently felt like Caspond's way of thinking was the best they could do.

With no one left inside the tent with him, Caspond buried his face in his hands.

●

What they managed to build was a fence that was all too simple, and while the west and north sides were complete, the south was unfinished, and the east hadn't even been started. They decided that rather than hole up in a place like that, it would be better to fight somewhere open where they could get into formation, so they abandoned their base and spread their troops across the flat land.

They decided to line up shoulder to shoulder.

Where Jaldabaoth showed up, that unit would be wiped out. In that case, the units on either side would ignore them and continue fighting the subhumans. That was the resolve with which they had chosen the formation. Remedios's paladins were to be a flying unit, able to station themselves anywhere. They would head to wherever Jaldabaoth appeared.

Neia's archers were also a flying unit. Neia felt there were two reasons for this. One was to allow Shizu, the King of Darkness's servant, to escape more easily, and the other was that if Shizu decided she wanted to fight Jaldabaoth after all, it wouldn't do to leave a hole in a unit that was assigned to a fixed location.

The unit had already discussed what they would do in the case that Jaldabaoth appeared.

Would they go to where they could take out subhumans, fall back to somewhere safe, or voluntarily fight the demon?

Everyone agreed.

They would go to where they could take out subhumans.

Certainly, their hatred for Jaldabaoth, the cause of all their hardship, ran deep. But not even the King of Darkness could defeat him. They had no delusions about their abilities. In order to inch closer to a strategic victory, it was best to pour their efforts into annihilating the subhumans. And they didn't want the king's servant, Shizu, to whom they owed so much, to die in vain, either.

Neia glared at the enemy forces from atop her horse.

In the previous battle, the subhuman alliance had been noticeably holey, but now they maintained a magnificent formation with no cracks. Likewise, the way they had been bunched up by race without divisions of arms had changed, and they were now lined up like a trained army.

Had she ever seen battle lines that projected such power? The rows of shields looked incomparably solid, and the glinting thicket of spears and swords was simply dazzling. While Jaldabaoth may have been a highly capable commander, this also spoke to his ability to capture hearts.

No—

Of course they obey him. How could anyone not after seeing how overwhelmingly powerful he is?

Many subhumans valued strength, so they were probably happy to fight on his side.

The battle started almost immediately.

Neia and her unit loosed arrows from the rear.

The volley of three thousand people loosing their shots all at once fell like rain.

In this battle, the humans hoped to score a swift victory by spreading out their positions—in their hope to eradicate the subhumans as quickly as possible.

They didn't hold back their heavy cavalry charge. With the fierceness of a unit with nowhere to run, the riders mounted a desperate attack. In response, the subhumans tightened up their defense.

They must have understood they only had one shot at this all-out assault—like wood being fed to a fire. The burned-up logs would only crumble to pieces.

It would be difficult for the humans, who were individually weaker than each subhuman, to break through the subhuman defense. No, it would have been doable if Jaldabaoth hadn't been there. But now the diverse races were organized so that their abilities complemented one another. Weaknesses were compensated for, and strengths were amplified.

The superiority they enjoyed several hours ago felt like a dream as they faced this new defensive prowess. They charged a few times, thrusted with their lances, and shot arrows, but the sturdy formation didn't falter in the slightest. On the contrary, the Sacred Kingdom side took greater damage.

Time passed moment by moment. They wouldn't be able to charge during the night. Well, they would probably be out of energy and strength before then and be thrown into confusion by the enemy's move.

And on top of that—

"Jaldabaoth has appeared in area 2-A! The Second Infantry Unit has been wiped out!"

"The Fourth Infantry Unit is half-gone!"

"The Sixth Spearman Unit is half-gone!"

—messengers brought battlefield news in loud voices.

"Now he's over there?!"

The battlefield had been split into several areas on Caspond's suggestion.

To make it even a little easier to command the troops, each area had been assigned a number, and though they were very rough designations, they at least provided some general organization.

Neia could see from where she was that—perhaps the troops nearby had run from Jaldabaoth—the lines were messy. Then the subhuman attack began, and the unit disintegrated.

This was the problem.

Jaldabaoth shows up one time and wields his power, and a five-hundred-person unit collapses, and nearly a thousand people die in total. Then the subhumans flood into the opening and cause even more damage.

If the subhumans would then get ahead of themselves, that would be great, but after they attacked, they retreated like a turtle pulling its head in. At that rate, the humans weren't able to turn it into a melee and make it harder for Jaldabaoth to use his power on them. This was surely another operation born of Jaldabaoth's perfect control over his troops.

Remedios's paladin unit rushed to area 2-A, but by the time they arrived, Jaldabaoth was already gone. He had teleported away and reappeared elsewhere as if taunting them.

This had been going on for a while now.

But the truth was, Neia and those around her didn't have any good ideas for how to cope. About all Neia and her unit could do was continue to rain arrows down on the subhumans.

Shizu merely stood next to Neia, keeping an eye on the battlefield. Her weapons couldn't shoot in an arc like a bow could, so she was missing this chance to put her skills on display.

About the time Neia's fingers had gotten sore from shooting, her quiver was empty. And it wasn't only her.

"Lady Baraja! Arrows! We have hardly any left!"

It wasn't as if they had infinite ammo.

"…Let's fall back and resupply."

On Neia's order, the unit fell back to where the supply unit was positioned.

Really, she would have liked to give her troops a break, but unfortunately, they didn't have the leisure to rest.

"Ready?"

"Yes, Lady Baraja. We can move anytime!"

"Then—"

She was about to shout, *Let's go*, when she spotted several scouts riding in from the west.

As soon as her eyes met the one leading them, he shouted, "A subhuman army is approaching from the west! Look sharp!"

"—Huh?"

Surprised, she turned around. If she squinted as if glaring into the distance, she could make out a faint cloud of dust and humanlike figures moving within it. It depended how fast they were going, but at that distance, she guessed it wouldn't take long for them to arrive.

What a terrible error.

They had been so focused on the fight with the subhumans in front of them that they had neglected the rear.

She wanted to believe it was a lie. She wanted to think it was those who had remained at Karinsha coming to reinforce them.

But she knew that couldn't be the case. If they were going to do that, they would have sent a fast horse ahead with the message.

Neia felt as though the ground was crumbling beneath her feet.

The news was just too depressing.

To pincer them with enemy reinforcements—that had been Jaldabaoth's aim.

He could stay back and have the subhumans fight. That way the humans would stick around to battle for their victory conditions. His objective had been to pin them to this spot.

In other words, he had foreseen them betting on him leaving if the subhumans were eradicated.

"Ha-ha! Well, that makes sense." Beltrán laughed as if he genuinely found it funny. As everyone let their gazes wander, wondering what had gotten into him, he regained his composure and said to Neia, "Master Caspond's idea was fatally mistaken. But really, why didn't we notice?"

"What do you mean by that?!"

"…Lady Baraja. It's obvious. If he controls the hills, then he can send reinforcements. Eradicating the subhumans here was never going to make Jaldabaoth retreat."

"Ahhh!"

It wasn't only Neia who understood, following his explanation. Others in hearing range groaned as well.

"We would need to drive the subhumans from this land and follow up with a counterattack on the hills. Then, finally, the subhumans would be eradicated, and we could learn whether Master Caspond's idea was right or not."

It made sense. Why hadn't she thought of that? He told her that answer, too.

"…We glimpsed the hope of salvation that his idea offered and jumped at it without thinking carefully enough."

Mounting a counterinvasion on the hills would be practically impossible. In other words…

"So there's…no way for the Sacred Kingdom to be saved?"

Silence reigned. The tumult of the battlefield sounded so far away.

"No…," Beltrán said awkwardly. "There is one way."

"Which is?!"

"…Jaldabaoth. We have to defeat Evil Emperor Jaldabaoth."

Despite hearing the perfect solution, no one could shout for joy. That was the most impossible thing in the world, and not being able to do it was the reason they had gone with Caspond's idea in the first place.

"…So we should have gone to search for His Majesty the King of Darkness first. We made the wrong choice."

If instead of retaking Karinsha, she and Shizu had gone to the hills, would this have been avoidable?

It was hard to say. Neia thought she had made the best choices she could. She had avoided recklessness and increased her chances of success.

But maybe they shouldn't have taken on this challenge.

If…

If…

If…

A number of ifs crossed her mind. When she thought that if maybe she had chosen just one of them…regret and guilt crashed over her like tidal waves.

Morale hit rock bottom. And it probably wasn't only Neia's unit.

This fight was over.

The conditions necessary for victory that formed the foundation of their plan had been shattered. Any further fighting was surely futile.

All they could do now was try to minimize the damage and figure out how to escape to safety. But that wasn't right.

Weakness was wickedness.

A weakling who couldn't save anyone was bad. That was why she had trained so hard.

She couldn't finish wicked.

How would she be able to show her face to absolute justice—His Majesty the King of Darkness, Ainz Ooal Gown?

Having made up her mind, Neia inadvertently voiced the thought in her heart.

"So this is the end, huh?"

The words came out louder than she expected. Whether those around her had heard what she said or they were thinking the same thing, they looked down.

This was as far as they would go.

The dream of liberating the Sacred Kingdom and saving the people was over.

Upon reflection, it was only with the power of the king that they had been able to dream at all. On their own, this was all they were capable of.

Neia knew it was no time to smile, but she did anyway. Then, regaining a somber expression, she turned to Shizu. "...Will you do me a favor and make a run for it?"

"......What about you, Neia?"

Neia stood tall. "I can't run! Having witnessed His Majesty the King of Darkness's great deeds, and as someone who has trained, I refuse to end as wickedness!"

From the corners of her eyes, Neia saw the others lift their heads.

"I won't run from him!"

Their faces were those of warriors once again.

They were faces of resolve. Faces the King of Darkness would be proud of.

"But...you... You're different... So we're entrusting our wishes to you. Maybe it's strange for us to entrust you with our gratitude for His Majesty...but please. Go find him, Shizu. You can use the members of our organization back in Karinsha however you choose. So..."

"......No worries."

Neia took the reply as an affirmative and breathed a sigh of relief.

But in the next moment, her expression warped with concern.

"......I don't need to go."

"Wh-what do you mean by that?"

"......Look."

Shizu was pointing toward the reinforcements—the various races of subhumans including both orcs and zerun—coming from the direction of Karinsha. When Neia squinted, she saw them all raise banners at once. It was...

"Huh?" Neia yelped in shock.

She couldn't believe her eyes, but no matter how many times she looked, the sight remained the same.

"......See? No need."

Neia knew that banner well.

It was the flag of the Nation of Darkness.

Proving that it wasn't a hallucination only she could see, her comrades gasped around her.

"That's the Nation of Darkness's flag, right? I think that's what you told us, Lady Baraja."

"Reinforcements from the Nation of Darkness? You did say there were subhumans there, right, Lady Baraja?"

They were in the middle of a war. At this very moment, lives were at stake, and Jaldabaoth was killing people.

Even so, Neia forgot all that and frantically tried to comprehend what was going on. What happened next caused a huge—truly huge—commotion.

The subhumans parted neatly in two as if they had rehearsed, and down the path that was created came a single undead.

A caster enveloped in a raven-black robe, riding a skeleton-like horse...

It was the hero Neia sought, the one she had been waiting for in her dreams.

"H-His Majesty the King of Darkness... No way..."

Neia wasn't sure if what she was seeing was reality or merely a dream.

But it was undeniably happening. This was no fantasy.

Her emotions exploded, leaving her unsure how she felt anymore.

But her field of vision filled with tears, and it was all she could do to wipe them away.

Shizu waved to the king. When he saw that, he steered his horse toward them.

The King of Darkness was approaching.

What should I say to him? Should I apologize for not going to his rescue? Will that be enough for him to forgive me? Before Neia could speak, the king drew near and nimbly dismounted.

"…Hmm. What a coincidence meeting you here, Miss Baraja. Did you think I was dead?"

"Y-your Majesty King of Darknesssss!" Tears overflowed nonstop. "I believed in you! Because of what Miss Shizu told me. I thought you were all right, but to see that you really— Waaaah!"

"Uhhh, mmhm. Uh…mm. Yeah. I see. I'm glad. Wait, 'Mi…'?"

Perhaps the King of Darkness was also happy to be reunited—his words trailed off.

"……Stop crying." Shizu pressed a handkerchief to Neia's face and then rubbed it hard. "…………More snot. That really is a shock."

"Oh…? Seems like you've made friends with Shizu, huh, Miss Baraja. I'm very happy to see that."

"Thanks to you, Your Majesty! Without Miss Shizu, I just… Thank you!"

Her emotions were so disrupted, she had lost track of what she was saying a while ago.

"I see… I didn't expect that… How have you been, Shizu?"

"…………Neia. She's my favorite… With her flavorful face."

"Please don't say it has flavor," Neia said as she rubbed the last tears from her eyes. "Your Majesty, there are so many things I want to ask you. More than anything…are you angry with us for not coming to rescue you? If so, I'll take full respon—"

"Miss Baraja." The king held up a hand to stop her. "What are you talking about? I'm pretty sure there's no reason for me to be angry with you…"

Neia's eyes overflowed with tears again. And it wasn't only her crying. Hearing the king's merciful reply, the people around her wept as well. The ones who had already had tears in their eyes sobbed.

The King of Darkness's shoulders moved slightly.

"...Uh, no need to cry, everyone. Isn't there something else you want to ask? You said you have a lot of questions, right? C'mon."

"Er, yes." After Shizu wiped her face again—having been kind enough to fold the snotty side of her handkerchief up—Neia asked a question. "A-are those subhumans soldiers from the Nation of Darkness?"

She didn't see any undead, but maybe the subhumans were just the ones out front?

"N— Well, I guess you could say that. I fell in the Abellion Hills. I added that area to the Nation of Darkness, so I guess they are from the Nation of Darkness."

Neia had no words.

Wow.

What other reaction could there be besides *wow*?

The hills were filled with all different types of subhumans, and the ruler had been Jaldabaoth's aide. Who besides the King of Darkness could deal with all that on his own as if it were nothing and conquer the area?

Neia trembled with excitement.

"And, well, it took a little while, but I rounded up the subhumans who had suffered under Jaldabaoth and led them here as an army—to settle the fight with him. Looks like I came at just the right time."

The King of Darkness's face was bone and didn't move at all. But Neia sensed a spirited smile.

"How very like you, Your Majesty!"

Beltrán approached, crying a storm of tears.

"Whoa, who are you?!"

Beltrán dropped with a thud to his knees. No, it wasn't only him. From all around Neia, the members of her organization approached the king and fairly threw themselves at his feet.

"We would expect nothing less, Your Majesty!"

"Brilliant, Your Majesty!"

Bathed in so many voices, even the king seemed to be caught a bit off guard.

"Oh, umm, hmm... Actually, there was something I wanted to ask you, Miss Baraja. Who are these people?"

"They're grateful for your compassion and want to repay you."

"That's right! You saved us, Your Majesty!"

"Yes, we responded to Lady Baraja's call in order to do whatever we can to repay our debt to you, Your Majesty, Great King of Darkness!"

Perhaps inspired by their agreement, Neia proudly declared, "And it's not just everyone here! There are many more!"

"Ohhh, I'm very happy to hear that, but...are they all like this?"

"Yes, that's right! Every one of us carries this much gratitude in our hearts!"

"I see, hmm... Thanks, everybody."

Everyone wept to hear his words of thanks and learn that their way of feeling indebted to him wasn't wrong; sobbing filled the air.

"...They're all crying because they're grateful to me?"

"Yes! That's right!"

"And you gathered them... You've, uh, grown a lot while I was gone, Miss Baraja."

"Thank you, Your Majesty!" The praise she received from the King of Darkness made Neia smile ear to ear.

"N-now, then... Miss Baraja. Have them stand up. I've returned to overwrite my loss... What happened to Jaldabaoth?"

"Oh! Right! Jaldabaoth is...."

As if waiting for that moment, flames erupted with a roar. The thought of how many Sacred Kingdom soldiers perished beneath them made her shudder.

"...I see. You don't even have to say the rest. It seems the time has come for me to fight him once more. Shizu!"

"...Yes, Lord Ainz."

"I'll handle this from here. You protect these people. Make sure they're ready to welcome me with applause upon my return!"

"Whooooo!" Everyone cheered.

"Listen! In the previous battle, I was careless. Outnumbered, low on mana... But not this time. Not even Jaldabaoth can summon that many demons so quickly. And my mana is full. There's nothing left that would cause me to lose! Wait here until I return victorious!"

Another roar went up when he proclaimed his absolute victory.

Then, his robe fluttering behind him, the king strode across a deserted field. As if compelled by his energy, everyone moved aside. They created a path.

"Your Majesty!"

At the sound of Neia's voice, the King of Darkness stopped and looked back at her over his shoulder.

"Defeat him!"

"Of course!"

The king set off walking again. His back receded into the distance. But Neia didn't feel lonely or scared. All she felt was the sort of safety a baby feels in their parents' arms. And it wasn't only Neia. Everyone who shared her beliefs felt the same way.

"......We won."

Standing next to her, Shizu said only that in a voice confident that the King of Darkness would be victorious. Neia agreed.

Eventually...fire blazed into the sky. And after it, darkness.

The pair clashed in midair as they had before.

There were no more battle cries.

Even the armies had halted their attacks to watch the sky.

Yes.

Everyone understood—that whoever won this fight, whichever side, had the authority to put an end to everything.

The battle had shifted to a divine realm where no normal person could set foot.

Light...
Darkness...
Fire...
Lightning...
Shooting stars...
Incomprehensible phenomena...
...all crashed together.
And then—

"Aaah!"

Neia cheered—because with her sharp eyes, she saw the flames scatter and the darkness descending.

Compared to the last fight, this one was over so quickly. It seemed a testament to the fact that if the king had possessed all his mana, if there hadn't been demon maids in the way, victory would have been this simple the first time.

"Miss Shizu!"

"......Like I said, Neia."

Shizu replied as if it was all a matter of course, and Neia grabbed her hands, shaking them up and down. But that wasn't enough.

She threw her arms around Shizu's little body and clapped her on the back.

Everyone could see that victory was theirs, and a huge cheer went up.

The King of Darkness slowly descended and alighted on the ground.

And when he raised a hand, the cheering thundered even louder.

Epilogue

Once the fight had been decided, the rest was simple. The subhumans were all out of morale, so it was just a matter of hunting down the dregs. The Sacred Kingdom lost almost no one; only subhumans were scattered across the earth.

Now that the enemy general, Jaldabaoth, had been defeated, there was nothing standing in the liberation army's way.

The city of Prato and the capital, Jobans, were retaken in the blink of an eye.

There was still the city of Limun farther west, and in the villages converted to prison camps, people were still suffering. But they had reached a major turning point.

The liberated capital erupted with joy, and the thrill hadn't abated even a whole day later. In fact, the excitement seemed to have actually grown.

But Neia and the rest of the liberation army leaders knew they faced a mountain of problems.

First: food. With everything devoured by the subhumans, food issues would be an obstacle for the Sacred Kingdom going forward.

Next: lives lost. That could be rephrased as "labor." If there were future engineers or scholars among those who had died, the loss of their technologies could prove catastrophic.

Then: materials. All the things that had been stolen or destroyed by subhumans would need to be remade, which would require a lot of resources.

Also: time. In order to retake the two seasons the subhumans had taken from them, they would have to work twice as hard.

They also had to root out the subhumans that might be lurking in their territory.

The many treasures thought to be stolen by the subhumans—magic items and other valuables—were missing. Subhumans had their own civilizations and adorned themselves with precious metals, so no one found it strange that they would collect human wealth. But not being able to figure out where it had all been taken was odd. They couldn't find any trace of an enemy transport unit.

Even with so many challenges ahead of them, some people probably just wanted to bask in happiness for the moment. They needed a rest in order to face the struggle awaiting them. And Neia accepted that.

But today was impossible. Today she couldn't bask in happiness.

Because today was a day of parting.

It was a terribly sad day.

In the eastern half of the capital on the city side of the main gate, a lone carriage waited. Contrary to its plain exterior, its interior was elegant and refined, and Neia was familiar with its outstanding functionality—right down to the cushions that shielded one's bottom from soreness during long journeys, which had impressed her in particular.

Yes.

This was the King of Darkness's carriage, which she had ridden along in during their return to the Sacred Kingdom.

That is to say, today was the day the King of Darkness was leaving the Sacred Kingdom and returning to his own country.

It wouldn't have been strange to find subhumans surrounding his carriage. He had united the Abellion Hills and converted many subhumans into allies for his fight against Jaldabaoth. Yet, not a single one was to be found, because he had sent them back to the hills.

And that wasn't something that had happened in the last day or so. No, he let them return home the day Jaldabaoth was defeated.

When asked why, the answer was one that took into account the feelings of the people of the Sacred Kingdom. "You don't want to move forward with them, do you?"

Neia was ruled by emotion.

Out of consideration for the mental state of the people here, he had sent his own soldiers home and chosen to stay with the Sacred Kingdom himself. No king would normally do that.

No, none but this king of kings, the benevolent King of Darkness.

And the members of Neia's organization, those who shared her beliefs, were filled with the same emotion.

So she and her fellow believers had taken it upon themselves to be his entourage. Since no one said a word of objection, that amounted to tacit approval. Of course, most of the fighting was over, and all they were doing was providing security for the king as he walked around, but Neia could still remember the looks on everyone's faces.

The joy of being able to walk near someone who had saved them, the pride of getting to accompany the hero who slayed Jaldabaoth, the happiness of waiting on the king they looked up to—their expressions were a mix of all those feelings.

Now, none of them was in her field of vision.

What she could see was the wall and main gate of the capital—and the road that led to Prato and beyond, to the Nation of Darkness.

"You're really returning today, Your Majesty? Many people are celebrating the liberation of the capital. I wouldn't be surprised if in a few days they wanted to hold a ceremony and invite you so they can express their gratitude to the one who contributed the most…"

Neia had asked a similar question several times. She was sure the answer would be the same. That she asked anyway had to be due to the woman in her.

"Yes, today I'll return to the Nation of Darkness. I'm not sure I'm cut out for ceremonies."

His last remark was so sudden that he rushed to give an exaggerated shrug of his shoulders so she wouldn't take it at face value.

His Majesty's sense of humor really is so awful.

"Very funny, Your Majesty."

"Right, exactly. It was a joke. A joke… But to tell the truth, I've done everything I came to do. So there's no longer any reason for me to stay. As king, I must lead my nation. If I stay away from the throne for far too long, Prime Minister Albedo will take me to task."

The image of that peerless beauty Neia had met only once came to mind. The woman was so gorgeous, she found her impossible to forget.

She doesn't seem like she would be that scary if she got mad. Or is it because she's so beautiful that the idea of her being angry is frightening…? I don't really think that's what His Majesty means, but I can't imagine her getting angry… In any case…I'm jealous…

His comment was one that could only be uttered regarding someone close to him, and for that reason, it would never be applied to her no matter how she wished for it, which only made her envy stronger. How happy she would have been to overhear the king she respected telling someone, *Neia will take me to task.*

"I see… It's a pity everyone from the Sacred Kingdom can't be here to see off the king who rescued our country."

The King of Darkness's departure had come up suddenly. This lonesome scene with no one there to see him off showed as much.

"I told Master Caspond I didn't want to be burdened with a huge commotion. This country has a lot of challenges ahead. Rather than wasting effort and supplies on my departure, I'd rather they be used for reconstruction."

"Your Majesty…"

Why do you have to go…?

If she clung to his leg and bawled, would he stay an extra day?

She was seized by the urge to do so but forced herself not to. It wouldn't be right to take any more advantage of his charity.

"Oh, uh, I don't mean in, like, a *looking down on you* way. Just that the Sacred Kingdom has lost so much. Really… Wealth and stuff. I kind of think they could have left a little more behind… The feeling I had is…that I want you to do your best without worrying about me—yes, that's right. And besides…this kingdom stabilizing will be good for the Nation of Darkness as a neighboring country, too. For trade in the future and so on."

He must have sensed Neia's feelings and hurried to console her. Usually, he was more dignified, but he sounded a bit out of his depth.

"Thank you, Your Majesty."

"Uh? Mm. Nah, don't mention it. I came to this country to acquire Jaldabaoth's demon maids. And in the end"—Shizu had been standing next to him in silence, practically concealing her presence, but he patted her on the back now—"I got them, as you can see. So the trip was worth it."

Neia was a little embarrassed that the Sacred Kingdom wasn't giving him anything at all.

Shizu, the demon maid, he had acquired on his own. And it wasn't only Neia who felt bad. All those who shared her beliefs agreed.

They considered giving something themselves, but then someone mentioned that it might actually be rude for people who weren't even representatives of the country to offer a king something, so the idea came to nothing in the end.

Neia wished Caspond would at least transfer something on the nation-to-nation level or sign a pact with terms that left the Sacred Kingdom slightly disadvantaged.

"…If you like, I could use a huge once-in-a-year spell to resurrect your parents."

"I appreciate it, Your Majesty…but I'll pass."

When they had liberated the capital, one of the prisoners said they had seen Neia's mother die in battle. She heard from them what a valiant fight it had been. Her mother probably wouldn't be upset to not be brought back to life.

And Neia had heard that resurrection magic required expensive catalysts. She probably couldn't afford it. The compassionate King of Darkness would probably do it free of charge, but she felt she had already personally benefited too much from his goodwill.

Still, the fact that the subhumans had apparently done away with the corpse and she never got to say good-bye was unfortunate.

"Talking forever only makes parting more painful. I should be on my way. Shizu, don't you have anything to say to Miss Baraja?"

"……See you."

"…! Yes! See you again."

Shizu offered her hand, so Neia took it.

And then neither one in particular let go first, but they parted.

"…Is that enough, you two?"

"……I'm…fine."

"Yes, Your Majesty."

"All right. Then, Shizu, let's go." With his foot on the step, the king turned and said to Neia, "…This country has a lot of struggles ahead. But… I'm sure you'll be able to tough it out. Let's meet again someday."

"Of course!"

The king went to enter the carriage. Neia called out to him without thinking.

"Your Majesty! Your Majesty King of Darkness!"

He stopped on the step and turned around. Neia swallowed, mustering her courage, and spoke in a quaking voice. "U-umm! May I call you…Lord Ainz?"

What a brazen request. She wouldn't have been surprised if he shouted at her for being an impudent foreigner.

"…Uh? Yeah, it's fine… Call me what you like."

"Thank you!" She bowed to the broad-minded king. When she looked up, Shizu was getting into the carriage. "Take care, Miss Shizu!"

"Mm-hmm!" Shizu gave her a thumbs-up and disappeared into the carriage.

The horse must have detected that the two had boarded. It neighed and set off on its own.

"Good-bye, Your Majesty!" Neia shouted after the carriage, no longer able to hide her tears. "Long live His Majesty the King of Darknesssss!"

It wasn't only her voice that raised the subsequent cheers.

The main gate wasn't the capital's only gate. Other believers had secretly gathered at other gates and were waiting outside to raise their voices in a prayer for the king's prosperous future.

"Huzzah!"

"Huzzah!"

"Huzzah!"

Then they frantically scattered flower petals they had brought with them.

The carriage drove through.

This wasn't enough to send off the one who had saved the Sacred Kingdom. But this was all Neia and those who understood her feelings were capable of.

The carriage gradually receded in the world blurred by tears.

Neia sniffled.

She was lonely.

She wished the king or Shizu had invited her to the Nation of Darkness. If they had, she might have given up everything to go with them.

But they hadn't.

It stung.

In the end, she was merely an attendant for while he was visiting her country. That was all he had thought of her.

A vortex of negative emotions threatened to swallow her up.

But no.

Neia would never forget those words. The King of Darkness had told her, *…This country has a lot of struggles ahead. But…I'm sure you'll be able to tough it out. Let's meet again someday.*

In other words, he had expectations for her.

He thought that despite the swirling chaos, she would be able to do a proper job rebuilding the country.

An era that felt both long and short, that had changed her life, was at its end. But this was also a beginning. There were so many things she had to do.

First, she had to work to repay His Majesty's kindness.

Then she had to get the country back on its feet. Justice and wickedness… She didn't know what they were before, but now she could define them with confidence.

Justice was the King of Darkness. And weakness was wickedness, so it was important to train and grow stronger.

Neia would spread her truth throughout the peaceful Sacred Kingdom.

"Lady Baraja, please dry your tears."

It was Beltrán.

She looked over and saw that his eyes were totally bloodshot. Maybe he had wiped his eyes before coming and was trying to hide it, but from the way his voice shook, it was obvious he had been crying.

"Right." She wiped her face hard, like Shizu had done.

"Lady Baraja. The people who witnessed the fight would like to hear the king's story. Many have even brought their families."

"I see. I'll tell them what a wonderful person His Majesty—Lord Ainz—is. And I'll talk about Shizu, too." Neia fixed her gaze ahead. "Parting is sad. But let's go, everyone! Let's let the people know that His Majesty is justice!"

"Yeah!"

Three thousand people raised their voices at once and followed Neia as she set off.

•

The carriage drove on.

The long job was over. Ainz had never experienced it before, but he figured this was what it was like to be stationed away from one's family for work. He had periodically returned to Nazarick, but it may have been the first time he was away for so long.

He had thrown the meat of ruling the Abellion Hills at Albedo, and anything further to do with the Sacred Kingdom he was leaving entirely to Demiurge.

In other words, the burden on his shoulders had decreased, and he relaxed to the greatest extent possible without Shizu noticing from where she sat across from him. Partway through, he had changed Demiurge's scenario to easy mode, but the exhaustion from the time he had spent in hard mode hadn't completely left him. Still, it was true he felt that relief specific to finishing off a job—and a matter that had been rather stalled out, at that.

Still, once he returned to Nazarick—E-Rantel—he would have to handle all the work that had piled up during the two seasons he was away, neither hurrying nor taking too long; once, thinking Albedo was keeping an eye on things so there would be no problem, he had simply stamped everything with his approval, and she said, "I'm impressed as always, Lord Ainz. What speedy decision-making skills," in what felt like a sarcastic way.

Yes. He had work waiting for him when he returned, but it wasn't as if that was the reason he wasn't using a Gate to go immediately.

Certainly not.

His intention was to teleport once he was out of sight, but it was still too soon. There was no benefit to showing his hand. Of course, the fact that the Hanzo, who was most definitely on the roof, didn't say anything and his anti-intelligence magic didn't activate should have meant that no one was watching them, but there could have been methods Ainz was unfamiliar with.

He figured that as long as he had time, it would be fine to wait to teleport until the line of sight was a little more obstructed.

Right. It wasn't that he wanted to put off reading documents that he wouldn't understand anyway as long as he could.

But if there was one problem…

Shizu hasn't said a word since we got in the carriage…

It had been the same with Neia—time with one other person in a carriage with no conversation made him extremely uncomfortable. With a man, he could have said whatever came to mind, but with a woman, he tried to take more care with his topic selection.

He had been hoping for a while now that Shizu would say something, but it didn't seem likely. Finally, unable to bear the silence, Ainz made up his mind to speak.

"Shizu, how was it working on your own away from Nazarick? Did you have any issues or things that should be handled better in the future?"

He started by asking for a report from his subordinate who had worked in isolation in the field.

"……I think……I did my best."

"I see. Good job hanging in there."

The conversation ended. That was it.

Though he waited briefly for it to continue, Shizu had nothing.

There wasn't really anywhere he could take things, having been told that she had done her best. *You didn't answer the part about issues encountered or potential improvements*, he thought, but that was the superficial processing of a boss. Probably she meant that she had worked hard, so he just needed to wait for the results. And that was a good thing—because it meant she hadn't run into many problems.

"……But," Shizu continued, "……it's hard to think for myself and operate……on my own."

"Yeah. You're right."

Up until this mission, Shizu had worked inside Nazarick, only doing what she was ordered to. This was the first time he had given her general instructions and made her decide things for herself to some extent, operating independently. Maybe it was a bit much. Maybe it would have been better to start with something simpler, but he also knew that she had achieved plenty.

"But now, circumstances are such that it wouldn't be at all strange for the Pleiades to be out and about. I'm sure the news that the demon maids have been brought under the King of Darkness's control will spread to other countries from the Sacred Kingdom. You may get orders to lead a group on a mission outside Nazarick in the future. This was good experience, right? But we should avoid such open-ended instructions. The person in charge needs to make sure—"

Having said that much, Ainz realized he was wringing his own neck; as the one in the top position at Nazarick, he was the one most likely to be giving orders.

I can't write a proper proposal. On the contrary, I'm sure I'm only capable of explaining superficial ideas, which will have Albedo and Demiurge furrowing their brows at me!

"—to play things by ear and write proposals that allow for some degree of wiggle room. After all, it's the ones on the ground who have the best grasp on the situation!"

"……Yes, I learned a lot this time not only following instructions."

"Yes, that's right. I'm sure you did. I understand that feeling very well."

As he was nodding, Ainz compared himself—with pain in his nonexistent stomach upon seeing Demiurge's instructions—to Shizu, who seemed to have gained something, and shed a few mental tears.

"By the way..." He changed the subject. If he continued along that line, he might have ended up shocking himself even more. "It seems like you became good friends with Miss Baraja when I wasn't looking. Weren't you sad to say good-bye?"

"......She's...my favorite."

"I see! That's great!" He reacted with genuine joy.

Satoru Suzuki never had children, but he felt like a dad hearing his kid had managed to finally make her first friend.

Well, I'm glad I resurrected her...but what does "favorite" mean in this case? Could it be that she means like a toy and not a peer?

Ainz cautiously asked, "...Is it safe to say you made a friend?"

Shizu cocked her head and thought for a moment but then answered, "......Yes."

Ainz felt as though this was a tremendous success, but the explosion of joy was immediately suppressed. Though he found that annoying, he realized that this was perhaps a first for Nazarick and was able to enjoy the slow-burning contentment of a friend outside of their home.

Most of the members of Nazarick had never been beyond its confines. So it was possible that they simply hadn't made friends and they would be perfectly capable of it if they got the chance.

Ainz certainly didn't count those with friends as superior. It could even be the case that friends were unnecessary.

But he did feel that perhaps it was better to have the opportunity to make them than not.

I had my guildmates in Ainz Ooal Gown. Maybe I should let the others go outside and give them free time so they get a chance to interact with others... Especially Mare and Aura. Or maybe everyone was born at the same time? Hrm...

"So did you promise you'd go back to visit Neia?"

"......No. This place is...far."

"Oh! You don't have to worry about that. I've made a note of several teleportation spots. You can go hang out whenever you want—using a Gate. Don't feel like you have to hold back! Anytime, anytime."

"……When I get some time…I will."

"Yeah! Time… I'll make sure you have some. I've been interested for a while in starting a vacation system. I'll give the Pleiades some time off, too. Maybe you could all go on a trip together. Already, the story is that you've all been put under my control, so there shouldn't be any problem with it."

Shizu thought for a moment and then shook her head back and forth. "……Nuisance."

"A nuisance, huh…?"

What does she mean by that? That they would bother Neia? Or that they would get in the way of her spending time with Neia? Or does she think the others wouldn't want to go?

"Well, if it's a nuisance, then don't worry about it. You can go on your own. By the way, I'm changing the topic, but I believe Miss Baraja's parents died, right? She wasn't upset about that?"

Apparently, Neia Baraja's parents had died. He felt like it would be all right to resurrect them if she wanted. And if she would be even more grateful…

Nah.

Frankly, at this point, there wasn't much value in bringing her parents back. He could tell from looking that she was plenty grateful. So he didn't need insurance. Plus, wands for raising the dead were rare; he wanted to conserve them as much as possible. And if he had Pestonia or someone use a resurrection spell, gold or precious stones would be consumed.

Honestly, the advantage they would gain wasn't worth it.

But if she's Shizu's friend, that makes it different. I don't mind doing something like that for a friend of Shizu's.

Neia had seemed close with her, and that's why he had brought up the subject to see how she—and Shizu—would react.

"……She……doesn't mind… And it's not good to give special treatment."

"Oh? I thought it would be something nice to remember us by…but… well, that's fine."

Actually, resurrecting people, and without a tidy corpse at that, could be a huge pain. There was the whole *How come you did it for them and not for me?* thing. And he couldn't have them asking for the Holy Lady to be resurrected. If he did, he was sure Demiurge would find a way of dealing with her, but there were too many downsides.

"If you're going to go, you can't read that book. You know that, right?"

"............Yes...I know. It's in the professor's room."

Shizu knew how all the gimmicks in Nazarick worked. He had never let her out of Nazarick before, since it would be too dangerous. He adjusted the situation with Control Amnesia.

Shizu's knowledge about the gimmicks was part of the backstory given to her by the player who created her. Ainz wasn't sure if magic would affect something like that, but when he tried it, the spell functioned as expected.

This was a feat he had been able to pull off thanks to practicing on the guinea pigs he had acquired; if he perfected the technique, he would be able to achieve amazing things.

That is, he realized he might have the power to touch the very core of each NPC. *What is the origin of memory? What is an NPC backstory, exactly?* Stuff like that. But that was merely Ainz's imagination talking, and it was far more likely nothing of the sort was possible. And to answer those questions, it might be necessary to master all the details of the spell and comprehend everything there is to know about human memory. In that case, he would probably require tons of guinea pigs and decades of training and research—and he'd have to resign himself to the idea that it could all come to nothing.

In any case, with Shizu's memories incorrect as they were now, she was a sort of trap.

If someone tried to use her to infiltrate Nazarick, they would definitely be in trouble.

"The professor...huh? Will the other Shizus activate?"

"......When the time comes."

Wait, they aren't just a gimmick? thought Ainz, but he didn't say so. It was similar to how the true identity of Santa Claus was shrouded in secret.

Satoru Suzuki had no memory of Santa coming to his house, but he had made an appearance in *Yggdrasil*...

"It was just the admins, though," he said with a wistful smile. When he realized Shizu was staring at him, he told her, "I was just talking to myself."

"......Your Majesty King of Darkness."

"Hmm?"

"......Your Majesty King of Darkness."

"...What's gotten into you, Shizu?"

She had been referring to him normally all this time, so to suddenly get called by his title sort of—well, really—confused him.

"......Was I being...overly familiar till now?"

"Wh-why would you say that? It's much weirder for you guys to call me 'Your Majesty.' Lord Ainz works fine. Really, you can take 'Lord' off. What about Mr. Ainz or something?"

"......That would be rude. I'd get yelled at."

"...Oh, well... In any case, you don't have to call me 'Your Majesty.'"

"......Understood."

"Oh, right. How did the rune thing I Messaged you about go?"

"......I did my best."

"Ah..."

It didn't seem like it had gone very well. Well, it probably didn't matter if it had ended in failure.

But maybe I should have waited to get back the bow and other items I lent her, thought Ainz absentmindedly as he looked at Shizu.

On his way, he had been accompanied by a glaring girl, and on the way back, an expressionless one. Both a bit eccentric.

The musing made Ainz crack a smile.

•

Caspond gazed out from the deepest chamber in the castle—the one that belonged to the holy king.

His coronation was coming up in a few days, so with the excuse that he wanted to relax, he refused to let anyone in—not even into the adjoining sitting room.

He knew for sure that Remedios would complain without reading the atmosphere, so he had her under house arrest. Well, no, not quite. He was having her rest at home because later he was planning to have her patrol for any subhumans lurking in the Sacred Kingdom.

His moving into this chamber before his coronation did give those hostile to him reason to attack. The reason he pushed the plan through anyhow was because the power struggle had already begun.

The point was to make his ascension a fait accompli before the opposition began interfering. To Caspond as he was now, without much knowledge of noble society, it was easier to have clear boundaries of who were enemies and who were allies. That was part of the reason he went ahead with the move.

"...If I take the throne without laying the groundwork with the other nobles, some of them will be offended. Especially southern nobles—the ones under me who haven't been harmed. And when they hear his voice, how will the people of the north, whom I fought alongside, react...?"

"Clear discontent will result, causing a rift that will split the Sacred Kingdom in two."

Caspond had been talking to himself, but a voice responded.

It was a soft voice that seemed to worm its way into people's hearts. It was the one who gave Caspond orders.

He turned around immediately, took a knee at the owner of the voice's feet, bowed his head, and then lifted it. "So good of you to come, Master Demiurge."

If he wasn't wearing a mask or changing form, he must have made sure the coast was clear.

"I was here picking up things to take to Nazarick anyway, so I stopped by. Are you having any problems at present?"

"None at all. Everything is going according to your plan, master."

When Caspond smiled, he got a faint grin back.

"Despite a few unexpected elements, thanks to Lord Ainz's efforts, we managed to complete phase one without any hitches. I expect a lot from you in the coming phase."

Even with his head lowered, Caspond knew that was a lie.

Demiurge didn't expect a thing out of him. But if he deviated from the rails that were set out, the course simply had to be corrected, and the plan would still be executed.

And there were probably plans for what would happen if Caspond's true nature was revealed. Among his instructions were some things he didn't understand the reasons for. He was sure they were in preparation for that sort of event.

The first phase of the plan was to bring the subhumans and Abellion Hills completely under Nation of Darkness rule. Any troublesome races were to be exterminated beforehand. And the other goal had been to spark a confrontation between the northern and southern parts of the Sacred Kingdom.

And phase two, led by Caspond, would be the clear confrontation and struggle.

Phase three was to eventually have the Nation of Darkness govern both realms.

"…Shall I keep my corpse, the tool for that purpose, here?"

"That won't be necessary. It's being stored in Nazarick. I'll bring it once the plan has reached that point."

The corpse of the real Caspond had been wrapped in a Shroud of Sleep and taken to Nazarick.

The magic item would prevent the body from decomposing. He had been captured and killed with an instadeath spell to make an extremely tidy corpse and was preserved before rigor mortis had even started to set in. He was even a bit warm still. With this corpse, anyone would think he had just died all of a sudden.

"Just to confirm, you know what to do as the next holy king, yes?"

"Yes, my intention is to make this a rich country worthy of presenting to Lord Ainz."

"Yes, that's right. But don't decrease the amount of discontent. Discontent is the perfect spice with which to welcome the next king."

"Yes, Master Demiurge." The Caspond doppelgänger asked about something that wasn't part of the plan. "By the way, how should I handle that girl?"

Understanding exactly who he was referring to from that question alone, Demiurge showed him a wholehearted smile for the first time.

"I once used the word *inscrutable* to describe Lord Ainz…and he really is. He prepared such a wonderful pawn for me. Her presence is likely to speed up my progress by a number of years."

It was hard to tell where Demiurge's narrow eyes were looking, but Caspond Doppel noticed them suddenly shift. When he realized they were directed at the wall—actually, beyond it—he remembered the capital's main gate was in that direction.

"I wanted to acquire someone who worshipped him…but to think such a deeply religious country would produce a girl like that… I was wondering why he told me that I could kill a girl he lent a weapon to, but it must have been to drive her into that mental state?"

Demiurge, delighted, wasn't directing the comment at anyone in particular. Caspond merely waited in silence for Demiurge's attention to return to him.

"I was right not to read too much into it and order her to be saved. But of course, no matter what I did, Lord Ainz would have compensated for it. That he said he was going to test my coping ability by thoughtlessly ruining the plan…and then set this up so well… I'd expect nothing less from the one who led the Supreme Beings. He shows me how inferior I am with his every move… Ho-ho, how cruel."

Demiurge shook his head, overcome with admiration. Silence reigned in the chamber. Eventually, as if to shake off his excitement, Demiurge adjusted his collar and tightened his necktie.

"Your position on the matter should be to support Neia Baraja with everything you've got. Do it visibly under the pretext of extending gratitude to Lord Ainz. That should further intensify the clash between north and south… I'll give you a detailed plan soon for what to do if someone interferes with her. Until then, operate from the positions I've just laid out."

"Yes, sir! ...And what will you do with her? She won't be the next leader, will she?"

If so, there were preparations to be made. That said, Demiurge would surely give him instructions if that were the case, so all he needed to do was follow them.

"That's not a bad idea, but I think it would be better to have her in a different role. I'm not sure if Lord Ainz wishes to be called a god or not, but if he does, we should probably start making arrangements. We can probably use her and her friends in experiments to do with worshipping Lord Ainz as a god."

"Yes, sir!"

"Now then, is there anything you want to confirm at this point?"

"Yes. The unnecessary woman, Remedios Custodio, is running around on pointless errands, but wouldn't it be safer to kill her?"

"No, we should leave her alive and let the nobles take their discontent out on her. That's why the first time we met, I made sure not to kill her. She belongs to a different department. As for the paladins, promote the deputy to commander and do with them what you will. Make good use of them."

"Understood!"

"We can get rid of her once the confrontation heats up, yes."

When Caspond acknowledged this, Demiurge ended the conversation and vanished using Greater Teleportation.

The demons lurking in the shadows, the Hanzos that Caspond couldn't possibly defeat, had been left for him to continue borrowing.

Having stood, Caspond Doppel looked out the window again.

He could only see the courtyard, but he imagined the city overflowing with joyful inhabitants. And he sneered.

"Yes, enjoy your happiness a little bit longer, my people."

OVERLORD
Character Profiles

Character **53**

Neia Baraja

Humanoid

The fanatic with the villainous eyes

Position —— Squire in the Sacred Kingdom
Liberation Army

Residence —— A nice area in Jobans
(lives with her family)

Class Levels —— Paladin ——————— **2** lv

Sacred Archer ———————— **3** lv

Evangelist ———————— **2** lv

Founder ———————— **4** lv

Birthday —— 1 Early Wind Moon

Hobby —— Talking about how wonderful
the King of Darkness is

| personal character |

Neia has changed so much that she gets another introduction. She died and lost levels. But at the same time, she survived the war and leveled up. Her class build isn't very efficient due to swapping out servant and so on, but it's a reflection of her many experiences, so it can't be helped. Neia herself doesn't realize she's using skills to influence people's thinking (and brainwash them). Her powers are still effective only on those with mental scars; those sorts of people feel saved by her words.

Character **54**

KELART CUSTODIO

HUMANOID

Fair face, foul heart

Position —— Highest-ranking priest in the Sacred Kingdom
and their leader

Residence —— A nice area in Jobans (lives with her family)

Class Levels —— Priestess ——————————— **?** lv

Holy Cleric ————————— **?** lv

Hierophant ————————— **?** lv

Etc.

Birthday —— 11 Early Water Moon

Hobby —— People watching (in meanings both
good and bad)

{ personal character }

The most elite pure priest in the region, whose power surpassed even that
of the Blue Roses. But as her true powers were kept secret, almost no one
knew. Her best friend (Calca) and family were very important to her, and
if someone was hostile toward them, she was more inclined to fight than
her elder sister and sometimes carried out cutthroat revenge plots with
no mercy. She usually seemed like she would forgive anyone with a smile,
but that was merely an act. She was the most feared woman in the Sacred
Kingdom and was always watching for ways to take out the nobles who
opposed Calca.

•

CASPOND BESSAREZ

HUMANOID

Mild brother of the Holy Lady

Position ——— Sacred Kingdom royalty

Residence ——— The castle in Jobans

Race Levels ——— Cleric ———————————— **?** lv

Sage ———————————— **?** lv

High Noble (regular) ———— **?** lv

Etc.

Birthday ——— 27 Late Fire Moon

Hobby ——— Reading (he especially seems to
like books about history)

{ personal character }

Though an outstanding individual, he realized he couldn't best his even more outstanding little sister, so he pursued knowledge for surviving in noble society. One could also say he was passive in the contest for power in their family and ended up yielding to her. He never regretted that, but he did wonder if she was really the right person for the job. If he had been holy king, he would have been able to pull strings behind the scenes and take other measures, so he may have been a better fit for the throne. He was one of the few members of the royal family Kelart didn't have issues with.

Character *56*

GUSTAV MONTAGNÉS

HUMANOID

You get used to the stomach pains

Position —— Deputy commander of the Sacred Kingdom Liberation Army

Residence —— A nice area in Jobans

Class Levels —— Paladin ———————————— **?** lv

Holy Knight ———————— **?** lv

Charisma (regular) ————— **?** lv

Etc.

Birthday —— 27 Late Wind Moon

Hobby —— Admiring little animals

{ personal character }

Of the two deputies, he's the one with no special skills with a sword, so it's easier for normal people to approach him compared to the other. (That said, he's still strong enough that an ordinary commoner would never be able to defeat him.) He often gets stomachaches, but having been impressed with how simply they can be cured with a spell, he would like to acquire faith magic. He bought a house that allows him to keep outside pets—cute squirrel-rabbit things called banias. Their names are Mircher and Amonna, and they are very important sources of comfort for his weary heart.

BEEBEEZEE

GROTESQUE

Glittering amethyst body

Position ——— Prince of the zerun

Residence ——— One of a thousand sinkhole caves in
the northern Abellion Hills

Class Levels ——— Zerun Lord (race) ——————— **?** lv

Wu Xing User ——————— **?** lv

Yin Master ——————— **?** lv

Etc.

Birthday ——— Winter 98

Hobby ——— Listening to stories

{ personal character }

The race has very few males. Those born male are instantly considered royalty. Males are precious, and they usually live their entire lives without ever leaving the nest, practically imprisoned. Since the prince tends to get fussed over, he is fairly confident about his body and even has some narcissistic tendencies. Incidentally, his race type is not an error. Zerun have a racial weakness that allows them to be affected by spells that work only on certain races, and for that reason, they are mistaken as subhumans, but they are actually grotesques.

THE
FORTY-ONE
SUPREME
BEINGS

BELLIVER

GROTESQUE

Big Eater

personal character

A magic swordsman by class, which meant he could switch between weapons and magic. But since it was predictable that he couldn't master both, he ended up being treated as a second-string member when the whole guild was present. That said, he was a skillful player and a capable gamer. In real life, he came into some inconvenient information about the huge conglomerate running the world and was silenced in a killing made to look like an accident. The information he possessed has been passed on to someone else.

Afterword

Thank you to everyone who has read this far. Did this volume feel heavy in your hand?

Those of you who read lying on your back must have struggled with the fear of what would happen if you dropped it.

This thirteenth volume was the first *Overlord* book to pass five hundred pages, and it did so by quite a lot. How did you like the story? I'm happy if even a few of you found it interesting.

But honestly, maybe I should have made this into Parts II and III. When I was editing, my brain got pretty tired reading it all at once. Reading chapters 4 and 5, and then the intermission, is about the right amount before sleeping for the night, I think. How about you?

Oh, and the other great thing about splitting this book in two would have been getting to see more of so-bin's wonderful illustrations!

But I doubt this will happen again, so it's not worth thinking about.

I always say that I'm going to write fewer pages, but this time it really was a bit much. The more pages, the longer every stage of the process takes, so the schedule keeps getting pushed. Not only that, but the chance of typos only goes up; there aren't really any benefits.

My goal for my next book is to go easy on the writer and readers alike.

*   *   *

I'd like to release the next volume in 2019, but I have to write one long thing before that, so there's no telling what will happen. If you could just leisurely wait, it would help me out. The third season of the anime will be on TV in the meantime, so I hope you'll enjoy that, too.

I really don't have much to write in the afterword these days. Back when I was a reader and I saw people saying that they didn't know what to write in afterwords, I would always think, *Write whatever you want as long as you write it*, but now that I'm in their shoes, I understand the struggle. What would you all write if you were me? Honestly...I feel like we don't need afterwords!

As always, many people helped make this possible. Thank you, and I hope you'll continue to humor me and my work.

April 2018

KUGANE MARUYAMA

Afterword by so-bin

I wish I could have done more OVERLORD art while it was on the air, but before I knew it, it was April. And I still have so many things to do...

so-bin

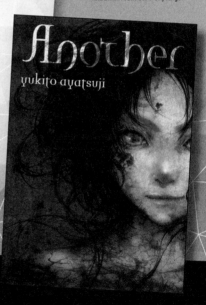